SALT MARSH SINNERS

Marian Mathews Hersrud

Although Naples, Florida, and some facilities are authentic, Rosewood Center and all characters are totally fictitious.

Copyright © 2013 Marian Mathews Hersrud
All rights reserved.

ISBN: 1493652427
ISBN 13: 9781493652426

To my incredibly wonderful, unique, and supportive family,
and to all retirement home residents who hear "use it or lose it"
and cheerfully follow directions.

ACKNOWLEDGEMENTS

How can I adequately thank my family, friends and consultants for their untiring support and expertise? The book would be flawed with errors, a total disaster, without their help. My gratitude is unending.

Law enforcement people answered questions and offered suggestions. Lt. Mike Foxx, detective Ray Wilkinson, dog trainer Lt. Harold Minch and retired officer Michael McCampbell provided information vital to the plot. The latter's "Call me any time," was a day brightener. Retired FBI agent Joseph Sheridan assigned my hero to his proper agency. Arbor Trace staff and residents provided essential data: Executive Director Dan Edenfield with specifications for my mythical high-rise, Becky Yocom, concierge's domain, Barbara Donovan, speech therapist for stuttering dialogue, Donna Skroski, cleaning staff regulations, Barbara Hogan, retired FBI agent, criminal investigation details, and Ginny Dill who led me through the final editing. *Naples Daily News* reporter Lipscomb and Fuller Funeral Home consultant, Jaqueline C. Trzyna, provided specific information. Jay Thisted of J & C Lamps suggested special designs. Carmen Gutierrez Bolger, Minneapolis artist, suggested appropriate names for my Cuban characters.

There would be no "*Salt Marsh Sinners*" without my grandson-in-law Jake Mort. A game warden who resided in Zapata, Texas, with his wife, my granddaughter Erica, he orchestrated my smuggling operation.

No book reaches publication without editors and proof readers. Rob Winslow, Arbor Trace resident, agreed to proof-read but added his editing skills. Joyce Wells, my faithful friend through all four novels is more than editor and proof reader. She's confidante and advisor.

To all of them, my undying thanks.

Other novels by
Marian Mathews Hersrud

Sweet Thunder

Spirits and Black Leather

Everybody Knew Pete

CHAPTER ONE

"Julie, come up to my penthouse, number 1842. I need you."

Julie Rogers, the concierge at Rosewood Center, an upscale retirement home in Naples, Florida, looked at her watch. It was five o'clock, her quitting time, but Frank Perruda in one of the four penthouses took precedence over her schedule.

"I'll be right up." She opened her purse, applied lipstick, and ran a comb through her blond hair. She greeted Rosita, her replacement, who had arrived in time for her to leave, then ran to Frank Perruda's private elevator.

"Glad you're here," Perruda said as he led her to a chair in his living room. "Would you like a drink?"

"Thanks, but no." She looked at her watch. "I'm through for the day at five o'clock, and I can't drink and drive home."

"Okay. I won't keep you, but sit down. I have a problem. It's personal and private. That's why I asked you to come here." Perruda settled his short, pudgy body into a chair across from Julie. His yellow polyester shirt, tucked into khaki shorts, hung below his overfed stomach.

Perruda took her hand. "I hate to admit this, but I think that Diane, my wife, is seeing somebody. I don't know who. I may hire a private detective, but I'd like to get some information first. You're at the concierge desk, and visitors have to sign in. I want you to watch and see if any men visit her here."

Julie twisted a lock of her hair and stared at him. "I can't do that, Mr. Perruda. That's against the rules."

"I'll pay you for that information, Julie." Perruda stood and faced her. "I just have to know."

"I'm sorry, but I can't. It's not ethical." She left her chair and edged toward the door. "I don't want to lose my job."

"I understand, so okay. Let's have a drink. I need one." He stood close to Julie and stroked her hair. "We could have a little drink. You don't have to leave."

Julie backed away toward the door. "I must go, Mr. Perruda."

"It's Frank, honey." He put his arms around her, kissed her, and with his right hand, reached under her skirt. "You don't have to leave. Let's have some fun." His breath was hot and heavy as he pressed his body closer.

Julie pulled away and raised her hand, ready to slap him. She stopped as he released her.

Perruda stepped back and looked at her with eyes watery and pleading. "Please excuse an old man," he said. "You're pretty, and I got problems." He sat in a chair and looked up at her. "I know Diane's seeing someone. What can I do?"

"I don't know, but I can't help."

Perruda shrugged his shoulders. "I understand." He reached for her hand. "Please sit down for just a minute. I won't make a pass at you. So many problems."

Julie sat and studied Frank Perruda. He looked as though demons were thrashing around in his head. His hands shook as he fumbled for a cigar and a match.

"What's wrong, Mr. Perruda? I can't help you with visitors, but—"

Perruda cut her off. "You can't help. It's a family thing. I've decided to change my will and leave my money to a special project. My three kids will be furious." He rose, leaned against the wall, and folded his arms. "My mind's made up, but there's trouble ahead."

"Family problems can be ugly." She stood and walked to the door. "I have to leave."

Perruda followed her. "Okay. Thanks for listening. We'll have that drink next time." He mouthed a kiss as the elevator door closed.

Julie leaned against the elevator car's wall and breathed deeply. This was her first encounter with a horny old man at Rosewood Center. She considered reporting him but knew it would be useless. As she rode to the lobby, Julie adjusted her skirt and shivered. She thought about Perruda. She had read her personal file of residents and knew he was the owner of Perruda's Fine Furnishings, and a five-year resident. He was seventy-eight years old and married to Diane, age unknown. She'd seen little of the Perrudas during those five years. Both he and his wife either swept through the lobby or came from the garage directly to their elevator. Now she knew Frank Perruda was a letch, and his wife was a slut. There would never be a "next time."

She returned to her desk, greeted Rosita, and unlocked her special file containing more detailed information. She studied Perruda's file. His son, James, and wife, Laura, lived at Luna de Ciel in Naples, a condominium on the beach. James managed the furniture store and was the emergency contact. Another son, Antonio, and his wife, Emma, lived in Minneapolis, and daughter, Carla, and husband, Phillip Stevens, in Boston. Frank Perruda's former residence was in Pelican Bay, an upscale Naples suburb.

Julie locked the file cabinet and checked her desk calendar. Friday, March 4.

She drove home, looking forward to a quiet weekend. Saturday and Sunday were filled with housework, a movie and dinner with friends, volunteer work, and Sunday church. After a painful divorce and worries about her future, Julie Graham Rogers had found her niche at Rosewood Center, and though her encounter with Frank Perruda had disturbed that niche, she knew the incident would soon fade into memory. She prepared dinner and enjoyed a movie on TV, a peaceful evening.

• • •

There would be no peace on Monday, March 7, at the home of James and Laura Perruda. Jim, Frank's elder son, knew the walls of their condo at Luna de Ciel in Naples might crumble when Laura heard the news. He entered Laura's computer room carrying a cup of coffee.

"Honey," Jim said as he put the coffee on her desk, "we received a letter from Mark Holtz, Dad's lawyer. Dad's cutting us out of his will."

"He's doing what?" Laura Perruda removed her earphones and did a one-eighty from desktop computer to husband. She stood and shook Jim's shoulders.

Jim carefully removed her grip from his Givenchy golf shirt. "Holtz sent this letter to all three of us, Tony, Carla and me. It's dated March third. That's last Thursday. This is Monday." Jim made circles on his forehead with his fingers. "He says Dad's changing his will, and we, his children, get nothing. He's leaving it to a special project. No reasons. We'll get a letter today spelling it out."

Laura stared at Jim. She opened her mouth, but no sound emerged. She sat down, turned, and stared at the monitor. "It's that bitch Diane, isn't it?"

Jim shrugged. "Not likely. As his second wife, she wouldn't get anything more than what's due under the law. I don't see her finger in this pie. My dad's seventy-eight. Maybe his mind is going. Last week he thought refugees from the Middle East were going to come ashore near Rosewood Center in Naples, Florida. They might be desperate people carrying guns. His penthouse might not be safe."

Laura sighed. "What can we do?"

"Call Tony and Carla. Have a family discussion."

Laura shook her head, blond ponytail whizzing around behind her. "Family discussions usually become family prizefights. Round two. Everybody in his own corner massaging his wounded ego."

"Yes, but this is a family situation. We're all involved, so there's no option."

"Maybe a brief respite from the cold in sunny, warm Naples might be enticing enough for them to forget egos and think like adults."

Jim nodded and looked out at the Gulf of Mexico from his eighth-floor apartment in Luna de Ciel. The view calmed inner turmoil, and he watched a flock of pelicans swoop down into the blue water. Waves lapped lazily onto the beach as a lone swimmer paddled slowly along the shoreline. A faint morning sun winked behind bits of white, puffy clouds. Peace. With his fingers Jim made circles on his forehead. God! To find that peace here in his condo!

• • •

Just two miles up the beach from Jim's condo at Luna de Ciel stood the eighteen-story retirement home, Rosewood Center, home of Francisco Perruda, Jim's father. Francisco, now Frank, was also the husband of second wife, Diane, and president and board chairman of Perruda Industries. He too looked out at his view and smiled. Here on the eighteenth floor, the view from his penthouse lanai was more spectacular as the horizon widened north, almost to Fort Myers, and south, almost to Marco Island. To an uninvolved onlooker, the smile hinted of smug supremacy, a gloat, an in-your-face-baby. To one who was involved, it could incite dread, trepidation, and a fear of what was to come.

He lay back on his chaise and thought about his meeting with Julie on Friday. He guessed he'd gone too far, at least for this first visit. Maybe she'd change her mind next time. He'd give her a few days and call her again.

"Frank, honey." Diane's raspy, fake southern drawl interrupted his brief reverie.

"I'm in the lanai," he called. "What do you want?"

"The plumber left his tools in my bathroom. You'll have to call somebody."

Frank sighed, picked up his cell phone, and called management. He then followed Diane's voice into her bedroom.

"It's okay. They'll send somebody up." He fumbled in the pocket of his bathrobe and removed a folded sheet of paper. "We need to talk. I'm asking my son, Jim, here for lunch. Call catering and order lunch for three."

He left the room quickly while Diane stood by her bed wearing only her pink tennis shorts, a pink bra, and a puzzled frown.

• • •

Tony Perruda's wife, Emma, sat at the kitchen table in Wayzata, Minnesota, and watched her husband as he threw the sports section of the *Minneapolis Tribune* on the floor. Knowing he was in no mood for small talk, she looked out at the snow-covered pine trees bordering their six-bedroom home on the shores of Lake Minnetonka. Their less affluent neighbors called it "Perruda's Palace" and watched carefully, ready to dodge to safety as Tony wheeled his new black Porsche convertible out of their four-car garage and onto the narrow streets of Wayzata. "Wild abandon," a bit trite, but accurate, described his frequent trips into town.

"More coffee?" Emma asked and rose to bring the silver carafe to the table. She hoped Tony wouldn't notice the dark circles under her eyes, her blond hair uncombed, needing a new perm and color.

"Coffee won't help. Damn! He's crazy!" He rose and paced the breakfast room, his bare feet slapping the Italian marble tiles. "He can't do this, Emma. Not to me. I'm his son, dammit!" He removed a letter from the pocket of his robe, studied it for the fifth time, and shoved it back inside.

As she poured coffee into two cups, Emma's hand shook. "Maybe he's senile, Tony. Maybe he doesn't know what he's doing."

"Yeah, like your crazy family. Good old Uncle George, who pinched his nurses and tried to fuck the aides?" He sat down, took his cup, drank, and spit it out. "Good God! When will you learn to make coffee?"

He threw his napkin at Emma, who caught and folded it, hands still shaking. After twenty-three years with Tony, she had perfected her reflexes. She stood and watched the sparrows huddled against the back fence. She was a sparrow too, she thought, stuck here in the snow and cold. She paused and reminded herself that sparrows could fly to a warmer climate. They didn't have to huddle as she did. Habit? A steady hope for a better relationship? A wish to return to life and love with Tony before marriage?

"Did you call your lawyer?" she asked.

"Am I an idiot? Of course I called. Jim's calling Dad's lawyer. I texted Carla in Boston too. Probably a waste of time, but she's my sister." He pushed a straggly bit of thick black hair away from his eyebrows. "How could I be so lucky? A brother who hates me, a sister who belongs in a home for the bewildered, and a father who hates all of us."

As he stood, his robe fell open, revealing a pudgy stomach hanging over his pajama pants. He rewrapped the robe, glared at Emma, and said, "I'm not going to sit back and watch my inheritance go down the toilet. I'm going to take the company jet and fly down there." He looked out at his snow-covered backyard. "Maybe I need to get out on a sandy beach."

• • •

"Bubbly, bubbly, bubbly." Carla Perruda Stevens swished the bath water around her. She was warm, contented, safe now. She reached for a red lollipop and chewed slowly. No hurry today. Philip had left for the office, and their two kids were in school. She was alone. She pushed aside her concerns regarding the letter and Phil's reaction and leaned back with a contented smile. Boston today meant a different life, not like the Boston she'd known as a child.

The bathtub in the corner was walled with mirrors. Carla looked at herself, soapy, wet, the ends of her long, brown, wavy hair dripping onto her shoulders. She made a face, stuck out her tongue, and laughed. Life was good. Philip's job didn't put them in the upper classes, but they were comfortable, and their children were happy in public schools. Her life was different now after the turmoils of childhood. Carla shuddered as she recalled her father's short-fuse temper, her mother quaking in the cellar, the screaming in Italian, a language she detested. Daddy made the rules and enforced them with his heavy, silver belt buckle. As a kid Carla learned to find safety in weakness, submission, and making herself invisible. School was torture also. A short, fat girl with a speech impediment was fair game in the crowded, cluttered, and downtrodden schools and streets of south Boston.

Carla sighed. It hadn't been easy, but she'd made it through and met Phil, who loved her in spite of her deficiencies. "Fat" became round and cuddly. "Short" meant an easy lift into bed, and a speech defect was minor as long as you could be understood. She'd seen the movie *The King's Speech* and had cried heavy, empathizing tears.

She gave another sigh as she recalled Phil's dinner conversation last night. His worries about his company's future and his own position had spilled over into a fretful harangue about the economy in general and Waverly Dechtonics in particular.

"I don't know what's going to happen. Everyone's on edge."

"I-i-it'll work out, honey," Carla said and brought dessert. The children giggled as Carla heaped caramel sauce on their bread pudding.

"I hope so, and it's good to know that your dad won't live forever."

Carla threw him a long look. "I d-d-don't want to th-th-think about an inheritance. Maybe I'm entitled to something after the h-h-hell he put me through, but it's over. Sure, he's l-l-l-loaded right now, him and that trophy wife in their f-f-f-f—" Carla stopped. Her lips didn't move.

"Slow down, honey," Phil said as he took her hand. "Just relax. It'll come."

Carla smiled and put her hand on her upper lip. "Thanks. I th-th-thought about their fancy penthouse. I d-d-don't trust him." She beckoned to Phil. "P-p-please come into the living room. I w-w-want to show you something."

They left the children at the table, and Carla took Phil's hand. "S-s-sit down. I want you to read this letter." She pulled a wrinkled envelope from her skirt pocket.

Phil read and reread. "He can't be serious! This is crazy! He can't do that!" He stood and threw the letter on the coffee table. "Do Tony and Jim know?"

"I haven't heard from J-J-J-Jim. He lives almost next d-d-d-door to Daddy. Maybe he can do s-s-something. D-D-Daddy hasn't made the ch-ch-change yet, according to the letter. He's just thinking about it."

"We can't let him do this, Carla. We have to do something." Phil sat, reread the letter, and shook his head. "No, he can't do this. We have to stop him."

As she lay back in the tub, Carla thought about last evening. Not to worry, she thought. A minor problem. She stood, reached for a towel as her iPhone made noises. She picked it up and saw a text message from Tony. Another sigh. Yes, he'd received the letter, and yes, something had to be done. Jim had called, adding another voice to family anger. He told Tony he'd have lunch with Dad and would call back. Carla drained the tub and dressed. A call to Jim might be wise, but she hated to use the phone, and action wasn't her strong suit. Better wait and learn from her brothers.

Her phone rang as she made the bed. "Carla, start packing." Phil's voice sounded serious, stern. "I just got airline tickets for Naples this afternoon. Your brother Tony called me, and he's on his way. We have to meet as soon as possible."

"B-b-b-but the k-k-k-kids, Phil. I have to f-f-find a sitter."

"Call our neighbor. This is an emergency. I'm on my way home now to pack. Our flight leaves at twelve thirty."

Carla held a dead phone and wondered what to do first, call a sitter or pack. Thirty minutes later her neighbor had been alerted, with instructions, and her suitcase was ready. Phil rushed from the garage to his bedroom, and Carla listened as he cursed her family, the lawyer, and his boss, who had urged patience, and a delayed flight.

• • •

Jim Perruda left his apartment at Luna de Ciel and drove slowly up Vanderbilt Drive to his father's penthouse at Rosewood Center. He dreaded a confrontation with the old man, and he'd rather be at the casino, where everyone enjoyed his company, made small talk, and didn't ask how much he'd won or lost. He left his car with the valet at the front door of Rosewood Center. Julie Rogers, the concierge, looked up from her desk and smiled.

"Good morning, Mr. Perruda. May I help you?"

"No," Jim answered. "I'm going to see my dad, so I'll just take their elevator." He paused and smiled at Julie. They'd met five years ago when his father moved to the penthouse. Julie, he learned, had been at her desk for three years prior to Perruda's arrival and was always a welcome sight. She dressed modestly, wore little makeup, but the effect was quiet elegance and a pleasant assurance. With blond hair that fell in soft waves about her face and sky-blue eyes partially hidden by blue-rimmed glasses, Julie was a concierge with class. Today he noticed a look of concern around her eyes, eyebrows a bit raised. God, did he display the kind of tension he felt inside?

Jim took his dad's private elevator to the penthouse. He admired a new painting above the polished mahogany table. Diane had an eye for good, original, and expensive artwork.

Frank opened the door and shook Jim's hand. "Glad you could come," he said. Jim greeted Diane, who stood close to her husband, one arm around his rotund waist. Frank removed the arm and put his hand on Jim's shoulder. "Would you like a Bloody Mary?" he asked.

"No thanks, Dad. We need to talk." Jim's glance at Diane read, "Leave us alone."

Diane shrugged and retreated to the kitchen.

Jim began with no preliminaries. "We received a letter from your lawyer saying you were changing your will. What's going on?"

Frank sat and looked up at his son. "I know it sounds crazy, but you kids don't need the money, and I've found something I've always wanted to do."

"I suppose we don't *need* the money, Dad," Jim said, stressing *need*, "but I think we're entitled…"

Frank struggled to his feet. "Entitled? What the hell do you mean? I brought you up from nothing, made a fortune for you. Even as a little kid, you were part of my work."

Jim snorted. "Yes, a part. In fourth grade I was cleaning toilets. Didn't have time for sports in high school because I got promoted from toilets to being your gofer. Do this! Bring that! You dragged Tony in too, but he was such a lazy son of a bitch that he didn't do much except flirt with the stenos. Carla was useless. Couldn't do anything because she couldn't even talk to people. Hell, being a part of your work, your rise to fame and fortune were torture. You robbed me of a happy life as a kid, and now you want to rob me of my inheritance that I damned well earned!"

Jim's face reddened, and his hands shook. He rubbed his temples with his fingers, stood, and walked out to the lanai. God, he'd said it all and meant every word. Did any of it get through to the old man?

He felt a hand on his shoulder. "Jim, you just see everything from your point of view. I got feelings too. I worked hard, and I made it. I made it myself. Nobody else gave a shit, not even you kids. Your mom was a nothing. Kept the house, but was there ever a kind word, a pat on the back? No, it was just me. I did it."

Jim removed his father's hand and stared at him. "So that's the way you see it."

"Yes. You're mad because you didn't have time for sports in high school, but I sent you to college. I never had the chance to go to college. My family had nothing. So you cleaned toilets. I cleaned streets. Don't get on the pity potty with me."

Jim said nothing and looked out at the Gulf, calm and peaceful. Maybe the old man wasn't so crazy after all.

Frank smiled. "So now you know I'm changing my will, but you don't know why. Let's have lunch, and I'll tell you about it."

They walked into the dining room, where the chef had prepared lunch—lobster bisque followed by a shrimp Caesar salad, garlic toast, and crème brulee. Frank ate slowly as he described his plan.

"I told you I'd never been to college. So now I'm going to buy one and have it named for me, Perruda University. It'll have everything, all university courses, a football team, lots of sports. All the teachers will be first-class, with fancy degrees. Nothing but the best."

"And where will this be?"

"In North Dakota."

Jim laughed. "Come on, Dad. You've never been there. You don't know anything about the place."

"Unimportant. I know what I'm doing, and I'm already working on the entrance, a big arch with 'Perruda University' in giant letters."

Jim finished his dessert, rose, and put his hand on his father's shoulder. His mind was a jumble of conflicting thoughts. This man was his father. Not a loving father. He thought about the heavy, silver belt buckle. A man who had worked hard, had been successful, but did he ever really care about his family? Jim pulled back his hand.

"If your mind's made up, there's nothing I can do. When are you finalizing your will?"

"Soon. My lawyer's putting everything together." He smiled at Jim. "You'll survive without that inheritance and maybe send your kids to Perruda University. Full tuition, of course. I don't believe in special favors."

Jim smiled woefully and shook his head. His dad didn't even know he had no children. He went to the kitchen, thanked Diane, and returned to the living room. He nodded to his father and left quickly. He's nuts, he thought. Committed and crazy. He rode the elevator down, nodded to Julie at her desk, and handed the valet a tip. He sat in his car, pulled out his cell phone, and called his wife.

"Laura, you won't believe this. He's taking our money and building a university in North Dakota."

Laura's response was a running tirade of four-letter words.

Jim replied, "I can't do anything. His mind's made up."

As soon as he closed his phone, his brother-in-law Phil called. "Carla and I are flying to Naples this afternoon. We'll take a cab from the airport and see you soon."

Jim remembered Tony's call an hour ago. He looked up at the eighteenth floor of Rosewood Center and knew his dad was in for a busy afternoon.

• • •

Frank Perruda didn't rise when his son Jim left the penthouse. Good riddance, he thought. His kids would never understand his intentions, never accept his decisions. Idiots! All they ever wanted from him was their allowance, money for cars, clothes, vacations in the Caribbean or the Riviera. But he knew what he was doing and where the money was. He'd made a killing in the furniture business while his neighbors laughed. Importing wood from India? Crazy! But Frank knew what his customers wanted, and as his business became more upscale, so did his profits. And the other stuff. Frank smiled as he thought about his furniture shipments from Mexico. Again his business associates laughed. They would never know what his imports contained or the size of his Swiss bank account.

"Frank, honey." Diane's voice from the kitchen sounded like chalk on a blackboard.

He groaned. "What?"

"I need to slip over to Nordstrom's. Call Felix and tell him to bring up the Bentley."

"Yes, love." Diane's appetite for the latest fashions amazed him. New clothes arrived weekly while thrift shop trucks hauled away last week's purchases. He chuckled to himself. He hadn't told her about his change in the will. As his wife, the law required a substantial settlement, but beyond that, she'd get nothing. Nothing! He knew she'd go through the settlement in record time, and then what? Of course she'd find another sucker like himself. She'd flatter, cajole, flirt, and make promises of undying, you-only love. And now he had suspicions about an affair. Damn! He'd been a sucker for five years. It was time to cut her off.

He watched as Diane swept out of the penthouse swathed in a pink above-the-knee dress. Her blond shoulder-length coiffeur and shapely size eight body with size thirty-eight breasts were prepared to seduce the sternest men who sat in the lobby waiting for transportation.

Frank watched her departure with relief. The sound of her voice irritated him. Either her fake southern drawl had swelled, or his hearing had improved. He took his special mobile phone from his pocket and punched in an international number.

"Gimme Pedro." He cracked the knuckles of his third left finger and waited. "Yeah? You got it? Good. Next week for sure, understand?" He used his throwaway phone with the card only for his private business calls. He turned on the television and spent a quiet afternoon thinking about Perruda University. He'd need a robe for the opening ceremonies, possibly a hood like the ones worn by those PhDs.

Salt Marsh Sinners

• • •

Behind her concierge desk, Julie watched Diane, who walked out of their private elevator and hurried into the lobby. The Bentley was parked under the porte cochere. As Diane walked by the concierge desk, Julie looked up and greeted her.

"Good afternoon, Mrs. Perruda. Lovely day, isn't it?"

"Yes, if you like heat and humidity." She brushed past the desk and drove away in the Bentley, tires screeching at the first turn.

Julie watched her departure and looked over her counter at two elderly men who obviously had noticed Mrs. Perruda's arrival and departure. She laughed. "You two have eyes that simply pop out of your heads."

Richard looked at Harry and winked. "Yup, that's a fact. She's some chick. Wish I were thirty years younger."

"You're not old, Mr. Kent," Julie said. "Think young and try your luck on the putting green. No sense sitting here on this beautiful day."

Julie enjoyed the old men's company but knew that any kind of activity was important. She also knew as some people aged, they became couch potatoes. "Use it or lose it" was heard in the exercise room, dining room, at the pool, and on the beach. Julie also knew that these two old men had contributed to the safety of the United States. Richard Kent, a nuclear scientist, had worked in Oak Ridge, Tennessee, on the atomic bomb and later at a hidden seaport helping to develop the atomic submarine. Harry Grimes had commanded a regiment that landed on Omaha Beach on June 6, D Day. His leadership under enemy fire and pounding waves had brought his men to an overhang farther from shore, where they could regroup and move ahead.

Rosewood Center was home to many unsung heroes and to some who kept their fame well hidden. These residents offered bits of information only when prodded. They didn't need any more accolades or medals. They'd been there, done that. Now they were content to recall privately the successes and, occasionally, the failures of their lives. Sometimes Julie felt like the proverbial bartender who listened to his customers' deepest secrets. Her desk in the center of the lobby was a natural place to stop and visit, and Julie's easy, open, and concerned manner encouraged reminiscences as residents remembered, relived, and recounted those experiences.

Julie had been at her desk for eight years and knew more about the inner lives of the residents than she really wanted to know. Mrs. Kingsley slept with the bachelor down the hall and needed to boast about her aging sex life to someone. You couldn't tell your best friends. It wasn't bridge table conversation, so you told Julie, knowing she'd never divulge that information. And that hussy, Diane Perruda! She'd stop at Julie's desk and repeat startling activities regarding her husband, whom she'd trapped into marriage.

"Being a night nurse pays off," she said. "Men are so helpless in the dark, especially after their wives have just died."

Julie dropped her concerns about Diane Perruda when her phone rang, and Frank's voice barked commands.

"Send someone up here to clear off lunch, and get someone else to pick up the plumber's tools. I called hours ago, but nobody came."

"Yes, Mr. Perruda. I'll take care of it right away." Julie made appropriate calls as visitors and tenants passed with the usual "How are you?" and "Have a nice day."

She looked up from her monitor at the reception desk and waved as Jim emerged from the Perrudas' private elevator. He waved to her but hurried to the door. She shrugged. No response was a standard reaction from anyone who visited the Perrudas. Maybe a private elevator put someone above the rest of the world.

Julie looked down at her computer and checked special operations. Peter Watson, executive director, kept Rosewood Center in running order and demanded professional and expert assistance from the staff. Julie admired his skills in dealing with all the problems that a retirement home is heir to. With an eye on storm warnings, the developers built the basement garage with knockout walls to cope with hurricanes and tsunamis. The first floor contained all working electrical equipment and was under constant surveillance. On that same floor was the lobby, magnificent in its early Victorian décor. Oriental rugs partially covered a parquet floor, and comfortable, velvet-upholstered armchairs grouped in conversational settings proclaimed peaceful elegance. Julie's six-foot-long mahogany desk faced the front door. A forty-two-inch-high, eight-foot-long counter topped with green Italian marble stood in front of her desk, and behind her, a forty-foot-long curved window offered a spectacular view of the mangrove salt marsh, an estuary, and the Gulf beyond.

The lobby was perfection in every detail of flooring, décor, lighting, and personnel. A luxurious dining room occupied the north end of the floor. It offered gourmet dining and catering service. A smaller snack bar provided light lunches. A two-hundred-seat theater filled the south end of the building. Its stage welcomed lecturers and musical groups, and a retractable screen offered weekly movies. Eighteen floors of apartments in several space categories, inhabited by aging residents with all varieties of ailments, meant constant vigilance and a staff that was efficient, caring, and available when needed.

A smooth-running retirement home runs on the oil of those who work in food and cleaning service—the cooks, wait staff, and housekeepers. Young women, many of them second- and third-generation Latinos, pushed their cleaning carts in and out of their designated apartments.

A small but well-equipped hospital stood next door, offering twenty-four-hour service. Nurses and aides were on duty, along with a resident doctor who was on call for emergencies. Each Rosewood Center apartment was well equipped with call buttons with strings attached in case a resident fell and couldn't reach the button. Response was immediate and reassuring. Younger residents might laugh at all of those precautions, but you didn't have to be eighty to lose your balance in the shower.

Julie looked up as Doris Johnson hobbled into the lobby and shoved her walker up close to the desk. She leaned over and put her hand on the counter.

"That's a lovely ring, Mrs. Johnson," Julie said.

"Yes, my husband bought it for me when we were in Australia. It's a fire opal."

Julie smiled. "Rings are my passion. I lost my grandmother's diamond engagement ring, and I've never forgiven myself."

"I'm sorry to hear that, and I'm also sorry about Cynthia Frost. I can't believe she would leave me here. She was to pick me up fifteen minutes ago, and she never called, and she isn't here. Can you call her?"

"Of course." Julie made the call and waited, as there was no response. "I'll call the hospital to check her unit. Please sit down. I'm sure there's nothing to worry about. Mrs. Frost may have forgotten and left without you."

As Julie called, Mrs. Johnson eased herself down into a chair, opened her purse, and studied a lipstick. Finally she opened it and applied a dab on her lips. She looked up and saw Julie watching her.

Mrs. Johnson laughed. "After eighty-one years, I know where my lips are, thank you."

Julie laughed too. "The people from the hospital will be right over, Mrs. Johnson. Would you like a magazine?"

"No, I'm too nervous to read."

A white-clad nurse arrived minutes later, followed by George, the handyman. They took directions and rushed to the elevator as Mrs. Johnson sat and stared at the ceiling. More minutes passed, and the phone rang.

"Yes? Oh, all right. I'll tell Mrs. Johnson." Julie stood and smiled. "It's okay. Nobody's there. They searched the apartment looking for Mrs. Frost, who might have fallen and couldn't call for help. Mrs. Frost's not in her apartment. George is checking the garage, so be patient."

As if on cue, George reappeared. "Her car's gone, so she's left," he said.

Mrs. Johnson pushed herself up, took her walker, and came to the desk. "Thanks, Julie. I guess she just forgot." She walked slowly to the elevator, and Julie shook her head. Residents sometimes forget, she thought. The nurse and George returned to their work, and the lobby was quiet.

• • •

The kitchen at the Perruda residence in Wayzata, Minnesota, was also quiet. Tony had flown off to Naples, Florida, and Emma was content. The clock on the kitchen wall coo-cooed eleven a.m. Tony hated that clock with its infernal bird tweets every hour. Because Emma's mother had given them the clock as a Christmas present, the birds continued to chirp merrily. Tony always gauged his breakfast carefully to avoid the chirping, while Emma laughed silently. After twenty-three years of marriage, she knew how to avoid discords with Tony. She had learned all about the Perruda family conflicts, but only after they were married. She had been shocked to hear of his brutal father's short temper and the belt with its sharp buckle he used on his two sons and one daughter. Tony's mother had cowered in the basement when Frank's temper rose to villainous heights. Tony and his older brother, Jim, had suffered through the beatings, stifling cries that only encouraged their father to continue his torture. Carla escaped more often but was beaten when her stuttering increased.

As tales of Tony's background emerged, Emma could understand her husband's own fury, but it didn't make her life any easier. She'd considered divorce often but always returned to her need to protect their two daughters and give them a normal home life with two parents. She would do anything to break the chain of Perruda violence, and she had succeeded. Their daughters entered their teens with no threats, no outbursts. She owed Tony that much. He too wanted a peaceful home for his daughters. Only when they were safely away from the house did he vent his anger and frustration on Emma.

The phone rang, interrupting her musings. She checked the clock. Eleven thirty. Twelve thirty in Naples. Tony was probably enjoying a Bloody Mary on the beach, maybe with a gorgeous blonde at his side.

"Hi. The trip went well. No problems. I'm going to see Dad this afternoon. I called Jim. He had lunch with Dad." Tony paused. Emma thought he'd hung up.

"He's crazy, Emma. He told Jim he's giving all his money to build a university in North Dakota. He says we don't deserve anything."

"What are you going to do?"

"I don't know. Maybe we can talk him out of it, but it's not likely. Carla and her husband, Phil, are flying in from Boston tomorrow. It sounds like a wild family reunion."

"When will you come home?"

"Who knows? I can't make any plans now. I'll check with you in a day or two. Hugs to the girls."

Emma replaced the phone and poured another cup of coffee. She sat and looked out at the soft, white snow in the backyard. It covered the bare limbs of the oak trees and nestled quietly on the branches of the pines. She sipped coffee and thought about lunch with Jane and Debby, friends since Delta Gamma sorority days at the University of Minnesota. She picked up the phone again, arranged for lunch, and left the kitchen. She looked again at the backyard. With Tony in Florida, her day was as peaceful as the quiet, white snow.

• • •

For Laura, Jim Perruda's wife in Naples, Florida, her day was anything but peaceful. As a busy Realtor with Brown and McCarthy, Naples's leading agency, she worked at home with her computer and displayed homes and condos to prospective buyers in her blue Lexus convertible. The routine sounded ideal for a fifty-three-year-old happily married woman, and she was envied by many of her co-workers. How could they see the true picture or know the inner workings of a marriage?

Laura had met Jim at Perruda's Fine Furnishings. One of her clients had asked her to find appropriate furniture for her new condo, so she drove to the store knowing it would have the kind of furniture her buyer would like. Jim came forward, introduced himself, and offered assistance. She gave him her business card and told him what she needed. She was impressed with Jim. Tall, good-looking, with the most beautiful brown eyes she'd ever seen.

Jim checked his watch and said he had time to see the condo and get a feel for the décor. Laura drove, and they were both enthusiastic about the furniture she'd suggested. Lunch followed, dinner the following week, concerts at the Philharmonic, and ultimately, a long weekend in Cancun, Mexico. Histories were exchanged. Both had been divorced with no children, both had attended college, he in Boston, she in Illinois. She met his father and was awed by the penthouse, private elevator, and Bentley. Jim traveled to Chicago and was introduced to her family: mother, father, and one sister who also worked as a Realtor.

Secrets were never disclosed. Jim didn't tell her about his addiction to gambling. He didn't mention the sponsored flights to Las Vegas, where gambling funds were unlimited as long as he followed the rules. He didn't tell her about his visits to the Indian casinos in various states and now in Immokalee, Florida.

Laura kept her own secrets. Her best friend Janet was more than a friend. She was Laura's confidant, soul mate, lover. Laura never questioned her own bisexuality. It was just who she was, and Janet accepted her love as she'd accepted other women. If Janet questioned her marriage to Jim, she never asked, and Laura never explained.

Now she sat at her computer and thought about Janet. Jim phoned to report his lunch with Frank and that he would be late for dinner. Laura knew he would be en route to the casino in Immokalee, always an outlet for anxiety and frustration.

She checked her watch and phoned Janet. "Hi. Yes, I'm free. I'll be right over. I can't wait to see you."

CHAPTER TWO

Russell Jones, a supervisory special agent with the Drug Enforcement Agency, looked out at the Gulf of Mexico from his lanai on the sixteenth floor of Rosewood Center. The morning sun cast a warm glow on the water. He sipped coffee, lay back on the chaise longue, and thought about his recent return to Naples. The flight from Washington, DC, had been delayed, and he hadn't been able to see his mother in the next apartment. She'd understand, but he was anxious to see her and learn if her Alzheimer's symptoms had worsened. An ugly disease.

As if to capitalize his thoughts, his cell phone rang, and heard his mother's voice. "Darling, I must see you. It's been months, and I can't find my nail file."

Russ smiled. "Mom, I just got in last night, but I was here two weeks ago. Look for your nail file in the bathroom, and if you can't find it, call me back. I'll be over soon, and we'll have breakfast together."

He hated the changes that continued to take place in his mother's mind. He remembered her as the gracious hostess who entertained lavishly in their Port Royal home or on their yacht anchored at the edge of their acreage on Naples Bay. And Dad, Llewellyn, a developer of golf course communities, a benefactor, a leader in the city of Naples that grew from a sleepy little fishing village into a beautiful city of lakes, parks, theaters and, because of his primary concerns, excellent schools and health care. He'd been honored before his death, and there was comfort in knowing that his genius for planning, executing, and caring had been recognized. It diminished the tragedy of his death.

Russ shuddered again as he recalled that night of worry, police and fire departments, the press, friends and strangers—everyone, it seemed, searching for his father. Dad had attended a symphony concert alone because his wife, Carolyn, had been ill, but he didn't come home.

Russ had been visiting his parents and decided to stay with his mother, whose fever had risen that evening. She'd needed him more than his father, who was in his usual seat at the symphony hall, surrounded by friends who loved Mozart almost as much as the nineteenth hole at their country club.

Russ checked his watch as the time between the last bars of the symphony and his father's failure to return home increased. At midnight he called 911, and the response was immediate and overwhelming. The call precipitated a search of massive proportions. Police, the fire department, reporters, and people who heard the sirens and learned the missing person's name joined in the hunt. At last, at four a.m., his car was found submerged in a canal. A group of neighbors had followed the zigzagging trail that ended on its banks. Rumors abounded. He was drunk. He committed suicide. An autopsy revealed a massive blood clot in his brain. He'd died instantly, and there was comfort in knowing he hadn't suffered, hadn't endured death by drowning. The funeral at an Episcopalian church, Trinity by the Cove, was the largest the city could remember.

Carolyn and Russell picked up the pieces of their lives. They'd already lost Mary Ellen, age thirteen, to acute leukemia, and now they faced a lonely and uncertain future. Russ, after graduation from Yale, had already established a career in law enforcement in Virginia, but was given time off to assist his mother during those trauma-drenched weeks following his father's death.

Carolyn stayed in their home for five years, sold it, moved to a penthouse on the Gulf, and lived there until her friends and personal physician recommended a move to a retirement home where care would be available if and when needed. Russ approved of each move and at age forty-two, he also considered a move to Rosewood Center during his frequent visits to Naples. Because of his mother, the age requirement was waived, and he was able to purchase a two-bedroom apartment next door. The arrangement was ideal for both of them.

Russ's cell phone rang again, interrupting his thoughts of the past. "Russ, have you seen my fingernail file? I can't find it."

"Why don't you look in a bathroom drawer, and if you can't find it, call me back."

He returned to the kitchen for a coffee refill. The calls were increasing, and he knew the need for a full-time caregiver was in the near future. He punched in the numbers of the concierge desk.

"Julie, this is Russ Jones in 1615. I'm going to need someone to help my mother, maybe full time. I don't know. I'll have to talk to her doctor. Meanwhile, do you have names of reliable people?"

Julie's response was clear, but concerned. "You'll have to call the director for that information, Mr. Jones. We're not allowed to make recommendations."

Russ called the office, spoke to the director, and wrote a list of reliable caregivers. He hoped he wouldn't need anyone immediately, but now he had pertinent information.

• • •

Julie sat at her concierge desk and thought about Russ. She remembered when he'd moved in last year. She'd liked what she saw—brown wavy hair, six feet four, maybe, and a polite but warm manner. She hoped he was single and might give her a second glance. At thirty-eight she knew who she was, her faults and virtues. Her ex-husband had reviewed her faults, overlooking her virtues, and after fifteen years of marriage, decided he could improve his situation where the grass was greener. The divorce was amicable, with no resentments, no arguments about finances. His medical practice thrived as did his relationship with one of his registered nurses. There were no children to complicate the settlement.

Julie stayed home licking her wounds for a year until a true friend urged her to get out, meet people, do something. Julie reassessed her faults and virtues as they related to employment. She liked to work out but wasn't a super jock. She liked to shop but didn't want to stand all day as a clerk. Her typing and computer skills needed upgrading. What did she like? People, interesting situations, new challenges.

When a friend's mother invited them to dine with her at her retirement home, Julie was impressed with Rosewood Center. The dining-room hostess and wait staff were bright and efficient. The food was exceptional, and the entire facility intrigued her. The next morning she met with the director, resume in hand. The director studied her resume, and Julie relaxed as the director asked questions. She learned their concierge had just retired, and would she be interested? A firm yes, and the appropriate paperwork was completed. Julie had a name tag, a list of instructions, and a chair behind the concierge desk.

Now, eight years later, Julie knew every resident by name, age, and past history. Each day brought a new challenge, a new resident, and sometimes, sadly, the loss of another. She mourned each death and enjoyed each special event. Rosewood Center was now her life.

Rosewood Center was in the middle of Monday morning chaos. Because a special team worked on Saturday and Sunday, Julie's desk was piled with sticky notes, each stuck to another, two stacks of phone messages, each marked "Urgent," and a sloppy mess of messages and notes of so many different colors and shapes that Julie twisted a blond curl and moaned.

George, the handyman, came to her desk and reached for his own pile of immediate problems. Washers didn't wash, toilets didn't flush, showers leaked, vertical blinds collapsed.

"Why does everything go wrong on weekends?" he asked.

Julie shook her head and twisted another curl. "Rosewood Center is inhabited by gremlins and bad spirits who only do their dirty work on Saturday and Sunday."

The phone rang. "Rosewood Center. This is Julie. May I help you?" Her voice was pleasant, her mood, frustrated.

"This is Russ Jones again, Julie. I hate to bother you, but could you please come up to my mother's apartment as soon as you can? I wouldn't ask if it weren't important."

"Of course. I'll be right up." She ran to the elevator.

Russ opened the door and took her hand. He looked as though he'd seen disaster, an earthquake, a flood. His hair was rumpled, his shirt and trousers covered with something dark and gooey.

"I probably should have called the hospital, but I don't want publicity. It's my mother. She's lost it, Julie."

He led her to a bedroom, where his mother lay on the floor next to the bed. She looked up at Julie and laughed. "Isn't this the silliest thing to be on the floor like this?"

Julie was so relieved to hear Mrs. Jones's voice that she laughed too. "Why are you on the floor, Mrs. Jones?"

"It's nice here, and the mice don't bother me. They like syrup, so I gave them some, but the bottle slipped, and now my dress is ruined."

Julie looked carefully and saw the woman's heavy blue wool dress and sweater were covered with syrup. She shook her head, and tears came as she remembered Mrs. Jones just last year. An agonizing change.

"Let's get you up now. The mice are gone, and we'll help you find something else to wear."

She and Russ lifted the old woman, and Julie carefully removed the dress and sweater. Russ found a robe, and together they eased her into a chair.

"Do you hurt anywhere?" Russ asked.

Carolyn Jones shook her head. "I just feel bad about the mice."

"I'll call housekeeping," Julie said. "I'm afraid her clothes are ruined. I'll find a bag and throw them down the trash chute."

Russ nodded. He knelt by his mother's chair and took her hand. "You're fine now."

Julie located a plastic bag, removed the clothes, and took them to the garbage chute in the hall. She returned to the bedroom, and as she looked around, she saw a diamond ring lying on the dresser. Startled, she recognized it as a twin of her grandmother's engagement ring, the one she'd lost years ago. So lovely, she thought. She followed noises in the kitchen and discovered Russ making coffee.

"Thanks for your help," he said. "I didn't know who to ask."

Julie smiled. "It's nice to be needed. What are you going to do?"

"I called one of the caregivers that Peter Watson recommended. I have to fly back to DC tonight."

Julie nodded. "I'm sure your mother will be fine with the help she needs." She watched Russ at the coffee maker. A handsome guy like that. Married? Living with someone? Kids?

Russ waved her to a seat at the table and brought coffee. She was startled when he took her hand, smiled, and said, "You've been so great. I've known you for almost a year, but I've never really seen you until this morning." He studied her now. "I'd like to buy lunch if you can get away." When Julie nodded, he added, almost to himself, "And I wish I didn't have to leave tonight."

Julie's stomach did cartwheels. She tried to remain calm, the concierge who took care of everyone else, herself invisible. "You needn't do that. I just wanted to help."

Russ rose, lifted her up, and kissed her forehead. "You did more than help. I'll pick you up at noon."

Julie floated to the door, down the elevator, and to her desk. She looked at those piles of urgencies and grinned. Here we go, she thought. How much could she accomplish before noon?

At one minute before noon, the front door opened. A man carrying an overcoat, dressed in a cashmere sweater, jeans, and

MBT sneakers, and pulling a wheeled overnight bag, stomped up to Julie's desk.

"Ring Frank Perruda's place. I'm his son, Tony. Just got off the plane from Minneapolis." As he twirled a diamond ring on his index finger and paced the lobby, he almost collided with Russ Jones. Tony glared at him. "Isn't there enough room for you, buddy?" he sneered.

Julie called from her desk. "Mr. Perruda asks you to come up." She gave him directions to the Perrudas' private elevator and stood to meet Russ.

"Sorry about that," Julie said. "Mr. Perruda must have been in a hurry." She took her purse, said good-bye to her replacement, and walked with Russ to his gray Buick. She leaned back next to him as they drove away.

"Hope you like clams," Russ said.

Julie, who would have liked anything he suggested, agreed. Lunch was rushed but easy as Julie told Russ about her job, the laughable and the sad and often the unusual. Mr. Evans in apartment 1256 owned a black Harley motorcycle, a Screamin' Eagle, that too often screamed around corners at two in the morning. Complaints multiplied until Mr. Evans agreed to rev up his engine only during daylight hours.

Russ countered with stories of several get-tough break-ins in Washington. He didn't detail his role, and Julie didn't ask. Private lives were alluded to briefly. Julie, a divorce. Russ, a death, too soon, too painful.

Julie was reluctant to leave, but her watch shouted "schedule." Back at her desk, she thanked her replacement and smiled at Russ.

"Call me if you need help. Your mother is a lovely person, and I'm sure the woman Peter recommended will be able to take care of her when you're not here." When he's not here, thought Julie, she'd miss him. Would he miss her?

Russ leaned on the counter in front of Julie's desk. As if to read her mind, he said, "I'll be back in two weeks unless there's something urgent. I'll interview the caregiver this afternoon, and she can begin working tomorrow morning early."

"That's reassuring, so don't worry. I leave at five o'clock, so I probably won't see you until you're back. Have a good flight, and thanks again for lunch. I loved it." Julie bit her lip. Should she have added "loved it"?

Russ waved as he walked to the elevator. "I loved it too," he called.

Mrs. Johnson, Cynthia Frost's forgotten friend, looked up from her chair by the window. She smiled at Julie. "What a nice young man," she said and winked at Julie.

• • •

Frank Perruda groaned when he heard his son Tony had arrived from Minneapolis. He didn't need the kid, didn't need any of his kids. All they ever wanted was money. They disliked Diane, his new wife, and made no effort to hide their resentments. Apparently they'd loved their mother, and when she died, he supposed they expected him to languish alone, lonely and miserable. Fat chance! Women liked Frank, young women, women with big tits and firm butts. He thought about Sally Torrino, who cooked Italian dishes and smothered him with oregano-flavored kisses. He had dropped her when he met Diane.

He remembered Diane's attributes when she came into his hospital room. Because he had a cold that threatened to develop into pneumonia, his doctor put him in the hospital. Diane, the night nurse, spent more time with him as his health improved. She'd bring his water, massage his shoulders. The massages moved downward as she whispered encouragement and concern. He was almost disappointed when the doctors told him he was well enough to leave. He and Diane spent their last night together closely locked in his hospital bed, and Frank's sexual needs were cared for by his willing partner.

As soon as Frank was released and returned to Rosewood Center, Diane became a frequent visitor, and his affair became common knowledge. Penthouse residents received more than the usual center curiosity. She fulfilled all of his needs in bed, on the davenport, against the wall, under the table, or wherever they found space. She whispered her love for him as she had done during his hospital stay. Frank had only one regret. Her strident daytime voice, with a pseudo-southern drawl, was an unpleasant contrast to her night nurse whispers, but her other attributes far outweighed his disappointment.

He reluctantly invited his two sons and one daughter to their wedding and was relieved when all three declined. Five years later, he could appreciate their reluctance. Diane became more demanding as time elapsed. More clothes, more jewelry, more entertainment. Now, with Diane here, Tony on his way to the penthouse, and Jim almost next door, he could relax in the knowledge that nobody in his family would profit by his death. They deserved nothing, and that's what they'd get!

The doorbell rang, interrupting his unpleasant memories. Diane opened the door, and Tony brushed past her to greet his father.

Frank left his chair in the lanai and extended his hand. "Nice of you to drop in. It's good to get away from the snow for a little while, right?"

"Yeah, it was piling up in the yard, and it's hard to find good guys who have snowblowers."

"How about some lunch? Jim was here this noon, and there might be something left."

"No thanks. My pilot and I stopped at Starbucks."

Frank was uncomfortable. He knew the reason for Tony's visit, and he didn't want to listen to any more crap. Jim had left in a huff, and here was Tony. Same song, second verse.

"Diane, call the concierge and reserve a guest room for Tony." He looked at his son. "For how many nights?"

"Maybe two or three. I haven't decided. I told Emma I'd be home sometime. She won't care."

As soon as Diane left to make the reservation, Tony threw his coat on a chair, sat down, and stared at his father. "We all got a letter from your lawyer, and that's why I came. You can't do this, Dad. We're entitled—"

"Entitled, entitled!" Frank walked over to Tony and stared down at him. "Nobody in this family is entitled to anything. I made it all, and that's my decision. All of you have comfortable incomes. Jim's taken over my business and is doing well. You've got a cushy job at the brokerage, and Carla's husband is a big cheese in his company. You don't need anything more from me. God knows I've given you enough all these years, with travel, clothes, big Christmas checks, and now you're entitled to more? Entitled, my ass!"

Frank walked out into the lanai. His hand shook as he lit a cigar. Just as he was about to sit, his cell phone rang. He pulled it from his pocket.

"Yes?" he shouted. "Who is this?"

"D-D-Dad, it's me, Carla."

Frank glared at his cell phone and looked back at Tony, who sat with his head in his hands.

"What do you want, Carla? I'm sorry I yelled. I got problems."

"I'm s-s-s-sorry, Daddy. I just wanted to tell you that Phil and I just l-l-landed at Fort Myers…" A long pause, then, "W-w-we want to talk to you about the l-l-l-lawyer's letter. Phil thought we sh-sh-should."

Frank cracked his knuckles, one by one. "Sure, come to Rosewood Center. I'll make a room reservation for you." His voice softened a bit. "Do you need a ride from the airport?"

"N-n-no. We'll find a taxi. Thanks anyway. B-b-b-bye."

Frank pocketed his cell phone and returned to the living room. Tony stood, and Frank realized how much the two of them resembled each other. Five foot ten, black hair that Frank colored and Tony permed, a pudgy stomach above the belt. There the resemblance ended because Tony would never understand his father's motives in changing his will. He also knew his recent business dealings would cause more tension, more controversy. Better to keep those items under wraps.

"That was Carla. She and Phil are coming this afternoon. It looks as though we're having a reunion."

Tony smirked. "Some reunion! Well, I'm here, so I'm going to move down to the guest room and go for a swim." He picked up his coat and pulled his suitcase to the door. "I'll call you later."

Frank sighed when his son closed the front door. A family reunion didn't mean a friendly get-together. It meant discord and confrontation.

• • •

Julie waded through the message piles and thought about Russ, nice thoughts that eased her busy schedule. She reserved the guest rooms Mr. Perruda had ordered and asked housekeeping to check them. She didn't need any Perruda complaints. At five o'clock she had completed her day's work and looked forward to a leisurely, simple dinner in front of the TV. She had recently purchased a home on Livingston Road. She liked the neighborhood, families with small children. New people had moved in next door, but Julie hadn't met them. One of her neighbors told her the new owners were from Canada.

She drove to her home and pushed the garage door opener. Nothing happened. Several tries, and the door remained shut. She walked to the front door and was surprised to see that it was ajar. Had she forgotten to lock it this morning? Anything's possible, she thought.

When she entered the house, she screamed, "Oh my God!" Two sofa pillows lay on the floor, their tassels matted and tangled. Someone had sat on a lounge chair and left a hollow on the seat. She walked to the kitchen and stared at her breakfast dish on the floor, milk from the cereal bowl spilled. She ran to the bedroom and opened her jewelry box. If her grandmother's cameo broach was gone, she'd kill herself, she thought. She opened the box and sighed with relief. Nothing was missing. She replaced the box in the bottom drawer of her dresser and went to the garage, where she saw the reason why the door hadn't opened. Someone had pushed a large, empty box against the door-opener mechanism.

She returned to the kitchen and called 911. Ten minutes later two uniformed policewomen arrived. Julie showed them the damage. Questions were asked, and the house searched. No fingerprints anywhere.

The women were sympathetic. "We couldn't find anything, but call us if this happens again," one of them said.

Julie thanked them, choked down some food, and later, tried to sleep with one eye open. At three o'clock both eyes closed.

• • •

Monday afternoon was a disaster for Jim Perruda. He'd left his father's penthouse seething with rage and frustration. Perruda University in North Dakota? His father must have slipped a cog. He'd had a busy day at Perruda's Fine Furnishings. It was the season in Naples when northern snowbirds flocked to warm, sandy beaches, and snowless golf courses. The store offered upscale furnishings that pleased their affluent visitors, and Jim knew what people wanted in their beach-front high-rises and golf course villas.

Tony called him at four o'clock. "Carla and Phil have arrived. We've all talked to Dad and got blasted with a tirade. Can we meet tonight at your condo?"

"Sure. I'll call Laura. We can order Chinese takeout." Jim hated to make the call but knew Tony's request made sense. They'd made the trip to Naples and met with their father. It was time to talk. Jim nodded. "You're right, Tony. We have to do something."

Jim grimaced as he tried to speak to his brother in a friendly manner. They'd never been close. Four years difference in their ages may have contributed to their disagreements, but life in the Perruda home was never conducive to warm relationships. Their father was able to cause trouble between the boys, praising one, blaming the other, and always with the threat of the heavy, silver belt buckle. Carla kept away from her brothers. They both taunted her, laughed at her speech defect. She spent most of her home life in the basement with her dolls.

Now they were to unite with a common problem. It wouldn't be easy. Lifelong resentments and struggles were difficult to overcome, but Jim, the eldest, would do his best to keep peace.

He called Laura. "I hate to ask, but Tony, Carla, and Phil want to meet tonight at our condo. Could you order Chinese takeout?"

Laura agreed to order dinner. "It's the best I can do on short notice, Jim. You're right. We have to do something. We'll order in some Chinese and talk."

He left the store at five thirty. Laura met him with a kiss. "I phoned a Chinese restaurant, and they'll deliver when I call them. Your sister, Carla, called and said they'd be here about seven o'clock." Laura laughed. "You'll have an hour to collect your thoughts."

Laura and Jim met their guests at the door with the usual welcoming conversation. "How was the trip?" "You look great." "Are the guest rooms all right?" Just chitchat. Nothing threatening.

Jim offered drinks and took orders as Tony, Carla, and Phil sat and looked out at the Gulf and the estuary beyond the lanai. As Jim filled requests, Laura called the Chinese restaurant. Dinner would arrive in half an hour.

Jim was tense as he served scotch, gin, and vodka cocktails. Nobody looked at anybody. Each one sat as though this was a stage, but nobody remembered his lines. Drinks eased some of the awkward pauses, and when dinner arrived, the mood was a bit more relaxed. But after dinner the same nervousness returned.

"Let's go into the living room," Jim said. "We all know why we're here, so let's get on with it." Five people rose as one and settled themselves. He continued, "You know I had lunch with Dad yesterday, and you know what his plans are for our futures. He may be out in left field somewhere, but his mind's made up, and there's nothing we can do to change it."

"Phil and I went to s-s-see him this afternoon when w-w-we arrived," Carla said. "Our plane was l-l-late, so we didn't have much t-t-t-time. We talked just a little about the will, and we knew r-r-r-right away his m-m-mind was made up. He w-w-wasn't going to change it."

"I think he's not himself right now," Phil said.

"He's crazy, all right," Tony said. "I have an idea. It's not a nice one, but you might as well hear me out." He stood and looked out at the lanai, not at the others. "Dad's lived a long life. Not a good one for his family, but he's made a fortune, and now he's going to cut us out of his will. All three of us have talked to him, and it's like talking to a wall, a brick wall."

"S-s-s-so what c-c-can we d-d-do?" Carla looked up at Tony.

"I guess we have to remove the wall."

Jim felt as though the temperature of the room had suddenly dropped twenty degrees. He stared at Tony, and silence like a black, smothering shroud fell into the room, covering all senses, all reality.

Jim was the first to speak. "Oh, good Lord! You mean…" He stood, walked around the room, and made circles on his forehead with his fingers. "There has to be another solution."

"Y-y-yes," Carla said. "Maybe we could have him c-c-c-committed." She looked at Tony, her eyes pleading.

"I hate this," Laura said. "Can't you find a way to change his mind, help him to understand how this is going to affect all of us?"

Tony looked at the others. "I don't like this any more than you do. I've thought of every other way to change the will, and I can't find another alternative."

Jim sat and stared at his brother. Beads of sweat appeared on his forehead. He stood again and walked out into the lanai. He saw lights moving beyond the shore, small craft filled with carefree boaters. He heard laughter, faint, airy. He looked back at his family and shuddered. The contrast was unfathomable, like the Gulf at its deepest levels.

"It's crazy," he said as he returned to the davenport. Laura, next to him, took his hand, her head down. Jim looked at Carla and Phil. They too sat, unmoving, heads bowed.

Jim stood. "Tony, what you're suggesting is unthinkable, vile, and—" He paused. "Illegal. You can't kill someone, especially your father, because you want his money."

"N-n-n-no!" Carla stood. "It's cr-cr-crazy!"

Tony sat and looked at each one. He sighed. "Maybe you're right. Maybe it's crazy." He stood again and walked slowly to the door. "Let's sleep on it."

Jim looked at his brother. "Who's going to sleep, Tony? You've given us nightmares."

Tony nodded. "I know." He turned to Laura. "Thanks for having us here tonight."

Laura shook her head. "I'd like to say I was glad to have you here. Now I'm not sure. When I married Jim, I didn't know his family, and now I almost wish I still didn't." She looked at Carla's husband, Phil, who stood with Carla, his arm around her waist. "Welcome to insanity, Phil. As in-laws, we're stuck and committed too."

"Yeah." His smile was one-sided, rueful. "Carla and I have a lot to talk and think about." He looked at his watch and at Jim. "We need to get back to our rooms at Rosewood Center. Frank made arrangements for us."

Laura went to the kitchen and called a taxi service. "The cab will be here in ten minutes," she said.

"Come back tomorrow for coffee at ten o'clock," Jim said. "We don't know when Dad will make the change in his will, but we'll need to make decisions while we're together."

As he walked with them to the door, he looked at Tony. "If Dad had known what we were going to talk about tonight, he'd have canceled the rooms and sent all of us to individual cells with padded walls and barred windows."

As soon as Jim's family left to wait in the lobby for a taxi, he and Laura went to the kitchen. The ordinary cleanup routine was a welcome change from the upheaval of Tony's proposal. They sorted recycling and trash and filled the dishwasher. Now the kitchen was clean, neat, and ready for tomorrow, a sharp contrast from Jim and Laura's minds, still cluttered, filled with rotting, leftover plans for murder.

"What are you going to do?" Laura asked. She sat at the table, her eyes pleading for answers.

"I don't know. At least we agreed to meet tomorrow." He smiled. "This is probably the first time Tony and I have agreed on anything."

"I watched the dynamics tonight, the body language and the obvious, alien relationships among you, Tony, and Carla. As kids, did you ever sympathize after the beatings or comfort Carla as she hid in the basement?"

Jim shook his head. "Dad drove a wedge between Tony and me. We had to protect ourselves. I still don't trust Tony. Too much water over the dam."

"And too many rocks below the surface."

• • •

No one spoke as Carla, Phil, and Tony shared a cab to Rosewood Center. Each person relived and reviewed his evening at Luna de Ciel. Thoughts were private, not to be shared.

Carla and Phil undressed quickly. "I'll sh-sh-sh-shower in the m-m-morning," Carla said. "I'm too t-t-tired after our flight from B-B-B-Boston, talking to D-D-D-Daddy this afternoon, and t-t-t-tonight at Jim's c-c-condo."

"I'll shower, and you sleep." He kissed her. "You know I love you, and I'll agree to whatever your family decides. I don't like this any more than you do, but we'll be in this together."

• • •

Tony found a flask of scotch in his suitcase, poured a double shot into a glass, and added a splash of water. He sat in the lanai and stared out at the Gulf. He knew his proposal made sense to everyone, but carrying out the deed would change that person's life forever. And what if the person were caught in the act? What if his father fought back? And how would he be killed? Oh God, he thought, there's just too much to think about. He sipped his drink, looked out at the Gulf, and stared at distant lights, stars, and ships. A half-moon peeked out behind a cloud. Astronaut Neil Armstrong walked there. "A small step," he'd said. Tony shivered. Was his step tonight a small one or a giant one in his family's future? The moon seemed to look back at him, a celestial mirror. "Hey, little speck down there. What did you do tonight? Who are you in this giant scheme of things?"

And who was he, Tony thought. The middle kid, a beaten, scared, little boy and now an adult, a minor success who used what he had to improve, augment, and, in some cases, reverse the directions of his fears. Emma and he had a reasonably good marriage, with two teenage daughters. He looked up at the moon and nodded. Just a little speck, but even specks deserve consideration.

His father's lawyer interrupted the life he'd created and enjoyed. It awakened him to the reality of his father's influence, and all his fears, pain, and need for recompense returned. He knew his suggestion was correct. His father's behavior today was as repugnant as it ever was, but now, as an adult, he could take appropriate action. He'd earned his inheritance through years of abuse.

He turned from justification to choosing the killer. Carla and Jim were also justified, and all three needed to face that reality together. As his thoughts turned to Carla, he knew she must be disqualified, but Phil, her husband, a strong, ex-prizefighter, could and would replace her. Jim, Phil, and Tony—three potential executioners. Each must choose his own method, each must have an airtight alibi, and most important, no one must know the killer's identity. Secrecy was vital to their mission's success.

He thought about drawing straws, coins, or cards. Cards, of course. Three kings—a spade, a heart, and a club. Each would draw, remember the suit, and he, Tony, would collect them, face down, and destroy them. With that decision in mind, he finished his drink. Oh God, there was just too much to think about. He went to the living room, turned on the TV, watched the final scenes of a murder mystery, and thought maybe he was in a murder mystery. Too bad the studio wasn't paying him. He went to his bedroom. Two hours later he fell asleep.

• • •

On Tuesday morning the family met at Jim's condo, drank coffee, and tried to stay alert.

Jim stood and looked at his brother. "It's time now to finish what we started last night. A decision has to be made before Dad decides to build a university in North Dakota with our money, so let's consider alternatives to Tony's suggestion."

"Y-y-yes," Carla said. "Maybe we could have him c-c-c-committed." She looked at Tony, her eyes filled with tears.

"I hate this," Laura said. "Can't you find a way to change his mind, help him to understand how this is going to affect all of us?"

Tony looked at the others. "I don't like this any more than you do. I've thought of every other way to change the will, and I can't find another alternative."

Jim sat and stared at his brother. Beads of sweat appeared on his forehead. "If there isn't an alternative, who's going to do it? I know you're right, Tony, but murder's a crime. We could all get life in a moldy old jail cell."

"Not if the crime's clean, and there's no suspect."

"Tony, we'd all be suspects. Once that will business is out, the police will grill each of us, and somebody could break and admit the truth." He wiped his forehead and looked at Carla, who put her head down and gripped Phil's hand.

Jim leaned back, his mind whirling. They needed that money. He'd earned it living with him all those years, still stuck with his demands, giving orders almost every day. Jim had no love for his father, not even respect, but he was a human being, and taking a life was almost unthinkable. But what else could they do?

He stood, walked around the room and turned to Tony. "I know it's wrong, but I think it has to be done. How could we do it, and how could we get away with it?"

"What about Diane?" Laura asked. "She's with Frank most of the time."

"She loves to shop, so it could be done during her shopping trips," Jim answered. He made circles on his forehead. "Here's another thought. Dad tells me that she watches TV every night. She goes into her bedroom with the TV and doesn't come out. Dad says sometimes he has to bang on the door to get her attention."

"That's important, but who's going to do it?" Phil asked.

"I've thought of that," Tony said. "It's up to you, Jim, and me. Carla, I'm sure you'd agree."

Carla nodded. "I-I-I couldn't d-d-d-do it. But who?"

Tony looked at Jim. "Do you have a pack of old playing cards? I want three kings, a heart, a spade, and a club. We draw, and the one who gets the spade king does the job. Not one of us will know who got the spade because I'll tear them up after we draw. All three of us should have an alibi of some sort. Only Jim lives in Naples, but he can find one."

"I j-j-j-just can't even think about it," Carla said. "He's our father. He wasn't a v-v-very good one, but still…" She stopped and wiped her eyes.

"He's not my father," Laura said, "but I can understand how you all feel." She stared at Jim. "But how do you kill someone? Even if it's your father or father-in-law, how can you do it?"

Jim answered. "You do it because there's no other way, no alternative. Oh, we could declare him too senile to make a will, but knowing our dear father, he'd make more sense to the doctors than we would. He's crafty and he's smart."

He went to the bedroom, returned with a pack of cards, and gave it to Tony. He watched as his brother sorted through the deck and put three cards in his pocket.

"B-b-but he's still our f-f-f-father. A human being," Carla said. "How can we even th-th-think about doing this?"

Phil took her hand. "Honey, if you can think of any other way to change his plans, let's hear it. I know this is a terrible thing to do, but what else can we do?"

"I know. I know. I d-d-don't know what else to do either."

Five heads were bowed, each with his own thoughts, dreads, and fears. No one spoke but each nodded.

Tony looked at each one. "Then it's decided, and we've all agreed. No backing out now." He watched as each person nodded. He took the three cards from his pocket. "The one who gets the spade can't tell anybody, not his wife, not his priest or minister. Not anybody." More nods. He offered cards, face down, to Phil and Jim and took the other. He gathered them up, face down, tore them into tiny pieces, took them into the kitchen, and turned on the disposal. Everyone heard the noise. Three blank faces stared into space.

• • •

Tony looked at the beach in front of the room Frank had reserved at Rosewood Center. Four hours had passed since he, Carla, and

Phil had left Jim's condo. They'd waited for the taxi, sitting in separate lobby chairs, staring at nothing. No one spoke, and when they arrived at Rosewood Center, they hurried into their rooms. Tony changed into his bathing suit and ran to the beach. He plunged into the water, hoping cool waves might clear his head. A decision had been made. Now that decision demanded action.

He looked back and saw Carla and Phil walking along the beach. He swam toward them. "The water's great. I'd like to stay longer," Tony said. "Maybe rent something on the beach."

"We'd like that too," Phil said. "Remember, Jim's wife is a Realtor. Maybe she could find a condo or even a small house for a short time, a week or two."

Tony pulled out his cell phone and punched in Laura's number. He explained their need and asked her to check her listings.

Her response was immediate. "You're in luck. I just had a cancellation this morning for a two-family unit on the beach near us. The price is out of sight, but it's the season."

"I'll ask Carla and Phil. Hold on." He looked at Phil. "Laura has something for us on the beach. It's expensive but available."

When Carla and Phil nodded, he spoke to Laura. "We'd like it. When can we move in?"

Tony listened, closed his phone, and said, "We can move in today. Let's drive over to Jim's and get the keys."

• • •

Russell Jones had left his mother at Rosewood Center on Monday afternoon and had taken the airport shuttle to Fort Myers. His four-fifteen flight was on time, and he had spent his travel time thinking about both his mother and Julie. His interview with the caregiver had been a success, and Marjory assured him she would carry out her responsibilities with concern for his mother. He gave her a list of phone numbers and instructions and left knowing that his mother would be cared for properly.

And then there was Julie. Russ smiled as he pictured her behind her desk, her blond hair, shoulder-length and wavy, her blue eyes that sparkled when she laughed, and ah, those legs! He wondered if she really appreciated her slim ankles and firm calves. She'd worn a white blouse with a light-blue scarf that matched her eyes, and her navy-blue skirt was exactly the right length. She'd plunged right in to assist his mother, even with the spilled syrup, and he knew she would continue to help in any situation, a double reassurance that all would be well during his absence.

He hadn't been that interested in a woman since Amy, his wife, died five years ago. His work with the Drug Enforcement Agency brought him into contact with many beautiful, talented young women, but no one had turned on any exciting vibes or sexual arousal for more than a day or two. There'd been that long weekend scuba diving in Key West and a week skiing in Aspen, but romance ended when the plane landed in Washington.

He thought again about Amy, their college romance, their wedding in Portland, Maine, her home. Both of them were involved in law enforcement, he with the DEA in Virginia, she with security at the Pentagon. A good marriage. They'd planned to have children, but cancer canceled their hopes. He pushed aside the agonies of her illness and returned to the present, here in seat 2A en route to Reagan International Airport.

Once inside the terminal, he called his mother. Marjory answered. His mother had eaten a good dinner catered by the restaurant service and had retired early. No problems. He wanted to call Julie, but thought it might be too soon, too presumptuous. Perhaps she was out on a date with some jock. He erased that thought and took a cab to his apartment at the Rotonda Condominiums in McLean, Virginia.

He was much too busy Tuesday morning to think about Naples. He arrived at his office in Arlington, Virginia, and immediately responded to calls, e-mail, and faxes that had arrived during his short time in Florida. He spent a busy day catching up on three cases in Alabama that had involved the DEA. As a

Salt Marsh Sinners

supervisory special agent who often worked with the FBI, he was called in often to assist with local crimes that involved a variety of drugs. He knew the complications that could arise between local law enforcement and the agency, and he kept a low profile unless he was asked to assist.

On Wednesday he thought about calling his mother, but Julie was on his mind. He could call Julie and ask about his mother. Easy, effortless, with no hidden agenda. Get real, Russ, he told himself. You really want to talk to Julie, don't you? He nodded to himself and made the call. Surprising how a voice can enrich a day! Julie's "Rosewood Center. May I help you?" was what he needed in the midst of Alabama's drug problems.

"It's good to hear your voice, Julie. I called to check on my mother."

"Your mother is fine, Russ, and Marjory is an excellent caregiver. They were outside this afternoon."

"Good. Please tell her I called if she asks. She doesn't remember when I come to Naples." He paused. "I hope to get back soon for another lunch with you."

"I'd like that, Russ, and don't worry about your mother. I'll call you if something goes wrong."

Russ smiled. Alabama's problems faded into a minor irritation.

• • •

Neither Laura nor Jim slept well Tuesday night. They ate breakfast hurriedly, and Jim drove to the furniture store, dodging mid-morning traffic. He was surprised to see his father at the store. Frank usually appeared about two o'clock in the afternoon.

He greeted Jim with a frown. "Glad you finally showed up," he grumbled. "We'll have lunch together. I only had burnt toast for breakfast, and Diane can't even make coffee."

Jim laughed. "Okay, Dad. Lunch at noon." He went to his office and sorted through invoices and memos, trying to keep his mind out of Monday night's dinner party and Tuesday's decision. What a meeting! They'd kill their father? Who was crazy now?

• • •

Frank was relieved that Jim's arrival had been late. He needed to get back into the receiving dock and check on the bar stools he'd ordered from his contact in Vera Cruz, Mexico.

His breakfast at home on Wednesday morning had been a disaster. Diane, who decided that a nursing career was more important than learning to cook, had somehow managed to boil an egg. Her coffee looked like the Ganges River in flood tide, so Frank took charge of the coffee maker. He read the morning newspaper while Diane struggled with making toast. Three batches burned in the toaster oven.

"Dammit, Diane, can't you even make toast?" Frank had asked.

Diane shrugged. "You do it. I don't have time."

Frank had taken over the task, finished his breakfast, and called for his car. "I'm going down to the store. I'll be home in time for dinner."

He had been relieved to get away from Diane. He had work to do at the store, work that didn't involve Jim or anyone else. Traffic was heavy, but he arrived at the store in time to go through the mail. Nothing interested him. Jim managed the necessary details, so he was able to spend his time in his own office handling private business. He'd done well. His shipments from Mexico had been successful. The store sold the merchandise he ordered, but not before he had time to readjust the items. Shipping drugs was a specialty, and he knew the people south of the border who were experts. He personally checked each one and paid them well. He'd learned the importance of a truck driver's attitude at the border. One hint of nervousness, and the border patrol was on the alert.

Salt Marsh Sinners

Today he awaited the arrival of six bar stools from Vera Cruz, Mexico. The truck would be driven to the border by a Mexican driver who would meet Perruda's driver, Patrick Davis, at McAllen, Texas. Patrick had worked for Frank Perruda for three years and had proved to be an excellent replacement for Frank's previous driver, who now languished in a prison cell in Nevada. People in law enforcement take a dim view of grand theft. Frank, with a fat wallet, was able to keep the Perruda name out of the proceedings.

The bar stools had been constructed in a small town near Vera Cruz. Each stool was upholstered in white leather, with four hollow chrome legs, and each leg would now contain plastic bags of cocaine. Frank intended to be at the receiving dock when the truck arrived. He had talked to Patrick on his disposable cell phone he used exclusively for his import transactions and was assured that on this Wednesday at three o'clock, the truck would arrive as planned.

Frank spent the morning checking the store's display rooms and greeting customers who had time to visit with Mr. Perruda, the distinguished owner of Perruda's Fine Furnishings. At noon Frank found Jim conferring with a young woman with vibrant red hair that matched her flaming red pantsuit. He waited as Jim wrote something on his business card. The woman walked slowly to the entrance, turned, and waved to Jim.

Frank watched her departure, then asked, "How about some lunch? I'm hungry."

Jim laughed. "I'm hungry too. Let's go to the mall. I don't have time for a leisurely martini lunch."

Conversation was limited because of the crowds of shoppers who stopped for a quick bite between Macy's and Sears. "Business was good this morning," Jim said as he ordered a chicken salad and iced tea.

"I'll be on the floor until about three o'clock if you need me," Frank said. He was relieved when Jim didn't bring up the subject of the will change. Apparently his children recognized the wisdom of his decision. He relaxed, knowing he was right, they were wrong, and now they knew it, all of them.

He checked his watch. Two o'clock. Patrick Davis should be arriving in an hour with the bar stools. He walked out to the receiving dock in the back of the store and watched his crews unloading truckloads of furniture. He sat down on a crate labeled "This Side Up" and waited. Ten minutes later his disposable cell phone rang.

"Yes? Hi, Pat. Where are you?" He leaned forward and cursed silently.

"I'm in northern Florida, Panama City. The truck leaked oil and had to be fixed. I'll get to Naples in a day or two."

"Dammit, Pat. I expected you to be here today. I need those stools. I've got contacts with deadlines. Shit! Come as soon as you can, and call me when you're close to Naples."

Frank didn't wait for an answer. He replaced his phone and glared at the trucks that were decently on schedule without any problems with a cocaine shipment. Damn! Life's a bitch, he thought. Diane's driving me crazy. My kids hate me, and now I'm in big trouble with Cynthia and her suppliers. I almost wish I was dead!

CHAPTER THREE

Wednesday was moving day for Tony, Carla, and Phil. They packed and met in the lobby of Rosewood Center. Julie accepted their credit cards and gave them receipts.

"I hope the rooms were all right," she said.

Tony answered. "They were fine. We're moving to a condo on the beach. Laura Perruda found us something." Tony realized he'd been impatient when he arrived on Monday, and this was a good time to show another side of his character, even though he had to grit his teeth to act the part of a warmhearted, kind, and sincere person. It wasn't easy after two days of pure hell. He smiled at Julie. "Will you call a cab for us?"

"I rented a car this morning," Phil said. "You can ride with us."

"Thanks. We can stop at Jim's condo. Laura will have the keys for us, I hope."

"After we get the keys, let's have lunch together." Phil said. "I'm hungry, and I think we can all use some strong coffee."

Laura met them at the door. "I have the keys for you, and here are the directions. I'd go with you, but I have an appointment. Jim's already left for the store." She gave Tony and Phil each a map of the location. "You can pay me with a credit card anytime."

Three hungry, tired, and nervous people thanked Laura and found the café Laura had suggested. Lunch with several cups of coffee revived them enough to locate the condo, unpack, and change into bathing suits.

"We can't do anything this afternoon," Tony said. "We might as well enjoy the beach." He led the way and plunged into the surf. Carla and Phil followed. They swam close to the shore for an hour, returned to the condo, showered and dressed, and sat in the great room staring down at the tile floor.

"I-I-I'm going to call home and check on the k-k-kids," Carla said and went into the bedroom.

In the kitchen Tony studied the coffee maker. He and Phil might find comfort in another cup. The previous occupant had left a can of coffee, and Tony made a pot. He returned to the living room with two mugs, handed one to Phil, and stared out at the Gulf. What could he say? Did you get the spade king? If I have it, I'd sound pretty silly. But he won't know I have it if I have it. If he has it, he won't say anything either.

Conversation slumped into weather conditions in Minneapolis and Boston, snow removal, and the difficulties of winter traffic. Carla joined them, and the conversation changed to problems with children under a neighbor's care. Mrs. Murphy reported the two children were all right, but there had been a head-lice scare at school, and she didn't know if the children would be sent home.

"I'd better call Emma," Tony said and went out to the lanai with his cell phone. He punched in his home number and listened to Emma's recorded voice.

"This is Emma. I've taken the children for a short vacation. The school has given them assignments. I don't know when we'll be back. Please leave your name, phone number, and a brief message."

Tony closed the phone and stared at the ceiling. Why would she leave with the kids? Where would she go? Damn! He returned inside and picked up his coffee mug. "Emma's taken the kids and gone somewhere," he said.

"Now you don't have to worry about hurrying home," Phil said. "Might as well enjoy a winter break here."

"I don't like this, Phil. It's not like Emma to go off without telling me. Maybe she went to see her stupid family. They don't like me much, and the feeling's mutual."

"Where do her parents live?"

"In some little dump in South Dakota."

"M-m-maybe they could t-t-tell us about where Daddy wants his college," Carla said. "Maybe you should c-c-call them."

"I'll think about it." Tony didn't want to think about it. He didn't want to think about Emma, the kids, and snow in the backyard. He wished he could turn his mind off completely.

• • •

Tony's wife, Emma, had relaxed briefly when her husband left their home in Wayzata, Minnesota, on Monday and had flown to Naples. She'd called her friends and made a luncheon date, but now her thoughts turned to a marriage that had somehow turned sour. They'd met at a fraternity dance at the University of Minnesota in Minneapolis. She'd loved Tony as soon as she looked at his curly black hair, brown eyes that promised love forever, and a mouth that could whisper sweet and beautiful words. She didn't know what Tony saw in her. Attractive, yes, with long blond hair that complemented her straight shoulders. Blue eyes that echoed a Nordic ancestry. But she was from the country, and he was from Boston and could choose any girl he wanted. Why me, she wondered, but her love for Tony overshadowed her question.

Their wedding in Dell Rapids, South Dakota, was not the beginning but definitely the end of a fairy tale. Tony conveniently forgot his home in Boston was hardly a prince's castle, and his father had abused his family. He'd deliberately replaced those memories with figments of his imagination, a happy home in a big city. Here in a small mid-western town, he felt superior, misunderstood, and completely out of place.

They moved to Minneapolis, where Tony gradually worked his way into the top sales division of a local brokerage firm. In their twenty-three years of marriage, they'd progressed from a small walk-up downtown to a modest home near Lake Calhoun to their present house in Wayzata, an upscale suburb of Minneapolis, on Lake Minnetonka.

Tony became more demanding and impatient as years went by, and his resentment of her small-town heritage grated. Emma's parents saw the change in their son-in-law's attitude, and their visits lessened. And so did Emma's sex life. Tony became less interested in pleasing her, and her orgasms decreased. Now there was little sexual activity, and Emma was almost relieved. She often wondered if Tony had found pleasure and excitement with another woman, but she wouldn't ask. A discussion of their sexual life could only lead to greater conflicts, and she didn't need more confrontations.

She was almost relieved when he flew to Naples. Lunch with her friends had been a welcome respite from family worries. They'd talked about the latest theater opening, the problems with city government, and minor disputes involving teenage children. Emma returned home, poured a glass of merlot, and thought about her future. She needed a change in her life, maybe a trip somewhere, but what about the girls? Emma checked her school calendar. Could lessons be provided so the girls could fly with her to…where? Someplace far from snow and her life with Tony.

She called the high school, visited with a counselor, and learned that lessons could indeed be provided for the girls. They were both honor students, and even a brief visit to a foreign country would be a rewarding experience for them. She would send the material home with the girls and give them instructions.

Emma called a travel agent friend and asked for suggestions. Her response was overwhelming. So much to see, so many mountains, temples, cathedrals, museums. Her friend filled her computer with brochures and personal ideas. When the girls returned from school, Emma had already selected Martinique as their destination. Because both girls were studying French, the French island was a perfect choice.

Packing was easy. Tank tops, shorts, bathing suits, and passports. The travel agent said although bookings were difficult at this time of year, she'd be able to put them on a Wednesday morning flight. She also booked them into a two-bedroom condo on the beach at Pointe de Bout. Emma received tickets, itinerary, and condo reservations by e-mail and quickly followed through with boarding passes. She didn't want to call Tony, who would probably start an argument, maybe even forbid her to go, so she left a voice mail on the phone. On Wednesday she and the girls waved good-bye to snowbanks and winter winds.

• • •

Frank Perruda sat on a crate in the shipping bay at Perruda's Fine Furnishings. His call to Patrick Davis, who was to bring the bar stools from the Mexican border in Texas, gave him heartburn and stomach cramps. A minor problem with the truck had delayed his plans for the day, and who knew when Pat would arrive?

"Damn," he muttered as he watched two workmen unload three dining-room sets and two grand pianos. He admired their strength and youth. He did that kind of work when he was young, he thought. Getting old wasn't fun, and now with his three kids screaming and wailing, life was even worse. And Diane! God, he must have been drugged from all those pills in the hospital. He looked back at the store. Good people took care of customers, and Jim handled all the major problems. Maybe life wasn't too bad after all. Pat wouldn't arrive today. Maybe he wouldn't go home this afternoon. Maybe he could find something or someone to fill time until Pat arrived.

He walked back inside and looked around. Jim and two salesmen were visiting with customers. The store looked professional but friendly, upscale but warm. In his office he sat at his desk and drew out a pocket-sized notebook. Wonder if Sally Torrino remembers me, he thought. He punched in her phone numbers and waited, hoping for recognition and availability.

Sally's response was almost more than Frank had hoped for. "Oh, Frankie, baby, how are you? Long time no see. When can I see you?"

Frank answered with a mixture of anxiety and fear. Diane would raise hell if she found out, but God, he wanted Sally now. He stood and rearranged his trousers. "I'll pick you up at your salon at five thirty. Save your evening for me."

He spent the rest of the afternoon visiting with customers and avoiding Jim. He wanted no questions and no reminders of family disputes. He called Diane and told her that he'd be busy with buyers all evening. He thought about Sally. She would love his plan for the university. He'd tell her after dinner, after they'd returned to her apartment, after they'd made love several times. He smiled and felt young again.

• • •

Back at her condo at Luna de Ciel, Laura, Jim's wife, sat at her computer and checked listings that looked appropriate for her abilities. She knew the market now and had a clientele of people who trusted her honesty. She was pleased to have found a condo for Jim's family, but last night's and this morning's events right here in her living room still gave her chills. Who drew the spade king? God, please don't let it be Jim, she prayed. She knew him so well, his faults and virtues. Could he really kill his own father? Of the three, Tony seemed to be the most capable. After all, it was his idea. Would he have stacked them to eliminate himself? So many questions whirled through her mind that she turned off the computer and drank leftover breakfast coffee.

Her brief time with Janet on Monday had been a delightful switch from family worries. She fondly remembered their first meeting at an art show on Fifth Avenue. Four blocks of the busiest street in downtown Naples were sealed off, and artists' tents lined the middle of the street. A festive time. Outdoor stands offered lemonade, Greek sandwiches, tacos, and other ethnic delights. Artisans from all over the world came with their work, and the street and sidewalks were filled with buyers and lookers. When Laura entered a tent that displayed framed watercolor and oil paintings of the Gulf of Mexico, she noticed a beach scene in watercolor that would do well in the guest bedroom. She stepped back to study the picture and bumped into a tall, willowy brunette who looked like a Paris model. When Laura excused herself, the woman laughed.

"Do you like it?"

"Yes," Laura answered. "Do you?"

"I should, because I painted it."

Laura, who couldn't draw a straight line, was impressed. "You have real talent. Do you live here?"

"Yes. I'm Janet Clark. Here's my card. If you want it, I'll reduce the price a bit."

Laura bought the painting and invited the artist to share a taco, and that was the start of their relationship. Janet invited her to visit her studio, and Laura recognized something special in her work. Janet's paintings were emotional on a flat surface, exciting on a canvas. Her colors were vibrant yet subdued, an enigma.

During Laura's third visit, Janet stroked Laura's hand as they sat together on the davenport. Laura looked at her, surprised, but how could this be? She felt a stirring she hadn't experienced in several months. She looked at Janet, and she knew theirs was not ever again to be a casual, platonic relationship.

Janet led her to her bedroom. When Janet shut the door behind her, Laura laughed. "If this were an old movie, that closed door would signify the end of the scene."

Janet bent over and kissed Laura's forehead. "But this isn't an old movie, and the fun has just begun." Now three years later, Laura and Janet arranged occasional weekends at art shows and spent as much time together as Laura could find with no questions asked. Her work as a Realtor gave her excuses for time away from home, and Jim with a full-time job and a need to gamble was too busy to notice her absences.

Today her schedule left no time for Janet. She had back-to-back appointments from ten o'clock this morning until five thirty this afternoon. She left the computer and dressed for her clients. As she applied makeup, she relaxed, knowing her mind would be so occupied with business that there would be no time to wallow in last night's nightmare.

• • •

Julie Rogers worked at her concierge desk at Rosewood Center caring for the needs and requests of the residents. She drove home after work on Wednesday, hoping there would be no more chaos, and as she parked in her garage and entered the house, she was relieved to find everything in its place, untouched.

The phone rang as she searched her freezer for something suitable for dinner. "Yes?" She listened as a woman introduced herself as Julie's new neighbor from Montreal.

"I wanted to call and tell you about what happened to your house Monday night, but I was afraid to call. May I come over?"

"Of course. I'd like to meet you."

Julie made coffee and forgot about dinner. Her curiosity was larger than her appetite. The doorbell rang, and Julie hurried to open the door.

A thirty-something woman wearing a blue warm-up suit smiled and shook her hand. "I'm so glad to meet you. I'm Lisette Mureau." She turned and pulled on a heavy leash behind her. "And this is Heidi, our Saint Bernard. She's the one who almost trashed your house."

"Oh." Julie was speechless. A dog had jammed the garage door, slept on a chair, played with her cushions, and messed up her kitchen? Julie found her voice. "How did she get in?"

"Heidi can push anything, and apparently your front door wasn't shut tight."

Julie thought about her usual hurried Monday morning departure. She'd opened the front door to retrieve the newspaper and had apparently forgotten to shut it tightly.

"I'm always rushed on Mondays. I work at a retirement home, and the weekend crew usually presents me with a mountain of leftover tasks." She waved her neighbor into the living room. "Would you like coffee? I just made it."

"Yes, thank you. I heard about the problem yesterday. One of your neighbors talked to the police who came to your house." She smiled and offered her hand. "I'm sorry that Heidi wasn't a good neighbor. It won't happen again. We're fencing our backyard."

Julie studied Heidi, the naughty Saint Bernard. She was about two-and-a-half feet tall, with a broad nose and a pink tongue that protruded from her wide mouth. Big brown eyes overwhelmed a muzzle big enough to swallow a squirrel in one bite. Long ears and heavy, golden fur rippled as she walked around the room.

"Sit," said Lisette. Heidi wagged her long bushy tail, upsetting a vase of daisies that stood on the coffee table.

When Julie returned from the kitchen with a roll of paper towels, Heidi sat by Lisette, her tail still in motion.

"I'm sorry," Lisette said. "Heidi isn't used to a lot of furniture. We try to keep our house Heidi-friendly."

"Don't worry, nothing's broken." Julie returned to the kitchen with two mugs and relaxed as they drank coffee together. Lisette would be a good neighbor. They shared their histories briefly, and Lisette invited Julie for dinner sometime the following week.

"We've just moved in, and we're rearranging and repainting the walls. I hope you won't mind the disorder, and I hope you like French cooking."

Julie, who had a passion for brioche, assured her that anything would be delightful. Lisette finished her coffee and left with a promise to meet again soon. When Julie returned to her freezer, she suddenly thought about Russ. She wanted to tell him about her experience with Heidi and now Lisette. Please call me, she asked silently, but she remembered she hadn't given him her home or cell phone numbers. She'd just have to wait and hope.

She spent the evening catching up on her e-mail and watching TV. Nothing exciting, and her day hadn't been overly stimulating. She fell asleep still hoping for a call from Russell Jones.

Thursday was a quiet day at Rosewood Center. The bus had taken many of the residents to an art exhibit in Tampa. Mrs. Johnson stopped at Julie's desk to model her new bathing suit.

"I talked to Cynthia yesterday and asked her why she left me," she said. "We'd planned to go shopping. She apologized and took me to lunch at the Turtle Club. We're still friends."

Julie laughed. "I'm glad you patched things up. It's not easy sometimes."

"That's true, but at our age, we don't have enough time to wallow in anger."

Mrs. Johnson waved good-bye and pushed her walker to the front door. George came by and picked up a few slips requesting minor repairs while Julie sipped coffee and thought about Russ again. She stopped thinking and punched in his mother's phone number.

Marjory, the caregiver, answered. "I'm glad you called. Mrs. Jones is fine, but I have a problem. My mother in Estero is ill, and I may have to go up to see her. I'll call Mr. Jones and tell him."

Julie was quick. "I can call him for you. I have his business number, but not his cell or landline."

"I'd appreciate that. Here are the numbers. If I have to go, it will only be for a short time, and Mrs. Jones manages very well. I really don't have to do much for her."

Julie called Russ's business phone and after hearing "Please hold" several times, heard his voice. "Russ Jones speaking."

"Hi, Russ. This is Julie at Rosewood Center. Everything's fine with your mother, so don't be alarmed. Marjory asked me to call you because her mother's ill, and she might have to leave briefly. She's not worried because your mother is doing so well."

Salt Marsh Sinners

"Thanks for calling. I wanted to call you anyway. How are you?"

He sounded so caring, so interested in her. Julie gulped. "I'm fine."

She told him about her encounter with Heidi, and Russ laughed. "I'm glad it was a dog, not a thief. I won't worry about Mother. I know this illness has ups and downs. She's up now, and that's good."

"How is your work?" Julie frowned at her stupid question. What could he say if it was classified?

"I'm flying to Indianapolis tomorrow for a few days." There was a pause. "I'd rather be flying to Naples to see you."

"I wish you were too, but you'll be back in a few weeks, I hope." Julie heard bleeps in the background.

"Sorry, I have to go. Stay in touch, and I'll see you soon."

The phone went dead, and so did Julie's hopes for Russ's quick return to Naples.

• • •

Russ Jones, relieved that his mother was safe and content, boarded his plane bound for Indianapolis. He was welcomed aboard by a smiling flight attendant and ushered to seat 2A. She stowed his carry-on and brought water and suggestions for other beverages. After lunch he thought about his assignment. He unlocked his briefcase and reread the information. It was all on a disk, of course, but he preferred the written word. Old-fashioned, he thought. Maybe I'm getting old too.

The owner of a major General Motors dealership in downtown Indianapolis had been shot and killed in the parking lot behind his building. It was obviously a case for the local authorities, but a further investigation revealed a cache of heroin stuffed inside one of the small motors that had been shipped from Mexico. Now it involved the DEA, and Russ was assigned to work with the Indianapolis Police Department.

After studying the material, he relocked his briefcase, rested his head against the seatback, and thought about Julie. He'd call from his hotel and set up a date. Two dates. Maybe three. He smiled and picked up his copies of *Time* and *Newsweek*. Later he had a short nap and awakened as the plane slowed for its approach into the Indianapolis airport.

He was met at the gate by a uniformed police officer and escorted through the crowd to a police car.

"The chief is anxious to meet you," the officer said. "The victim was well-known here, so the rumor factory is working overtime. His widow has already hired a crew of eager young lawyers to clear her husband's name, and we don't even know who killed him or how or why the drugs appeared at the dealership."

"I suppose the press is on your tail asking questions and interviewing the family."

"Yeah, and they get in our way sometimes. We want to find the killer like yesterday, and the reporters want to drag it out. Makes great copy for the media."

Russ laughed. "It's the same everywhere. Maybe I can run interference for the chief." He sat back and thought about his recent cases. Similar in some ways, yet totally different in many procedures and outcomes.

He was ushered into the police chief's office, and the two men reviewed the case together. Russ became completely immersed in the murder. He met and admired the work of the police and detectives who spent hours on investigation, interrogation, and research. Timing was important, but careful attention to all details was essential in solving the case.

Russ spent a week in Indianapolis and was relieved and satisfied when the killer was identified and arrested. The wife of the victim grieved but knew justice had been served. After a thorough investigation, Russ had uncovered a drug trafficking operation, and arrests were made quickly. The victim's son was now the automobile dealership's new owner, and life in Indianapolis had, at least for the present, returned to its normal routine.

Salt Marsh Sinners

Russ called Julie but was unable to reach her. He'd try later. He returned to Washington tired but content. Working with competent, dedicated men and women was challenging, sometimes humbling, and he'd been an important segment of that team. His report would be welcomed as a success. Sometimes you win one, he thought. Trite but true.

• • •

Patrick Davis, the driver of Frank Perruda's truck, slouched in a booth at Bill's Diner, his legs sprawled out under the table. It was Tuesday. He'd made it from the border in McAllen, Texas, to Panama City, Florida, before the truck began to leak oil. Now all he could do was watch the body shop across the street and wait. He leaned back, and his shaved, bald head covered by a red Boston Red Sox cap, rested on the back of his chair. He looked sideways across the street at the body shop. His truck, packed with six precious bar stools that held packets of cocaine hidden in the stools' hollow chrome legs, had been hoisted up onto a lift in the garage. Patrick worried. God, what if the truck fell off? He sat up, ate a bowl of chili, drank three cups of coffee, and thought about his situation. His call to Frank Perruda hadn't helped. Frank was mad as usual. He was mad most of the time these days.

Patrick sat back and thought about his three years with Frank Perruda. He'd heard about Frank from Frank's brother Luigi, who was involved in safer but still illegal activities in Rochester, New York. Patrick had driven for Luigi, but after too many bouts with icy roads and fog, he wanted clear vision without snow and ice. Frank hired him to pick up a load of dining-room furniture in McAllen, Texas, and drive it to his furniture store in Naples, Florida. He was to meet his Mexican truck just this side of the border. It was so easy. There were no hidden drugs. The second trip was a bit more difficult because cocaine was hidden in the legs of a davenport. Again, the driver knew what to do.

He'd arranged to follow a decoy truck that contained thirty-five pounds of marijuana. While that vehicle was pulled over and searched thoroughly, the Mexican truck was eased through with minimal inspection.

Patrick learned new techniques, and his many trips to McAllen became routine, the truck filled with cocaine-hidden furniture, Patrick's mind filled with worry, anxiety, and fear. Patrick had hoped for success on this trip, and it had proved successful. Now all he needed was to get to Naples as soon as possible.

As Patrick watched the body shop, he remembered another shop in San Antonio, Texas, his hometown. The shop sold bikes, shiny, fancy bikes with lots of speeds and chrome, the kind his mother could never afford. He was thirteen years old, and the bike was brand new, red with white markings. He wanted it, so he waited until the shop's owner turned his back, grabbed the bike, and rode away. Three hours of hell followed, with the owner, the police, his mother, and grandmother all involved.

"Shame on you!" said his grandmother, pointing a long, thin finger at his skinny chest.

"How could you do this, Patrick?" his mother wailed. "But somebody should have locked up those bikes."

For Patrick it was just another ordeal, with his mother defending him, blaming the authorities and the shop owner who ought to keep his bikes out of the reach of innocent young boys. Maybe the father he never knew might have reacted differently. Who knows? His mother was always there to protect him, no matter what he did. When he dropped out of high school, it was because the principal was too strict. When he forged a check with his mother's signature, he was only playing, officer. Don't send him away. I'll watch over him.

Patrick was twenty-two when his mother died of cancer, and he was left with no one to help him. He worked at several places, never rising above the lowest positions. His sense of time didn't conform to office or café hours. And work? Less was best. He had one special attribute, however. He could drive anything, anytime. He drove for pizzerias, florists, and postal services, but because he was strong physically, his favorite job was hauling furniture. He'd found his niche in the world of trucking, and he was content.

At last, at four o'clock, he watched as his truck was lowered from the hoist. He brushed cracker crumbs from his knee-length denim shorts and sleeveless T-shirt and walked across the street. He paid the mechanic with cash and slid up onto the driver's seat.

He pulled out his cell phone and called Frank. "I'm leaving Panama City now," Patrick said. "The truck's fixed, and the cargo's safe. I won't get to Naples until tomorrow sometime. I'll drive to the store and call you."

"Okay. I'll wait for your call. And for God's sake, don't get picked up for speeding. Another hour or so on the road isn't that important."

Pat pocketed his cell and thought about his transactions with Frank. The money was never enough to cover the worry and fear that accompanied his trips. He could rot in jail, and Frank wouldn't give a damn. He'd find another sucker to do his dirty work. Maybe it was time for a little chat. He liked the old man, however, in spite of his resentments over money. Maybe together they could work something out that would be more acceptable, something more for Patrick. Hauling drugs was risky business. Frank owed him for the chances he took. Patrick smiled as he thought about a salary increase, and the smile broadened as he thought about his future, far from Naples and Frank Perruda. Because Patrick hadn't given Frank an exact arrival date, he called his friend, Chuck, in Tampa.

"Hi. I had trouble in Panama City, but now I can stop in Tampa. I want to schedule the trip we discussed last month. I really want to leave Naples, and you said you could help."

Patrick listened as Chuck offered a bed and detailed plans. "I can take you to Tampa in my boat, Pat. That's the first step."

Patrick's mind whirled as he listened to Chuck. Sure, he could stay in Naples demanding higher pay, but he'd rather move, find another job, another location, a new life.

• • •

Carla, her husband, Phil, and brother, Tony, spent Wednesday and Thursday on the beach. They dined at restaurants on Fifth Avenue, shopped at Saks and Nordstrom's, and were bored. Thursday evening they sat watching TV. Carla had made popcorn. They chewed and yawned.

Finally Tony said, "I think I'll drive down to Key West tomorrow for the weekend. Dad isn't going to do anything about his will now, and I'd like to get away."

"That's a good idea," Phil said. "Maybe Carla and I will drive up to Orlando and visit Disney World. We'd be back here on Monday."

Carla interrupted. "I w-w-want to call home again, Phil. I'm wondering about the lice p-p-problem." She went to the bedroom and returned a few minutes later. "Bad news. I c-c-called, and all the k-k-kids are being sent home. I can't leave Mrs. M-M-Murphy with our kids. She has three of her own. I th-th-think I should fly home if I can get a t-t-ticket. You could drop me off on the way to Orlando."

Before Phil could answer, Carla called the agent Laura had suggested, mentioned a family emergency, and was booked on a Friday morning flight to Boston. Phil sat and put his head in his hands.

"I don't like you leaving like this, Carla. I know I can't help much at home, but going to Orlando alone won't be much fun."

"I know, b-b-b-but maybe I can make other arrangements for the k-k-kids and meet you in Orlando. M-m-maybe on Sunday."

"Okay, and try to get back soon."

Plans for the weekend livened their evening, and they retired with three travel plans whirling in their minds. Too much togetherness had been wearing. Tony never did like Phil very much, and Carla's speech defect drove him crazy. Carla and Phil were glad to get away from Tony. His bragging about his career and his scathing remarks about Emma and her family were grating. None of the three spoke about Tony's plan for killing Frank Perruda. The one who drew the spade king would forever keep his silence. There was no reason to discuss it.

Tony got up early Friday morning and called Jim. "We're planning to take off today, Jim. I'm going to Key West for the weekend. Phil is dropping Carla off at the airport on the way to Orlando. Their kids are out of school, and Carla's worried about the sitter. Maybe she can fly back on Sunday and meet Phil in Orlando. We've enjoyed the beach, but we need a diversion." He stopped and thought about Tuesday night. "I don't think Dad is going to make that will change right now, so we have some time to enjoy Florida."

"That makes sense. I may take time off too. Laura's busy with some condo sales, and there's a new casino in Vegas."

And one of them thought, *if I do it this weekend, I'll have established my alibi.*

CHAPTER FOUR

The dispatcher at the sheriff's office took the call at 10:15 p.m. on Friday, March 5. She heard a woman's raspy voice screaming.

"Help! I heard voices. A fight, I think. Hurry!"

"Of course. What's your name, and where are you?"

"I'm Diane Perruda at Rosewood Center. Can you send someone right away? Hurry!"

"We'll be right there." The woman's voice was calm, giving the police time to reach Rosewood Center. Within ten minutes Peter Watson, the executive director of Rosewood Center, had been called, and two police cars stopped at the center's front entrance. Two police officers, a man and a woman, ran to the entrance and were met by Watson who led them to the Perrudas' private elevator. Diane met them at the door dressed in a short nightgown with a transparent robe. Anyone but the officer would have terminated the search, his eyes glued to Mrs. Perruda's size thirty-eight cleavage. He didn't stop.

"Where is the fight?" asked Callahan, the officer.

"In there." She led them down a long hallway and stopped at the last door.

The officers and Diane paused and listened. "I don't hear anything," Callahan said. "Stay back, Mrs. Perruda." He reached for his gun and aimed as he slowly opened the door. The hall light was on, and that was enough to see the body of a man lying on the bed. His mouth was open, and his eyes stared straight up.

Diane screamed. "Oh, God! Oh, damn! Frank!" She turned to Callahan. "He's dead, isn't he?"

Callahan nodded. "I think so." He looked around the room, empty except for the dead man. He took out his iPhone and called headquarters. "We have a dead person here. Call the emergency people." He turned to Diane who stood transfixed, her eyes glued to Frank's body. "We'll go back to the living room and wait for the ambulance. Don't touch anything."

He took her arm and led her out of the room and motioned her to a chair. "Wait here for the EMTs. We'll be in the bedroom."

Diane sat and stared at Callahan. "Don't mess everything up," she said and shook her finger at him. "I don't want you people tearing up the place, for God's sake." Her last words were a raspy scream.

Callahan patted her shoulder. "Don't worry. We'll be careful."

Diane shrugged, pulled her robe together, and moved to the davenport where she could watch the bedroom door.

Within minutes, the penthouse was filled with two EMTs, two firefighters, and the medical examiner who rushed to the bedroom. Callahan met them at the door. "I've taken pictures but haven't touched or moved anything."

Callahan, his assistant, the medical examiner, and two EMTs worked carefully. Callahan took more photos and used a video camera to complete his task.

Amanda Rieger, his assistant, walked to the windows and opened the draperies. "No one could have escaped this way," she said. "It's straight down eighteen floors, and there's no balcony or lanai here."

"Don't jump to conclusions until the guys have had a chance to examine the body. He may have died a natural death."

"That's doubtful," an EMT said. "There's a pillow on the floor. It's covered with some blood and what looks like saliva. Look at the body's mouth. There's blood around the lips, and blood vessels around the eyes have ruptured. Even without an autopsy, I'd say he was smothered."

"By persons unknown," Callahan added. "Amanda, we'll dust the room for fingerprints and check everything in the room. I want to know if robbery is apparent."

He returned to the living room and dismissed the firefighters. There'd been no sign of fire, and their medical assistance wasn't needed. Diane sat staring into space. No words came.

Callahan noticed that Diane's upper arms were muscular. A weight lifter maybe. Sexy and strong, Callahan thought, and he wondered about their marriage. She was much younger than her husband. Would she benefit from his death?

"We're checking the room, and the technicians are taking care of the body. After the medical examiner has checked the body here, he'll take it to our county medical examiner's building." He paused and used a softer approach. "You shouldn't be alone tonight. We can call for a caregiver."

"No, I'll be all right. I used to be a night nurse, so I'm accustomed to sleepless nights."

"Okay, but here's a number to call if you need someone."

Diane took the card. "Thanks. I'll call if I need help."

Callahan returned to the bedroom. The medics had already moved the body onto a stretcher and were ready to leave. They'd stepped carefully around the pillow that lay by the bed.

"We'll have a report for you in the morning," a medic said to Callahan.

They lifted the stretcher and walked to the front door with the medical examiner. Diane watched their exit but remained on the davenport. She wrapped her arms around her chest and moaned softly.

Callahan and Amanda left the bedroom, shut the door, and sealed it with yellow tape. "We should probably tape the entire apartment, Mrs. Perruda, but right now, this will be enough. Don't move anything, please. Tomorrow we'll have more people here." He sat in a chair close to Diane and turned to Amanda. "You can leave now. I won't be long."

Amanda nodded her agreement and left.

Callahan studied Mrs. Perruda. She seemed more at ease. "I know it's late," he said, "but I'd like to ask you a few questions. Do you mind?" He removed a tape recorder from his pocket.

"That's all right. I won't sleep tonight anyway."

"Where were you this evening?"

"I went to my bedroom after dinner to watch TV. Frank wasn't in a good mood. He was mad at his kids because they didn't like his new will." Her smile was quizzical, wry. "He was going to disinherit all three of them and build a university in North Dakota. They came down here to complain."

"That's important information." Callahan brushed back his red hair. "Did he say anything about expecting a visitor?"

"No, and I didn't hear anyone come in. Of course the TV was on, and my bedroom isn't near the front door."

"Where are his children now?"

"The oldest, Jim, lives in Naples at Luna de Ciel. He runs the store. His brother, Tony, and his sister, Carla, and her husband, Phil, arrived on Monday. Tony lives in Minneapolis, and Carla and Phil in Boston. Jim's wife, Laura, is a Realtor and found them a condo on the beach. I don't have the address."

"Did your husband change his will?"

"I don't think so. He didn't have time." Diane leaned back on the davenport, stared at the ceiling, then turned and glared at Callahan. "One of those horrible people killed him. I know it."

"It's possible, but we don't know." Callahan stood. "We'll find the killer, Mrs. Perruda. Try to get some sleep."

He left the apartment and shook his head as he went to the elevator. The next of kin were obviously suspects, but what about Mrs. Perruda? She said she was in her bedroom watching TV, but they only had her word with no witnesses. As he rode to the lobby, he also considered it might be someone else, someone Frank knew, not family.

A twenty-something man stopped Callahan as he walked to the front door. "Excuse me, but I'm Trevor Johnson from the

Naples Daily News. We got the 911 call on our police scanner, and they sent me."

Callahan sighed. "Okay. You need a story, but I haven't much information. You can't use the victim's name until the next of kin have been notified, and I don't know when that will be.

Johnson punched his iPhone. "Male?"

Callahan nodded. "He was seventy-eight years old, and he died. Period."

"Thanks. I hope to get this in tomorrow's paper."

• • •

Diane watched Callahan leave. She locked the front door and went to her bedroom. She turned on the TV. Any noise would be welcome, anything to take her mind off tonight's horror. A car chase appeared on the screen. Brakes squealed. Sirens wailed. Diane turned it off, and as she paced the floor, reality struck like a lightning bolt. She screamed and fell onto her bed. She buried her head in a pillow and sobbed deep, pit-of-the-stomach, wrenching sobs. Frank was dead. No time to say good-bye. No time to reflect and remember the good times.

She sat up, sniffed, and wiped her eyes. Yes, there were good times, and Frank had been generous. She liked the clothes, the Bentley, the affluence he could afford, and yes, she liked his waking her with a cup of coffee and a gleam in his eye. His age hadn't diminished his sexual desires. But now Frank was gone, Larry was available, and she wanted to add another chapter to her manuscript.

She picked up her cell phone and punched numbers. A man answered.

"Sugar honey," Diane said. "Frank's dead." She listened, and her shoulders relaxed. "Yes, I know. We can be together soon. I'll be busy with the police and funeral arrangements now. Just wait for me."

She turned off the light, climbed into bed, and fell asleep at once.

• • •

Sheriff Jack Ryder sat behind his desk on Saturday morning at the Collier County Sheriff's Office on Airport Road and drank his usual eight o'clock mug of coffee. He moved his nameplate back and forth, back and forth, and studied his title, Sheriff John Ryder. How proud he was eight years ago when he was elected, but now, having to deal with the killing of a prominent businessman, he felt more trepidation and less pride. He thought about the murder scene, the body of Frank Perruda stretched out on his bed, dead eyes staring at his killer. His deputies had given him a detailed report. They'd searched the penthouse thoroughly over the screams and threats of Mrs. Perruda.

"You can't just come in here and tear everything apart," she'd yelled. "Maybe he isn't dead. Are you sure he's dead?"

God, that woman would drive any husband to an early death. His deputies had explained to her for the fourth time the details of the medical examiner's examination. Frank Perruda did not die of a heart attack or a stroke. He had been suffocated. There were no fingerprints anywhere, and as far as Mrs. Perruda knew, nothing had been stolen. How did the killer enter the building, and how did he or she escape? Sheriff Ryder replaced the plaque and buzzed his second in command, Arturo Lopez.

"Can you come to my office? I want to review what we know about the Perruda case and talk about what our next step should be."

Lopez entered and sat down in front of the sheriff's desk. His black hair slicked back from his forehead and steely black eyes echoed his Latino heritage. "What have you got, Jack? We didn't get much at the penthouse."

"No, but Mrs. Perruda told Callahan her husband intended to change his will, disinherit his kids, and build a university in North Dakota."

Lopez laughed. "The guy must have been nuts. Why would he do that, and in North Dakota?"

"Beats me, but now we have three suspects. The eldest, James, lives here and runs the furniture store. Tony is a broker in Minneapolis, and the daughter, Carla, lives in Boston. They arrived on Monday, and their father was killed on Friday."

"You'll bring them in, of course. Maybe we could play good cop, bad cop, like they do on TV."

Ryder laughed. "I don't want either role, thank you. I've assigned the interviews to Officer Doyle and Detective O'Hara, and they'll start with James." He buzzed the front desk, gave instructions, and listened as the phone rang at the James Perruda residence at Luna de Ciel.

Laura's tense monotone answered. "Yes? This is Laura Perruda."

"This is Sheriff Ryder. Sorry to bother you, Mrs. Perruda, but we need to speak to your husband. We have bad news. His father was killed last night."

"Oh dear God!" Laura exclaimed. "It isn't true!"

"I'm sorry, but it's true, and we need to notify all of his next of kin. I need to speak to your husband."

"He isn't here. He flew to Las Vegas yesterday. He'll probably be home sometime tomorrow, as he's always at the store early on Monday."

"Do you have his cell phone number?"

"No, and it wouldn't help. He left his cell phone here on his desk."

"We'll check airlines and hotels. We need to notify the family before we can give out any information to the media."

"I understand. I'll ask him to call you if I hear from him."

"Mrs. Perruda, do you know how we can locate your husband's brother and his sister? We've called both their homes in

Minneapolis and Boston. Tony's phone left a voice message, and no one answered in Boston."

"Yes, I can help. They wanted to stay in Naples, and I found them a condo on the beach. Unfortunately there's no landline, as the owners didn't want it used. Renters have taken advantage of the phone and used it for long distance. Tony and Carla have cell phones, but I don't have those numbers. I can give you the address."

Ryder wrote the address and said, "We can get a warrant and access their numbers, but that takes time. Thanks for your help."

He replaced the phone. What was his next step? He couldn't call Diane, Perruda's wife. She didn't know much last night. He shook his head. The media was calling, and he couldn't release anything until the family had been notified. He called a deputy and gave him the sons' and daughter's names and the address.

"Find them," he ordered. He leaned back in his chair, scratched the back of his head, and swore silently.

• • •

Laura made coffee and sat at the kitchen table. Where was Jim? Did he use Las Vegas as an alibi for murder? Questions with no answers whirled through her head.

At ten o'clock the phone rang. "This is Sheriff Ryder again. We've checked all airline manifests and lodgings in Las Vegas. If he's there, he used an alias. We can put out an APB, but I'd rather not at this time."

Laura's voice portrayed anxiety, fear, and total innocence. "I don't know who to contact. If something's happened to Jim…" Her voice trailed off into silence.

"If he calls, contact us immediately. He needs to know about his father's death."

Laura paced the floor, her slippers slapping on the kitchen floor tiles. She drank more coffee and watched the clock.

An hour later the phone rang. "Jim, where are you? The police can't find you, and something terrible has happened, and I've been so worried, and…"

"Hey, just a minute, Laura. I'm fine. Nothing to worry about. What's happened?"

Laura breathed deeply. "Your dad died last night, honey. The police came because Diane called 911."

"Oh God! How did he die?"

"They think he was murdered." Laura paused. "Where are you?" She was calm now. Jim wasn't dead, but he certainly wasn't in Las Vegas.

"I changed my plans, but I'll come home as soon as I can. Don't worry. I'm okay."

The phone was dead, perhaps hiding his location, activities, and—oh, please no! Was he his father's killer? Was he with someone? Did he know about Janet? Their married lives had taken separate routes, he at the store and the casino, she with her computer and Janet. It was time to assess their marriage. Perhaps Frank's death might be a catalyst for renewal.

• • •

Saturday was Julie's favorite morning. The weekend crew would be there to handle weekend problems, and she could relax at home, catch the news on TV, and enjoy a leisurely cup of coffee. Peter Watson's voice on her phone ended Saturday morning's lotus land.

"Julie, can you please come to the center at once? We need you."

"Of course. I'll be there." Julie dressed quickly and drank her coffee at stop signs.

The concierge desk was a hub of activity. Watson met her at the door and explained the situation as he ushered her through a crowd of concerned residents, each with a theory, a knowledge of the killer, and a need to be heard right now! Julie began responding to phone calls as she removed her jacket.

"Yes, Mr. Perruda died last night. No, we don't know the cause of his death." She looked up at Peter and added, "We'll have a printed statement as soon as we have the information."

Peter nodded. What else could be said? Julie answered as many questions as she could, and the crowd gradually moved off. They'd watched the police cars coming and going, the teams of deputies tramping through the lobby to the stairs and elevators. The sheriff, a rare visitor, was given special acknowledgement.

Mrs. Johnson pushed her walker up to Julie's desk. "I'm glad Mr. Perruda died in his bed. What if he'd drowned? We couldn't have used the pool for weeks."

Julie laughed. A day brightener was welcome.

Peter pulled a chair behind the counter and slumped down. "What a night and morning!" he exclaimed. "I got the police call about twenty minutes after ten last night. Diane Perruda called 911 at about ten fifteen, and the police were here in minutes."

"Did you see the body?"

"No. I led the police, two of them, up to the penthouse. Mrs. Perruda was screaming. Two EMTs arrived, firefighters, then the medical examiner. It was crazy. I didn't stay, Julie. I couldn't do anything, and they didn't need me. I had no information for them. I'd worked late in my office and heard nothing, saw nothing."

"Did any of his family show up? A son and daughter flew here on Monday, and Jim, of course, lives just down the street."

"I haven't seen any of them. They'll be notified, of course."

Julie's first thought was of Russ, who could probably solve the mystery in minutes, but reality took over, and Julie's thought modified into actual possibilities. Russ didn't even know the Perrudas and wouldn't know how to reach the family. She wanted to call him, but a busy schedule and common sense kept her away from the phone.

She was surprised to see Diane Perruda leave her private elevator and come to the desk. She wore a pink sheath that ended above her knees. Hair and makeup were perfection.

"Ask Felix to bring up the Bentley, please," Diane said.

"Please" was a new word in Diane's vocabulary. Julie was startled as she made the call. "We're so sorry about your husband. Everyone here is concerned. If you need anything or anybody, please let us know."

Diane nodded. "I need to buy something black."

She left, and Julie shook her head, wondering if Diane Perruda had any family or friends in Naples. She hadn't noticed many callers.

• • •

Jim Perruda sat in the passenger seat next to the pilot. He'd hired Collier Air Inc. to fly him and Rita to Atlantic City. It was so easy to use Las Vegas as an alibi, and Rita had been available on short notice. He didn't know Rita had just bounced off a torrid romance suddenly grown cold and was open to any suggestion that might restore her self-image. They spent most of Friday and Saturday in bed or at the casinos. No one would ever know about their trip. They'd used a charter service and fake identifications at the hotel. Now all of their precautions had been a waste of time. They might as well have sent a plane flying low along the shore in Naples, towing a banner behind announcing their rendezvous.

Rita, in the seat behind Jim, stroked his head. "Don't worry, sweetie. You'll think of something."

Jim turned and kissed the top of her head. He had noticed her flaming red hair during her first visit to the store, gave her his card, found her address, and called the next day. Rita laughed at his sudden interest and accepted his invitation. For Jim, their weekend had been a joyous escape from the tension at home. Now that escape was, at the least, embarrassing, and it could lead, at the worst, to divorce proceedings.

Jim turned to the pilot and asked him to hurry. The pilot nodded and made preparations for takeoff.

As soon as they landed in Naples, Jim paid for Rita's cab, promising to call her next week. He found his car at the parking lot and drove home.

It was now late afternoon. He parked, grabbed his carry-on, and took the elevator to his condo. He unlocked the front door and stood uncertainly. What could he say? How would Laura respond?

"Hi, honey, I'm home."

"That's obvious." Laura came from the bedroom and stared at Jim. No welcome smile, not that he'd expected one.

Jim felt remorse, sort of—anxiety, yeah. "Tell me about Dad." He listened as Laura gave him the report she'd received from the sheriff.

"You must call Sheriff Ryder. He's working today, trying to find you and your family. I gave him the address of the condo they'd rented. Maybe he's found them."

Jim called and was relieved to hear another voice. "I made a change in my travel plans," Jim said. "I flew home as soon as I could."

"Come to my office tomorrow morning. Eight o'clock. Here's the address."

Jim wrote on a note pad and promised to be on time. He replaced the phone and sat in the lanai next to Laura.

"Now at least you know that I didn't draw the spade king," he said. "I'm guilty of betraying you, but I didn't kill my dad."

"I've had time to think, and I'm confused and…" She stared at Jim. "I'm damn mad!" She stood and looked out at the Gulf. "I know you weren't alone this weekend, and that hurts. I don't want to know who it was, and I don't want particulars." She turned to him. "I just want to know if we still have a marriage and if it's worth saving."

Jim lowered his head. "God, Laura, I don't know. I still love you even more than I did ten years ago, but that's not enough for either of us. You have your business. I have mine. We lead separate lives. Is that a marriage?"

"I don't know, and with your father's death, we're both going to be involved with the police and lawyers. Let's put this on the back burner and take care of death, not life."

Jim nodded. Laura was right to delay more discussion. Now he thought about his father. Which one had killed him? Tony said he was going to Key West, and Phil, Carla's husband, planned to drive to Orlando. Which one used his alibi?

They ate dinner silently. Laura had given him all the facts as she knew them, and he'd learn more tomorrow. He dreaded an interview with the sheriff. He'd never faced an interrogation, didn't even recognize the address he'd been given. Would it be taped or photographed? Would they ask about his family's part in the murder? Damn Tony, he thought. They must have all been crazy to agree to his plan. He didn't want to implicate either Tony or Phil, so what could he say?

He went to the guest room, undressed down to his jockeys, and tried to sleep. His mind did cartwheels. If he admitted he'd been in Atlantic City and could prove it, either Tony or Phil would be guilty. He didn't like his brother much. They'd been rivals as children, and Tony usually blamed Jim for his own foolish pranks. But he was still his brother. He didn't know Phil well, but his sister's husband deserved consideration.

He got up and knocked on Laura's door. "If you're not asleep, I need advice. I'm lost."

"Come in. I'm not asleep."

Jim sat on the end of her bed. "I have to lie to the sheriff. If I tell the truth, they can verify it, and that leaves Tony and Phil as suspects. Is that fair?"

"I don't know what's fair. You have a dysfunctional family, Jim, and you're part of it. I don't know if a lie can be accepted as truth, and you'd flunk a lie detector test. Try it anyway tomorrow and see what happens."

"Okay. Try to sleep. Maybe I can too." He left and tossed the rest of the night.

The next morning he bumbled his way into the kitchen and made coffee, half asleep. He didn't want to call his brother and sister. They probably weren't back from their trips anyway, and his mind was so cluttered with his own problems that he couldn't endure any more complications. They'd learn soon enough about Frank's death, and one of them would have to lie. He smiled wryly to himself. Now they'd have time to invent more alibis if they needed them.

• • •

Sheriff Ryder seldom ordered Sunday morning interrogations and wished that Frank Perruda had got himself killed during a weekday. His officers had made a thorough examination of the Perrudas' penthouse and, with the sheriff's orders, had removed the yellow tape. Mrs. Perruda had been a nuisance during the procedure, warning them of any damage or breakage. The officers were relieved to finish their assignment.

Sheriff Ryder drank coffee, scratched the back of his head, and thought about the interview with James Perruda. Officer Doyle and Detective O'Hara would handle it, but he might drive to headquarters and look in on them through the one-way window. He studied Friday night's report. No fingerprints, no forced entry, and no robbery. Motive? The will, of course. What else? The department would have many hours of interrogations before the killer's identification.

• • •

Jim followed directions to police headquarters on Horseshoe Drive. The one-story building was set back several blocks from Airport

Road on a tree-lined, two-lane street. Officer Doyle met Jim at the door, introduced himself, and led him to a room that contained a six-foot-long table and three chairs. Jim saw the ceiling cameras and the window, blank for him, visible for those inside. He'd seen enough scenes like this one on TV. Now he was part of a real one.

Officer Doyle introduced Detective O'Hara, and the three men sat down at the table. Doyle began, his voice conveying assurance and concern. "I know this is difficult for you. Have you been able to contact your brother and sister?"

"No. They're out of town, and each promised to return tonight or tomorrow morning. I haven't called them."

Jim noticed a raised eyebrow and a quizzical expression.

"You have our sympathies in the death of your father."

"Thanks. It's especially hard for me because we worked together for so many years."

"Yes. This is just a preliminary interview. We don't need a sworn statement yet. We'll get that later. Right now we just need to know a few facts. We have your name, age, and address, and we know you are the manager of Perruda's Fine Furnishings. Are you the owner?"

"Yes. Dad turned it over to me about eight years ago. He said a partnership could last just so long, and now it was my turn to run the business."

"And you agreed. What about your relationship with your father?"

Until now, Jim had been relaxed. Wary but relaxed. He paused and thought about the question. Should he tell Doyle about the beatings, the accusations, the misery he'd endured? Those admissions would surely implicate him, and he had enough worries because of the will change.

"We got along. Dad wasn't a really warm person, but there were no major problems."

Did he sound sincere? Suddenly he felt warm and uncomfortable. He loosened his tie and saw O'Hara watch his gesture. Oops, he thought. He needed to stay calm and honest.

"Okay. Now let's talk about your father's death. Where were you Friday night about ten o'clock?"

"I told my family I was going to Las Vegas, but I changed my mind."

"Where did you go?"

Jim sat back and thought again. The question he dreaded. "I guess I'll have to take the Fifth on that one. I can't answer."

Doyle stood and shook his head. "That's all for now. You may go, but we'll be in touch."

Jim rose, knees unsteady. He'd made it through for now. Maybe a miracle would occur before they called him again.

He went to his car and called Laura on his cell phone. "Hi. I'm leaving the sheriff's office and going to the store. They asked me about the weekend, and I pleaded the Fifth. I didn't know what else to do."

"You were right, and you're safe for now. I have calls to make, so you can fix dinner for yourself or eat out. I don't know when I'll be home."

Jim knew any more discussion was useless. He drove to the store and sorted through his mail. At noon he went out to the receiving dock to check on new furniture shipments. His unloading crew had left for lunch. He walked around, saw two new shipments, and looked up at the twenty-foot ceiling. The shipping area walls were lined with shelves. Jim noticed a new shipment on the top shelf, six chrome-legged bar stools. He didn't remember the order, so he climbed a ladder to check the invoice number. As he moved a stool, the one next to it tipped over and fell to the floor. Jim swore and climbed back down.

The stool lay on the floor with one of its four legs broken. He bent over to get a closer look and was startled to see a mound of white powder surrounding the leg. He stooped, dipped a finger into the powder, and licked. My God! It wasn't flour or sugar, but it was familiar. He thought back to a pool party he and Laura had attended. Someone had brought cocaine, and he'd taken a few sniffs. He'd liked the sensation. Wow! He sat back on his heels and thought about the source and the one who had ordered the shipment. Hurriedly he swept up the drug and flushed it down the toilet.

He carried the bar stool and its broken leg back to his office and shut the door. He looked through his invoices and found no record of six bar stools. Had his father ordered them? He went to Frank's office and studied invoices. Yes, there it was! A shipment from Vera Cruz, Mexico. Jim drew circles on his forehead with his fingers and thought about several shipments from Mexico his father had ordered. His father was in the drug business big-time, and he knew nothing about it. What else didn't he know about his father?

He returned to his office and removed the other three legs. After a thorough search, he discovered fifteen packets of cocaine. Now he had to bring down the other stools before his people returned. He retrieved the stools carefully and brought them to his office. He removed the legs off each one and now stared at ninety-five plastic bags of cocaine. He gathered up the bags and stuffed them into his safe. With a small tool, he was able to repair the broken leg and return all six to the top shelf.

During lunch at Starbucks, he considered his future. Frank must have amassed a fortune by now. Where was the money? His inheritance would be a pittance compared to drug money probably hidden in a Swiss bank account or in a bank on Grand Cayman. Admittedly, he should inform his family, but it was such a great secret, at least for now.

He returned to the receiving dock, where two men worked unpacking furniture boxes.

"I see some bar stools on the top shelf," he said to the older man. "When did they arrive?"

"A guy brought them here on Thursday. Mr. Perruda met him, and they moved the stools into a corner. We were planning to leave them there, but a big shipment was due that afternoon. After Mr. Perruda and the driver left, we moved them up to the top shelf to make room for the new shipment."

"Thanks. You were right to move them." Jim returned to his office wearing a puzzled frown. Who was the driver? When was his father planning to remove the drugs? Who was his father's contact? Questions loomed and swirled through Jim's mind.

Were there drugs in his father's penthouse? Jim drove to Rosewood Center, hoping Diane would be out. He noticed Julie at her desk, really noticed her. He'd seen her many times but hadn't stopped to visit. Now, with his marriage probably on the rocks, a new relationship had potential.

"Hi. I'm going up to my dad's apartment. It's going to be weird without him."

"Yes, and we're sorry about your loss. Is there anything I can do?"

"Thanks for asking. Not right now, but maybe later." Jim leaned on the counter. "We haven't been formally introduced, but I'm Jim, and you're Julie. Nice."

Julie laughed.

"What do you do after work?" Jim asked.

"I go home usually. I bought a house last year."

"Family?"

"I live alone. No kids." Julie paused. "I guess I shouldn't be telling anyone I'm alone."

Jim laughed. "Not to worry. Your secret is safe with me. Maybe we could have dinner after work some night. I'd like to know you better."

Jim noticed an awkward pause. Maybe he'd gone too far, too soon.

Julie smiled. "I'd like dinner, but you're married, and I'm a divorcee. Not a good combination."

"You're right for now, but don't forget the invitation. We never know what's next."

He left and went up to the penthouse. He rang the bell, and when no one answered, he used his key. He went to Frank's bedroom and studied the medicines in the pharmacy bottles. He removed the lids, sniffing each one. Nothing. He searched through drawers and closets. Nothing. In the kitchen he removed pots and pans, looking behind each item. Nothing. Again, he drew circles on his forehead. If there were no drugs here, Frank must have sold them as soon as they arrived.

He drove back to the store and sorted through the invoices in his father's desk. He saw six invoices from Mexico, some from Vera Cruz, others from San Miguel de Allende. The dates included all of the last six months. His father had made no attempt to conceal the invoices. He must have removed the drugs immediately and sold them, and because he had disposed of the drugs himself, he had no reason to worry about anyone else interfering with his transactions.

Jim sat in his father's chair and thought about the millions Frank must have amassed in the drug trade. Millions! Where was the money? Jim called his father's lawyer, Mark Holtz. Frank had already named him executor in his will. Checking his father's bank account would be no problem. When Holtz reported the balance in his father's bank account, Jim's heart dropped to the floor. Ten thousand dollars? A pittance! Perhaps Frank had a savings account, certificates of deposit? No, not in his estate. The lawyer assured Jim a full account would be given when the estate was settled. Holtz asked Jim to locate his brother and sister. He wanted all three of them present when Frank's will would be read. Frank's wife would attend, of course.

Jim's call to the lawyer gave him no clues. If his father had accounts in a Swiss bank or on the islands, he knew getting his hands on such an amount would be difficult, maybe impossible. He left Frank's office and paced the floor. He endured the rest of the afternoon and wondered how he could survive the rest of his life. Laura might leave. Rita had been a delightful respite from family problems, but he wasn't interested in a second weekend. Her red hair had covered a limited mind, and they had nothing in common. Sex wasn't enough. He reached in his pocket and tore up her business card. He sat back and stared at his safe. Ninety-five packets of cocaine, and only he knew the exact number. He opened the safe and hid one packet in the bottom drawer of his desk.

∴

Tony Perruda returned to Naples Monday afternoon. He unlocked the condo, unpacked, and poured a scotch on the rocks. He'd called Jim's home and listened as Laura told him of his father's death.

"It won't be aired until you three have been notified, so let's hope that Carla and Phil will come back today. Jim has already been questioned by the sheriff's department. You and Carla will have to appear too. It's a mess, Tony. You've put your family in jeopardy."

"We had to do it. I'm sorry." Tony wasn't sorry. They had faced a stone wall, and the only way to move ahead was to remove the wall. "Ask Jim to call me when he comes home."

"He may not come home. Call him at the store."

"All right." Tony poured another scotch. Why wouldn't Jim come home? He called the store. "I'm back. I called Laura. Carla and Phil aren't here. Do you want to meet for dinner?" Tony kept his voice in a monotone, shoving aside screams of anger, worry, and unspoken threats of doom. His alibi was safe until a thorough investigation took place. With luck, law enforcement might be understaffed. He listened as Jim agreed to meet him for dinner.

"If Phil and Carla return, I'll invite them."

Tony replaced his phone and thought about his wife, Emma, wondering again where she was, why she'd left. Damn, he missed her! Something new for him. She'd always been there, even when he didn't need her. Now he felt a void in his life, an emptiness he couldn't comprehend.

He heard a key turn in the front door and greeted Phil. "I'm meeting Jim for dinner. Where's Carla?" he asked.

"She's still in Boston. The hair problem was more serious than she had expected, so now she's shampooing the kids three times a day. She hopes to get back here in a day or two." Phil took his suitcase to his bedroom and returned to join Tony in a drink. "To life," he said and touched Tony's glass.

"To life," Tony echoed. The words chilled. "It's not life, Phil. My dad was killed Friday night."

Phil stared at his brother-in-law. "Oh, no!" He finished his drink and went to the kitchen.

Tony watched Phil as he returned with another drink. "I need this," Tony said and walked into the lanai. "I'll wait here for Jim."

• • •

Jim drove to the beach-front condo and suggested a quiet restaurant in Old Naples. He remembered his interrogation and wondered how Tony and Phil would react to the ordeal. Which one had killed Frank? The question plagued him, gnawed into his brain, burrowed into its center.

As he drove downtown, he said, "I gave your cell phone number to the sheriff's office, Tony, so they'll call you tomorrow." He wanted to warn them but held back. Each man needed to follow his own gut feelings and control his own fears.

• • •

No one spoke during the drive downtown. Each man, deep in his own thoughts, kept a distance, a barrier. Each of them regarded the others as the murderer, and the one who drew the spade king had his own set of worries. Three men united in a common bond of silence but separate in thoughts of Frank Perruda's death.

Jim thought, I can't admit that I couldn't have killed my father because I was in Atlantic City with Rita. I can't reveal my whereabouts, as that leaves only two suspects for the police. It wouldn't be fair to either Tony or Phil. We're in this together.

Tony thought, whether I drew the spade king or not, I can't tell anyone where I was.

Phil thought, if I drew the spade king, I'd lie about my whereabouts. If I didn't draw it, I'd still have to lie.

CHAPTER FIVE

The phone next to Tony's bed rang at eight o'clock Tuesday morning. Tony rolled over and answered, his voice groggy and hushed.

"Mr. Perruda, this is Sheriff Ryder's office. Please come to police headquarters on Horseshoe Drive at nine thirty this morning." The caller gave location instructions as Tony wrote hastily. "Is Philip Stevens there?"

"Yes, he arrived late yesterday."

"Ask him to be here at ten thirty. We'll contact your sister later."

Tony scribbled the address on a note pad. "We'll be there." He struggled to his feet, walked down the hall, and knocked on Phil's bedroom door. "Time to get up. The fuzz wants to talk to us. I'll make coffee."

Tony had time only for a quick shower before leaving. "I hate this, Phil. Maybe I'll see you before your interview if I'm still intact. I wonder if they do waterboarding here."

Phil, still in his pajamas, sat at the kitchen table and sipped coffee. "I guess none of us looked beyond a solution to your dad's changing his will. Good luck. I wish I had words of encouragement and good advice. Right now I'm too befuddled to think straight." He sighed. "I'll be glad when Carla returns. I miss her."

"I miss Emma too," Tony said and was awed by his admission. Had he ever missed her before this morning? No, because she was always there when he needed her. Now she was away somewhere in the world with their daughters while his world was hanging in shreds of confusion, close to panic. He hurried to his car and followed directions to police headquarters.

The building was located at the end of a narrow street in a wooded area. It looked like any ordinary office building until a row of police cars in the parking area announced "Law Enforcement." He entered and waited until an officer opened a door leading to yet another door. Inside he saw a six-foot-long table, three chairs, two people, a uniformed policeman and a man wearing a white shirt and chinos. Cameras hung from the four corners of the room. Tony turned to see a window with no view. Who was behind it? He smiled wanly and sat while his knees shook.

The man in street clothes spoke. "I'm Detective O'Hara, and this is Officer Doyle." He smiled at Tony, sat, and made notes on a yellow legal pad. He brought out a recording device and placed it close to Tony. His introductory questions were asked informally, and Tony relaxed. He answered truthfully as his name, age, residence, and employment were recorded.

"Mr. Perruda, where were you when your father was killed?"

Tony jerked upright in his chair. "I don't even know exactly when my father was killed." He looked directly at the detective. "I left Naples Friday afternoon and just returned yesterday. I got some information from my sister-in-law Laura, Jim's wife, but it was sketchy."

"Have you contacted Diane, your father's wife?"

"No. I don't know her well and…" Tony trailed off, then added slowly, "I haven't had time to call her."

He sensed unasked questions concerning relationships, but he sat back and waited for more questions, ones that he could either answer truthfully or fabricate with ease.

Officer Doyle looked up from his notes. "Your father was killed around ten o'clock Friday night. Again, Mr. Perruda, where were you?"

Tony answered carefully. "I drove to Key West. I needed a change of scene." He felt as though he were out in left field

Salt Marsh Sinners

at the Dome in Minneapolis playing with the Minnesota Twins baseball team. Doyle at bat sent out questions his way, and Tony fielded them easily. Yeah, he could strike out the batter! No, he didn't remember where he stayed. So many bed and breakfast homes in Key West. No, he didn't meet anyone who could identify him. You know how it is in Key West. Everyone's friendly, out for a good time, nobody cares who you are.

Yes, he planned to come back to Naples Monday afternoon. Of course he didn't know about his dad's death until he got here. Last night? His brother and brother-in-law and he went out for dinner.

Detective O'Hara leaned forward. "Mr. Perruda, did your father have any enemies, anyone who hated him enough to kill him?"

"I don't know anyone who would kill him. I live in Minneapolis and don't come to Naples often. I don't know a lot about my father's friends or enemies."

A light went on in Tony's head. He added, "When my dad married Diane, our relationship went to hell. She grabbed my dad because he had money. She was nothing until she married him. Just a nurse, for God's sake!"

"And she would profit by her husband's death," Doyle added. "We'll look into that." He and O'Hara stood, and Tony followed, his shaking knees betraying a calm exterior.

"That's all for now," Doyle said. He checked his watch. "We'll talk to Philip Stevens, your brother-in-law, soon. You may go, but don't leave Naples. We have work to do now that your dad's next of kin have been informed, and you will be busy too. The news media wants information, and you'll want to write an obituary. Funeral arrangements must be made. Your father's body is at the medical examiner's building, where an autopsy was performed. Now the body can be moved to a funeral home. You'll have papers to sign, people to see."

Tony was escorted out of the building. He shook hands with the officer who accompanied him and walked alone to his car.

Now in the driver's seat, he felt nauseated. He couldn't throw up, he thought, and swallowed the bile that rose in his throat. His hands shook as he started the car. Had they believed his story? He sighed. It had been tough, but his remarks about Diane surely must have stirred an interest in her. They could point fingers, all three of them.

As he drove out of the parking lot, he passed Phil on his way to headquarters. Tony didn't wave, didn't stop. He had nothing to say.

He drove back to the condo and spent the rest of the morning on the beach. He didn't want to talk to Jim and wished Emma were here. She'd understand. Maybe they'd have sex again. He watched the waves as they broke against the sand, and waves of desire and despair washed over him. He wanted his inheritance, but he wanted Emma more. He waded in the water close to shore and dreamed of skating rinks and snowbanks, he and Emma together, rolling in the snow, just one big sexy snowball.

• • •

Phil Stevens drove into the parking lot at headquarters and passed his brother-in-law's car. He noticed Tony's steely brown eyes that looked straight ahead. He wished he could have stopped Tony and asked him about his interview. Phil had never been to police headquarters in Boston, never had a speeding ticket. A high-school tragedy hadn't involved law enforcement. Now he was up to his eyeballs in a murder! Damn Tony and all the Perrudas! Yes, even Carla! He parked next to a sheriff's vehicle, turned off the ignition, and wondered how he had got himself into such a predicament.

He adjusted his rearview mirror and looked at himself. The same gray-brown eyes stared back at him. His bulbous nose, broken three times by opponents in the ring, ruddy cheeks, heavy eyebrows, all there. Outwardly he hadn't changed. Now, thanks to Carla, he faced a new challenge that twisted, wrenched, and tore into his guts.

Phil sat for a moment remembering his first encounter with Carla. He had rented a tuxedo for his high school's senior prom and was uncomfortable and nervous. His muscles, an asset in the boxing ring, bulged under his shirt.

"Do you want to dance?" he asked, and his date smiled and took his hand. Four bars of music, and Phil's ankles were bashed by his date's black patent-leather sandals. He needed a partner on the dance floor, not an opponent on the soccer field. Oh, joyous deliverance! His date stumbled on the dance floor, and he bumped into Carla and her partner. Phil grinned and apologized. The music stopped and, hoping for a bailout, Phil suggested they trade partners. Carla wore a pink organdy gown that accented her short, pudgy figure. She smiled at him as the music began, and Phil was hooked. He didn't know what hit him or why. Carla would never be the poster girl for his senior class, and she stuttered as they introduced themselves, but she looked so helpless, needing someone. Phil had nurtured wounded puppies and helped his friend's little sister with her homework. The oldest in the family, Phil was the caregiver. When Carla looked up at him and smiled, he knew she would be his next puppy or someone's little sister.

When the music stopped again, Phil led Carla to her seat by the wall. "You're Italian?" he asked. Carla nodded.

"Me too, but my great-grandfather changed his name when he landed at Ellis Island. 'No more Stefanelli,' he said. He wanted to be an American, so he changed his name to Stevens."

Their friendship ripened during the years that Phil worked his way through college, majoring in engineering. He met her family and wondered how she survived. She met his family, and Phil was proud of the difference. His parents worked hard and gave their children love, roots, and wings. They saw little of Carla's family and were relieved when her father and brother Jim moved to Florida to open a new furniture store.

Theirs was a good marriage with much love. Their two children did well in school, and his job with Waverly Dechtonics had meant a series of promotions and a comfortable income. He worked out at the neighborhood gym but stayed out of the ring. Some nights he awakened in a cold sweat, an agonized scream filling the bedroom, and he shuddered as he recalled that night of terror and guilt, the gnawing wild dog of memory.

Three fights were scheduled, and his was to be the last event. He and his opponent had sparred together for a year. Friends in high school, enemies in the ring. That night they circled and punched for six rounds. No clear victory for either one. What went wrong? How did a carefully plotted, fair fight become a debacle? Phil didn't understand the sudden change, the need to win at any cost. His fists became weapons, and when his opponent backed away, a bestial howl erupted from Phil's anguished gut.

The referee called the fight, and Phil was led to his corner. He failed to choke back monstrous tears that flooded his towel. His opponent was bloodied and battered, his nose mashed against his cheekbones, and his eyes swollen and half-shut. He staggered and fell onto a corner of the ring. His neck hit the sharp edge of a bucket, severing his jugular vein, and the floor became a red lake of blood. His friend lost his life, and Phil lost his desire to become the heavyweight champion of the world.

Now he sat in his car in a parking lot next to a sheriff's vehicle. His sweaty hands shook, and his legs wobbled as he walked to the building. He wished he were back in Boston, that he'd never come to Naples, never faced involvement in a family murder. God! And escape was impossible. He had no choice but to enter the building and sit face-to-face with law enforcement.

Officer Doyle met him at the front door, introduced himself, and led him to the interrogation room. He'd seen them on TV, a fantasy land thousands of light years away from his own reality. Another man, Detective O'Hara, joined them, and the questions began. Phil had nothing to hide about his background, address, and employment.

Doyle adjusted a tape recorder and turned to look at Phil. "Where were you on Friday night at approximately ten o'clock?"

Phil bit a nail on his right ring finger. "I was in Orlando. My wife and I planned to drive up together, but she had to fly home and. . ." Phil, now inconveniently nervous, described in detail the situation at the children's school. He couldn't stop talking.

O'Hara interrupted him. "Yes, we understand. Where did you stay? We can, of course, check all the motels in the area, but we'd rather hear it from you."

"I can't remember. I was so upset about Carla."

"Is that your final statement regarding your whereabouts, Mr. Stevens?"

"I guess so. I'm sorry." Phil bit another fingernail.

Doyle and O'Hara stood. Both men stared down at Phil. Doyle turned off the tape recorder.

"That's all," he said. "We'll call you again soon."

Phil stood and walked with Doyle to the door. He hated what he had said, how he had reacted, and he knew in time he'd have to make a confession. They'd get it out of him.

• • •

Sheriff Ryder unlocked his office door at seven thirty Wednesday morning. Officer Doyle had texted a report of his interrogations of James and Tony Perruda and Philip Stevens. They'd been almost identical regarding their whereabouts Friday night. James had invoked the Fifth, and the other two just couldn't remember. James lived in Naples and owned a furniture store. Perhaps a visit from the sheriff might instill enough fear to move him into a confession of sorts. He buzzed Lopez and asked him to come in.

"Art, we're getting nowhere with the Perruda family. I'd like to call on James at the furniture store, scare him a little, maybe threaten. If you're not busy, we could go about ten o'clock."

"I'd like to join you. The case is a real puzzle. James takes the Fifth, and the other two tell us they can't remember exactly where they were in Key West and Orlando. They're prime suspects."

At nine thirty, Sheriff Ryder went to the parking lot and found Lopez with two black Labradors on leashes. "Why the dogs?" Ryder asked.

Lopez laughed. "They're drug dogs, and I'm the sitter. I'm stuck with them because the guy who works with them called in sick. We might as well take them with us. Maybe Perruda likes dogs and might be more willing to talk."

Ryder groaned. "All right. We'll take the van and put the dogs in back."

They drove to the store and parked at the curb. Lopez opened the door for the dogs and joined Ryder at the store's front entrance. They were met by a saleswoman who directed them to Jim's office. The dogs followed Lopez obediently, and Lopez said, "The dogs are better trained than my kids. They'd be climbing all over the furniture."

Jim rose as the two men stopped in front of his office. Sheriff Ryder introduced himself. "We spoke on the phone. This is a difficult time for you, but I must tell you that your taking the Fifth makes our work much harder." He nodded to Lopez. "Officer Lopez has read your testimony also and wanted to be here." Ryder noticed a wariness in Jim.

"Why are the dogs here?" Jim asked.

Lopez told him about their trainer's illness. "I hope you don't mind. They're housebroken."

Jim laughed. "Okay. Would you like to look around the store?"

"Yes, if you have time," Ryder said.

Jim led them through the furniture rooms, and the dogs followed. "Back here is the receiving dock where we unload the furniture," Jim said as they moved away from the display rooms. "It's a busy place."

Ryder and Lopez followed Jim. When they reached the center of the area, the dogs sat down and stared at a spot on the floor.

"What's with the dogs?" Jim asked.

"They're drug dogs, Mr. Perruda," Ryder said. "They're trained in what we call 'passive alert.'" He was quick to notice that Jim suddenly looked up at furniture on the top shelf and just as quickly lowered his eyes. "I think we've seen enough today," Ryder added. "Thanks for your time."

Ryder didn't see another pair of eyes that looked up at the stools, Jeff Parker, an employee who worked in that area unloading and setting up the merchandise, who watched the dogs from behind a load of crates and studied each stool carefully before returning to his work.

Ryder and Lopez walked with Jim through the store, the dogs at Lopez's side. They shook hands and walked to the car. Lopez opened the back door for the dogs.

"I think we've got a new angle here, Art," Ryder said. "Those dogs smelled drugs. We'll need a search warrant. Jim looked up at some stools on the top shelf. I'm sure he didn't mean to. It was just a sudden, spontaneous reaction."

"If it's drugs, we'll want the DEA in on the case."

Ryder nodded. "See if you can find someone in the area."

They returned to headquarters, and Lopez contacted the DEA. He returned to Ryder's office, sporting a grin from ear to ear. "You won't believe this, but a DEA supervisory special agent lives at Rosewood Center, next door to his mother. I got a full report. His name is Russell Jones."

"Good. Call him now. We need him."

• • •

Jim Perruda stood at the front door of Perruda's Fine Furnishings and watched Sheriff Ryder and Officer Lopez pull away from the curb. Had Ryder been honest regarding the dogs? Did they suspect a possible drug presence in the store? He returned to his office and stared at his safe that contained the bags of cocaine. What should he do with them? His father had a dealer. Frank wouldn't have used his landline at home. A special cell phone, of course. How could he trace his father's calls? He needed to find that phone. He hated to call Diane, but funeral arrangements must be made, and now he'd have a reason to see her.

"Hi, Diane. This is Jim. We need to talk. I'd like to see you about noon if you're not busy."

Diane's voice was a raspy monotone. "You can come."

At noon Jim stopped at Julie's desk. "Hi. Have you been bothered by the press or the cops because of my dad's death?"

Julie shook her head. "We've had a few calls from the news media. They can't print anything without knowing the names of the next of kin. A reporter gave me his card. You should call him." She gave him a *Naples Daily News* business card.

"I'll call. Thanks." He was relieved Julie hadn't brushed him off after she had declined his dinner invitation. Maybe dinner together was still possible. He smiled and rode the private elevator to the eighteenth floor. He rang the doorbell.

Diane opened the door, an unwelcome glare in her eyes.

"I don't know what you want, and I'm busy, but come in."

Jim sat down on the sofa. He noticed that Diane held a coffee mug in one hand and a cigarette in the other. She didn't look busy.

She stood in front of Jim with her hands on her hips, coffee mug and cigarette dangling.

"Well?"

Jim leaned back on the sofa as though he had time to relax. "I just need to know about funeral arrangements. Have you called a funeral home?"

"No. You should do that. I don't know anything about funerals."

Jim sighed. "Okay. I'll call Fullers and get back to you. I'll call the church too. Did you and Dad attend one?"

"He went to a Catholic church somewhere. I don't know."

Jim frowned. It was now all in his lap. He'd call Laura and pray she would help with the funeral. "I need to have Dad's cell phones. It's business."

Diane went to Frank's bedroom while Jim looked around the living room, and memories of that visit flooded his mind—the arguments, the lunch, the lack of agreement. Now he felt high-level guilt, wishing their last time together had been less confrontational, more cordial. The room was different now. Diane must have called an interior decorator as soon as Frank stopped breathing! New furniture, new draperies, all with a jungle motif and none of it from Perruda's Fine Furnishings. She hadn't wasted time or money.

Diane returned with two cell phones. "Frank used one for his business and the other for social calls. Take them but bring them back when you're finished."

Jim pocketed the phones. "Thanks. I'll call as soon as we've made the funeral arrangements. Maybe one of us should give a eulogy." He left shaking his head. Diane would have the penthouse, but he knew after the funeral, he'd never set foot in it again.

He returned to his office and checked the addresses on one phone. The names were business acquaintances and friends, most of them familiar. He checked the second phone and knew at once this was a "burn" phone, a disposable phone with no listings of any kind. He tossed it into his wastebasket and swore. The old man had covered his tracks completely. Now his only hope was a call from his dad's dealer, and that was unlikely. Maybe Laura might have advice. Maybe one of her clients was a drug dealer. Fat chance, but he wanted to see her. He punched in his home phone number and hoped for a reasonable reply, even a reply of any sort.

"Oh, hi, Laura," he said. "I'd like to pick your brain. How about having dinner with me tonight?"

"Um." Jim could almost hear her brain asking questions. "Okay," she said. "Pick me up at six, and we'll go somewhere."

His next call was to the *Naples Daily News* reporter, Trevor Johnson. He explained the delay in contacting the paper, and Johnson asked questions regarding his father and the Perruda family.

"We'd like to have an obituary today," Johnson said. "We've been waiting for an okay to print a more detailed report of your father's death but couldn't do anything until all of you had been notified. It's been difficult, Mr. Perruda."

"I'm sorry, and I'll get you an obituary this afternoon."

When all three men were back in Naples, cell phone numbers had been exchanged. Jim called his brother. "Tony, the *Naples Daily News* wants an obituary today. Will you do that? I gave them the facts they wanted regarding Dad's death. Now I need your help."

Jim was surprised to hear Tony's response. "Sure, I'll do that. Give me an address and the name of your contact."

Jim gave Tony the information and smiled. He and Tony had never cared much for each other, and their father hadn't encouraged familiarity or even respect. Perhaps now there was a chance for mutual concerns. Hey, he might even like the guy!

Jim replaced the phone and looked at his safe. Ninety-five bags of cocaine. He was glad those damn drug dogs hadn't entered his office. They'd have had a field day!

His next call was to the Catholic Church. After thirty minutes of discussion, a funeral service was arranged. Would Jim care to do a eulogy? He'd give it thought and get back to them. He decided to talk to Laura tonight about a eulogy. Maybe she would help.

• • •

Russell Jones sat at his desk at DEA headquarters in Arlington, Virginia, and listened as Sheriff Jack Ryder in Naples, Florida, explained their need for DEA input and assistance.

"We have a murder on our hands, and now we're seeing a connection with drugs."

Russ checked his calendar and found an empty space. "Yes, I can leave this afternoon. I'll meet you in your office."

A case in Naples! How convenient! He'd see his mother and Julie at the government's expense. His secretary made flight arrangements, and he was in the air at two o'clock. Sheriff Ryder had faxed enough data to keep him occupied during the flight. Many suspects but no real evidence. He remembered his case in Indianapolis. A businessman smuggling drugs. Perhaps it could happen again in Naples. He hadn't met the victim or his family, but everyone knew about them. Rosewood Center residents were interested in one another, and the rumor department worked overtime.

The Collier County Courthouse was just minutes from the Naples airport. He paid the cab fare, and with briefcase and carry-on, he hurried to the sheriff's office. Sheriff Ryder welcomed him, and the two men reviewed the case.

"It's sticky, Russ," Ryder said. "The Perrudas are well-known here. Son Jim took the Fifth, and Tony, the younger brother, and Philip Stevens, their brother-in-law, both say they can't remember anything. The old man didn't live long enough to change his will, so they're all viable suspects."

"How did you learn about the change in Frank's will?"

"His wife, Diane, told Officer Callahan about it. Maybe she wants to blame one of them for his murder."

"You suspect drugs are involved in the case?"

"Yes. That's why we called you." Ryder told Russ about their experience with the dogs. "Our drug dogs targeted a spot on the floor of their receiving dock, and Jim looked up at some furniture on the top shelf. I want to visit the store again with you. We may need a search warrant, but I'd like to keep this casual if possible."

Russ nodded. "We may not need a warrant. I'm a Rosewood Center resident. The connection might be enough for a friendly conversation. I'll ask my secretary to call Jim and make an appointment for tomorrow morning."

He and the sheriff set a time for the next morning's visit, and Russ hurried to the center. En route, Russ called the concierge desk.

"Rosewood Center. May I help you?"

Julie's voice bounced into Russ's head like dazzling silver stars. "Hi. This is Russ, and I'm in Naples. How about dinner tonight?"

"I'd love it. When did you arrive?"

"This afternoon. I'm on my way to the center now. I'll see you in about five minutes." He sat back in the taxi and smiled. Julie and his mother. Life was good.

When he stopped at the concierge desk, Julie stood to meet him, and he knew his weeks of waiting to see her had only added to the excitement of seeing her again.

"I'll be back down here after I've seen my mother," he said. "Where would you like to have dinner?"

"I'll find a good spot, and I'll drive." Julie smiled. "I'm so glad you're here."

Russ blew her a kiss as he went to the elevator. Marjory opened his mother's door, and he rushed to his mother's chair. He kissed her cheek and sat on the floor in front of her chair. He noticed a faraway look in her eyes. God! Didn't she know him?

"Oh, Russell," she exclaimed. "How good to see you."

Relieved, he looked up and smiled. "It's good to be home, Mom. I'll be here for a few days, so we'll have time together."

Russ stayed with her for half an hour and promised to return the next day. He unlocked his apartment, stowed his carry-on and briefcase, and returned to Julie's desk as she answered one last call before closing time.

They drove to a restaurant on Fifth Avenue and between courses, filled in the blanks. Julie told him about Heidi, the Saint Bernard next door, and Russ gave a brief account of his assignment in Indianapolis.

"Let's drive to the municipal pier after dinner," Russ said. "I need a sunset over the Gulf."

The pier was crowded. Tourists with children and natives with fishing gear strolled along the walkway. On the beach below them, people swam, waded, and walked along the white sandy beach. Watching the sunset was ritual for both tourists and natives, and Julie and Russ held hands as they watched those last seconds before the sun fell beneath the horizon.

"I never tire of sunsets," Julie said.

"You're right, and I miss them." He turned to Julie . "I miss lots of things, but most of all, I miss you."

"I miss you too. I'm glad you're home."

Russ said little during the drive back to Rosewood Center. He wanted Julie tonight, all night. Did she want him? And if she did, would she stay the night and make excuses to her boss the next morning? Maybe they should drive to her home, and later he could take a cab to the center. Suddenly Russ felt as awkward as a middle-school student on his first date.

Julie solved his problem. "Let's go back to my house. I'll make cappuccino."

She drove home, opened her garage door, and parked. She turned to Russ, and instantly their arms were around each other. Russ breathed her perfume as he kissed her. Kisses multiplied as they held each other. Together they walked into Julie's bedroom.

"I think I wanted you that first day when I moved to Rosewood Center," Russ said. "I've wasted too much time."

"I wanted you too, but I couldn't climb over the counter and force you onto the lobby floor."

Russ laughed between kisses as they undressed each other and fell onto Julie's bed. For Russ, it was a dream come true, a fantasy he'd envisioned and a desire fulfilled. His years alone faded into oblivion. Julie's body, warm and eager, matched his own frantic movements, and as they lay back, breathing deeply, he thought about a symphony he'd loved. Each member of the symphony had played as one, just as he and Julie had tonight, and the music they made together transcended one player's performance into a magnificent whole. Beautiful, exotic, rhythmic, complete.

CHAPTER SIX

Julie and Russ awoke three times during the night with the same "Oh my God! This is heaven!" experience. By seven o'clock the next morning, they were sublimely content.

"Shall we share a shower?" Russ asked as he nuzzled her neck.

"Sure," Julie answered.

Breakfast was hurried as they charted their return to Rosewood Center. "I'll park my car in my usual spot," Julie said, "and we'll take separate elevators. No one will know where we were last night."

"Sounds logical. Lunch?"

"I'd love it. Somehow we didn't have time for much conversation last night." She giggled.

Russ rode with Julie to the center. Only one horn bothered them as Julie maneuvered through traffic with Russ's hand caressing her upper thigh. They kissed quickly in the garage and went to their elevators, relieved no one was there, not even Felix, who guarded the place as though it was his own private abode.

Russ shaved and changed before stopping at his mother's apartment. Marjory met him with a finger on her lips.

"Your mother's asleep. She had a bad night. Thought her mice were leaving, and she cried."

"I'll be back later," Russ said. "I'm sorry. Does this happen often?"

"No, but it's expected."

At nine o'clock Russ called Perruda's Fine Furnishings and asked for Jim. He introduced himself and said, "I'd like to see you this morning if you have time. It's urgent."

He sensed nervousness in Jim's reply. "Come about ten o'clock."

As he walked to Jim's office, Russ admired the store's layout and furniture. He was confident that a rapport with Jim was possible, and his own experiences with this kind of situation gave him the confidence he needed to put Jim at ease.

• • •

Jim stood as Russell Jones walked into his office. They hadn't met, but Jim had learned about the Jones family, Carolyn and Llewellyn, who had helped to bring Naples into its present position of cultural and commercial excellence.

"How can I help you, Russ?" he asked. "I know you live at Rosewood Center when you're not in Washington or Virginia, and you're with the DEA. Is this a personal or business visit?"

Russ smiled. "Both, I guess. I'm sorry about your father. I lost mine several years ago, and there's still a cavity in my life."

"Yes, it's not easy. So why are you here, and what are we going to talk about?" Jim was nervous and wanted to finish the conversation even before it began. He had asked questions from friends who knew the family and learned that Russ was a special agent with the DEA. God! Was he here because of those damned dogs?

Russ confirmed his suspicions when he said, "Sheriff Ryder called me yesterday and asked that I assist in solving your father's murder. I've worked with this kind of situation, so let's be open. I was asked to help because Ryder suspects a drug connection. Your dad may have been an innocent victim of a drug cartel. We both know the dogs reacted to the presence of drugs in your receiving dock area, and you suspected the source."

Jim listened in horror as Russ stated facts that chilled his whole being. What could he say? Something about Russ, however, gave Jim a feeling of confidence and trust. What did he owe his father anyway? And what did he really know about his father's transactions? Maybe together, he and Russ might solve the problem, and maybe, just maybe, Russ could find the money for him, those millions his father had secretly amassed.

"Russ, I want to help you, and perhaps we can help each other. My dad imported furniture from Mexico, and I'm sure each of those shipments contained drugs. The last shipment arrived two days before he was killed. I don't know who brought them or anything about the transaction."

Jim told Russ about the "burn phone" and his total innocence about his father's drug involvement. "I don't know where he put the money. And he must have made a killing. I don't know who his contacts were. All I know is when one of those bar stools fell and broke, cocaine was hidden in the leg. I swept it up, but the dogs still smelled it." He smiled. "I guess I should have scrubbed the floor."

Russ laughed. "Maybe, but now we both know something, and maybe we can find the source of your father's operation. Can I see the stools?"

"Of course." He led Russ to the receiving dock and asked an employee to bring down one of the stools.

Russ studied it, removed one of the legs, sniffed and nodded. "I can smell cocaine. Where is it now?"

Jim wondered if he should tell him the truth or make up a story. Common sense prevailed. Russ was too smart and too experienced to accept a fabrication. "I put the drugs in my safe." He led Russ back to his office and opened the safe. Ninety-four bags were moved onto his desk.

Russ studied them, opened, and sniffed. He checked the weight as he balanced them in each hand. "The weight is about the same in each bag, and that's a big shipment. This was a professional job. Do you have invoices?"

"I do." He gave them to Russ, who read each one carefully. There were no addresses, no identification of shipping origin or carrier. The paper was standard.

Russ sighed. "This won't be easy, but nothing's impossible. I'd like to take the drugs and the invoices for analysis. I need a receipt for everything. It should be in writing."

Jim made notes and gave Russ a written statement regarding the transfer of drugs and invoices. "I'd like to keep this confidential," Jim said. "No one in my family knows anything about this, and I don't want them to be informed."

"I understand and agree with you. Confidentiality is part of my job."

"Thanks," Jim said and shook Russ's hand.

• • •

Another person in Naples was concerned about the drug shipment and its present location. She had buyers ready. Everything was in place for its usual transaction. She'd called Frank and learned the shipment was delayed.

"The stuff is in six bar stools. I'll call you as soon as they arrive," he had said and kept his promise.

He called her on Thursday. "I'm tied up with family right now, but the stools are safe here. We'll wait until Sunday when the store is closed."

"How about tonight?"

"Evenings are out. You know that. The police patrol the area, and if anything unusual occurs, they're right there. Sunday is better."

She reluctantly agreed and waited until she picked up Saturday's copy of the *Naples Daily News*. My God! A brief report of a death on the front page! No name was given, but the age, sex, and address of the victim assured her that Frank Perruda was dead.

She needed to get her hands on that drug shipment. Maybe she could go to the store as an innocent buyer and purchase the stools. Meanwhile, she'd have to call her people and tell them to wait. No, there were no problems. It was merely a delay. Stay cool.

She thought about the situation and laughed. Now she wouldn't have to pay Frank one penny, and all the profits would be hers. She'd miss Frank, but he was a pain in the ass at times. She knew Frank's supplier in Mexico, and she had connections with people who would buy the drugs, people who knew the system.

She relaxed, poured a glass of merlot, and smiled. Maybe she'd attend the funeral.

• • •

On Martinique, a French island in the Caribbean, Emma Perruda and her two daughters sat on the beach at Pointe de Bout. It was Tuesday, March 15. Their two weeks in the sun were almost half over, and already the girls spent more time discussing their school projects and friends than practicing their conversational French with the natives. Emma didn't know why, but she missed Tony. There was no one to resent, no one to hide from or glare at. And there was no soft, warm body next to hers in bed.

Although she hadn't had an orgasm for months, she remembered that exquisite agony. Perhaps their separation now might change future encounters in the bedroom.

"Girls," she said, "let's go to town for dinner tonight. A French menu will be good practice for you, and someone else's cooking will be good for me."

They drove to the town at four o'clock and wandered the streets. Emma was intrigued by a furniture store that displayed bedroom sets manufactured in France. The craftsmanship was excellent and the design, unique. She priced four pieces, inquired about shipping, and decided, even at that price, the purchase was wise. She hoped Tony would appreciate a change in their bedroom's décor. She gave the manager her credit card and address.

"*Oui, madame, c'est bon. Merci.*"

They found a small café with a menu posted on the front window. As they studied the offerings, a heavyset woman dressed in a wild floral print dress came to the door.

"*Bon soir, mesdames. Entrez, s'il vous plait.*"

Although the dinner was pleasant and the atmosphere charming, Emma noticed that the girls fidgeted and picked at their food. "What's wrong?" she asked.

Kimberley, the older one spoke. "Mom, we've had a great week, but we're homesick. There's nothing to do, and we miss our friends."

Emma thought for a moment. "I understand," she said. "I'll see if we can go home sooner." Ordinarily, she would have refused a change in their vacation, but she too was homesick. She hated to admit she missed Tony, and her curiosity regarding his father's behavior took precedence over added expense. She called her travel agent, who checked the computer for several minutes before she reported three empty seats on Thursday's flight to Minneapolis.

"There's a charge for changing flights. Is that all right?"

"It's not a problem," Emma said, and she and the girls began to pack. Their last day on the island would be special now, not just another day in the sun.

They returned home on schedule, and Emma went to the phone to check messages. She had set up a message on the phone and purposely left her cell phone at home. She hadn't wanted to talk to Tony, didn't want to hear anything about his family in Naples. She listened to her messages. Nothing from Tony. She heard long pauses accompanied by deep breathing and assumed the breath was Tony's. She debated a call. No, he probably didn't want to talk to her. Yes, she needed to learn about his trip. "Yes" won.

Tony's hello was impatient and gruff.

"Hi, I'm home. Are you still in Naples?"

"Yes. I'm glad you called. Where the hell have you been?"

Emma laughed. It was the old Tony, the one she knew too well.

• • •

When Tony heard Emma's voice on his cell phone, he felt strange and alien emotions. God! He had missed her. Incredible. And he needed her. Extremely incredible.

"It's been hell here, Emma. I don't know where to begin. I met Dad and tried to talk him out of changing his will, but he wouldn't listen. He wouldn't listen to Jim or Carla either."

"So what happened?"

Tony paused. Of course he couldn't tell her about his scheme with the three kings from his deck of cards. She'd probably assume he'd killed his father, and he didn't need accusations.

"I went to Key West for a few days, and while I was there, Dad was killed. Murdered in his bed."

"How dreadful! Who killed him?"

"We don't know. Jim, Phil, and I made plans to spend a long weekend away from Naples. Phil dropped Carla off at the airport on his way to Orlando. She flew home to take care of their kids because of a health problem in school."

"So all of you were gone when your father was killed?"

"Of course," Tony snapped. Hell! She sounded just like Detective O'Hara.

"I didn't mean to upset you, Tony. Where are you staying?"

"Jim's wife found us a condo on the beach." He stopped to think. He missed Emma, and maybe she'd be more understanding if she were here with the family. "Why don't you fly down? You could be here for the funeral on Saturday. Jim's making arrangements, and I'm helping him with a eulogy."

"I'd like to come. I'm still packed from our trip."

Tony sneered. "And where were you?"

He heard a chuckle. "I took the girls to Martinique, so I'm already beach acclimated."

"Good. Bring your bathing suit, shorts, and something appropriate for the funeral."

Tony smiled as he pocketed his phone. He needed to get his mind off murder and interrogations. Seeing Emma would be a pleasant diversion.

• • •

Russ parked at the entrance of Rosewood Center and waited at the counter while Julie completed a visit with Mrs. Johnson.

She introduced Russ. "He's Mrs. Jones's son, visiting from Virginia."

"I know your mother," Mrs. Johnson said. "We worked together on fund-raisers for the Philharmonic. We were both League members. I don't go anymore. It's too difficult with the walker, and we have many younger members now."

"Do you attend any of the programs?"

"Of course. We have a bus that drives us to many of the performances. I still have season tickets for the Pops concerts." She laughed. "I used to attend the classical series, but I kept falling asleep." She stopped laughing and studied Russ. "I hope you're here to find out who killed Mr. Perruda. We don't like this sort of thing in our community. It's bad press."

Russ was surprised to hear her speak about his mission. Did everyone know about his work?

"I'll do what I can. Why did you think I was here on business?"

Mrs. Johnson laughed again. "My grandson, Trevor, is a reporter for the *Naples Daily News*. He's what we euphemistically call 'an investigative reporter.' I call him a snoop."

Russ smiled and motioned to Julie. "Do you have time for lunch?"

Julie picked up the hint, stood, and waved good-bye to Mrs. Johnson.

As they walked out of the lobby, Russ said, "That was a shocker. Does everyone in the center know what I do?"

"No, but many of those folks have nothing else to do. It's not malicious." She snuggled up to Russ, and her movements started a wildfire in his insides. He kissed her deeply.

"It's so good." He straightened his clothes and started the car. "Now, where's lunch?"

"Let's go to the Turtle Club. We can have lunch on the beach."

They were ushered to a beachside table, and as they sat back and watched swimmers and sunbathers, a woman with a cane walked by and nodded to Julie. "That's Mrs. Frost," Julie said. "She lives at Rosewood Center and forgot to pick up Mrs. Johnson last week. We had a crisis until George the handyman, Felix, and the hospital staff decided Mrs. Frost was alive and well, just forgetful."

"Ah, the joys of retirement homes. Do you ever have burnout?"

Julie shook her head. "The residents are dear friends, and Peter Watson and the staff are easy and compatible. It's strenuous sometimes, but nothing's perfect all the time. What about you? Do you get stressed out?"

"Mine is a different kind of work. I only get calls when there's trouble, so it's stressful already." He smiled. "But I like my work too, and I also like the people I work with. I think we're both people people, like the song." He sang a few bars from Barbara Streisand's CD. "Will I see you after work? You could come to my apartment as soon as you're through, and we could have a drink and go out for dinner after…" He took her hand. "You don't have to hurry home, do you?"

He liked it when Julie blushed. "No, I don't have to hurry. I'll come up after five."

Russ whistled more of Streisand after he left Julie at her desk and unlocked his apartment. He called Perruda's Fine Furnishings and asked for Jim. "This is important. Are the stools still there?"

"I'll check. Hang on."

Jim returned a few minutes later. "Yes, they're still on the top shelf."

"Good. If anyone buys them, we'll have a lead to follow. Alert your sales staff."

"We'll watch for a sale."

Russ opened his laptop and searched for recent drug arrests, specifically those involving shipments from Mexico. So many hits! The border was a busy place. There were no documented arrests giving a Naples destination and no drivers' names. The search was futile. He took the bags of cocaine from his safe in the closet and stuffed them in his briefcase. He wanted to give these to the sheriff and went back to the lobby.

"I'll see you later," he said to Julie and drove to the courthouse.

Sheriff Ryder offered coffee, and he and Russ discussed the case. "The stools are our only lead now," Russ said.

"Correct. When Jim Perruda met with Officer Doyle and Detective O'Hara, he wouldn't give his whereabouts on the night his father was killed, so maybe he did kill his father. My instincts tell me he's innocent, but you never know for sure." Sheriff Ryder scratched the back of his head. "Jim's still a suspect, along with his brother, Tony, and brother-in-law, Philip Stevens. We'll bring them in again tomorrow. There's his sister also. Philip says she flew back to Boston, but we haven't checked the manifests."

Ryder buzzed Officer Lopez. "Get me flight manifests for Boston flights on March eleventh. I'm looking for Carla or Mrs. Philip Stevens." He sat back and sipped coffee. "What else do we have?"

"Not much." Russ was uncomfortable. Here he was with an unsolved crime, and all he could concentrate on was Julie. Her warmth, her body, her whole being from brain to toes. The government was footing the bill, and he was in love.

Ryder gave him more information about Perruda's death, including the reports from Officer Callahan and the medical examiner. As he finished, Lopez called to say that Carla Stevens was a passenger on American Airlines on March 11. Hers was a one-way ticket.

"That's strange," Ryder said. "Wasn't she planning to return here?"

"Maybe she didn't know when she'd be back, and of course she wouldn't know her father would be killed the next day."

"Or that her husband may have killed him."

"Right," Russ said. "I'm too suspicious. Guess it goes with the job. With only a slight hint of trouble, I could suspect your mother of selling drugs." He opened his briefcase. "Jim Perruda gave me these cocaine packets, and I want you to store them. I have a safe in my apartment, but this is evidence in the Perruda case."

"We'll keep them here, neatly identified. Come with me."

They walked to a room containing boxes, files, and locked storage. Ryder signed forms and gave one to Russ. He placed the bags in a safe and locked it. Russ sighed, relieved the bags were out of his possession.

He left the courthouse and drove to Old Naples, where he recognized a familiar jewelry store. The owner welcomed him and showed him an assortment of rings.

"A sapphire would be her color," Russ said. He looked at several and chose one in a classic silver setting and carried it back to the center. He parked in the garage and took an elevator. He'd see Julie later. He stopped at his mother's apartment and rang the bell. He was pleased to see his mother at the door, eyes bright and clear.

"My dear Russell," she said. "Come in, and we'll have tea. Marjory just left to visit friends."

Russ was glad to see a positive change. He accepted a cup of hot tea and relaxed. "Do you remember Julie, our concierge?"

"Oh yes. Such a sweet girl."

"I like her too, Mother. I haven't felt like this since Amy died. Maybe there's a future for us."

"That would be lovely." Mrs. Jones finished her tea and put the cup on the floor. Her eyes lost their clarity, and she stumbled as she stood. "I must tell the mice. They'll be interested."

Russ groaned. In and out, up and down. Sadly, he took his mother's hand. "I'm sure the mice already know. I'll stay until Marjory returns."

He sat with her until Marjory opened the door an hour later. She noticed the change in Mrs. Jones. "I'm sorry, Russ. She was fine when I left."

"I know. It's the disease. We've had a nice visit."

He returned to his apartment and reviewed the Perruda case file. Drug shipments were the new wrinkle in the case that brought him into the investigation. What's next, he asked as he checked his watch and waited impatiently for five o'clock.

• • •

Carla Perruda's husband, Phil, sat in a chair at the central library on Orange Blossom Drive. He had used a computer to check his stocks and to send e-mails to his office. He went out on the patio and called Carla. Damn, but he wished she'd come back!

"How are the kids, and when can you get here?" he asked.

"I d-d-don't know. Maybe t-t-tomorrow. School started t-t-today, and the k-k-kids' heads are clean. M-m-m-m-m—."

"Wait a minute, honey. You'll find the word."

Phil heard a soft moan. "I m-m-miss you. I know you d-d-didn't kill my d-d-dad. You c-c-couldn't."

Phil smiled at her naivety. He'd killed in the ring. He recognized his anger, usually well hidden but still there, crouching, ready to spring if the situation arose. That night at Jim's home, the situation had arisen, and he knew what was expected of him, of all three of them. Did Jim and Tony know the same anger, dread, and fear?

He thought about his interrogation with Doyle and O'Hara. They'd call him in again, and he'd go through the same agony. How long could he maintain a cool head and a calm facade?

"Just get here soon. The funeral will be on Saturday."

"I'll call for a r-r-reservation t-t-tomorrow."

Phil pocketed his phone and prayed for an empty seat on a plane bound for Naples. He bit a fingernail. Carla's family could drive a guy crazy. She was sane enough, although he could sense something in her body language that indicated hidden emotions and thoughts, but her brothers were off the wall. Jim seemed harmless, but he knew about the gambling. Tony was bossy, compulsive, maybe bipolar. Their wives must be nuts too, he thought. Otherwise, how could they survive?

He left the library and located a bowling alley. He didn't want to go back to the condo. He'd had enough of the Perrudas for today.

• • •

Diane Perruda paced the living-room floor. She was still stuck with the Perruda family and hoped the funeral would be the last event in her life as Frank's wife and now widow. There'd be legal involvements, of course. She thought about Frank's will-changing intentions, now impossible. Unfortunately, those damn kids would still receive their inheritance. It wouldn't affect her share, but she wished that none of them would get a penny. Rotten people who treated her like scum. So righteous and self-assured outwardly and so corrupt inwardly. She knew about Jim's gambling and Tony's mean streak. Carla was pathetic. None of them deserved anything. She was the grieving window, she thought. She should get it all.

The phone rang, interrupting her musings. "Yes? Oh, hello, Sheriff." She listened and stroked her neck. "Yes, I can come tomorrow."

She scribbled the address and stuck out her tongue at the phone. They would probably treat her like a common criminal. She knew their kind. Mean, sexist, aggressive. They'd probably try to rape her just to get a confession. She'd tell them a good story, make them crawl. She went to her closet and spent half an hour choosing the right dress. Black would be appropriate. Short, however. She'd give those bums at headquarters a look at a real woman. They'd all want her, and she'd laugh at them.

She thought about her lover and decided to call. She could use the landline now. It was all hers, and she didn't have to check on Frank anymore. She smiled and punched in a number.

"Hi, sugar honey," she said, breathless, anxious. She listened and exchanged plans and promises.

"We'll be together soon. The funeral will be on Saturday. I'll have to meet with the lawyer and the cops, but there's nothing to worry about. I want to see you like crazy."

The next morning she dressed in her new black sheath and drove to headquarters. Officer Doyle and Detective O'Hara met her at the door and escorted her to the interrogation room.

Diane smiled and took Doyle's hand. "I hope this won't be a terrible ordeal. I've lost my darling husband, and I'm scared." She wiped an invisible tear. "The killer's out there somewhere. Maybe I'm next."

"Don't worry, Mrs. Perruda. This won't take long. We just need some more information." Doyle removed her hand and ushered her to a chair. He turned on a tape recorder and sat across from her at the table.

"Please state your full name, age, and residence."

Diane gave her full name, took a few years off her age, and added her address. She answered more questions involving her education and employment. "You can check with the hospital. They have my records."

Detective O'Hara asked, "Will you give us a full report of your activities on the night your husband was killed?"

"I already gave the information to the officer that night," Diane snapped, her raspy voice loud, each word stressed. "I don't want to go through it again." She crossed her right leg, giving the officers a startling view of her upper thigh.

"All right," O'Hara said. "We'll just ask a few questions. Do you always stay in your bedroom in the evening with the door closed, watching television?"

"When we didn't go out, that's what I did. Frank was a sports nut, and I got sick of baseball. I don't know an inning from a first half or whatever they call it." She smiled at the detective. "I like situation comedies, romance, and reality shows. Something sexy and funny."

"What were you watching at about nine thirty until ten o'clock?"

Salt Marsh Sinners

"Hell, how should I know? I don't remember." She glared at O'Hara. "What difference does it make?"

"It makes a great deal of difference," Officer Doyle said. "If you can't remember what you watched, how do we know you were in your bedroom watching television?"

O'Hara stood and looked down at her. "It would be easy to slip into your husband's room while he was asleep and use a pillow to suffocate him."

Diane stood and put her face two inches away from O'Hara's nose. "Damn you!" she shouted. "You have no right to accuse me. I loved Frank. I gave him everything he wanted." She stared at Doyle. "And he wanted a lot." She put both hands on her hips and massaged them. "Yeah, he got what he wanted."

Doyle's eyes were glued to her cleavage. "Ah yes, well, let's sit down and work together. We don't intend to charge you with your husband's murder, but we have to look at every possibility." He looked at his notes. "You accused your husband's sons and daughter of the murder. Why?"

"Frank intended to disinherit his kids and build a university. Jim, the oldest, lives here and came for lunch that week. He and Frank had a heated discussion, and Jim walked out. His brother, Tony, flew down from Minneapolis that day, and so did his sister in Boston. I heard Tony and his father discuss the will, and Tony was mad."

"Mad enough to kill?"

"Yeah, you bet. He's mean."

"I'm sure you know they have alibis. They say they all left Naples Friday morning for the weekend."

"I wouldn't believe anything those people tell you. They're horrible." She put her head down on the table and covered her ears. "They treat me like dirt." She plugged in her pseudo-southern accent. "Here I am taking care of their dear old father so they don't have to lift a pinkie for him, and what do I get? Nothing!"

She raised her head and looked at Doyle, eyes full of tears. "I didn't kill Frank, honest. You know one of those kids did him in. Just get the killer and put him or her behind bars for the rest of his life. Bread and water. Solitary. Nothing's bad enough for them."

She stood and faced Doyle. "Can I go now? I haven't anything more to say."

Doyle nodded. "That's all for today, Mrs. Perruda, but don't leave town. We'll talk later."

He and O'Hara escorted her out of the building, and she walked slowly to her car. She sat with both hands on the wheel and relived her ordeal at headquarters. Had she been convincing? Had they believed her innocence? She pulled down the sun visor and looked in the mirror. She smiled. Yes, she'd given them what they needed. A little thigh, a little tear, and lots of blame-shifting.

• • •

Julie watched the clock and cleared her desk as the hour hand moved slowly to five and the minute hand, just as slowly, moved to twelve. She combed her hair and added a bit of scent. As she walked to the elevator, Executive Director Peter Watson stopped her. "Frank Perruda's obituary was in this morning's paper. Will you make an announcement for the front table stating our condolences and the funeral information?"

"I'll have it on the table tomorrow morning."

"I want it there now, Julie. It's important."

Julie smiled outside and sighed inside. She returned to her desk, and fifteen minutes later, the announcement was placed on the table. She ran to the elevator and straight into Russ's arms.

They kissed and walked together into Russ's bedroom. No preliminaries. Their desires were magically mutual.

An hour later Julie murmured, "Mmm," as they breathed deeply in unison. "Lovely, so lovely."

They whispered together as though someone might hear, love thoughts, loneliness forgotten.

Salt Marsh Sinners

Russ left the bed and returned with a ring box. "This is for you because it matches your eyes."

Julie opened the box and exclaimed, "Oh, darling, you must have known how much I adore rings." She put it on her right ring finger. "So beautiful. Thank you."

"It's not an engagement ring." He paused. "Yet," he added. "You don't know me well enough for a commitment."

Julie lay back on the pillow and stared at the ceiling. No, she didn't know him well enough. She had thought she knew her former husband, but she didn't, and when another woman became a threat, she realized knowing someone for only six months wasn't enough for a lifetime together. She knew she'd made a mistake with her first marriage and didn't want to rush into a second one.

"You're right, honey, and you don't know me well enough either." She turned and kissed him. "I do love you, and I want this to be real for both of us. I'll wear your ring, and we'll be together as much as possible." She sang into his ear, "You tell me your dream, and I'll tell you mine."

"That's a beautiful old song. My mom used to sing it to my dad." He sighed. "I wonder if she remembers it."

"Of course she'll remember. It's her short-term memory that's gone." She smoothed Russ's hair and kissed his forehead. "I know you worry about her, but she has no pain, and Marjory takes good care of her. You're both lucky."

"You're right, and now I'm hungry." He looked at his watch. "What's your choice for dinner?"

"Let's buy takeout and go to my house. I can check my mail and do martinis."

"That's a great idea, but we should take two cars."

"Or you could ride with me, pack a toothbrush, and go home in the morning."

"I like your suggestion better." They dressed and went to Julie's car. Chinese takeout, martinis, and Julie's bed. A blissful interlude.

CHAPTER SEVEN

On Friday morning Jim hurried to Perruda's Fine Furnishings, hoping to find his father's hidden treasure. His visit with Russell Jones gave him the opportunity to broaden his search. Surely the DEA had sources and the know-how to locate his father's drug money. Meanwhile he'd work with his customers and watch for a bar stool buyer. If that person had read of Frank's death, he might assume the drugs were still in the stools. Frank wouldn't have had time to remove the drugs and sell them to his dealer. His father hadn't had time to change his will either. A smirk appeared on Jim's face. They'd taken care of that problem, he thought, and either Tony or Phil could take credit for the operation. Which one? He was almost glad he'd taken Rita to Atlantic City. At least Laura knew he was innocent of his father's death.

He looked up from his desk as one of his salesmen knocked, entered quickly, and said, "There's a man out front who wants to look at bar stools. Shall I show him the ones in the receiving dock?"

Jim jumped up. "Yes. I'll follow you. This is important."

He walked with the salesman, who spoke to the customer. "We have six very fine stools in the rear of the store that were imported from Mexico. Would you like to see them?"

Jim studied the man. Short, stocky, bald head, muscular. A gold loop earring in his right ear. Obviously a drug dealer.

"Yeah, I'd like to look at them. I'm opening a new biker bar, and I need something sturdy. Nothing fancy. I seen pictures of art deco, and I kinda like that."

Jim joined in. "The stools would be perfect for you." He turned to his salesman. "Tim, you take this man…" He paused and looked at the customer. "May I have your name?"

"Sure. I'm Sam Kolinsky. Just moved here from Frisco."

Jim watched as Tim led Kolinsky to the receiving dock, then he rushed to his office and called Russ. "We've got a bite. A big one."

"I'll be right there," Russ said. "Hold him if you can."

Jim walked back and watched as a workman climbed up to the top shelf and brought down one of the stools. Kolinsky looked it over, checked the cushion, lifted himself up, and sat on it. "I like it. How much?"

Jim did a quick figure in his head. "The stools are one hundred dollars each. It's a bargain because they were handcrafted especially for us."

Kolinsky took out his iPod and rubbed it. "Okay. How about delivery? I need them early next week."

"If you pay for them now, we don't charge for delivery," Jim said. "Let's go back to my office, and I'll get your address."

Jim walked slowly, hoping Russ would arrive before the sale was completed. He ushered the man to a chair and spent several minutes at his computer.

Jim turned and watched Kolinsky as he peeled off six $100 bills from his wallet. "There's sales tax, of course," Jim said and reached for his calculator. He seemed to have trouble with the numbers. Several times he added, canceled, reworked, canceled.

Kolinsky fidgeted. "I can help you. It's six percent, right?"

"Yes," Jim said. "I had a bad night."

Kolinsky laughed. "Too much of the booze, maybe. Six percent is thirty-six dollars." He pulled more money from his wallet. "That should take care of it. Here's my address." He took a business card from his pocket. "I haven't had time to get new cards," he said. "Here's my new address."

Jim looked at the card. "That's in Everglades City. We have to charge for delivery because it's thirty-five miles from Naples, and I'll need to find out when our truck can make the delivery." He left his office and walked slowly back to the receiving dock.

When he returned, he was relieved to see Russ enter the building. Jim beckoned and said, "Our customer is in my office. He says he's opening a bar in Everglades City. I don't trust him, of course. I'm sure he's our man."

"I don't want to meet him, Jim. I just want to watch, and when he leaves, you can give me the details. I'll inform the sheriff, and he'll get a team together. Probably a SWAT team. This is good news."

Jim returned to his office. "I spoke with our driver, and he can deliver the stools on Monday. We have to charge seventy-five dollars for the delivery. Gas is expensive."

"No problem," Kolinsky said. "I'll give the guys a beer for their trouble."

Jim flinched. The man was too friendly. He was hamming it up for his benefit, he thought. What an act!

As soon as Kolinsky left, Jim and Russ discussed their next move. "I called Sheriff Ryder while you were finishing the sale," Russ said. "He'll organize a SWAT team because the guy could be dangerous. I want the team to follow your van and wait until the stools have been unloaded and the buyer has signed the bill. As soon as the van leaves, Ryder's people will enter, fully armed and ready for trouble."

Jim sat as his desk. "The stools will be safe in the receiving dock until Monday," he said. "Where are the drugs?"

"I took them to the courthouse, and they're locked up. I want to study those invoices carefully. They're in my briefcase."

"Good. I'm glad the drugs are safely put away. We wouldn't want to lose any." Jim suppressed a grin, knowing one bag was safely tucked away in his desk. Suddenly he pounded his fist on the desk and stood. "That guy could have murdered my dad!" he exclaimed. "They must have met at Dad's house. How else would he have known about the drug shipment?"

"You could be right, but don't jump to conclusions. If he's the killer, we'll learn soon enough. Stay cool and don't worry."

As soon as Russ left, Jim relaxed. Connecting his dad's murder with the drug trade would turn law enforcement away from family accusations. He really didn't care much for Tony. He hardly knew his brother-in-law, but they were both family, and he was stuck with them.

He changed mental gears and called his brother. "Have you written a eulogy, Tony? We'll need it for the funeral tomorrow."

"No, I'm not going to write one. I really tried, and nothing worked. We know what we had to do, and anything I'd say would sound hollow and fake. We don't need a eulogy anyway. Forget it."

"Okay. No eulogy. Have you heard from Emma?"

"Yes. She finally called and is flying here this afternoon." Tony laughed. "She took the girls to Martinique for a week, so she's already packed for a Florida vacation."

Jim put the phone down and thought about the funeral. Laura had talked to the priest, and the funeral home had worked with her on a program for the service. She and Jim had discussed cremation but Jim, knowing his father, decided upon a traditional burial. At two o'clock he'd had enough of Perruda's Fine Furnishings. He left the store and drove to the casino.

• • •

Carla, at home in Boston, packed as soon as she'd received Phil's call on Thursday, but she wasn't able to get a reservation until Friday.

She called her neighbor, her faithful sitter. "I d-d-d-don't know when I'll get b-b-b-back." Her neighbor assured her the kids would be fine. Not to worry.

Phil's call on Thursday had been puzzling. "I'm so glad you're coming," he said. "It's pretty tense here. Tony grumbles most of the time. Jim's busy at the store. Thanks to Tony's scheme, we're all worried, don't know who's guilty. We can't even talk openly. It's like the dead horse in the living room. We just walk around like zombies pretending it's not there."

"I'm anxious to g-g-g-bet back too. The g-g-girls have m-m-missed being in school, worried about their hair. Shampooing twice a d-d-d-day has taken up most of my t-t-t-time."

"I don't know when I can come home. Have you found a sitter?" Phil asked.

"Yes, the n-n-n-neighbor is taking them. Our children are about the s-s-s-same age, so it's no p-p-p-problem for her. We trade child c-c-care. When did you l-l-l-leave Orlando?"

"I came back on Monday. Orlando wasn't much fun without you."

He had to emphasize his innocence to Carla and to the police. Any hint of a discrepancy would implicate both of them. Together in Naples, they could smooth out the details. God, he hated to involve his wife in the murder. She was so violently opposed to her brother's scheme, but she was the sister. No escape.

"I'll meet your two-thirty plane," he said and wrote carrier and flight number. He relaxed, knowing Carla would be here tomorrow. Maybe after the funeral, they could sneak off for a few days, tell the sheriff and the lawyer they needed a break.

• • •

Emma, Tony's wife, back home from Martinique, asked a friend to stay with the girls for a few days. The girls protested. "Mom, we're old enough to stay alone."

"I know, but I have enough problems right now, and I can't handle any more. Please, just this once."

Reluctantly they agreed, and Emma's friend moved in.

Emma's flight to Naples was on time, and Tony met her at baggage claim. She was startled when Tony hugged and kissed her.

"I'm so glad you're here, honey," he said. "It's been hell."

Emma put her hand on his cheek. "I missed you too. I'm so sorry about your dad. Was it really murder?"

"Yes, and the cops think, because he was planning to change his will, one of us killed him." He led her to his car, stowed her suitcase, and they left the airport.

Emma was puzzled by Tony's statement. She knew he was angry and had come to Naples to talk to his father. But murder? Unthinkable! However, a small gnawing fear entered her thoughts. Tony's temper was sudden and sometimes violent. She remembered his anger that morning before he flew to Naples. If a bad cup of coffee could set him off, a change in his father's will could lead to *murder*! She moved closer to the car door and closed her eyes. Oh, please, no, she prayed.

Tony gave her a brief account of his father's death and his interrogation. "I don't know what's next. Jim said he took the Fifth, and I don't know why. Phil was questioned too, and of course Carla will be brought in for questioning. It's a mess."

When they arrived at the condo, Emma was pleased with the location. She unpacked and found Tony and Phil in the lanai.

Phil stood and kissed her cheek. "I'm picking Carla up in an hour," he said. "She had to fly home because of a health problem at school."

"I'll glad she's coming. We can all go out for dinner tonight. Tony, call Jim. Maybe he and Laura can join us."

Emma wanted to bring the family together and try to assimilate the situation. The Perrudas were all in a turmoil that extended beyond their father's death. She sensed a reserve, a tenseness in Phil, and Tony seemed to be on edge. His report was sketchy, and his voice betrayed worry that bordered on confusion.

Salt Marsh Sinners

Tony punched in Jim's number and suggested dinner. "Okay, we'll miss you," he said and closed his phone. "They're busy. Jim said he'd see us tomorrow at the funeral."

Emma shook her head. "I'm sorry." She was disappointed and decided a swim in the Gulf might soothe her concerns.

The water was warm and relaxing. She returned to the condo, showered and dressed for dinner. She applied makeup, pulled her long blond hair into a bun, and secured it with an orange comb that matched her dress. She smiled at the mirror. Answers would be found, and the family would survive.

Carla and Phil arrived at six o'clock. "I'm so glad to see you, Carla," Emma said as she hugged her sister-in-law. "It's been two years since we met in New York."

"I'm g-g-glad to be here," Carla said. "It's a sad time, but it's g-g-g-good to be with f-f-f-family."

Tony mixed drinks, and after a leisurely happy hour, dinner on the wharf completed their evening. Emma crawled into bed beside Tony and stroked his shoulder. He responded quickly, and Emma discovered she was multi-orgasmic.

• • •

Frank Perruda's funeral was held at Saint William Catholic Church at two o'clock on Saturday, March 19, one week after his death. At one thirty the family was ushered into a private room next to the sanctuary. Comfortable chairs, a tray filled with coffee cups and cookies, and two coffee urns labeled "regular" and "decaf" offered solace and sympathy. Diane wore a black silk Valentino suit and a matching wide-brimmed hat. Black nylons and black pumps with six-inch heels completed her costume. The others were attired properly, with less elegance.

Jim fussed with his tie, and Laura used a mirror from her purse for a last-minute checkup. Tony fidgeted and ran his fingers through his black hair. Emma frowned at her mirror and applied lipstick. Phil put his hand under his collar and shook his head. Carla cried.

Half an hour later, the family was led to two front pews as the organ began the opening hymn. Carla looked back and was pleased to see most of the pews were filled. Her eyes were red, and tears fell. She remembered that night at Jim's condo when Tony suggested the unthinkable. Who did it? She shivered and moved closer to Phil.

The casket was covered by a blanket of red roses. Laura had made the choice, along with all other plans, and Carla smiled through tears. Roses were the perfect flowers for her dad. The priest conducted the service and spoke briefly about Frank, a member of the community, giving his time to worthy causes. The service ended with the congregation singing "Amazing Grace." Two men from the funeral home moved the casket up the center aisle, followed by family members. Two limousines were at the curb to take the family to the cemetery. Carla watched a darkening sky and hoped rain would be delayed until after the interment.

A white canopy covered the gravesite, and as the priest read the brief service, claps of thunder drowned out his words. Carla stood close to Phil as the casket was slowly lowered into the ground. Suddenly there was a brilliant flash of light, followed immediately by a deafening roar of thunder. Carla grabbed Phil's shoulders and moaned.

"That was close," Phil said. "Are you all right, Carla?"

She nodded and looked at the others, who stood at the gravesite.

Diane's arms were around the priest, who pried them loose and patted her shoulder.

Tony and Emma clung together, and Jim held Laura's hand. The priest smiled at the family and continued the service. As he closed his prayer book, he said, "God has sent a message to all of us. Life is short and unpredictable. Our brother Frank is at peace now."

"Let's go back to the center for coffee," Laura said. "I talked to Julie, the concierge, and she arranged a small reception for us."

Carla nodded. "I think we all need a cup of strong coffee." She stopped and turned to Phil. "I'm almost afraid to think about it, but I'm not stuttering."

Phil put his arm around Carla and kissed her. "It's a blessing, honey." He looked at the priest. "God moves in mysterious ways, and today my wife had been given a new life."

The priest took Carla's hand and made the sign of the cross on her forehead. He bowed his head and whispered a prayer that only Carla could hear.

Emma took Carla's hand. "Sometimes a shock can create a miracle. The casket and that bolt of lightning together could change anything. I worked with a speech therapist last year who acknowledged the possibility of a real transformation."

"It's a miracle," Carla said. "I pray and hope it lasts." She walked to the limo with Phil, clutching his hand. She had felt a presence, experienced a miracle, but she felt a curtain had been drawn in her mind, something left unsaid, unknown. Behind that curtain was a mysterious, unfathomable shadow, almost sinister. Carla pushed it away, shook her head, looked up at Phil and smiled. Her new gift outweighed anything behind that curtain.

• • •

The family returned to Rosewood Center. Diane led the way. This was her home, and the man in the casket was her husband. She removed her hat and poured coffee. Taking a cup to a corner table, she studied all the Perrudas. Tony was a smartass, and Emma was a mouse. Carla and Phil were pathetic. He looked like an ex-prizefighter, and she looked like a little frump. Laura was too bossy, too self-assured. Jim might be interesting in bed.

She looked forward to life without any Perrudas. Frank had provided for her in their prenuptial agreement. Money was no problem, and she already had a suitable replacement for Frank. Too bad he had to die, but for the living, life went on.

• • •

Julie drove home from Rosewood Center after preparing refreshments for the family. She had attended the funeral and admired and felt compassion for the Perrudas, who must be suffering now, wondering who had killed their father.

As she sat at her kitchen table and read the front page of the *Naples Daily News*, she heard a scratching at the front door, accompanied by whines and low barks. She opened it and fell to the floor as a Saint Bernard rushed at her, placing two huge, muddy feet on her white blouse. She looked up at the dog.

"Heidi!" she exclaimed. "How did you get out? Where's Lisette?" Heidi licked Julie's cheek.

As Julie got up from the floor, Heidi raised her front paws again. "Down, Heidi," Julie ordered.

Heidi sat, big brown eyes shining, big pink tongue moving up and down. Julie laughed. Her next-door neighbor's dog must have dug her way out from under her backyard fence and sought refuge at Julie's home.

"Stay!" Julie reached for her closest phone. "Lisette, Heidi's here. She needs you."

Lisette appeared in minutes, leash in hand. She stared at Heidi.

"*Mechent chien*," she said. "Naughty dog! I'm so sorry. I'll wash your blouse and clean up the floor. Heidi must have dug under the fence. Now we'll have to put stones around the entire backyard." She sighed and smiled. "At least you have a dog friend."

"Don't Saint Bernards carry flasks of whiskey around their necks? I could use a drink right now. Do you have time?"

"Yes. Heidi doesn't have a flask, so you can make me a drink while I take her home." She attached the leash to Heidi's collar and pulled her gently.

Salt Marsh Sinners

Julie laughed. "I'll do martinis. Hurry back." She went to the kitchen and made the drinks. When Lisette returned, Julie said, "I want to give you my house key. If I lock myself out, you'll be there to rescue me."

"Good idea. I'll give you one of mine. I'm not infallible."

Julie spent the evening watching television, hoping Russ would call. She twirled her ring and smiled. Theirs would be a careful, comfortable relationship. No strings and no disappointments.

• • •

On Saturday afternoon Jeff Parker, one of the workers in the receiving dock, greeted his boss, Jim Perruda, who had just returned from his father's funeral. "Sorry about your dad," Jeff said.

"Thanks, it was a nice service. A storm interrupted the interment. We had coffee at Rosewood Center."

Jeff watched Jim leave the area, and went to a truck that had just arrived. He was a good worker but had an uncontrollable urge to eavesdrop. He listened to conversations between workers, chats between customers and salespeople, and he had listened carefully and safely behind a crate whenever a white, unmarked truck drove to the receiving dock. Frank Perruda was always there to meet the truck. Although Jeff never met the driver, he was alert whenever Frank appeared.

Last week, when Perruda entered the area, Jeff knew the white truck would soon arrive. He hid behind a crate and watched as the truck stopped, and the driver opened the rear door. He unloaded six bar stools.

"Careful of the legs," Frank said. Jeff heard them discuss the border crossing. No sweat. The Mexican driver had turned the truck over to Perruda's driver and went to a car on the Mexican side. Jeff heard the word *snow*. A weather condition? Jeff smiled. Cocaine. He had kept his secret and listened again on Friday when Jim and Sam Kolinsky discussed a delivery on Monday.

Now on Saturday, he knew he had to take those stools apart before the delivery. He could make a killing with the stuff. He had friends who knew the real users. Because he didn't know the drugs had been removed during his lunch break, a plan emerged in Jeff's brain. He could hide a key to the back door and enter the store late Sunday night. With a flashlight he could conceal his presence, bring down the stools, and fill his pockets with white gold.

Jeff arrived at the store at midnight Sunday night. Using his key he opened the door, found a ladder, and placed it against the shelves that held the bar stools. He used his flashlight as little as possible, and as he climbed up to the top shelf, he couldn't see another person enter the building, dressed in a black sweat suit, black tennis shoes, and a black cap.

Just as Jeff reached for one of the stools, he felt the ladder move away from the shelf. He screamed as he fell backward. First his head and shoulders, followed by his torso, smashed onto the cement floor. The ladder fell on top of his mangled body. His pain was intense, and waves of agony and terror hit him as he lay under the ladder. The assailant knelt beside him. The last thing Jeff Parker saw in his life as he lay under the ladder, helpless on the cement floor, were two eyes glaring down at him as an eight-inch blade was plunged into his chest. The cement floor suddenly became a puddle of Jeff Parker's red blood.

The assailant left the body, replaced the ladder, and brought a stool down to the floor. The bubble wrap was removed, and a leg unscrewed. Nothing. A hollow tube. Quickly the other three legs were exposed, with the same result. The killer cursed silently, returned the stool to the top shelf, and left the building.

Ten minutes later a squad car drove through the alley behind Perruda's Fine Furnishings.

"Everything looks okay," the driver said.

"Yeah," his partner said. "Too bad about the old man. I hope we catch the guy who killed him."

Salt Marsh Sinners

• • •

Russ had spent a quiet Saturday visiting his mother and reviewing his Perruda case notes. He didn't attend Frank Perruda's funeral, didn't know the man, and didn't want to be associated with the family in any way. He hated to admit it, even to himself, but with all his involvements since he'd arrived back in Naples, a quiet evening at home would be welcome. He kissed his mother good-night, ate a quick takeout hamburger at Wendy's, and drove back to his apartment.

He turned on the TV, hit the mute button, and called Julie. Her voice thrilled him, but he was too burned out to change his plans for the evening.

"Hi. I'm home catching up on some work."

"And I'm paying bills and cleaning cupboards. Not an exciting Saturday night for either of us."

"You're right, so how about an exciting Sunday?"

"I'm going to church," she said. "Do you want to join me?"

"I could use some spiritual guidance. I'll pick you up."

They drove to Trinity-by-the Cove, an Episcopalian church near Russ's childhood home. It was good to be back. He was pleased to see three friends who exchanged recent histories and introduced their families. Russ enjoyed sharing Julie with his friends. She was stunning in a white sleeveless dress with a pale blue scarf at her neck. Blue earrings matched her sapphire ring.

"Brunch at the Ritz?" Russ suggested.

Julie's reply was an enthusiastic yes.

They left the car with a valet at the hotel entrance and found a table near the beach. They ordered Bloody Marys and eggs Benedict. As they sat together, Julie looked up and greeted a couple who walked past their table.

The blond woman wore yellow shorts and a matching blouse. The blond coloring was obviously artificial, and she was nervous as she greeted Julie in a raspy voice.

"Hi. I want you to meet Larry Fischer. He's my accountant. Frank always took care of everything, so I need help."

Fischer seemed to be as nervous as the woman. He smiled at Julie but said nothing. Julie introduced Russ to Diane Perruda, Frank's wife, and Russ stood and shook her hand.

"I'm glad to meet you, and I'm sorry about your loss. We're neighbors. I live on the sixteenth floor."

Diane smiled. "That's nice." She took Larry's hand and led him to another table.

When Diane was out of listening range, Russ said, "That's a surprise. Is she always that sexy?"

"You're very perceptive. Yes, and sometimes rude. Maybe penthouse people are different."

Russ shook his head and sipped his drink. Some chick, he thought. Did she murder her husband? He wanted to discuss the problem with Sheriff Ryder. If she killed him, the drugs probably wouldn't have been involved, and his work on the case would end. He'd have to return to Virginia and live without Julie. He shook his head again. No, Diane was obviously not her husband's killer.

Russ and Julie spent the entire day together. Russ's bedroom took precedence, followed by Julie's bedroom and her pool. Chinese takeout and a movie with popcorn completed a quietly spectacular Sunday.

He returned to Rosewood Center at midnight and was awakened at eight o'clock Monday morning by a phone call.

"Mr. Jones, this is Lloyd Callahan at police headquarters. We have a murder that may be connected to the case you're working on with Sheriff Ryder. One of the workers at Perruda's furniture store, Jeff Parker, was found this morning, stabbed to death on the floor of the receiving dock. He was killed around midnight last night. No clues."

"Was he related to the Perrudas?"

"No. Jim Perruda gave us a statement saying the man had been an employee at the store for five years with no record of violence or any kind of trouble. Parker's wife is coming in at nine o'clock this morning. Can you be here?"

Salt Marsh Sinners

"Yes, I'll come. I know the address."

He dressed hurriedly, drove to police headquarters on Horseshoe Drive, and was met by Callahan, who led him to Police Chief Gordon Turner's office.

"I was called to investigate Frank Perruda's murder on March twelfth," Callahan said, "so I'm familiar with the case. I'm sure there's a connection here."

"Ugly business," Russ said. "The sheriff brought me in because of the drugs that were found at the store."

"We all need a lot of help with this one," Callahan said. "We're glad you're here. Chief Turner is anxious to meet you."

Russ was greeted by Chief Turner, a tall man of African American descent. He shook Russ's hand.

"I'm glad to meet you, Mr. Jones," Turner said. "I've been talking to the wife of the man who was killed last night."

He introduced Russ to a twenty-something woman who cried openly. "I don't know what happened," she said between sobs. "Jeff left the house about nine o'clock last night. He was kind of nervous, but I didn't think much about it. He likes to go to late movies, so I went to bed about ten o'clock."

"You called 911 at four thirty-two this morning."

"Yes. I woke up about that time. Jeff wasn't home, and I was worried."

Turner spoke to Russ. "The patrol car found him. Mrs. Parker told the dispatcher he was employed at the store, so that was the first place they looked." He gave Russ several pictures. "Not a pretty sight. We're sorry, Mrs. Parker. I wish it hadn't happened."

Mrs. Parker wiped her eyes. "We just got married two months ago. Will you call his parents? I can't do it."

"Of course." Turner buzzed Callahan.

Mrs. Parker gave him two phone numbers, stood, and said. "I want to go home."

"We'll take you. Your information is all we need now. We'll call when we have a lead on Jeff's murder." Turner took her hand. "I hate this, and I'm sorry."

"I'm sorry too," she said and left the office.

"I wonder why Parker was in the receiving dock," Russ said. "We've been so interested in the bar stool shipment that maybe we're not checking other reasons for his being there."

"We considered that possibility, but when we examined the stools, we found Parker's fingerprints on one of them. We also found his fingerprints on a ladder, so he must have used it to reach for a stool. The medical examiner's report indicates bruises and broken bones on his body that must have occurred from a fall, but that didn't kill him. He was killed by being stabbed in the chest, and he died instantly."

Russ shook his head. "I want to visit the store and talk to Jim. He may have some thoughts about Jeff Parker, why he was at the store Sunday night. Maybe he knew about the drug shipment, but he didn't know Jim had removed the cocaine."

"And how did he know about the drugs? Maybe Jim will have some knowledge about the man. Call me after your visit."

Russ left headquarters and drove to the store. Jim led him to the back area and said, "Jeff was a good worker, but he was nosy. He liked to listen when I'd speak to an employee, and it was offensive sometimes."

"So he may have listened when the stools arrived. I want to talk to some of his co-workers."

Russ's conversations with two of Jim's employees confirmed his assumptions. There was ample room for hiding places in the area. Large crates and boxes filled the bay. Parker could have heard the conversation when the stools were delivered. Jim had told Russ he had discovered the drugs during lunch break, so of course Parker wouldn't know the drugs were gone.

So why was he killed? Someone else wanted the drugs, someone else who also didn't know the drugs were no longer in the stools. Who was that someone? Someone strong enough to smother Frank Perruda? Russ shook his head, bewildered and angry. The Indianapolis case was easily solved. This one had more questions than answers.

CHAPTER EIGHT

Sheriff Ryder had spent most of Saturday choosing members of the Special Weapons and Tactics team. He selected Lloyd Callahan and Amanda Rieger, who were part of the team that investigated Frank Perruda's murder. They might want to join this operation. Ryder chose six other officers who were experienced in SWAT teamwork and asked the eight team members to be in his office at seven thirty Monday morning.

The team arrived on schedule and listened as Ryder gave them a complete history of the stools and a format for the operation.

"The stools will be loaded onto a truck and will leave the store at one o'clock this afternoon, so be here at twelve o'clock," Ryder said. "We're fairly certain that Sam Kolinsky is involved in the drug trade in Collier County. We've checked his background and learned that he had one drug arrest in Los Angeles before moving to San Francisco. He bought the stools instantly, paid cash, and ordered a delivery today."

Callahan asked, "Do we have a search warrant?"

"Yes. It's a no-knock warrant. You're authorized to follow that action."

"The usual weapons and gear, I suppose," said Thompson, the commander of the team.

"Yes, you'll have MP-five and AR-fifteen rifles and the usual clothing. Those lead-bearing vests are heavy and hot in this weather, but we can't take chances. This man could be armed and dangerous."

"This is new to me," Amanda said. "I've seen pictures of SWAT teams that have torn up the place, and I don't want to do that."

Ryder laughed. "Not to worry. You're to search and secure everything. There won't be any mess."

"How do we handle Kolinsky?" Callahan asked.

"I'm relying on your good judgment when you enter the bar. You'll search Kolinsky for concealed weapons, of course, but don't overreact. You and Rieger should follow behind and take orders from Thompson. These people are experienced. They'll know what to do."

Because Chief Turner had told him about Jim Perruda's pleading the Fifth, Ryder was reluctant to call him regarding the stool shipment.

"We're powerless," Turner had said. "Just don't trust him with the family jewels. He's hiding something."

"Right, but he has to know our plans." Ryder sighed and called Jim at the store.

"When will your truck leave the store?" Ryder asked.

"We plan to load up and leave here at one o'clock. Will the team come here and follow the truck?"

"Yes, they'll be at the loading dock at twelve forty-five. When they arrive at the bar in Everglades City, they'll wait until the stools have been unloaded and your workers have left before entering. We don't want innocent people injured."

"I understand, and I'll be here when you arrive."

Ryder's next call was to Russ Jones. Ryder gave him all the details of the plan and asked him to follow the team.

"We want the DEA in on this, Russ. It's a drug raid."

"I'll be there on time. Thanks for the call."

Ryder sat back in his chair, knowing everything was in place. It was time for a coffee break.

• • •

Supervisory Special Agent Russ Jones listened to the sheriff and planned to be at the store's receiving dock at twelve thirty. He spent the morning with his mother, who was in an "up" mode. He told her about Julie again, hoping she'd remember.

"I'm so happy you have found someone, my dear," Mrs. Jones said. "It's not right to be alone." She sighed. "Marjory is good company, but she's not your father. I miss him terribly."

Russ nodded. "I miss him too. He was special."

Marjory came from the kitchen with a pot of tea and a plate of scones. Russ relaxed until eleven o'clock. It was time for a quick lunch and preparation for the afternoon's raid. When he returned to his apartment, he remembered his conversation with Sheriff Ryder as they discussed their suspicions. Was Sam Kolinsky a druggie or an innocent guy who needed bar stools?

At twelve twenty, he drove through the alley behind the furniture store and parked near the next establishment. The SWAT team vehicle would require prime space. He walked to Jim Perruda's office.

"I wanted to see you before the team arrives," Russ said. "I'd like your assessment of Sam Kolinsky."

"I think he's suspicious, Russ. He seemed overly friendly, and he certainly was dressed for the part." Jim gave Russ a description of the man, and Russ nodded.

"You can't always tell a man's character by his dress. I've met millionaires who looked like street thugs."

"You're right," Jim said, "but I'm anxious to learn who killed my dad, and it just might be Sam Kolinsky."

Russ noticed an eagerness in Jim to find the killer, coupled with uneasiness. Jim paced the floor in his office, walked out onto the designer rooms, returned, and sat staring at the ceiling. He said nothing.

Russ stood, knowing there was more to this operation than a SWAT raid. He knew about Jim's pleading the Fifth, but he'd been open about the drugs, urging Russ to find a safe hiding place.

"I'll go back to the receiving dock and watch for the team," Russ said. "I'll see you later." The more Russ thought about Jim's body language, the more unsure and skeptical he became, but the sheriff was convinced the raid was necessary, a positive sign. Perhaps, he thought, he'd had thought overload.

At twelve thirty, a man climbed a ladder to the top shelf and began to bring the stools to the floor. He and another worker loaded them into the truck and waited for the team. Promptly at one o'clock, a black armored van pulled up in the alley behind the store, and Officer Bill Thompson, the commander of the team, visited with the driver.

"We'll follow you to Everglades City and will park about a block behind you. We don't want to arouse any suspicions. Kolinsky may be watching for you, and we want the stools unloaded and in his possession before we go in."

The driver nodded and climbed into the truck.

After Russ had watched the loading, he approached Thompson, the commander of the team, and introduced himself. "Sheriff Ryder wanted me to follow you. I know your procedure, and I won't interfere or get in your way."

Thompson laughed. "Glad to have the DEA on the team, Mr. Jones. It's your baby too."

Russ went to his car, donned a flak vest, added a blue blazer, checked his Glock, and followed the team.

The thirty-five-mile drive to Everglades City was uneventful. Russ kept a reasonable distance behind the team and noticed they too stayed back from the truck. They didn't want to look like a procession.

The truck driver with the bar's address led the team to a side street close to the center of town. He stopped at a building painted in blazing orange. Above the front door of the building, a ten-foot red sign announced "Sam's Roarin' Twenties Bar and Grill."

The driver and his partner unloaded the stools and brought them into the bar. The SWAT team parked, followed by Russ, half a block behind them. He watched as the truck driver and his partner left the building about ten minutes later. They turned and waved to someone inside. The stools had been delivered.

Now the team moved quickly. Thompson kicked in the front door as he raised his rifle. The others followed rapidly. Two black Labrador dogs followed the team.

Russ sat in his car for five minutes before he walked to the bar. He stepped through the open door and looked at chaos. He saw a stocky man in a stained white apron arguing with Thompson. Other members of the team, armed and alert, searched the bar thoroughly. Tables and chairs were up-ended, cabinets and standing shelves were subjects of thorough inspection. Liquor bottles and oven doors were opened.

The two black Labrador dogs followed Thompson. Russ knew about "passive alert" and watched the dogs, trained to locate drugs of any kind. The dogs sniffed the stools, sat, and stared. Drugs had been hidden in those chrome legs, and the scent still lingered.

Russ moved closer to Thompson and listened as he spoke to the man in the apron. "Mr. Kolinsky," Thompson said, "I've already told you we're here because those stools contained bags of cocaine imported from Mexico."

"How the hell should I know that?" Kolinsky asked. "You guys are nuts to barge in here. Look at this mess! I bought those stools because I needed them. I'm not a user. Gave it up years ago. And you searched me like I was carrying concealed weapons! I'm innocent, for God's sake!"

Kolinsky looked at Russ. "Who the hell are you?" he asked.

For the first time in his official life, Russ was tongue-tied. The letters "DEA" could scare an already nervous, angry man. "The sheriff asked me to be here. Don't worry."

He turned to Thompson. "Has your team searched enough?"

Thompson looked tired and upset. "I'll give us about thirty more minutes." He looked at Kolinsky. "If we don't find anything, we'll put everything back. You'll never know we were here."

"I'll bet," Kolinsky sneered. "I've seen enough TV to know what you guys do."

"This isn't TV, Kolinsky. This is the real world."

Russ admired Thompson's handling of the bar owner. He knew the commander of the team carried a great responsibility, not only for his team, but also for all the citizens of Collier County.

Russ turned over a chair and sat. He watched as each member of the team returned to the bar area. "Everything is okay upstairs," one team member said. Others returned and gave the same report.

"Okay," Thompson said. He looked at Kolinsky. "I'm taking full responsibility to tell you we've found nothing here. We'll secure everything." To the team members, he said. "Okay, let's clean up the place." He pulled out his iPhone, called the sheriff's office, and gave a full report of the raid.

Russ helped the others replace the furniture and all other items that had been moved and thoroughly searched. Kolinsky sat on a stool and watched the activity. When all eight team members had finished, the bar looked ready for business, clean and neat.

Kolinsky half smiled at Thompson. "How about a beer before you leave?"

Thompson laughed. "Thanks, but we can't drink on duty. I'll stop in when I'm not working."

Russ stood and followed the team. Kolinsky stopped him at the door. "I don't know who you are, but I'll bet you're FBI."

Russ smiled. "Why do you think I'm FBI?"

Kolinsky winked. "I watch TV. You're a dead ringer for an FBI agent on my favorite crime program."

"Very perceptive, but don't believe everything you watch on TV." Russ shook hands with Kolinsky. "I'll be back someday with my girlfriend."

As he walked to his car, he saw about ten people across the street who must have watched the operation from a safe distance.

Russ smiled. He'd bet Kolinsky's bar would be a center of curiosity and an immediate success.

• • •

Sheriff Ryder sat at his desk at four o'clock Monday afternoon and rubbed the back of his neck. Thompson's report of the raid meant law enforcement was back at the starting gate. Who killed Frank Perruda and Jeff Parker, and why? In Parker's case someone wanted the drugs, someone who didn't know the drugs had been removed. That someone must have been involved in other transactions with Frank Perruda.

He called Lopez and asked for a complete report of all persons in Collier County who were or are presently involved in any part of a drug situation or crime.

"Sure," Lopez said. "The list will be a long one. I'll get busy right away."

Ryder called Police Chief Turner. "Do you have any more information regarding Parker's death?" Ryder said. "We were glad to receive your fax report this morning. It's obvious that Parker was going after the drugs."

"Yes," Turner said, "and so was the killer."

"We're checking all drug-related incidents in the county, Gordon. I'm hoping we'll find a connection somewhere. I'll keep you informed."

"Thanks. Maybe the pieces of the puzzle will come together."

Ryder's next call was to Russ Jones. He listened as Russ gave him his version of the SWAT team raid. "They did their job remarkably well, and there were no hard feelings after they'd cleaned the building."

"Our people are well trained," Ryder said. "I'm glad you were there as a witness."

Russ laughed. "It was an interesting afternoon, Jack, but we didn't solve any crimes. No killers, no drugs, no users. Total *nada*."

"We don't always win, but we don't give up. We're checking all drug-related crimes in the county now. Would the DEA have more information for us?"

"I'll check and call you back. Maybe we'll find more information, and maybe not. It's worth a try. I'll see you tomorrow."

Ryder replaced his phone as Arturo Lopez walked through Sheriff Ryder's open door with several sheets of computer printouts.

"We've gone through the files thoroughly," Lopez said. "We made a list of possible suspects, and there are a lot of them. We never seem to get ahead of the pushers and the big dealers. Most of the users aren't worth investigating. They're just poor souls who got hooked. It's *muy triste*."

Ryder nodded. "We can't give up, Art." He took the printouts. "Thanks for your work." He looked at the wall clock. "It's six o'clock. Time to go home."

Lopez left, and Ryder put the papers into his briefcase, his homework for the evening.

• • •

Jim Perruda had watched the van, the SWAT team, and Russell Jones drive through the alley en route to Everglades City. He was relieved to see an empty space where the stools had been. Ugly memories of Jeff Parker's death the night before surged through his already anxiety-ridden brain. He walked back to his office, sat at his computer, and opened his e-mail.

He jumped up, startled, as someone behind him placed two soft, feminine hands across his eyes. He sniffed a familiar scent. Rita!

He turned and gave a small smile. "Oh, hi," he said. "This is a surprise."

He walked to his door and shut it as Rita put her arms around him.

"You promised to call when we landed," Rita said, "and over a week has passed." She stroked his hair. "I've missed you."

Jim cleared his throat and backed away. "You know my dad died. He was murdered, Rita, and it's been hell ever since." Jim refused to give her any details. "You look great. What have you been doing?"

He really didn't want to know, but he had to say something. He looked at her and shook his head. She wore a bright-orange too-tight T-shirt above bright-orange shorts. Orange sandals and a streak of orange through her red hair completed her attire.

"My job at the clinic was terminated, so I'm having a hard time, financially, I mean."

With an orange tissue, she carefully dabbed her eyes to avoid dripping mascara.

Jim groaned silently. He should have suspected the reason for her visit. Blackmail! Oh God, that's all he needed!

"I could loan you some money temporarily—no interest, of course. Would that help?"

Rita kissed him, her tongue moving across his upper lip. "You're sweet, Jim baby. Five thousand would do nicely." She sat down and crossed her legs. "I promise I won't ask you again. It's a bad time for me too." She smiled. "We did have fun in Atlantic City, didn't we?"

"Yes," Jim admitted but remembered the consequences. Laura might never forgive him, and he had to plead the Fifth with the police to protect his family. He could feel beads of sweat on his forehead, and his chest felt uncomfortably hot.

He sat down in front of her and took her hands. "Look," he said, "we had a really great weekend, but it's over, Rita. I really love my wife, and I probably ruined my marriage."

"Yeah, I've heard it all before." She stood. "I'll take five thousand. Maybe I'll pay you back, and maybe I won't." She shook her head. "You guys are all alike. A roll in the hay to break the monotony, then back to the wife." She waited as Jim wrote a check and gave it to her. "I won't see you again, Jim. You're not worth another trip, even in a chartered plane."

She walked out, not waiting for Jim's reply.

Jim leaned back in his chair and wiped his forehead. Did she really intend to stay out of his life? Another worry on top of all the others. When would he find peace?

• • •

Russ called DEA headquarters in Arlington, Virginia, and asked for a complete printout of drug cases in Collier County. He was convinced this was not an isolated drug operation involving two or three people. Frank had been importing drugs for at least six months, and Russ believed many pushers and users could be identified.

He picked up his briefcase, visited his mother for half an hour, and was at Julie's desk at five o'clock.

"I have a surprise for you," Julie said. "We're going to have dinner at my house tonight. I made a casserole."

"Sounds great. I'll follow you in my car and leave later tonight. I have to be at the courthouse early in the morning, and I don't want to wake you."

Julie's casserole, Caesar salad, and asparagus, followed by apple pie, were a delight for Russ, who was tired of restaurant food. Their after-dinner activity delighted him even more. Julie was an accomplished partner and knew what Russ liked. Russ knew what Julie liked. Together it was magic each time.

At eleven thirty, Russ turned over in bed, kissed Julie, got up, and dressed.

"I need to get home," he said. "I wish I could stay all night, but my car in your driveway in the morning might raise your neighbors' eyebrows."

"I hate to see you leave, but there's still tomorrow." Julie took a robe and followed him to the door. "Watch out for stray dogs and cats. Call me tomorrow." She blew a kiss, and Russ drove home to Rosewood Center. He parked, locked the car, and took his briefcase into the lobby. It was deserted.

He took the elevator to the sixteenth floor and walked to his apartment. He held his key and paused. An alert charged through his brain, and he didn't know why. The door looked all right, but the minute he stepped inside and turned on the foyer light, the alert became a glaring red beacon. The living room had been vandalized. He took his Glock 22 from its holster, ready to meet the intruder, and gazed, horrified, at the chaos. Sofa and chair cushions had been slit open and the contents scattered. Rugs had been thrown onto furniture. Lamps lay on the floor, surprisingly unbroken. Pictures were askew on the walls, as though someone was looking for a wall safe.

Russ groaned and swore. Whoever had committed this crime had done it quietly. No one in the building could have heard a sound. He stepped over the litter and went to his bedroom, his weapon off safety, and aimed. It had been thoroughly trashed. His bed had been torn apart, the mattress and box spring in shreds. All drawers had been emptied, the contents scattered. His closet was a horror of pockets torn open, jacket linings ripped, and the floor covered with all of his clothes. Only hangers remained on the rods.

He made a quick tour of the apartment, stepping over the trash. The apartment was empty. The perpetrators had fled.

He removed his cell phone and called 911. He identified himself and gave his address. "My apartment has been vandalized, and I need someone to investigate. I'll meet you at the front door because it's locked." He stopped to think again. "Don't use a siren. I don't want to alarm the residents."

He took a quick look into his bathroom and swore again. A walk to the kitchen produced more groans. Because the police would arrive soon, he had no time to look further. He needed to be at the front door when they arrived.

In the lobby he waited three minutes before a silent, unlit police car stopped at the entrance. Russ opened the door, and two men entered. Introductions were exchanged, and Russ led them to his apartment.

The officers were as startled as Russ had been. "What a mess!" one exclaimed. The men made notes on their iPads as Russ led them through each room. The bathrooms drew their attention. All pill bottles, anything that might contain a drug of any kind, were emptied.

The officers donned gloves and dusted for fingerprints, but found none.

Officer Mahoney took pictures of the apartment. Each room was thoroughly photographed. When he had completed his task, he said, "It looks like someone was looking for drugs, Mr. Jones. We've seen this kind of damage in drug-related cases. Not unusual but just plain ugly."

"I guess I'll have to sleep at my mother's apartment tonight. Will you want a report in the morning?"

"Yes," Mahoney said. "Can you come to the sheriff's office?"

"Sure. I'll be there." Russ shook his head. "The person who did this was experienced or frantic, maybe both."

"Yeah," Mahoney said, "and sometimes you never find the culprit."

"We'll find this one," Russ said. "I'm sure of it."

When the officers left, Russ stumbled through the living room into his bedroom. He was able to locate his shaver and a toothbrush. He picked up his briefcase and locked the door behind him. In the hall he opened his briefcase containing the invoices and other material relating to the case. He patted it and smiled. The criminal had found nothing.

He unlocked his mother's apartment next door and tiptoed into the den. He opened the sleeper sofa, undressed, and fell asleep in his jockey shorts.

The next morning he surprised Marjory as he appeared, shaved and dressed. She came from her bedroom, covered her mouth, and suppressed a scream.

"Oh, Russ, you scared me," she said.

"Sorry," he said and explained the reason for his presence. "I'm going to the sheriff's office now to make a report."

"Do you want coffee before you go?"

"No. I'll grab something downtown." He stopped and called his insurance company and was relieved to learn an adjuster could meet him at his apartment at eleven o'clock.

He took his briefcase and stopped at Starbucks for coffee and a scone. At the courthouse he went to Sheriff Ryder's office.

Sheriff Jack Ryder met him and offered condolences. Officer Mahoney's report had been thorough and chilling.

"I'm sorry, Russ," Ryder said. "It was obviously a drug search, and we usually can't find the guilty party."

"We'll find this one, Jack. It may take time, but we'll find him."

"Good. I hope you're right. I have some papers here for you to sign. Just routine stuff."

"No problem." Russ signed. "I want to study your printouts and see if they agree with what I expect to hear from DEA headquarters. We may be able to zero in on likely suspects."

"I hope so." Ryder gave him several computer sheets. "You can take these home and study them."

Russ laughed. "I don't have a home, Jack. Remember?"

"Okay, you can use our conference room. It's private."

He led Russ to the conference room and brought a carafe of coffee and a mug. "You might need this. Good luck."

Russ spent an hour studying the printouts. Three names interested him. Jose Fuentes, Joshua Carlson, aka George Peterson, and Rufus Jones. He hoped he and Rufus weren't related. All three men had been convicted of marijuana possession and had served short terms in the county jail. All the others were too old to commit two murders and trash his apartment, were out of town at the specific times, or were still in prison. He punched addresses and phone numbers into his iPhone and returned to Ryder's office.

"Thanks for the coffee, Jack. I found three names of guys who might have committed murder. I took their names and addresses, and I'll see them now."

"Do you want someone with you?" Ryder asked. "I know you usually work as a team. I can send an officer."

"I can handle this alone. I don't want to alarm or threaten these guys. We'll have a friendly chat this time." He added, "I didn't contribute anything to yesterday's raid in Everglades City. Maybe I can help now."

He thought about his briefcase, which held the invoices and other important material. "I have to meet an insurance adjuster at eleven o'clock before I check out the men, so I'd like to leave my briefcase with you."

"I'll guard it with my life," Ryder said and put the briefcase in his desk drawer and locked it. "And, Russ," he said, "call if there's trouble."

"I'll be prepared. Don't worry."

Russ drove home and met with the adjuster, who photographed everything and took notes.

"It's bad, Mr. Jones," the adjuster said. "We'll do our best to help you."

Russ thanked him and led him through and over the clutter to the front door. He returned and checked the yellow pages for companies who remove damaged and unsalable items. He called several before he found people who could remove everything that day. Russ gave them directions to the service entrance.

Julie should see this, he thought, and called her desk. She responded quickly and ran to his apartment.

"Oh, Russ, how horrible!" she cried. She hugged him. "Can I help?"

"No, a company is coming soon to remove the mess. You can direct them when they arrive."

Julie nodded, kissed him, and returned to her desk.

Russ found a broom and dustpan and tried to clean his bathroom floor. No liquids had been spilled, so the work wasn't tedious. He filled a wastebasket with trash. He folded towels and straightened the shower door. The bathroom began to look presentable.

At two o'clock he received a call from Julie. "The men are here to remove your furniture, sweets. I'll send them up."

Russ stepped over the mess and admitted two heavyset men who might have been on a wrestling team in their free time.

"Wow!" one of them said. "You really took a hit! They must have been looking for gold."

"No, drugs," Russ said, "and they didn't find any."

The men loaded everything into wheeled carts, and Russ counted fifteen trips to their truck. Within an hour Russ's apartment was nearly bare. He signed the bill and sat down on a kitchen chair that had been spared. Other chairs had survived, and the kitchen table was intact. He straightened pictures and moved lamps from the floor to their rightful tables. The living room looked empty but neat. He'd call the center's cleaning service to finish the job.

Russ checked his watch. It was three o'clock. He'd have time for one or two interviews before dinner. He locked his apartment, went downstairs and spoke to Julie.

"I'm going to talk to some people. If I get back in time, we could have dinner, but don't wait for me."

"That's all right," Julie said. "I have leftovers from last night. Don't worry."

Russ drove to the first address on his list, Jose Fuentes, who lived in Golden Gate, an eastern suburb of Naples. He found the house set back in a trashed yard surrounded by Southern pines and palmettos. Russ fingered his Glock 22 in its shoulder holster and walked to the front door of a small brown wood-siding house. Four front windows were dirty and discolored.

A five-foot-eight, swarthy-complexioned man with greasy black hair answered Russ's knock. "Yeah? What do you want?"

"Are you Jose Fuentes?"

"What's it to you?" the man paused. "Yeah, I'm Jose." He studied Russ. "And I'm clean. Did my time. I'm not buying if you're selling."

Russ laughed. "I'm not selling, but I'd like to ask you a few questions." He pulled out his DEA identification badge, knowing the man would respond with some respect, maybe fear, because he'd had experience with law enforcement.

"Okay, come in," Fuentes said.

Russ sat down on a weathered davenport and pulled out his iPhone. "I'm looking for someone who can remember his activities on Friday, March 11. Where were you?"

"That was a long time ago. Let me think." Fuentes scratched his head. "I took my mother to Miami about that time to see some relatives. Do you want me to call her?"

"Yes. I'd like to talk to her. Does she speak English?"

"Yeah, a little. If you talk slow, she'll understand."

He pulled out a cell phone and punched in a number. He waited, then said, "*Madre, tengo un hombre aci.*" He gave the phone to Russ.

Russ spoke slowly as he asked her about her trip to Miami.

"*Si*. We go." She paused. "I check time." She paused again. "*Vamos al marzo undecimo.*"

"*Muchas gracias,*" Russ said and returned the phone to Fuentes. "I guess you're not the man we're looking for, but maybe you can help me."

"I don't see my old friends anymore, but I'll help if I can. Would you like a beer?"

"No, thanks." He studied Fuentes. "A furniture owner was killed on March 11. He lived at Rosewood Center and was importing drugs from Mexico. We don't know who the buyer was or who bought them from the buyer. Do you know anyone who might have been involved?"

Fuentes shook his head. "No, I gotta stay clean, so I stay away from those guys. Sorry."

"I understand." He gave Fuentes his business card. "If you do remember someone, call me."

"I will." Fuentes didn't rise when Russ left. There was nothing more to say.

CHAPTER NINE

Russ drove away from Jose Fuentes's house and checked his list and his watch. It was five thirty. He had time for one more stop. Joshua Carlson, aka George Peterson, lived in an area south of Golden Gate and according to Russ's GPS, not far from Fuentes's house. It was, however, the season when traffic multiplied. He finally found the house after two detours and three dead ends. It was set back from the road amid a tangle of live oak trees, and it needed paint and lawn service. Although he wasn't expecting trouble, he checked his Glock 22 before he knocked. He waited for several minutes until a tall man wearing a gray beard, torn gray T-shirt, and black shorts opened the door.

"Yeah? What do you want?"

"I don't want to bother you, but I need help finding some people." Russ looked inside and groaned silently. The room was littered with beer cans, overflowing ashtrays, and paper plates filled with leftover pizza.

He hesitated. The man hadn't welcomed him, and the place was a mess. Before he could change his mind and walk to his car, the man said, "You can come in, but we don't like company much."

Russ walked into the room. "I won't stay long. I just need some information. Are you Joshua Carlson?"

"Who wants to know?"

"Several law and drug enforcement people." Russ paused and looked around. He didn't see anyone else. Maybe the guy was just a slob. "We're investigating a murder that took place the night of March 11. Maybe you can help us identify anyone who might have been around at that time." He forced a smile. "I don't suppose you can remember where you were that night."

Carlson laughed. "Is this a joke? What's with you guys? Do you think I'd tell you even if I could remember?" He laughed. "And I can't."

"I know the murder took place over a week ago, but maybe you can remember." Russ paused. "Look, Carlson, I'm just trying to do my job, and I need help."

"You came to the wrong place, mister." He picked up a can of beer and swallowed.

Russ knew Carlson wouldn't offer any information. He was stuck inside the house, and he knew it was time to leave with no further questions. How could he terminate the conversation?

Carlson put down his beer and stared at Russ. "Why did you come here? Who are you working for?" He walked to the door, blocking it, and turned to face Russ. "You're not leaving until I get some answers."

Russ walked to one side of the door, hoping to distract the man and make his escape. "Okay, you're on a list of guys who do drugs. It's no secret that you did time two years ago for possession and selling. It's not private information, Carlson. That's why I'm here."

"So I did time. What's that got to do with the murder?"

"The victim was buying drugs in Mexico and smuggling them across the border."

Carlson laughed. "I don't need Mexican drugs. We have enough right here."

Russ moved closer to Carlson and the door. "Okay. You can't remember where you were, so—"

The sentence ended as he was rushed from behind and knocked to the floor. As he struggled for his gun, his attacker kicked him in his lower back. Russ turned slowly, and he was kicked again, viciously, in his groin. He doubled up in pain and tried again to reach his gun. This time the attacker's kick was aimed at his right shoulder.

Russ groaned and looked up. The attacker was a muscle-bound, forty-something man with shaggy blond hair that fell to his shoulders, covering some of his tattoos.

He kicked Russ again, pulled him up, and tried to hit him with a clenched fist. Russ responded quickly. In spite of the blows, he fumbled for his gun, but the man saw his movement and grabbed the gun before Russ could touch it. As the man stared at Russ, he palmed the gun back and forth, right hand to left hand, almost caressing it. Now Russ knew that his attacker was an experienced killer. Would he shoot while Carlson laughed?

"Don't move," the man said, aiming the gun at Russ's forehead.

Russ ducked and quickly lunged at the man, beating his fists into his attacker's eyes and nose.

Carlson stepped behind Russ and grabbed both arms. Russ tried to break away, but his assailant saw his chance and began an onslaught of fists and kicks. Russ fell to the floor, hitting a marble-topped table with jagged edges. His left arm caught on the table, and as he fell, he felt his arm snap above the elbow. He screamed, and his attacker hit him again. Russ lay on the floor, conscious of nothing but the overpowering pain, until everything faded into a black void.

• • •

Carlson looked at his brother, the attacker. "Hank, that was dumb. He's a cop, maybe FBI. We don't need this right now. My old lady's coming tomorrow, and now we got a problem." He bent down and frisked Russ's inert body. "Here's his wallet. I'll keep it and look at it later. What are we gonna do with him?"

Hank swore. "We can get rid of him, but I like his gun. I think it's a Glock 22. I always wanted one, so I'm gonna keep it."

"Okay, but we've got to do something soon before he wakes up."

"We could dump him in Naples Bay."

"Naw, it's still daylight. Somebody would see us. We got to move him away from here. How about Everglades City?"

"Yeah," Hank said. He smiled and pounded his brother on the back.

"We'll wait until it's almost dark," Joshua said. "We don't want anybody following us. By the time we get to Everglades City, it'll be dark enough to dump him."

"Yeah," Hank said, "but if we let him live, he can identify us."

"No chance. We're outta here as soon as Trixie comes. They'll never find us. I got connections and fake passports."

"What about his car?"

"When we get back, we'll drive it into a canal," Joshua said.

Together they carried Russ to Joshua's car, opened the trunk, and shoved him in. Carlson shut the trunk, and the two men drove away.

• • •

Russ moaned. He shifted his legs, but there was little room. He wiggled his toes, and tried to move his arms. Pain shot through him like knife blades. He lay still and braced himself against the jarring. He heard the sound of a motor. He was jammed into a car, probably a trunk. Where were they taking him? He thought about the two men, dangerous criminals who seemed intent on killing him. He had made a big mistake, he thought. He should have called Ryder and told him his destination. He should have taken someone with him. He'd never messed up before on an assignment, but he hadn't expected trouble.

His pain was so intense that he passed out several times. At last the car stopped. He heard a trunk door open. Arms lifted him up, carried him, dropped him. Conscious now, he shut his eyes and stayed limp. If he had any chance of survival, he had to remain quiet until he could get away. He heard the men talking.

"What will we do with him?" his attacker asked. "We could dump him in the Gulf."

"Hank, you know we're movin' out in a coupla days. Nobody's gonna find us, so what's the point of killin' him? We could get life if we're caught."

"You're right," Hank said, "and nobody's gonna know where he came from. You got his wallet. Nobody's gonna know who he is. I took his watch too." He laughed.

Russ was relieved to know he wasn't intended to be a drowned corpse floating in the Gulf. He stayed inert as the men discussed his fate.

"Let's move him into that grove of palmettos," Carlson said. "He's hidden and maybe he'll die before anybody finds him."

Russ was carried and dropped onto a stump. He kept his position in spite of sudden pain in his back. His life depended upon stillness. As he lay there, he heard the men move away. A car's engine started, and Russ heard the sound of a motor diminishing into silence.

He tried to sit up, but was in such pain that he could only roll over away from the stump. He felt his left arm and knew it was broken. He opened his eyes, but one didn't respond. He touched it and felt a soft mass. It was swollen shut. The pain in his back increased, but he knew he had to move. He didn't want to die in a palmetto patch. He lifted his knees and slowly pushed himself toward a light that shone faintly in the distance. Where was he? As his one good eye became adjusted to darkness, he saw faint outlines of a road near the palmettos. He crawled, cradling his left arm, to the side of the road and pulled himself toward the light.

Progress was slow as he half staggered, half crawled, on two knees and one arm. An hour passed, and Russ was close to the light. He could make out a few buildings. A sign above a building close to the road read, "Everglades City Recycling." Russ smiled. He knew someone in Everglades City. Sam Kolinsky. If he could make it to his bar, he'd be safe. He sat down and breathed deeply. Pain shot through him in waves of agony. A sling would ease the pain. He removed his belt, and with his teeth, managed to support his arm, but how far could he travel without passing out? He knew he'd lost blood.

He staggered and crawled, staggered and crawled, too weak to remain upright for more than a few minutes. He thought about his cell phone and reached into his pocket. His phone and wallet were both gone. If he died here on the road, no one would know who he was. He thought about Julie. She'd miss him. Maybe she'd find someone else. No. She couldn't do that, he thought. He had to survive. He pushed himself farther and found a bench under a palm tree. He pulled himself up and sat, moaning, almost crying. After a short rest, he tried standing and found he could walk a few steps before crawling again.

Another hour passed, and he was close to Sam's Roarin' Twenties Bar and Grill. As he staggered forward, he saw a light. On his knees he reached the front door and pounded with his fist.

"Help me." His voice was only a whisper, but the door opened. Russ saw a pair of stained tennis shoes. "Sam, it's me, the DEA guy," he whispered.

"Holy cow!" Sam exclaimed.

Russ fainted, regained consciousness, and fainted again. In a daze, he felt nothing as Sam cut open his left jacket sleeve, swabbed the break, and wrapped a towel around his arm. At last Russ awoke and felt a cool cloth on his face.

"Sam," he whispered.

"Yeah, it's me. Somebody did a real number on you. I've called 911. The ambulance will be here soon."

It wasn't long before he was placed on a stretcher and moved into the ambulance. Oxygen tubes were inserted in his nose, a needle into his arm, and soothing words came from an EMT.

He drifted off again and was jolted as he was carried out of the ambulance.

"We're taking you to the nearest hospital in Naples," a voice said. "It's on Collier Boulevard."

In a blissful daze, Russ felt little as he was rushed to the emergency room.

"Can you hear me?" a voice asked.

Russ mumbled his name and address and passed out again. An hour later he awakened and knew he was in a hospital room. A nurse adjusted his intravenous tube. He tried to move his left arm and found it strapped into a sling. The nurse gave him a glass of water with a straw, and Russ sipped eagerly.

"Thanks," he whispered.

"I'm glad you're awake, Mr. Jones. You're at Physicians Regional, and there's someone here to see you. He's been very impatient. We couldn't allow visitors until you were fully awake."

Russ looked up and recognized Sheriff Jack Ryder. He stretched out his right hand, and Ryder took it.

"My God," Ryder said. "You got yourself into a real mess. They could have killed you."

Russ nodded and spoke slowly with swollen lips. "Yeah, I knew better. Call me stupid, but don't call Arlington."

Ryder laughed. "Okay, but don't do this again. It puts a strain on my people. It wasn't easy. They had your Glock 22 and would have used it if they'd had time. Our team moves fast."

Russ understood most of what Ryder said. "You got them?"

"Yes. The Carlson brothers won't attack anyone for at least twenty years. The Justice Department takes a dim view of attempted murder of DEA agents. But they didn't kill Frank Perruda. After an hour in our conference room, Joshua admitted they were in New Orleans that week with their sister, who was in the hospital to correct a botched-up abortion. We checked with the hospital. The men weren't here when Frank Perruda was killed." Ryder put his hand on Russ's right shoulder. "You're going to be all right in a few days."

Russ nodded. "I must look awful. Do you have a mirror?"

"No, but you have a right eye that's swollen shut, and you're black and blue everywhere. Your left arm has a compound fracture. Do you hurt badly?"

"A little. My knees hurt. I'm sore all over, and I didn't find out anything about their being involved in Frank Perruda's murder."

"Now you know they weren't here, but that doesn't clear them from beating you up. They wanted you dead, Russ."

He gave him a plastic bag. "Here's your wallet, your Glock, your watch, and your cell phone." He stood to leave. At the door he said, "For God's sake, don't lose them again!"

As soon as Ryder left, Russ opened the bag and called Julie on his cell phone. "I'm okay, but I'm at Physician's Regional with a broken arm and some bruises."

"I'll come after five. Don't go away."

Russ laughed. "I'll wait for you."

• • •

Julie was shocked to hear Russ's voice, hoarse and weak, on the phone. Her day was long as she waited until five o'clock. She arrived at the hospital and was directed to Russ's room. When she opened the door, she suppressed a scream with tightly closed lips. Russ's face was a mass of bruises, his hair matted and dirty. She rushed to the side of the bed and bent to kiss him. Russ shook his head, and Julie realized his lips were swollen. She put her head down beside his and cried.

"I'm so sorry," she said between sobs. "What have they done to you?"

"I was an idiot," Russ mumbled. "Didn't think. Dumb."

"I called the sheriff's office, told him about us, and he gave me some information, but I wasn't expecting so many bruises." She kissed his forehead.

Russ moaned. "I crawled. My knees hurt. I hurt all over." He smiled at Julie. "But I'll be all right in a day or two. Don't worry."

"I'll worry until you're healed, honey. It's my nature." She stood up. "You need to rest, so I'm going now, and I'll be back tomorrow."

Russ mouthed a kiss, and as she left his room, she sobbed. Russ would mend, but he'd gone through hell. First his trashed apartment, and now his battered body. How would he react after he recovered?

• • •

On Tuesday morning, March 22, Officer Doyle and Detective O'Hara sat in a conference room at police headquarters. They drank coffee and discussed the Perruda interrogations.

"We got nowhere last week, Mike," Doyle said, "and I'm sure they won't change their stories next time."

O'Hara nodded. "I think it's time to change our approach. We can lie. Usually they can't, but we're getting a royal runaround." O'Hara studied his coffee mug. "Those two men, Tony Perruda and Phil Stevens, the daughter's husband, are in this together. Supposing we change that."

"You mean break them up?"

"Yes," O'Hara said. "What if we tell Tony Perruda that Stevens has ratted and put the blame on him?"

"It might work. I haven't noticed any close family relationships during the sessions. Maybe they're not a loving family, and giving Perruda that information might trigger a real confession."

"It's worth a try. Tony Perruda's coming in this afternoon. Let's set it up."

• • •

Tony Perruda and his wife, Emma, sat on beach chairs and watched the sunset. It was Monday, March 21. Tony had been in Naples since March eighth and had met with his interrogators twice. He was tired of making up the same story, repeating each detail until his brain hurt. He was also tired of Naples. The weather never changed, the Gulf was refreshing, but he didn't need any more sunsets. He remembered his last bout with Doyle and O'Hara. His answers were identical, and they finally gave up and sent him home.

"I have to see them again tomorrow, Emma, and I'm sick of it. Maybe the statute of limitations or something has run out. Anything to get them off my back."

Tony realized he had to tell Emma about his plan to kill his father, even though she'd never understand such violence, and he didn't need any more recriminations. His sister was already angry, wondering why they had all agreed upon such drastic measures. What was money anyway, she'd asked. But the plan was a good one. He had no regrets.

"I'm going to end all this crap with the law, Emma," he said. "Start packing. We're going home."

The next afternoon Tony drove to police headquarters and sat down again with Doyle and O'Hara. He took out a nail clipper and studied his fingers.

"Mr. Perruda," Doyle said, "we don't need to go through the same questions again. We have your story, twice now. We don't need it again."

"That's right," O'Hara said. "We have other evidence." He sat down close to Tony. "When Philip Stevens was here last week, he finally broke down. He said he was sorry, but he had to implicate his brother-in-law."

Tony looked up, put the clippers in his pocket, and stared at O'Hara. "What do you mean? What did Phil say?"

"He said you didn't go to Key West. He thinks you stayed in Naples and probably killed your father."

Tony jumped up and looked down at O'Hara. "That's a damned lie!"

"We're just reporting his transcript, Tony," Doyle said.

Tony sat down, elbows on the table, his hands on his ears. "Damn Phil!" he cried. "What does he know? He probably killed my dad and is looking for someone else to blame."

"That's possible," O'Hara said, "but we have his statement." He stood and looked down at Tony. "Did he tell the truth?"

"Hell, no! He's crazy!" Tony stood and walked to the door. "I'm not going to listen to any more of this. You know where to find me."

Doyle and O'Hara followed him out. "We'll be in touch," Doyle said. "Don't leave town."

Tony ran to his car and drove to the condo. He opened the door and saw his brother-in-law in the lanai reading a magazine. "Phil," he called. "Where are the girls?"

"They went shopping."

"Good. I just got back from headquarters, and they told me what you said last week."

Phil looked up. "Yeah? It was the same old stuff."

"Damn you!" Tony yelled. "It wasn't the same old stuff. You told them I killed my dad!"

Phil stood and jabbed his fist into Tony's chest. "I did no such thing, dammit!"

"I don't believe you. The police have your transcript."

"Did you read it?"

"Hell, no. Why should I? It's on your record, Phil." Tony walked around the lanai and came back to stand nose to nose with Phil. "You're a dirty, rotten, dumb ex-prizefighter. You never were good enough for my sister, and now you turn against a family that helped you get started with your company."

Phil sat down. "What do you mean?"

"It's true. Jim had connections in Boston, and he knew the president of Waverly Dechtonics. He put in a good word for you, and you got the job. You owe the Perrudas, Phil, and this is the thanks we get!"

Phil stood and walked into the living room. "I'm not going to listen to any more of this," he called back to Tony. "I'm going to pack up, and Carla and I are moving out. We'll find another condo. I'll call Laura. She can find us something." He went into his bedroom, and Tony heard him throwing clothes into a suitcase.

"Good riddance," Tony called. He never liked Phil, he thought. He wasn't good enough for Carla. Tony sat down in the lanai and thought again. He knew Phil had killed an opponent in the ring. He could have killed again, and Frank was Carla's father, not his. Tony walked into the kitchen and made coffee. Yeah, he could turn the tables on him and clear himself. They couldn't prove his original story about his time in Key West, and he could put the blame on Phil.

He took his coffee into the living room as Emma and Carla came in from their shopping tour. Each had four boxes and giggled as they greeted Tony.

"We had a glorious time," Emma said. "Nordstrom's had that magic word in their window, *sale*. We couldn't resist it."

Carla laughed. "There's nothing like a new outfit to lift a girl's spirits." She looked around. "Where's Phil?"

"He's packing. You can talk to him."

Carla rushed into their bedroom and shut the door.

"What's going on?" Emma asked. "Are they leaving?"

Tony nodded. "Phil and I have a problem, and it doesn't concern you."

Emma sat down. "I don't understand. Is it something about your dad's murder?"

"Indirectly. Don't worry about it." He went to the kitchen and brought her a cup of coffee. "I don't know how long we'll have to stay here. I want to go home, but it won't be soon, thanks to Phil Stevens." Tony ground his teeth. He'd like to kill him, he thought, but thought again. Phil was his sister's husband, therefore immune to being murdered.

Phil and Carla came from the bedroom, suitcases in hand. "I called Laura," Phil said. "She's found us a small condo down the street."

He and Carla walked to the front door. Carla looked back at her brother. "I don't know what's going on," she said. "If it concerns that first night we were here, Monday night's dinner at

Salt Marsh Sinners

Laura and Jim's condo at Luna de Ciel, Tony, you can take full responsibility."

When the door closed behind them, Emma said, "Tony, what did she mean? Monday was the day you arrived. What happened that night?"

Tony ground his teeth again. "I didn't want to tell you, but now you need to know." He gave her a full report, the three kings, the meaning of the spade king. "I know it sounds crazy, Emma, but I knew we had to do something to keep my dad from changing his will. We all were entitled to our inheritance, and his plan for a university in North Dakota was idiotic. I think he was losing it."

"Did everyone agree?"

"No, we had a long discussion and slept on it. Carla was against it at first, but finally agreed. We all made up alibis for that weekend, allowing the spade king holder to do the job. Jim was going to Las Vegas, Phil was going to Orlando and would meet Carla when she returned from Boston, and I was going to Key West."

"And did all three of you reach your destinations?"

"Jim pleaded the Fifth, so I don't know if he went to Vegas or somewhere else. He's never told us. I can't tell you where Phil and I went."

"Why not? I'm your wife. I can't testify against you even if I wanted to." Emma took his hand. "I love you, Tony. Sometimes it's not easy, but we can still have a great marriage. That's what I want."

"I want that too, Emma, but I can't tell you anything more. It's all between Phil and me right now."

"What happened?"

Tony sighed. "You may as well know. He lied to the cops and said I didn't go to Key West. You know what the cops will think? I'm in deep water, thanks to my dear brother-in-law."

"When will you be called in again?"

"I don't know. It's hell, Emma. I want to go home, and I'm stuck here." He took her hand. "You should leave. There's nothing you can do here, and the girls probably need you."

"I don't want to leave. The girls are all right."

"No, I want you to go home. I'm not good company, and I have to settle things with Phil." He took her hand and kissed her. "And I don't want to ruin your friendship with Carla."

Emma nodded. "I know you're right. I don't want to leave, but I'll call a travel agent."

She pulled out her cell phone and left to find a phone book.

Tony sat alone on the sofa and cursed Phil and the entire situation. He needed to justify his part in his family's unanimous decision. Details slipped away. The memory was too painful. Emma returned. "Thanks to a cancellation, I have a reservation for tomorrow." She sat next to Tony. "I do hate to leave, honey, but I'm no good to you here. It's a mess, and I have no useful advice. You'll just have to figure it out yourself." She took his hand. "Don't be too hard on Phil. Maybe he was desperate. Did they pressure him into making that statement? You don't know what kind of tactics they used."

Tony shrugged. "You might be right. We'll work it out." He stood and looked down at Emma. "But he's made trouble for me, and I'm not going to take this lying down. I'll get even somehow."

"Take a nap or go for a swim. Let's go out for dinner tonight and forget about Phil. I want our last evening together to be pleasant, with no more rehashing of your interrogation."

"I'd like to forget it too. I'm going to the beach."

• • •

Carla and Phil drove to Jim's condo and picked up the keys on Laura's desk. "You people are so lucky," Laura said. "Two cancellations are rare during the season. You'll like the new place." She looked up from her computer. "It's none of my business, but why are you leaving Tony and Emma?"

Salt Marsh Sinners

Phil bristled. "I could ask you why Jim took the Fifth. Doyle told me what he did."

He noticed Laura's face turn from a healthy tan to beet red.

"That's none of your business, Phil," she said with a wry smile. "Everybody has secrets, thanks to Tony's little scheme. The Perrudas were never a close family, and now the rift widens. I don't like it as an in-law, and I'm sure you don't either for the same reason. I hate this, Phil."

Carla spoke up. "It's true that we all aren't compatible. Our father pitted Tony against Jim, Jim against Tony. I'd run down to the basement and hide. He didn't pay much attention to me. I don't remember when I started to stutter." She paused. "I wonder if he ever really liked us. It's sad, isn't it?"

Phil put his arm around his wife. "You're safe now, and we should all pull together. It's Tony's fault, and I don't know if I can pull together with the rest of you, not after what's happened."

"And you won't tell me why you're moving," Laura said. She gave Phil the keys. "You'd better go now. We can't be honest, and I'm busy." She turned back to her computer.

Carla and Phil drove to their new residence. Phil kept his resentments to himself. Carla and Tony were Perrudas, and even though their relationships were strained, they were still family.

• • •

Russ Jones spent two days in the hospital recovering from his beating. His bruises began to fade, his knees scabbed over, and his sight returned as the swelling decreased. His left arm hurt, but his pride hurt worse. He knew he had messed up and disgraced the DEA. If Ryder blabs, he thought, he'd probably be demoted to teaching the evils of marijuana to kids in middle school.

Officer Arturo Lopez came to the hospital to check him out. "We have your car at the courthouse," he said. "You can pick it up there."

When he left, Russ thanked the hospital staff and breathed fresh air as he walked to Lopez's car.

"It's good to be going home," he said. Suddenly he remembered the condition of "home." Where could he go, he thought. Julie's house? His mother's apartment? He opted for his first choice and called Julie on his cell phone.

"Of course, Russ. I want you to come. I have a guest room, and you can stay as long as you like."

Russ heard the words "guest room" and was puzzled. Was she through with him because of his messing up with the Carlsons? He'd have to ask. They'd always been honest with each other.

Lopez parked at the courthouse, and Russ went to the sheriff's office. Ryder welcomed him like the prodigal son, gave him his briefcase and keys to his, car and asked him to stop in as soon as he felt better.

"I don't know what I'm going to do, Jack," Russ said. "My apartment has been trashed. Someone hoped to find drugs and failed. I've been beaten up, and now we know the Carlsons weren't involved in the murder of Frank Perruda. What's worse is I haven't accomplished a damn thing. I'm going to stay a few days with my girlfriend, Julie, and then return to Virginia."

"I understand," the sheriff said, "but I hate to see you go."

"You won't miss me. I didn't even meet Rufus Jones, the third guy on my list. I thought we might be related."

"I doubt that," Ryder said. "He's black, and he couldn't have been involved anyway, because he lost a leg last year from diabetes and is in a wheelchair."

"So my list of three suspects was worse than useless." He picked up his briefcase and walked to the door.

"I'll keep you informed," Ryder said and waved. "And I hope you'll be back."

Russ thought about Julie and his mother. He needed Julie, and his mother needed him. "I will, and we'll be in touch."

It was three o'clock when Russ arrived at Rosewood Center. Julie rose from her desk, and even though a few residents were seated in the lobby, Russ came around the counter and hugged her.

Mrs. Johnson pushed her walker up to the counter. "Aha, we have a romance going on," she said. She winked at Russ. "You look like you've been in a fight, but Julie will take care of you, I'll bet."

Russ laughed. "Yes, and I need all the tender, loving care I can get."

To Julie he said, "I'm going to look in on my mother. I'll be back at five."

Russ found his mother a bit more confused. She knew him but looked away. "It's cold here, and the mice are coming for dinner."

Marjory came from the kitchen and shook her head. She beckoned Russ into the kitchen. "I'm worried, Russ. She doesn't eat regularly, so I try different dishes." She smiled. "But other days she's more lucid than I am."

"I'm glad you're here. I'm going back to Virginia in a few days, but you can call me anytime, and I'll come back."

She looked at Russ with his bruised face and his left arm in a sling. "You had a problem with your apartment, and now you've had more trouble."

"Yeah, but I'll be all right."

He returned to his mother's side and spent the afternoon reminiscing. Mrs. Jones remembered parties, fund-raisers for the Philharmonic Orchestra, and little Russell growing up. It was a quiet time for Russ, as he relaxed for the first time since he knocked on Carlson's door.

Just before five o'clock, he kissed his mother and went to the guest bedroom to pick up his shaver and toothbrush. He followed up with a return to his apartment for a change of clothes. He groaned as he looked around his home. A few lamp tables stood alone in the living room. The carpeting and tile were dirty. His bedroom held only a bedside table and reading lamp. He took his clothes and left quickly.

At five o'clock he went to the lobby to meet Julie. She finished a phone call and picked up her purse. "Let's stop and get takeout tonight, okay?"

Dinner was Chinese with chopsticks and a variety of dishes. Russ helped with cleanup, and both watched TV. Julie made popcorn, but Russ's jaw was still too tender to enjoy it.

At ten o'clock he yawned and stood. "I'm still too tired, honey. I need to go to bed."

He paused. "You mentioned the guest room. Am I being evicted?"

Julie laughed. "Of course not. I thought you'd be more comfortable. You're still in a recovery mode."

"I guess you're right, but if I get too lonesome, move over."

CHAPTER TEN

On Wednesday, March 23, Laura Perruda, sat at her computer at Luna de Ciel, drank coffee, and stared out of the window. Jim had moved into the guest room, and they exchanged only basic conversation. She knew he had spent the weekend of his father's death with another woman. He hadn't admitted it, but it was obvious.

She was tired of rentals, demanding clients, and especially Jim's family. Because she was the Realtor, *of course she could make reservations for Carla and Phil.* She gritted her teeth. It was time for her to think about Laura, and Laura thought about Janet. She needed her now.

"I'm glad you called," Janet said. "I'm free today. I just finished my commissioned painting, so let's play. I'll pick you up at noon."

Lunch on the beach at the Turtle Club was followed by a quick run-through at Saks. They liked a new brand of shorts, but they weren't interested in shopping. It was time for Janet's bedroom. Laura needed to unload all her anxieties and frustrations. Although she knew Janet had never been turned on by the male sex, she also knew her friend was perceptive and willing to listen.

Janet's bed offered a fulfilling, glorious respite from Laura's miseries. Janet was sensual and caring, a combination of beauty and soul-sharing. Jim, the man, could never comprehend this kind of a relationship. She was lucky, Laura thought as she fondled Janet's breasts, to have two completely different kinds of love in her life.

She returned home refreshed and ready to face dinner with Jim if he returned. Sometimes he appeared unannounced, and tonight was one of those times.

"Hi," he said. "Am I too late for dinner?"

Laura laughed. "I have a casserole in the oven. You can do the martinis."

Jim went to the bar and returned with two drinks. He sat at the kitchen table, sipped his drink, and looked at his wife. "Laura, we need to talk. This last week has been hell, and it's getting worse."

"What's wrong now?"

Jim slouched in his chair. "You knew I wasn't alone in Atlantic City and said you didn't want to know anything more." He made circles on his forehead with his fingers. "I have to tell you now because I think I'm being blackmailed."

Laura put down her drink and looked at him. She stood and put her hands on her hips. "I should feel sorry for you, but I don't. If she's that kind, your taste in women is pathetic." She drank most of her martini in one gulp. "Did you give her some money?"

He nodded. "She came to the store. Said she needed a loan. I gave her five thousand dollars."

"Will she ask for more?"

"That's what is bothering me. She said maybe she'd return the money, but I doubt it." He looked up at Laura. "What can I do? The whole idea was wrong. I must have been out of my mind."

"Is she pretty?" Laura feared the answer, but she had to know.

"If you like red hair." He put his head on the table and banged his forehead. "I'm sorry, and I don't know what to do."

Laura paced the floor and thought about Jim and their marriage. Most of it was good, even great. They shared ideas, vacations, and interests. If they disagreed, adult patience and wisdom prevailed. Suddenly she knew she didn't want to lose him.

She lifted Jim's head. "Look at me," she said. "I know what to do. If she comes back, call me and stall her until I arrive. It'll be a woman-to-woman thing, and she'll be shoe leather when I finish with her." She smiled at her husband. "I love you, Jim."

She sat down in front of him, looked at the ceiling, and thought about her life with Jim. She had Janet, and Jim had a redheaded gold digger. She remembered when she and Jim had their late-night conversation. She'd said the past was on the back burner because of Frank's death, and dealing with the present was more important. Now the past wasn't even on the stove. It was out in a trash bin somewhere faraway.

"Let's have dinner," she said and raised an eyebrow as she smiled. "Dessert will be in our bedroom."

• • •

The next morning Jim rolled over in bed next to Laura and nuzzled her neck. "I haven't slept this well for ages, honey. You're a magician."

She giggled. "You were a good instructor in the art of magic." She cuddled and moved her hands over his body.

"Mmm," Jim purred. He wanted Laura again, but as he caressed her body, the phone rang. "Damn!" he muttered and picked up the phone. He heard a familiar voice and whispered to Laura, "It's Mark Holtz, Dad's lawyer. I wonder why it took him so long."

Laura kissed him. "Be nice," she said.

"I know this is late," Holtz said, "but I've been swamped with company. Cousins I didn't know arrived with no place to stay. Living in paradise isn't always enjoyable. My wife and I finally locked the house and flew to Nassau."

"I understand," Jim said. "Are you ready to settle my father's estate?"

"Yes. Will you call the family together, Diane and Tony Perruda and Carla Stevens? We'll meet tomorrow morning at ten o'clock at my office."

"Do you want in-laws?"

"That's up to you. Sometimes they muddy the waters."

"I'll think about it, and I'll call the family."

The magic was gone with the phone call. He and Laura prepared for the day, enjoyed breakfast together, and made plans for a special dinner downtown. He drove to the store feeling like a new man, a lucky man.

He sat at his desk and checked e-mails and invoices. An hour later he turned around and looked down at the drawer that held one of the plastic bags he'd rescued from his father's cocaine shipment. He felt great, he thought. A little snort of coke might make him feel even greater. He opened the drawer, removed the packet, and discovered that a little sniff did indeed raise his enjoyment level. It would also heighten his tolerance level as he made calls to the family.

He punched in Diane Perruda's number, and she responded eagerly. "I wondered what took him so long. Nobody's that busy. I'll be there at ten." She broke the connection before Jim had time to explain.

He called Tony's cell phone. "I took Emma to the airport yesterday," Tony said. "She needs to be with the girls, and I don't know how long I'll be here."

Jim gave him the information, and Tony agreed to be present. "Are in-laws included?" he asked. "I don't want to see Phil right now."

Jim was puzzled but didn't ask questions. "Laura thinks it's better if she and Phil aren't there. It will be just you, Carla, Diane, and I."

His next call to Carla's cell was even more puzzling. "Yes, I'll come," she said. "But Tony really made a mess of things. I'll try to be civil."

His task completed, Jim spent the day with a mild high. At five thirty he returned to Luna de Ciel for a special dinner with Laura. His marriage was intact, the estate would be settled, and, he hoped, a substantial sum of money would be his. He continued to fret over his father's drug cache. Where was that money, and how could he find it? He had no answers.

Salt Marsh Sinners

• • •

Russ awoke Friday morning to the sound of water running. Seconds later he remembered he was in Julie's guest room. He looked at the bedside clock. Six thirty. Julie was showering. He got up and walked into her bathroom.

"Good morning," he called through the shower door. "I slept well and feel much better."

"I'm glad," Julie replied. "Will you hand me a towel?"

What was it about a towel that felt as though they were together again? He smiled, found a towel, and tossed it over the shower door. He turned and looked in the mirror, and all of his *joie de vivre* faded. His face still showed the bruises and battering he'd endured, and again he felt remorse and guilt. He glared at his image. Idiot, he thought, and returned to the guest room. Dressing and making his bed were difficult because of the sling holding his broken left arm.

He knew it was time to put his life back in order, and he didn't know where to begin. His apartment needed furniture, and he needed time to heal. He wanted to thank Sam Kolinsky in Everglades City for saving his life. He wanted to thank Sheriff Ryder and Arturo Lopez, Ryder's assistant. He wanted to thank God, Julie, and the hospital staff. It was a large order, so he had to start at once.

He and Julie shared breakfast and plans for the day. "I have a board meeting at ten o'clock," she said. "Some of the residents are still upset about Frank Perruda's murder. Mrs. Perkins worries she might be next. Peter Watson, our executive director, has been busy assuring everyone this was an isolated case. No one else was in danger."

Russ shook his head. "I wasn't any help in solving the case, and as time goes by, it's more difficult."

"What are you going to do now?"

Russ drank his coffee and thought about a possible schedule in the midst of his turmoil. "First I need to furnish my apartment.

If you're free on Saturday, we could visit Jim's furniture store. I'd like to see him again before I leave."

Julie looked surprised and startled. "Are you going back to Virginia soon?"

Russ sighed. "I need to tie up some loose ends here, but I haven't helped solve the case." He slumped in his chair. "I've even made the situation worse." He stood and paced the kitchen. "I have another idea I want to try out with an FBI friend. Maybe I'll find an answer."

"I'll miss you terribly, but I understand." She rose and put her arms around him. "I love you so much. Please come back soon."

Russ kissed her. "I love you too, and of course I'll be back. But before I go, we have work to do. After shopping I want to drive to Everglades City. Maybe Sam will feed us."

Julie laughed. "If he can't, we can eat at the Rod and Gun Club."

• • •

Mark Holtz, Frank Perruda's lawyer, watched the clock that hung among six framed diplomas and certificates of outstanding achievement. He'd graduated from Harvard, attended conferences and national meetings of the American Bar Association. During his practice in Des Moines, Iowa, and later in Naples, Florida, he found his legal interest in estate planning and wills of all kinds. He cared about his clients, and today he was guilt ridden. He'd neglected Frank Perruda's estate because of family boarders whom he secretly called "moochers." Now he would do penance as he prepared for his ten o'clock meeting with the Perruda family. He'd met Diane when she and Frank planned their prenuptial agreement, and he was worried. He'd had enough experience with clients to recognize a grasping second wife, and he had done his best to protect Frank. He'd met Jim briefly but didn't know Carla or Tony. He was curious about their relationships. He knew an estate can sometimes bring out the worst in people, and he hoped today's meeting would be amicable.

He stood and welcomed the family as they arrived separately, obviously each in his own car. Not a positive sign. Diane, dressed in an above-the-knee black dress that barely covered her breasts, smiled at him and sat far from the other chairs. She took a mirror from her purse and applied more lipstick.

Jim arrived, shook hands with Holtz, and sat as far as possible from Diane. Carla walked in with Tony. She didn't speak to her brother and sat in a chair at the back of the conference room.

The lawyer noticed the seating arrangement and knew this would not be a joyous occasion. Perhaps he'd learn more as the meeting progressed.

"Would anyone care for coffee?" he asked.

Tony raised his hand. "Yes, I'd like a cup."

Holtz called and ordered two cups. "Let's get started," he said. He gave each one a copy of the will. "We'll go through it together, and you may ask questions at any time."

The family members fidgeted as they read two pages of legalese. At last names were given. Each of his three children was to receive a sizable inheritance in cash, stocks, and tax-free bonds. Diane would keep the penthouse with a monthly stipend. If she remarried, the penthouse and stipend would become the property of each of his three children.

"What?" Diane stood and screamed at the lawyer. "Monthly? Didn't he trust me with a yearly income?"

"I'm only reading his wishes, Mrs. Perruda."

Tony stood and glared at Diane. "Maybe you can take it up with him in your next life, but you probably won't be going to the same place."

Carla giggled, and Jim shook his head. Holtz noticed the family had no sympathy for their father's angry widow.

The secretary brought coffee, and Holtz was glad for a respite. He gave Tony a cup, and sipped his own.

"We'll continue if you don't mind." He glared at Diane and Tony. "You'll see the rest of Frank's estate is to be divided among six charities and foundations, four in Naples and two in Boston."

He set his coffee down and stood. "If there are no more questions, I'll finalize the will and distribute the funds that Frank requested." He walked to the door. "Please excuse me. I have another appointment." He shook his head as he left the family. The word *dysfunctional* formed in his mind.

• • •

Carla had sat at the back of the room and watched the three Perrudas leave separately. She didn't want to visit with them, and when Holtz left the office, she remained in her chair reliving recent events. When Holtz returned, she left quickly and went to her car. She was pleased to receive her inheritance, but as she remembered Tony's plan to murder her father before he changed his will, she felt her money was tainted, almost unwelcome. She knew, however, because of the economic crisis, her husband's job could be terminated, and the money would be welcome. She wouldn't refuse it.

She hadn't asked questions or commented during the reading of the will. She had nothing to offer, and she was angry with her brothers, angry with herself. How could she have agreed, finally, to the plan? And who had killed her father? Please, not Phil, she prayed. It was Tony's idea. He should have drawn the spade king.

She remembered her father's interment and the lightning. Now she was freed from stuttering. It was too amazing to comprehend. Maybe her father's soul recanted its cruelty as his body was lowered into the ground. Maybe the Holy Spirit wanted to help her. With those thoughts in mind, she made the sign of the cross and smiled.

As she left the lawyer's office, she thought about Laura. Theirs had never been a close relationship. Jim was the older brother, and the age difference contributed to a lack of communication. Emma, Tony's wife, had returned to Minneapolis, and she needed to talk to someone, preferably female. She sat in her car and punched in Laura's number on her cell phone.

"Are you alone?" she asked. "I'd like to see you."

"Please come," Laura said. "We'll have a glass of wine and talk."

Carla was uneasy. She hadn't been in Laura and Jim's condo since Tony's plan was accepted.

"Dad's lawyer read the will to us," Carla said. "Jim can give you the details." She sat rigidly on a chair and folded her hands. "There's trouble between my husband and Tony. I don't know the reason."

"Let's go out on the lanai. I'll bring the wine." Laura rose and went to the kitchen as Carla walked to the lanai, sat, and looked out at the Gulf. Waves lapped lazily onto the shore as a flock of tiny brown sandpipers scurried along the sand.

Laura returned with two wineglasses. "It's a Chardonnay. I hope you like it." She sat across from Carla. "Now what shall we discuss?"

Carla sipped before she spoke. "You know, Laura, we're a crazy, mixed-up family. I used to hide in the basement, listening to shouts and screams. My dad was a tyrant, and it's spilled over into his family."

"What about your mother?"

"She was afraid of my dad and didn't want to cross him. Sometimes she'd join me in the basement, and we'd cry together. She was a good Catholic. It was 'until death do us part.'"

"But you and Phil have a good marriage."

"Yes, and we have two wonderful children. I've been blessed." Carla chewed her lower lip. "What's bothering me now is all the secrecy. At police headquarters your Jim wouldn't answer any questions. Tony and Phil won't tell where they were that weekend, and now those two aren't speaking."

"I can tell you Jim's secret if you promise not to tell your husband, not anyone. I need to tell someone. It's been eating me like a shark in my stomach."

"Have you talked to Jim?"

"Yes, we finally had an open discussion. I feel better now, but the pain is still there."

Laura looked out at the Gulf and spoke slowly. "Jim didn't go to Las Vegas. He flew in a private plane to Atlantic City with another woman." She shook her head. "It's been hard, Carla, but together we're going to mend. Jim's remorseful. He wouldn't talk to the police because if he told them about his escapade, only Phil and Tony would be charged in your father's death."

Carla stroked Laura's hand. "That's a terrible situation for both of you."

"Yes. Jim and Tony have never been chummy, and Jim hardly knows Phil, but Phil is your husband, so he's also family."

"So now it's down to two," Carla said. She took a tissue from her purse and wiped her eyes. "We should never have agreed to Tony's plan. He's to blame for all of this."

"But we did agree, so we're all guilty. We can't lay it all on Tony."

Carla sighed. "I suppose you're right. What do we do now?"

"We'll have another glass of wine, maybe two more. No one could blame us for getting royally smashed!"

"I have to drive home, so one more is my limit."

Laura laughed. "But I'm not going anywhere." She went to the kitchen and returned with the wine bottle.

• • •

Russ spent the rest of the day visiting his mother and studying the material he'd received from Sheriff Ryder regarding the murders of Frank Perruda and Jeff Parker, Jim Perruda's employee. He read the invoices Jim had given him. The most recent one listed a davenport.

Russ called Jim at the furniture store. "I'm looking at the invoices, and if the davenport is still at the store, I'd like to see it."

"Of course. I'd like to check it too, if it's still here."

At Perruda's Fine Furnishings, Russ met Jim, and together they walked into the davenport section.

"After you called," Jim said, "I checked our stock. The davenport hasn't been sold."

"Good. Let's look at it. I'm sure it held a supply of Mexican drugs when it arrived."

They located the davenport, and Russ read the tag, "*Hecho en Mexico.*"

"That's it," he said.

Together they studied the three cushions and could find no signs of tampering. Jim tossed them on the floor, and they checked the rest of the davenport. Russ touched the back left corner and found a two-inch slit that had been carefully replaced with matching thread.

"This is it, Jim," Russ said. "Look at the workmanship. Unless you were looking carefully, you'd never see it."

Jim laughed. "Good. Now we can sell it at full price." He became serious. "I checked the other invoice copies. Two upholstered chairs arrived and were sold within the week. If they were still here, I'm sure we'd find the same repair work."

"Can you check the sales? I want to know if the chairs still contain drugs, or if they'd been repaired."

"I'll have my secretary find the sales receipts. It may take time to reach the buyers."

"Yes, and it may not be important, but we need to know." He paused. "I wonder how long your father was involved in these transactions."

"I don't know. We have those invoices, but he could have hidden others, and if he had a Swiss bank account, I can't open it without proper identification."

"That's a standard practice. I'm sorry, Jim." Russ shook his head. They walked to Jim's office. "I'm returning to Virginia on

Sunday, but I'll be back. My mother's here and…" He paused. "I've found a special friend."

"Good for you. Anyone I know?"

"You may have met her. It's Julie Rogers, the concierge at Rosewood Center."

Jim raised an eyebrow. "We met when I visited my dad."

"Thanks for your help," Russ said. "Julie and I will be back here tomorrow. I have to refurnish much of my apartment, and I need female assistance."

"We'll be glad to help you. What's the occasion?"

Russ gave him a brief report of the damage. "Someone was looking for drugs. That's why the upholstered furniture and beds were torn apart. My apartment isn't livable." He shook his head. "I'm sorry I haven't solved your father's murder, but I'm not giving up."

He left the store and returned to Rosewood Center for a visit with his mother. On his way out, he stopped at Julie's desk. "How about dinner tonight? You name the restaurant."

Julie smiled. "Let's find a restaurant on Naples Bay."

"I'm making a plane reservation for Sunday," Russ said. "I hate to leave you, but I may be able to find the killer."

"I hope you'll be safe next time."

"No confrontations, I promise."

• • •

Julie and Russ shared a leisurely breakfast Saturday morning before Russ returned to his apartment to pack for his Virginia trip on Sunday. Julie cleaned her house and washed clothes, her usual Saturday activity. She needed to keep her body and mind busy. Russ would be gone, and she would be alone, wishing he were here. She turned on the radio. Any kind of music would fill her ears as she worked.

Russ returned at one o'clock. He'd seen his mother and packed. "Mom wants you to visit her," he said. "I'm only taking a carry-on. My jackets were so badly ripped, they can't be mended."

They left her house and drove to the furniture store. Julie was nervous thinking about Jim Perruda's dinner invitation. She hoped he forgot he ever knew her.

Jim greeted her with a smile, and Julie was relieved when he asked a saleswoman to work with them. They spent two hours selecting furniture. Julie and Russ agreed on most of his choices, although she'd never have purchased the eight-inch statue of Venus with a clock glued to her navel. Russ laughed. "It's so bad, I couldn't resist it."

Julie laughed. "I hope you and Venus will be a happy couple."

They finished shopping, and Julie snuggled up to Russ as he drove to Everglades City.

"I don't want this day to end," she said, "but I'll be strong."

"We'll both be strong, and we can talk, text, and e-mail."

"But it won't be the same."

Russ slowed and parked by the side of the road. He put his arms around her and kissed her deeply. "Let's just think about today, Julie. It's ours together."

He released her and drove onto the highway. "I can't hold your hand and drive because of my sling."

Julie laughed. "When you return, you won't have a sling."

When Russ passed the road he'd followed on his knees and one arm, he described his progress to Julie.

"How could you remember your destination? You must have been almost dead."

"I kept thinking of you. I couldn't die and leave you."

Julie stroked his arm. She couldn't find words to express her love for him. She only knew there must be a life for them together.

Russ stopped in front of Sam's bar, a building painted in glaring orange with a massive sign above the door, "Sam's Roarin' Twenties Bar and Grill." Sam greeted them and hugged Russ.

"You look a lot better than you did the last time you were here," Sam said. He turned to Julie. "You must be the reason he kept going."

"Yes," Russ said. "And I wanted to see you again, Sam, to thank you for saving my life."

Sam grinned. "You were a mess, all right, but I remembered you during the SWAT raid. You didn't take part, but you helped straighten the place." Sam looked at Julie. "He's FBI, ain't he? I can tell 'em every time."

Julie laughed and looked at Russ. "Well?"

"Not FBI, Sam. I'm with the Drug Enforcement Agency," Russ said. "They brought me in because of the drugs, but I haven't succeeded."

"I'm sure you tried," Sam said. "How about a beer on the house?"

"Not on the house. I'm buying. Do you serve meals?"

"Not yet. My chef comes next week."

Julie and Russ enjoyed their beer and visited with Sam. They promised to return and drove to the Rod and Gun Club for dinner.

Later, Russ drove back to Naples with Julie curled up beside him.

"You can't sleep in the guest room tonight," Julie said and wished the night could go on forever.

The next morning Julie and Russ went to church, ate brunch, and returned to her house. Russ packed his few belongings into his carry-on as Julie sat on his bed and thought of strategies to delay his departure. She found none. She'd have to accept the inevitable.

• • •

Sally Turrino, the woman Frank had phoned just two days before he was murdered, combed out her last customer's permanent at the Shear Beauty Salon on Fifth Avenue. It was five thirty Saturday afternoon, and she had no plans for the weekend. At age seventy-one, she was husbandless, dateless, and bitterly alone.

She walked to the counter with her customer. "Would you like to schedule an appointment for next week?"

"Put me down for nine thirty on Friday."

She wrote the date and gave the woman a copy. After she ushered the customer to the front door and locked it behind her, Sally returned to her station and sat in the customers' chair. Chin resting on her open hand, she thought about Frank Perruda. Theirs had been a special relationship until that grasping hussy Diane snagged him. After his marriage Frank's calls were less frequent, and his visits dropped to zero.

Sally's wistful sigh said it all. They'd met at the Italian Club in Naples and shared memories of their youth in South Boston. As their relationship blossomed, Sally hoped to become Mrs. Frank Perruda, but his pneumonia and ensuing romance with his nurse, Diane, sent all of Sally's hopes down the sewer.

She had been thrilled when he had called and asked to see her. Perhaps the old flame could be rekindled. They had spent a memorable afternoon and evening together. Frank's sexual drives hadn't decreased, and Sally had responded with equal emotion. Afterward she baked a pizza, and they talked. He asked about her life, and she admitted there wasn't much to tell. Her four children were busy in four different states. She adored her grandchildren, but her own life in Naples was uneventful.

They shared a bottle of Chianti at her kitchen table, and Frank stroked her hand.

"I need to talk to someone, Sally. I'm importing some drugs from Mexico. I'm making a fortune, but it's risky business, and I'm worried."

She listened as he told her about his furniture orders and drug sales. He gave her a complete report and named names.

"So far it's okay, but I need to plan ahead." He cracked the knuckles of his left hand.

"Does your family know?"

"Hell, no. They'd just want a piece of the action. This is just between us. You're the only one I can trust, baby-doll."

"My lips are sealed," she said. "Your secrets are safe with me."

Frank stroked her hand. "I think Diane's seeing somebody, and my kids want all they can get." He laughed as he told her about changing his will. "They think I'm nuts."

"Building a university isn't crazy, Frank. Think of all the kids who'll graduate, maybe go on to save the world."

"You're the only one who agrees with me." He sipped wine and removed a thick envelope from his pocket. "This is for you to keep, Sally. It's confidential. Don't tell anyone. Even my family hasn't a clue."

He walked to the door, his arm around Sally's ample waist. "I knew you'd understand." He kissed her and stroked her breasts. "I'm not in any trouble now, but if something should happen to me, wait a few months, open the envelope, and follow instructions."

"You'll be all right, and we'll be together again soon. I'll save this for your next visit." She kissed him. "I wish I could help you."

Frank smiled and stroked her upper thigh. "You've already helped." He pulled her close and put his arms around her. "Keep the envelope for me."

"Sure. When will I see you again?"

"Next week, I hope."

They kissed, and Sally watched as he drove away. He'd promised to call her again, and her hopes had soared until she read of his death in the *Naples Daily News*. She was shocked and sickened. Was he killed because of his drug dealings, or did someone in his family put an end to his plans for Perruda University? At his funeral she sat in a back pew and wept silently. No one knew him as she did, a powerful yet caring man who could turn a seventy-one-year-old woman into a sexually active twenty-year-old.

Sally remembered his story, kept the envelope and his secrets. "Wait a few months," he'd said. Now she sat in the salon, wondering what to do with the rest of her life. Frank's information weighed heavily as she balanced a visit with law enforcement against secrecy and continued worry.

She'd keep his secrets and follow his instructions. She left the salon and stopped at a neighborhood bar. A glass of wine might lift her spirits, at least temporarily.

• • •

On Sunday afternoon Russ rode with Julie to the Fort Myers International Airport. He'd seen his mother and assured Marjory he was available at any time.

Marjory wasn't worried. "She's doing well now. I'm not expecting any major problems."

As Julie maneuvered through traffic, Russ turned and kept his right hand on her upper thigh. "Good-byes are too painful," he said. "As soon as you stop at the terminal, I'm going to kiss you and run like hell to my plane."

Julie nodded. "And I'll drive home and hate being without you."

As promised, he raced inside the terminal and went through security before Julie left the airport. His flight to Reagan International was happily on time, and he arrived at his apartment in Tyson's Corner, Virginia, in time for dinner. When he unpacked that evening, his thoughts were full of Julie, but when he opened his briefcase, it was time to consider his plan to discover the identity of the murderer. That guy has to be somewhere, he thought. We'll find him.

The next morning, he took a cab to DEA headquarters in Arlington, Virginia. He was greeted warmly by staff members, and his secretary hugged him.

"We've missed you, Mr. Jones. We're glad you're back." She brought coffee and a stack of mail. "People are still buying stamps." She laughed and left his office.

By noon Russ had caught up with his mail and checked e-mails. He had stayed in contact with the agency during his time in Naples, and now at his desk, he found little additional information.

At twelve o'clock he called his close friend, Dwight Holbrook, a former college classmate and now a supervisory special agent with the FBI. Dwight had joined the bureau two years before Russ's employment at DEA. Now Russ needed an attentive ear.

"Hello, I'm back," Russ said when Dwight answered. "Do you have time for lunch?"

"Of course. Take the Metro, and I'll meet you here."

Lunch was a lobster roll and Caesar salad at a local eatery, and conversation was lively. Dwight had just returned from Colombia, South America. There had been rumors of a possible terrorist attack, and he had been sent to investigate.

"I was there last year," Russ said. "The DEA needed to work on the marijuana farm problem, and we tried to convert the natives. We suggested corn, sweet potatoes, and soybeans and promised large sums of money for a change in crop production."

"Is it working?" Dwight asked.

"It's too early to tell. We have to go back often to reassure them. It's always an uphill struggle, but we can't give up." He sipped iced tea and looked at his friend. "I've been working on a case in Naples, Florida, and I'm stuck. I need help."

Keeping his voice down, he said, "Two murders that involve drugs. No leads. It's a dead end."

"What are you going to do?"

"I'd like to fly down to the FBI's Identification Division building that keeps their civil and criminal files, but they won't let me in without your help."

"I can arrange it, Russ, and I'm free for a few days. I'd like to join you, but we need clearance from the bureau. We can't just walk in with your DEA identification." Dwight scratched his head. "I'm going to call the director at the bureau. Maybe he and your boss can work it out together."

Russ smiled. "Can you set us up for a trip tomorrow morning?"

"I'll try, and I'll call you as soon as I get clearance."

"Thanks. I know this is unusual, but so is the whole damned situation in Naples."

Russ gave his friend a brief account of the murders, the hidden drugs, and his encounter with a local user. "I went through a complete list of suspects at the sheriff's office, and nothing came up. I'm sure the FBI has a more comprehensive list, and I need it."

He and Holbrook left the restaurant. Holbrook took a cab back to the J. Edgar Hoover Building on Pennsylvania Avenue, and Russ returned to the agency in Arlington. He spent the afternoon following up on agency business and kept one ear open for Holbrook's call.

At four thirty Holbrook called. "You won't believe this, but I was able to talk to the director personally. He listened and said he'd call your agency's administrator. It's an outside chance, but I'm hopeful, Russ. I'll call again as soon as I have more information."

"Thanks, Dwight." Russ wiped his forehead and grinned. Maybe Lady Luck was on his side.

Half an hour later, Dwight called again. "We're all set. I'll meet you in my office at nine o'clock tomorrow morning."

The two-hour flight to West Virginia was uneventful. The pilot set the chopper down on the helipad near the Identification Division building, and the men walked the short distance to the main entrance. With proper identification they were escorted to the central office and briefed regarding procedures.

"I was here last year," Holbrook said. "It's impressive. My dad remembers when Hoover moved the building out of Washington. I guess there wasn't enough room at the bureau."

A staff member brought coffee. "Do you want to look at the civil file?" he asked.

"No," Holbrook answered. "We need to study the criminal file in the dungeon. We're looking for a killer."

The staff member led them down to a lower level. The area was fenced in from floor to ceiling and guarded by an armed attendant. Russ and Dwight were admitted after a thorough identification check.

"This will be a tedious job, but the killer has to be here somewhere," Russ said. He had given Dwight a detailed account of the murders, his trashed apartment, and his encounter with the Carlson brothers. Dwight would know how to proceed.

The men spent the day searching through drug-related cases and culprits. The Naples cases weren't current enough to consider.

"Those guys would have to be a hundred years old by now," Dwight said.

"And nobody knew about Frank Perruda's drug operation. He obviously had a stable of professionals who knew all the angles, all the right people."

"I found two names that might have a connection to your case," Holbrook said. "One lived in Ocala for three years and did time for doping horses. The other went to prison for armed robbery in Orlando. He's been paroled."

"I'll put those two in my iPhone." Russ took pictures. "I found only one name, but it's so remote, it probably isn't worth keeping."

"Who is it?"

"John Thurston. He drowned in a lake at the border between Texas and Mexico, but his body was never recovered." He aimed his iPhone at the file. "I'll keep it anyway. Anything's possible."

They replaced the files, returned to the reception area, and walked to the helipad. As the helicopter lifted off, Russ sighed. "We didn't learn much on this trip, but thanks for setting it up."

"Worth a try. How about dinner tonight? There's a new restaurant near Watergate."

• • •

At his desk at police headquarters, Chief Gordon Turner scratched his head as he studied the latest reports of the murder of Jeff Parker, Perruda's employee. Damn. There were no clues and no suspects. His interview with Parker's widow had offered no further information. Officers Callahan and Rieger had questioned all the personnel who worked at the furniture store and learned nothing. The entire receiving dock area had been dusted for fingerprints and checked for broken windows and scratched door locks. No signs of a forced entry. No murder weapon. The place was clean.

Chief Turner tried to picture the event. Parker would have known about the bar stools containing cocaine. He'd have a key and a flashlight. He'd have worn gloves, pushed the ladder against the shelves, and climbed to the top. Did he remove a stool and try to carry it down to the floor? If so, the killer would have replaced it.

And what about the killer? He too knew the stools contained cocaine. He'd have known about Frank's drug shipments, and must have known the patrol car's schedule. He'd had a key. Did he expect to find Parker at the store? Why did he carry a knife? He must have expected trouble from somebody. Parker? All six stools were in place on the top shelf. Had Parker checked and returned them, or did the killer do the job?

Turner sat back in his chair. There must be a key, something they had missed. He shook his head. Even the DEA couldn't solve this one.

CHAPTER ELEVEN

Frank Perruda's distributor, Cynthia Frost, a resident at Rosewood Center, sat at a table in Barnes & Noble's lunch area and thought about his murder. She was stunned and frustrated. She'd like to kill the guy who murdered Frank and ruined her operation. She and Frank had created a successful drug trafficking business in Naples. He had worked with his Mexican partners, who ordered the pieces for Perruda's Fine Furnishings and had purchased the best cocaine. It was a professional organization of people who knew the system, all the details, from buying the drugs, sealing them in furniture, and getting them through border crossings, undetected and ready for pickup in the United States.

With expert communication she had received the shipments, paid Frank the usual millions, and had sold them to her organization of drug dealers in southwest Florida. She and Frank had worked together for five years perfecting their operation, and now he was gone, murdered by some punk who probably wanted to make a quick fortune.

She received another blow when she discovered the cocaine in the stools had been removed. She could have sold the stuff herself without having to pay Frank.

She returned to her apartment at Rosewood Center. With difficulty she had kept a low profile. Doris Johnson could have discovered her operation when the distributor forgot their shopping date, making her miss her appointment with Doris Johnson. When Mrs. Johnson had asked the staff for help, they had searched Cynthia's apartment. Luckily, the distributor kept all incriminating objects and files well hidden. They'd found nothing, and she was safe. Meanwhile she continued to cover her tracks.

She mixed a scotch and soda, sat in the lanai, and recalled her frantic search of that DEA's apartment. She knew the cocaine was no longer in the legs of the bar stools, but where was it? Logic told her Russell Jones, Mrs. Jones's son, a DEA agent, had hidden it in his apartment. She had observed his goings and comings from a comfortable high-backed chair in the lobby and listened to conversations with Julie and others. His schedule was perfect for the apartment search. With a skeleton key and the right tools, she'd searched carefully. She kept her actions as quiet as possible, turning and slitting cushions and bedding, emptying pill bottles, jars, anything that might contain the drugs. It was a difficult and worthless task. There were no drugs. Now she knew the drugs were stored somewhere else. She'd have to start over with a new supply before her buyers found other sources.

She returned to the kitchen and made notes. Without Frank furniture shipments were no longer possible. She'd need a different hiding place for the drugs. She picked up a magazine and looked through the advertisements. Lamps and chandeliers were splashed across several pages. She scribbled designs on a note pad, and a new method of concealment formed in her mind.

Two buyers had asked about the next shipment. It was time to call Pedro in Vera Cruz. She punched in his numbers.

When Pedro answered, the distributor said, "Frank's dead. We can't use furniture now."

"We can do lamps and pictures," Pedro said. "I like the ones we paint on black velvet. I saw a poodle—"

She cut him off. "No pictures on black velvet, Pedro. We need something classy. I have a friend in Naples who owns a shop that sells accessories. Tell me about the lamps."

"The bases could be large and hollow."

"Too obvious. How about the shades?"

Pedro paused. "Maybe we could hang tassels, pendants. I've seen some."

The distributor smiled. "You could make them with colored plastic. Glass is too heavy. Send me a design. I need it today, not tomorrow."

The distributor called two buyers. She assured them that new shipments of the same outstanding quality would arrive soon. She couldn't give them an exact date, but she'd keep them informed. She smiled. Her network would spread the news.

She called her friend Sharon, who owned the accessory shop. "I may be able to import some table lamps from Mexico. Chandeliers are also a possibility. Are you interested?"

"Yes. Many of my customers have asked about Mexican imports."

"I'll call when I have something to show you. I know a designer in Vera Cruz." She pocketed her phone and stretched out on a chaise. The sun edged toward the horizon, and puffy clouds in soft shades of orange, peach, and lilac escorted the sun on its westward journey. A tranquil setting merged with unsettling thoughts, problems that needed solutions, people and places yet unknown. She reached for a yellow legal-sized pad and laid out possibilities, new contacts, new merchandise, and a new delivery system. As she scribbled, her thoughts focused on a future bright with success.

She thought about her apartment here at Rosewood Center. The residents' every need could be filled. Felix, who guarded the garage, was a trusted ally, and she paid him well for his information. The wait staff and chefs were exceptional. George was on call for minor repairs, and the cleaning service was efficient. She thought about the girls who came weekly. Most of them were Latinos. The distributor smiled again as new ideas whirled in her mind. With her new operation, Spanish-speaking young women might be an asset.

• • •

Edilia Perez Prado, a member of the housekeeping staff at Rosewood Center, slouched in her chair at her sister Olga Prado Zayas's breakfast table. She studied her plate of enchiladas stuffed with scrambled eggs and sausage and swallowed with difficulty. She didn't want to insult Olga by throwing up.

She stood and took her plate to the kitchen before her sister returned. She ducked past Olga, whose eyes were fixed on the griddle, scraped her enchilada into the sink, and hurried into the bathroom. She leaned against the wall and stared into a mirror. She looked exactly what she was, an eighteen-year-old girl with long black hair that fell softly below her shoulders, black eyes that blinked back her tears and a café-au-lait complexion. Pretty, troubled, anxious, it was all there staring back at her.

She combed her hair, applied lipstick, and returned to the kitchen. Olga and her husband, Marcos Mendieta Zayas, had finished breakfast.

"Thanks for breakfast, Olga," Edilia said, forcing a smile. "You're so good to let me stay with you until I can afford a place of my own."

"You're welcome to stay," Olga said. She put her hand on Edilia's shoulder. "We want you with us."

"We shouldn't interfere," Marcos said, "but we're worried about your relationship with Tomas Fuentes. You're safer here, Edie."

Edilia put her head on Olga's arm. "I know how you feel, and I'm worried too." She began to cry. "I have to make decisions and change my life. I know now that I was wrong about him."

"Love is crazy, *querida*," Olga said. "When you're in love, you don't see the bad stuff. Tomas is handsome and all the girls fall for him."

"I was thrilled when he chose me." Edilia sniffed. "I didn't know about his temper and the drugs." She put her arms around both Olga and Marcos. "And now it's too late."

"What do you mean?" Marcos asked.

Salt Marsh Sinners

Edilia looked at her brother-in-law and sobbed. "In about eight months, I'm going to have his baby. I'm sick, and he doesn't want the baby and won't help me. I have to work, and my boss at Rosewood Center doesn't like pregnant cleaning staff." She sniffed again.

Olga gave her a tissue and rubbed her back. "But you have us and our kids. Our mom and dad in Miami love babies too. You're not alone, *querida,* and we love you."

Marcos looked at his watch. "Yes, but now I must go to work." He laughed. "We'll have another family member to care for." He took Edilia's hand. "Edie, will you give me a ride to the maintenance building at Pelican Marsh? My car blew a tire yesterday."

"Sure," Edilia answered and blew her nose. "Should I pick you up after work?"

"No, my car will be ready this afternoon."

As they left the house, Edilia thought about her housekeeping job at Rosewood Center and wondered how many more months she could work. Her boss and head housekeeper, Shirley Green, had informed her cleaning crew that she didn't approve of unmarried, pregnant, young women. Legally, of course, she couldn't fire anyone for pregnancy, but she could make her life miserable. Edilia frowned as she thought about concealing her pregnancy for at least six more months. She also remembered Tomas's reaction when she told him about the baby.

"What do you mean, you're pregnant? I thought you were on the pill," Tomas had yelled as they sat together on the edge of his bed.

"I couldn't afford to take them, and you promised to use a condom, remember?"

Tomas glared at her. "I don't remember. It's all your fault." He'd risen, finished a half-smoked cigarette, and blew smoke in her face.

Now Edilia realized that their relationship, so full of promise, had died that day and was buried with all her hopes and dreams.

Her brother-in law interrupted her memory. "Will you be here for dinner?" he asked.

Edilia returned to the present. "No, I'm going downtown with some friends. Don't wait up for me. I'll be late."

As she eased into early-morning traffic, Edilia asked, "How is your work at Pelican Marsh?"

"It's hard work mowing and trimming, but the pay isn't bad, and I work with good, honest guys."

"I like the people I work with too. I've been there just six months, but I've met nice people, the girls I work with and the people I clean for."

Edilia stopped at the Pelican Marsh gate, and Marcos opened his car door. "You're a good driver. Did you learn in Miami?"

"Yes. I took lessons, and now I can drive any vehicle." She laughed. "I can even double-clutch, but there isn't much call for it on I-Seventy-Five."

As he left her car, Marcos blew her a kiss. Edilia blew another and drove to Rosewood Center. She parked in the staff garage and signed in at Shirley Green's office.

As Edilia put on her smock and picked up her cleaning equipment, Shirley said, "You will do Mrs. Murphy's apartment, number 1046. When you have finished, I want you to clean the hall on that floor. Vacuum the carpet, dust the furniture, and wipe the baseboards."

Edilia nodded and pushed her cleaning cart to the staff elevator. She stopped on the tenth floor and knocked at apartment 1046. When no one answered, Edilia used her key and started working. She began in the kitchen and two hours later had completed her assignment.

As Edilia walked to the door, Mrs. Murphy returned. She looked around and smiled. "You did well. Thank you for coming. I hope to see you again next week."

"I hope to come back, but Mrs. Green schedules our work. You could ask for me."

Salt Marsh Sinners

She pushed her cleaning cart into the hall and wondered where to begin cleaning. The hall extended from the fire wall in the center of the building to the opposite wall, a seemingly endless expanse. She was tired and thirsty after cleaning Mrs. Murphy's apartment, and the carpet looked soft and comfortable. She pushed her cart to the fire wall, removed a bottle of water, and slipped to the floor. She leaned against the wall and closed her eyes.

"Are you all right?"

Edilia opened her eyes and stared at ten pink, pedicured toes encased in black sandals. She stood, a guilty grin on her face.

"I'm okay. I just finished Mrs. Murphy's apartment and took a break before working in the hall."

She admired the toes' owner, an elderly woman dressed in a gray, long-sleeved, spangled T-shirt and black slacks. Her gray hair was combed back into a chignon. An aquiline nose, well-shaped eyebrows above soft blue eyes.

"I'm Cynthia Frost, and I need a little touch-up in my kitchen. If you have time after your work in the hall, maybe you could help me. I'm in apartment 1038."

"If there's time, I'll ring your bell," Edilia said as she started dusting the furniture. Two hours flew by as she dusted, wiped the baseboards, and vacuumed the carpet. It was almost noon, but Mrs. Frost had said she needed a touch-up. Maybe it wouldn't take long.

She rang the bell at 1038, and Mrs. Frost led her to the kitchen. "I only need a clean sink and counter tops," she said. "Do you have time?"

"No problem." Edilia worked quickly, and Mrs. Frost's sink and counter tops glistened.

"I know we aren't supposed to tip." Mrs. Frost slipped paper currency into Edilia's smock. "Don't tell anyone. It's our secret."

Edilia blushed, removed the money, and placed it on the counter. "I can't take it, but thank you." She took her cleaning supplies and put them in her cart. "I can come whenever you call Mrs. Green." She left the apartment and went to the lunchroom.

The afternoon assignments didn't require heavy lifting, and Edilia worked quickly and carefully. She returned her supplies and smock to the workroom and went to the staff garage.

She was startled to see Tomas. "It's about time you showed up," he said as he smoked a cigarette and stood by her left front bumper. "You got plans for tonight?"

"I'm going out with some friends." Edilia didn't want to give details or continue the conversation. He'd treated her like dirt the last time they were together, and she didn't want any more abuse.

Tomas grabbed her arm and pulled her close. "Break the date. You're going with me."

Edilia removed his arm and glared. "I'm not going with you, so just leave. I don't want to be with you right now, Tomas. There's nothing to discuss."

"Yes there is, baby." He gripped her arm again, forcefully now. "So you got knocked up. How do I know I'm the father? I'll bet you've got lots of guys besides me."

Edilia glared at him. "Maybe we should have a test, Tomas. You're the father, and you know it." Unwelcome tears dripped down her cheeks. "I've always been your girl and nobody else's."

Tomas released her arm and backed away. "Yeah, I know that. I just wish you weren't pregnant." He paused and bit his lip. "You could get rid of the thing. You don't have to go through with it."

The tears stopped, and Edilia stared at him. "What? You must be crazy! It's our baby, and I'm going to have it. I'd never have an abortion, so face it, Tomas." She laughed. "You're going to be a father whether you like it or not."

She pushed him away and opened her car door. "Have a nice night, Daddy, and don't come here again."

She drove away and didn't look back. Her future with Tomas was uncertain. She'd get through her pregnancy with Olga's and Marcos's help, and maybe fatherhood might change Tomas.

Maybe he'd love her again. They'd get married and have a home together with a baby to love and protect.

Her next week at Rosewood Center was filled with special assignments. Both Mrs. Murphy and Mrs. Frost had asked for her, and it was easy to work on the same floor without pushing her cleaning cart in and out of service elevators. Mrs. Frost gave her time out for coffee and was interested in Edilia's life at home.

"I live with my sister and brother-in-law now," Edilia said, "but I plan to have a place of my own." She told Mrs. Frost about her parents in Miami, who encouraged her to continue her education.

"Dad insisted that I take driving, swimming, and typing lessons, his important three R's."

"Tell me about your driving," Mrs. Frost said. "I may need a driver for special occasions."

"It was an intensive course. We had to drive all makes of cars and trucks." Edilia laughed. "We drove in all kinds of weather except snow."

"Do you have any vacation time?"

"I'll have two weeks, but I don't know when."

"You can finish the kitchen, and we'll talk later," Mrs. Frost said. She took her purse. "I have an appointment. Please lock the door when you leave."

Edilia smiled, followed instructions, and locked the apartment at five o'clock.

On Thursday evening Mrs. Frost called Edilia. "I need a driver to pick up an order from Mexico. Can you take time off?"

"I can ask Mrs. Green. We have two weeks of vacation, but we haven't received a schedule. I can ask her tomorrow."

"Good." She paused. "This is confidential, Edilia. Make up a story about your leaving. We'll talk later."

Edilia closed her cell phone and thought about the trip. She hoped Mrs. Green would give her vacation time on short notice. Mrs. Frost hadn't given her a date, but Edilia sensed the trip would be scheduled in a few days.

• • •

Three days later Cynthia Frost received a call from Pedro in Vera Cruz. "I'm sending you by overnight express two samples of pendants that can be filled with small amounts of cocaine. I can't promise the kilos that Mr. Perruda received, but you will have enough to make a good profit."

"How many pendants will hang on each lampshade?"

"Ten on the large ones and seven on the smaller ones. I am sending you a picture of the shades with pendants. They will look nice."

"What colors?"

"Dark colors. Black, brown, purple."

"Good. I will talk to my store manager."

She closed her phone and mixed a scotch and soda. She walked to her lanai and toasted the setting sun. She was back in business.

The next morning she received a call from Pedro. "I called my friend in San Miguel. She makes lamps and chandeliers. Here is her phone number."

Cynthia sat back and smiled. No one would suspect lampshades if they could be made to conceal drugs, and chandeliers could be made with the hollow pendants.

She called and listened as Pedro's friend described her plan. "We can make softback shades with three layers. Black on the outside, gold on the inside, and in between, a quilted fabric."

"Why quilting? That costs more."

"Pedro said he wants to place drugs inside the shades. Without quilting, the drugs will all fall to the bottom of the shade."

Cynthia gasped. "Pedro told you about the drugs?"

"Your secret is safe with me. Pedro and I work together."

"Okay. How many can you make? I need eight lamps, and maybe chandeliers with hollow pendants."

"We already have lamps and chandeliers. We can do shades and pendants in six days. Bubbles might work on the chandeliers. I'll talk to Pedro."

Relieved but anxious, Cynthia spent three days contacting her buyers, assuring them that top-quality cocaine would soon be available. On the following Monday, Pedro called to say the shipment was ready.

"We will not meet your driver at McAllen, Texas," Pedro said. "It will be too hard to transfer the shipment. Our driver will have a fake visa and will drive to Houston. If all goes well, he will meet your driver at a warehouse east of Houston on Highway Ten. Here is the address."

As Cynthia wrote, she asked, "When will your driver leave Vera Cruz?"

"Tomorrow. Your driver should call this number when he arrives at Beaumont. This will give our driver time to meet at the warehouse."

Cynthia wrote more notes. "My driver will have the money for you." She wrote the amount and planned a trip to her bank.

On Thursday evening Mrs. Frost called Edilia. "The shipment from Mexico is ready. Can you take time off and pick up the shipment in Houston, Texas?"

"I can ask Mrs. Green tomorrow."

"Good." She paused. "This is confidential, Edilia. We'll talk later."

• • •

Two days later the date was confirmed. Edilia called Mrs. Green. "I hate to change my schedule so soon, but my family needs me. Can you find a replacement for next week?"

"I can." Mrs. Green's voice wasn't pleasant.

"I hope I'll have my job when I return."

Mrs. Green's voice was softer. "Of course. You're one of my best girls."

Edilia was relieved to know she'd have her job, and Mrs. Frost had promised a reward for her driving.

Edilia was back at Mrs. Frost's apartment the next day for detailed and final instructions.

"The rented truck is in the staff parking garage. You can drive there early tomorrow morning and leave your car." She gave Edilia the keys, a map, credit card, cell phone, and an envelope. "The map shows your route to Houston. It's about twelve hundred miles one way, so you'll need to stay in a motel en route. The envelope contains travel money and the warehouse address."

Edilia was puzzled. "I need to know more about the trip, what I am to bring back, and why this is a secret mission."

"The less you know, the better it will be for you." She gave Edilia a note. "When you reach Beaumont, Texas, call this number. The driver from Mexico will have several boxes for you and will transfer them into your truck."

As Edilia walked to Mrs. Frost's front door, she turned back. "Should I call you with my return time?"

Mrs. Frost nodded. "Call me when you leave Houston."

Edilia drove back to Olga's home, her mind swirling with unasked questions. Why was this a secret trip? What was in those boxes? Why wasn't she informed? She couldn't explain her planned absence to Olga and Marcos. Stories formed in her head—a friend in trouble, a shopping trip, a need to hide from Tomas. None of them made sense, but she needed an excuse.

When she arrived at the house, her worries ended. A note on the kitchen table read, "Marcos's brother is sick. We've gone to Miami." Edilia added a note explaining her absence.

The next morning she climbed into the truck and drove north. The first four hours were uneventful as she adjusted to a new vehicle. She relaxed and welcomed new highways and new scenery. She stopped at a motel in Mobile, Alabama, ate dinner at a nearby restaurant, set her alarm, and fell into bed.

Salt Marsh Sinners

The next day was another uneventful drive to Beaumont, Texas, where she stopped and called the number Mrs. Frost had given her.

A heavily accented voice answered. "I am Ramon. You are the driver? You are in Beaumont?"

"Yes. Where are you?"

"I am in Texas City. It is four o'clock. I will meet you at the warehouse in an hour."

Edilia followed directions and parked at a lot next to the warehouse. It was four thirty. She leaned back and was asleep when her truck door opened. She awoke and smiled at a south-of-the-border young man. "You're Ramon?"

"Yes. You are the driver?"

"I'm Edilia, and I know trucks." She climbed down and was startled when Ramon embraced her and kissed both cheeks.

"I wasn't expecting such a pretty young lady. We have much to talk about. Let's have a drink after we load your truck."

Edilia shook her head. "I can't stay. I want to drive back to Lake Charles tonight." Edilia felt her nose growing like Pinocchio's.

"*Lo siento. Es muy triste.*"

"I'm sorry too, but I'm tired and don't feel good. Maybe next time." Edilia wanted to stay, but something was wrong inside. She had been nauseated, but now she felt slight pains. Nothing serious, she told herself.

Ramon kissed her hand. "If you must go, I will help you move the boxes."

Edilia stared at him. "I was told you would move the boxes."

Ramon laughed. "We will do it together. They are heavy."

She paused, wondering if she should reveal her pregnancy, but he wouldn't understand. "All right. Let's get started."

Because Ramon had backed up behind Edilia's truck, the distance between them was minimal, but the boxes were heavy. Edilia perspired as she lifted and moved twenty boxes. Ramon helped, but the effort was more than she had expected. Thirty minutes later the transfer was completed, and Edilia was anxious to start the return trip. She shook hands with Ramon before he could embrace her again.

"Good luck with your drive home," she said. "*Adios.*"

"*Adios, querida.*" He put his arms around here and kissed her forehead. "*Vaya con Dios.*"

As soon as Edilia drove away from the warehouse, she felt a sharp lower-body pain. She gasped, and the pain subsided. Five minutes later the pain hit her again but stopped in a few seconds. She studied the map. If she could reach Beaumont, she'd stop and rest.

The pain hit her again as she drove onto an exit ramp leading into Beaumont. She parked at a gas station and convenience store and, holding her stomach, ran into the store.

"Can I help you, honey?" asked a woman behind the cashier's counter.

"The ladies room," Edilia gasped. She followed the woman's directions and closed the door behind her.

• • •

From behind the counter, Gladys saw the young woman as she staggered out of the ladies room.

"You need to sit down," she said and led her to a cushioned chair behind the counter. She gave the girl a bottle of water and stroked her shoulder. "What happened? Can I help?"

The girl shook her head. "I'll be all right, but I think I just had a miscarriage."

"Oh my God!" Gladys exclaimed. "I'm going to call my doctor."

"Please don't. I'll be okay, and I have to be in Naples, Florida, tomorrow."

"I don't think so," Gladys said and pulled out her cell phone.

• • •

Edilia wakened in alien surroundings. Everything was white—the walls, bed linens, curtains. As she tried to rise, a soft hand took hers. "It's all right, Edilia. I'm Gladys, and you're in the hospital."

Edilia moaned. "What happened, and how do you know my name?"

"You fainted, and we brought you here. We had to look through your purse to get your name and address." She smiled. "You'll be fine."

Edilia was confused and agitated. "I have to get back to Naples. I can't stay." She looked up at the woman. "I remember leaving the truck and running to the bathroom." She pushed herself up. "Did I lock the truck?"

"We locked it. Henry moved it to our parking area. It's safe there." She stroked Edilia's hand. "You had a miscarriage, remember?"

Edilia nodded.

"You're all right now. Our doctor examined you and said all you needed was rest. How do you feel?"

Edilia lay back on the bed and stared at the ceiling. "I'm okay. I need to get home, deliver the stuff in the truck, and…" She gulped. "Tell Tomas he won't be a father." She sobbed and looked at Gladys. "He didn't want the baby."

"Sometimes a miscarriage means it wasn't meant to be. How did you feel these last weeks?"

"Nauseated, kind of sick."

"I'm not a doctor, but I'm sure you were lucky to lose the baby now."

Edilia sat up. She understood what Gladys said, and although the pain of loss was deep and acute, she knew wallowing in despair would not bring the baby back. It was time to get on with her life.

"You're probably right." She smiled at Gladys. "When can I go home?"

As if cued in, a doctor entered the room, greeted Gladys, and studied his patient. "You're fine now, Edilia. You can dress and sign out. No further treatment is necessary." He took her hand. "You are a lucky girl, Edilia. In these cases, the fetus isn't growing properly. Did you have any problems?"

Edilia nodded. "I've been nauseated, didn't feel good. I had to lift some boxes in Houston, and I felt worse."

"Lifting may have triggered the miscarriage, but it would have occurred very soon."

She smiled at the doctor and Gladys. "I think I understand. Now I need to pay for my treatment and get home."

As soon as the doctor left, Edilia stood, and Gladys helped her dress. "I'll drive you to your truck, and I hope I see you again."

They stopped at the desk, and Edilia paid the bill with Mrs. Frost's credit card. An hour later she was back on the highway. Her mind was clear, and her intense pain was gone. She turned on the radio, hoping the sound of music would dull the loss that sank its claws into every inch of her body. She drove long hours and stopped at a motel in Mobile, Alabama. As she settled into bed, she called Mrs. Frost. "I've been delayed," she said. "I needed hospital care in Beaumont."

Edilia heard an exasperated sigh. "You must get back tomorrow. I don't care how long you'll be on the road. Just hurry."

Edilia frowned as she replaced the phone. Mrs. Frost hadn't asked about her need for hospital care, and her only concern was a prompt return to Naples. Edilia stared at the ceiling. No questions. No sympathy. She'd have a long drive tomorrow, with no comforting welcome at Rosewood Center.

The trip from Mobile to Naples was happily uneventful. She called Mrs. Frost on the outskirts of Tampa. "Come to the garage and wait for Felix. He'll help with the boxes." She cut the connection.

Edilia followed instructions and watched Felix leave his office near the elevators.

"We'll do this together," he said. "I'll take the heavy ones."

"Thanks. I had trouble with them." Edilia smiled. "It's good to be home."

They took the boxes to the freight elevator and pushed two heavily laden carts to Mrs. Frost's door. She opened it quickly, and Felix left with instructions to tell no one.

Edilia watched Mrs. Frost as she inspected two boxes. "Everything looks all right," she said. "You can go now."

Edilia didn't move. "You said you'd pay me when I returned."

"I didn't expect to have a hospital bill, Edilia. That's the money you would have received."

Edilia opened her mouth, but no words came. At last she found her tongue. "I could have died, Mrs. Frost. I had a miscarriage after lifting all those boxes."

"If I'd known you were pregnant, I've never have hired you. So go now. We've both learned a good lesson." She pushed Edilia to the door and put a small wad of bills in her hand. "Keep this, and don't tell anyone about the trip. You promised, remember?"

Edilia nodded. "No one would believe it anyway."

CHAPTER TWELVE

Jim Perruda sat at his desk at Perruda's Fine Furnishings and watched his customers as they wandered through the showrooms. He thought about Tony and Phil, who also faced interrogations at police headquarters. For Jim the sessions were torture, and he wondered how long he could stall Officer Doyle and Detective O'Hara. *Where were you the night your father was murdered?* The question gnawed at his stomach like an ugly vulture.

His phone rang. "Hi, Tony," he said as he heard his brother's voice. "What's up?"

"Phil told the cops that I lied about my trip to Key West the weekend of our dad's murder. Why would he do that?"

"I don't know. Stay cool and wait for an explanation. I'll talk to you later."

Jim didn't want to hear any more family trouble. He said good-bye and thought about his own problems. He had successfully steered his interrogations at police headquarters into a stone wall of "I can't answer," but how long could he delay his confession? He sighed, opened the bottom drawer of his desk, and removed the packet of cocaine. A sniff, and ah, the euphoria, the dreams of pleasures beyond his troubled world. He thought about the millions his father had accumulated, all buried in a bank account somewhere out of reach. Although his inheritance was enough to keep him in his accustomed lifestyle, he'd have preferred to own a yacht and a private jet. Fortunately, his father hadn't had time to change the will that excluded his children. A university in North Dakota? He should have been committed. If he could have proved his father was incapable of logical thought, he might have been saved from death. Jim smiled wryly. His dad would have laughed at any examination, and his sanity and safety would have been intact. He sighed as he put the packet of cocaine in his pocket.

Rita, his companion in Atlantic City, was a threat, not a lover. Laura was great, but the word *wife* lacked excitement. He had to admit their night together had been ecstatic, so what was missing? Because Jim wanted a diversion, the baccarat tables in Immokalee beckoned. He picked up the phone.

"Hi, Laura. I won't be home for dinner tonight. Don't wait up." He paused. "Now that we've talked, I feel great. Don't worry about me." He smiled as he opened his packet of cocaine. The path to the casino was smooth.

He lost heavily at the baccarat tables. He left that area and spent two hours at the bar. Martinis eased the pain of an empty wallet. He left the casino at ten o'clock and considered his options. Home was okay but ordinary. Hey, what about Julie? He pulled out her business card and found her address. She'd be lonesome without that DEA guy, Russ Jones.

Because cocaine and gin hampered his vision and reasoning, he nearly collided with four oncoming cars and got lost three times as he tried to focus on the traffic and Julie's address. At last he found her house and rang the bell. Minutes later the door was unlocked, and he saw Julie as she opened the door just a few inches. She wore a heavy robe and a surprised expression.

"Hello, Jim," she said. "I expected to see Lisette, my next-door neighbor."

"Hi, I'm not Lisette." He smiled. "I wanted to see you." He reeled as he pushed open the door. He grabbed Julie's arm and kicked the door shut behind him. He pushed her into the living room. When he reached the davenport, he held her arm and sat.

"I had to see you," he said, slurring his words. He pushed himself up and grabbed her with both arms. She tried to push him away, but he held her, kissing her lips, her hair, and her ears as he pulled her robe open.

Julie struggled to get free. "Don't, Jim, please," she begged. "You shouldn't be here. Go home."

Jim laughed and released her. "I thought we'd have a nightcap together."

She wrapped her robe tightly around her, and as she reached for the telephone, he grabbed her hand. "Don't," he said. "Just a little kiss."

He pushed her onto the davenport, laughed at her screams, and pulled open her robe.

• • •

Lisette Mureau and her husband, Henri, sat in front of the television and yawned together. "It's eleven thirty," Lisette said. "Time for bed."

Suddenly Heidi, their Saint Bernard, raced into the living room, barking and growling. She put her teeth around Lisette's hand and pulled.

"Ouch!" Lisette cried. She stood and followed Heidi to the front door. "What is wrong with the dog?" she asked.

"I don't know, but I think we should let her go. She knows something we don't understand. Maybe it's Julie. Take the key."

They ran with Heidi across their lawn to Julie's home. She barked and scratched at the door. Henri unlocked the door, and Heidi rushed ahead, barking and growling. Lisette and Henri heard screams as they followed Heidi into the living room.

"Oh, *mon Dieu*!" Henri exclaimed.

A man knelt above Julie on the davenport, gripping her arms with his fists. Her robe was open, and the man's trousers and shorts hung below his knees. Henri ran to the davenport, but Heidi charged ahead, and with her mouth wide open, she bit down firmly on the man's bare buttocks. The man screamed and swore as he fell forward onto Julie, his arms flailing wildly.

Lisette heard a cacophony of sound, a trio of Heidi's barks, Julie's soprano screams, and the attacker's baritone as he yelled and swore.

"Lisette, call 911!" Henri yelled.

His wife called, and in a voice trembling with horror, gave a report of attempted rape and the address.

Henri tried to grab the attacker, but Heidi was too quick for him As Julie pushed Jim onto the floor, Heidi rushed at him again. The man screamed as the dog found the same target for her teeth. Julie pushed herself up from the davenport and staggered into Lisette's arms. She pulled her robe together and tried to talk, but no words came, only sobs and moans.

Lisette held Julie and stroked her shoulders. She looked down at her dog. "Come, Heidi. Sit." Heidi released the man and sat.

The attacker reeled as he tried to stand. He put his hand on his buttocks and blood spattered onto the floor. He grabbed his trousers, wrapped them around his body, and staggered to the davenport. With his head between his hands, he moaned and cried.

Seconds later sirens wailed, and Henri ran to the front door. Two police cars were parked in the driveway, and four uniformed policemen ran into the living room. Two of them pulled Jim to his feet, and his trousers fell to the floor. Jim screamed as they handcuffed him and shoved him onto a chair.

An officer ran to Julie. "Are you all right? Did he finish the job?"

Julie shook her head. She stood and hugged herself. "I'm okay." The words were interrupted with sobs.

Jim looked as though he had lost all of his strength. He looked at Julie, tears streaking down his face.

"Oh God, I'm sorry, Julie. I didn't mean to hurt you. I didn't mean…" He looked back at the policemen. "I wouldn't hurt her, honest."

Heidi growled and came to Julie. She nuzzled Julie's hand, and when Julie sat, Heidi put her head on her lap. Julie patted her.

"You saved me, Heidi. Thank you." She looked at the officers. "I know this man. He's Jim Perruda. His dad was killed. I work…" She paused and sobbed. "He didn't rape me. Heidi stopped him." She looked at her attacker. "I know you, Jim. I knew your dad." She cried as she patted Heidi.

An officer put his hand on Julie's shoulder. "We have to take him to the hospital, Mrs. Rogers. He's performed a criminal act, but he'll need hospital care." The officer looked at Jim's body and added, "He's already paid a heavy price." Two officers snickered.

Julie shook her head. "He was drunk. I won't sleep tonight, but neither will he." She stood and glared at her attacker. "Go with the officers, Jim. I won't press charges, but I never want to see you again."

"We need to fill out a report," an officer said. "I'm Officer Kelley." He pulled out a tape recorder and a note pad. "It won't take long." He turned to the other men. "You three take him to the hospital, and I'll follow." He turned to Henri. "Has your dog received rabies shots?"

"We're from Canada, and Heidi received shots before we crossed the border."

"Good. Perruda won't need them."

Lisette and Henri watched as the officers helped Jim into his shorts and trousers and led him to the front door. Jim's steps were unsteady. He looked back at Julie.

"I'm sorry," he said.

As Julie completed the report, the officer said, "If you change your mind, please call." He gave her his card. "Rape is a crime, even attempted rape. You could have been killed."

"I know, but he was drunk or high on something. I'm sure he's going to suffer enough without a prison sentence."

The officer shrugged. "It's your decision now, but a crime has been committed. Charges will probably be filed."

After the officers left, Lisette went to the kitchen. "I know where you keep the whiskey. We'll have a drink." She returned with three glasses. "You shouldn't be alone tonight. Would you like Heidi or me to stay?"

"I'd like Heidi," Julie said. "Will she stay with me?"

"Of course," Henri said as he sipped his drink, "but she'll use most of your bed."

• • •

Laura sat in front of the television at their Luna de Ciel condo. It was midnight. Jim hadn't returned, and the late-night shows were filled with car chases and murder. When the phone rang, a chill shook her body. No sixth sense was needed. Jim was in trouble.

She listened to her husband as a greater calamity exploded in her ears. "You what? You're where? Oh my God!" As she heard details, horror and anxiety filled her mind. "I'll be right there," she said.

She drove to the courthouse, and an officer escorted her to the jail next door. He unlocked the door of Jim's cell. "You can go in," he said. "We'll be near if you need us."

Laura looked at Jim, who sat on a bed, one rump higher than the other. She sat on a chair and stared at her husband. Was this really Jim, this miserable, disheveled, dirty hunk of humanity?

"Oh God, Jim. I worried, but I didn't expect this." She looked around, almost surprised. Was this Jim in a prison cell? Rape? Oh please, no!

She didn't want to stay or ask questions. She stood and looked down at Jim. "I'll call your dad's lawyer, Mark Holtz. He'll know what to do." She walked to the cell door. "Maybe he can arrange for bail, maybe even get you off. I don't know." She called to the officer and left her husband in his cell.

Salt Marsh Sinners

The gears in Laura's mind were on neutral as she walked to the office. How could she process this situation, how to make some sense of Jim's escapade? She had no answers.

"Mrs. Perruda." A voice jolted her into reality. It was one in the morning. Jim was in a prison cell, and she, his wife, stood at the counter at the county jail.

"What should I do?" Laura leaned on the counter, her head between her hands.

"Call your lawyer in the morning," the officer said. "Your husband needs to sleep, and you can't do anything for him."

Laura nodded. "I'll go home. Thanks."

Hot cocoa and two sleeping pills did nothing, and Laura stared at the bedroom ceiling until seven in the morning. She showered, made coffee, and called Mark Holtz.

She explained the situation and listened as Holtz's voice portrayed amazement and disappointment. "I've known the family for many years, Mrs. Perruda. Jim's behavior is beyond comprehension. I'll see him this morning. You should be with me."

Laura sighed. "I'd rather not. I was there last night, and I have nothing more to say."

"All right. I'll call you after I've seen him."

Laura drank coffee and stared at the Gulf. Waders, swimmers, and bodies stretched out on the sand. Naples as usual. No tsunamis or hurricanes. Only the gentle wash of waves upon the sand. Laura could almost smell the lotions, cigarette smoke and decaying shell life. She turned back to her coffee mug and mouthed curses at her husband as she picked up the phone.

"Janet, it's Laura. I need you."

• • •

Cynthia Frost needed Felix, her assistant. She called his extension, the garage at Rosewood Center.

"I want to deliver the lamps and chandeliers this afternoon. When are you available?"

She listened. "Three o'clock will be perfect. Come to my apartment, and we'll pack the truck."

She returned to her kitchen table to finish the assembly work. She had removed the lampshades' inner linings with care. Now forty-eight sealed packets were ready for distribution. She had removed all pendants and bubbles from the chandeliers and, with a miniature scale, measured their contents. She filled packets with cocaine and added them to the others. She smiled as she shook out her hands. The work had been tedious and painstaking.

After she rechecked the shades and chandeliers and repacked them, she called the store.

"Chez Nous. This is Sharon. May I help you?"

"This is Cynthia Frost. The lamps and chandeliers are here. I can deliver them this afternoon. They're lovely. You'll be pleased." Now the way was clear for calls to her buyers.

• • •

Edilia Perez Prado sipped her breakfast coffee at her sister-in-law's kitchen table. Her hands shook as she held the cup. "I have to tell you what happened, Olga. I promised Mrs. Frost I'd keep her secret, but she cheated me. It's not a secret now."

Olga patted Edilia's shoulder. "We were in Miami while you were gone and had just come home when you arrived. What happened?"

Edilia sighed. "I drove a truck to Houston and picked up a load for Mrs. Frost. The driver came from Mexico and wanted me to stay with him." She giggled. "He was cute, but I couldn't stay." She stood and put her arms around Olga. "I was sick. I had a miscarriage in Beaumont."

"Oh, *querida*, I'm so sorry." Olga stroked Edilia's back.

"A lady took me to the hospital. I was there all night and left the next morning. I'm okay. The doctor said it would have happened sooner or later."

"Mrs. Frost must have been worried about you."

Edilia sniffed. "She didn't care, said my hospital bill was my wages for the trip. When I told her about the miscarriage, she gave me two hundred dollars."

"I'm glad she gave you something." Olga poured more coffee. "What was the cargo?"

"I don't know. We moved lots of boxes from his truck into mine."

Edilia's cell phone buzzed. "Yes? Hi, Tomas."

She didn't want to see him. He'd laugh at the miscarriage, relieved. She remembered his anger and accusations concerning her pregnancy and knew their relationship was over, dead, decayed beyond recovery. She also remembered his arms around her, his kisses, deep, breathless, filled with his wanting her and, she admitted, her wanting him. As she listened to his voice, her longing for him was stronger than her anger. She still loved him.

"We need to talk," Tomas said. "I missed you. When can we meet?"

Edilia smiled and looked back at Olga. "Come here this morning. We'll talk."

As soon as the conversation ended, Olga put her arms around Edilia. "I know you'll go back to Tomas, but please, Edilia, know that Tomas is a user. He uses drugs, and he uses women."

Edilia nodded. "But maybe he'll be different now. I'll tell him about the baby, and," she looked at Olga, "there won't be another. I promise."

"Okay, but be careful. I'm going to work. When Tomas comes, use your head, not your heart."

Edilia nodded. "Don't worry. My head's on straight."

• • •

Tomas Fuentes replaced his phone and drove to Marcos's home. He was eager to see Edilia and take her back with him to his apartment. It would be like old times. Maybe he could convince her to have an abortion. Being a father wasn't his style.

When she opened the door, he knew she was his. Her arms outstretched, her smile, her lips half-open.

"Baby," he said and reached for her. But, hey, how come she pushed him away? Tomas was startled.

"I'm glad you're here," she said. "I have news for you."

Tomas's insides hurt as he listened. The trip to Houston, the cargo from Mexico. Tomas interrupted. "I suppose you went to bed with the driver."

He felt a slap on his cheek. What was it with his woman? "So, okay. Then what happened?"

She described the rest of her trip, the miscarriage, the hospital. Tomas was stunned, but what the hell, there wasn't a baby anymore. *Muchas gracias.* He tried to kiss her and received another slap.

He sat on the davenport and looked up at her. "How come you hit me? You're okay, and I'll bet you got a lot of money for the trip."

Edilia sat beside him and took his hand. "It's been a bad time, Tomas. The long drive, losing the baby, and now there's not much money."

"Why?"

"Mrs. Frost gave me just two hundred dollars. She said the hospital bill was my payment, but she'd give me two hundred as a favor." She cried, and Tomas gave her a tissue.

"Who is Mrs. Frost? I can get that money for you." Tomas stood and folded his arms across his chest. "No dame is going to cheat my baby."

Edilia reached up for his hand. "Forget it. She lives at Rosewood Center where I work. Mrs. Green gave me time off, and I can't take chances."

Tomas shrugged and pulled Edilia to her feet. "Let's forget everything now." He kissed her and caressed her breasts.

Salt Marsh Sinners

Edilia pulled away. "Not now, Tomas. I'm not ready." She smiled. "I'll be all right. I just need time."

Tomas put his hands in his jeans pockets. "Okay. How about dinner tonight?"

Edilia nodded, and Tomas knew she'd be his again after dinner. He returned to his car and checked his watch. Eleven o'clock, two hours before his job at the store. He opened the glove compartment and removed a packet of cocaine. A quick sniff and he'd be ready for work. He needed to buy more, but his dealer said there was a problem. His supply was running low. He expected a new shipment from Mexico, but didn't know the exact date.

He sat in his car and thought about his uncle, Jose Fuentes. He lived in the area, and he used to do drugs. Maybe he'd know where to find the good stuff.

He parked and pushed open his uncle's door. "Hi. It's me, Tomas."

He expected a warm greeting, not an icy stare. "What do you want, Tomas? I don't see you unless you want something."

Tomas laughed. "You know me, Uncle Jose. And I do want something. Remember how we used to do stuff together?" Tomas sprawled on a chair. "I could use some coke right now. Something's happened to my guy."

Jose looked down at his nephew. "Something's happening here. A narc, Russell Jones, came to see me. He was investigating a murder. Drugs were involved, so he was called in. It could mean a crackdown."

Tomas stood. "Who got killed?"

"Frank Perruda. He owned a furniture store. I read the obituary. He lived in Rosewood Center, a fancy layout. Real uptown."

"Rosewood Center?" Tomas put his hands on his uncle's shoulders. "What else did he say?"

"Nothing else. Said he had to make another call. I told him I was clean and didn't have anything to do with druggies." Jose patted his nephew's back. "I didn't tell him about you. I hoped you weren't using anymore." He sighed. "Guess I was wrong to hope."

"I'll quit soon, but now I really need it."

"I can't help you, Tomas. This might be a good time to get the monkey off your back."

Tomas walked to the door and turned to Jose. "Don't worry about me. I'm okay." He walked to his car, lit a cigarette, and studied his hands. No shakes. He really was okay. He thought about Rosewood Center. Frank Perruda lived there. Maybe he imported Mexican drugs, and somebody killed him. Maybe Mrs. Frost. Edilia could have been transporting Mexican drugs from Houston. He knew about "source" cities. Better to bring them there than to make the switch at a border town. Tomas sat up and scratched his right ear. My God! Edilia could have been arrested and searched. They'd have found the stuff. She'd be in jail for life! God, she'd have told the authorities about him, and he'd be in jail too! Tomas's hands shook. He needed coke now.

• • •

Felix sat in his office next to his garage at Rosewood Center. "His" because he cared for each car, knew its personalities, how many miles per gallon, when it needed an oil change. Mrs. Jones's car was used occasionally by her caregiver, Marjory. The Buick belonging to Mrs. Jones's son, Russell, was driven briefly during his visits to Naples. Julie's car, parked in the concierge's slot, needed new tires. Diane's Bentley needed a new transmission. He'd watched her revved-up takeoffs and wondered how long the car's motor would survive. He smiled as he hoped she'd be downtown in the middle of rush hour when her car quit. She'd scream, swear, and flirt with any man who came to assist.

His phone rang, and he heard Mrs. Frost's anxious voice. "It's three o'clock, and I'm ready to deliver the boxes to my friend's shop, Chez Nous. Will you bring a luggage cart?"

Salt Marsh Sinners

Felix sighed. He'd moved them from her truck to her apartment. Now he'd move them back again.

He brought the luggage cart and loaded the boxes into the truck. Mrs. Frost smiled. "You drive, and I'll ride with you." She took her cane and followed him.

Felix parked in the alley behind the store on Fifth Avenue, and Cynthia went to the back door. She returned with a young man whose dark skin was richly tattooed. "Sharon wants you to put the boxes in the back room," Cynthia said and returned to the store.

"I'm glad you're here," Felix said to the young man. "I've moved these damned boxes too many times."

The man laughed. "Tell me about it."

"The boxes came from Mexico. I had to bring them to Mrs. Frost's apartment so she could check the merchandise. Then I had to haul them back to the truck."

"How did they get to Naples?"

Felix was surprised at the young man's interest. Why would he care? "A driver picked them up in Houston." Oops, Felix thought. He shouldn't have given information to a stranger.

Felix carried the lighter boxes into the storage room. The kid looked strong. He could handle the heavy ones.

"The boxes have been opened," the young man said.

"They were checked at the border. The border patrol always looks for drugs."

Together they unpacked the boxes. The six, two-tiered chandeliers were made of wrought iron painted in shades of gray-green. Three chandeliers were decorated with opaque bubbles. The other three held pendants in dark green. The pottery bases of the eight table lamps resembled animals in different poses, three on their hind legs, three asleep, and two ready to pounce. The young man laughed.

"Somebody must have been snorting when he made these bases."

Felix laughed too. "I guess that's surrealism."

When the work was finished, both he and the young man went into the store.

Cynthia took Felix's hand. "Sharon, this is Felix, who helps me."

"You've met Tomas, my helper?"

"We unloaded the truck together." Felix smiled at Tomas. "You carried the heaviest boxes."

Tomas laughed. "No problem."

Felix noticed that Tomas studied Cynthia, watched her as she and Sharon walked back to an office. Something bothered Felix. He couldn't put a handle on it, but he was uneasy.

"Do you work here every day?" Felix asked Tomas.

"In the afternoons. I work at a chickee hut in the morning and at Mel's Diner. Gotta earn big bucks."

"What do you do with all that money? Are you in school?"

"Maybe someday I'll find time for night classes." Tomas looked serious and troubled as he added. "I need money for special things, stuff that helps me get through those long hours." He stared at Felix. "You know what I mean. Maybe you can help."

Felix sat and scratched his ear. "I maybe could find something for you." He looked toward Cynthia as she bent over at Sharon's desk. "Mrs. Frost might know someone who can help you. Shall I ask her?"

"Not now. It's too obvious. Wait till you get home." He scribbled on a note pad. "Here's my phone number. I could use some coke real soon."

Felix pocketed the note. "I'll talk to her." He noticed Tomas's hand shook as he wrote his number. The kid needed drugs, and Cynthia could provide them. Felix shook his head. He hated the drug racket, but Cynthia was a generous employer. He looked up at Tomas, who chewed a nail as he paced back and forth. A victim, a loser.

Cynthia left Sharon's desk. "We can leave now. She'll check the merchandise and send a check." With her cane she limped to the back door. Felix followed and opened the truck door for her.

Before they reached Rosewood Center, Felix reported his conversation with Tomas. "I don't like it, Cynthia. I'm sure he knows about the shipment. Does he know your driver?"

"I don't know. I'll call her."

"Not now. The girl might be suspicious."

"You're right, but I'm also afraid she may have said enough about her trip to alert Tomas. If he's a user and needs cocaine, he'll fill in the blanks."

"What now?"

"I'm sorry, but the kid has to be silenced. He knows too much."

"But won't his girlfriend, your driver, be suspicious if he turns up missing?"

"He could be forced to make an excuse for his absence. I'm counting on you, Felix. You're good at these things."

"I don't like it, Cynthia. The kid's young. He could have a life."

"What kind of a life? He's a loser. You can do it, Felix. I'm relying on you."

Felix drove the truck into a convenience store's parking area and stopped. "I can't do this, Cynthia. He's just a kid, and the risk of being charged with murder is more than I can handle."

Cynthia laughed. "Yes, you ran away last time in Chicago. I hate to threaten, Felix, but you owe me one, and we're in this together. Think about it. Tomas could put us both behind bars if he's allowed to live. There's too much at stake here."

Felix nodded and pulled out into the traffic. "You're right. It has to be done."

As he drove, he thought about how to proceed. Tomas's body would be found in an obscure wooded area near Immokalee, Florida, far from the casino and habitation. By the time they'd reached Rosewood Center, a plan formed in his mind. A dinner invitation after work, a drive to Immokalee, a silencer on his gun.

He parked the truck at the staff parking garage, and he and Cynthia walked back to the center's garage.

"I'll take the truck back tomorrow," he said, "and I'll take care of Tomas." He turned to Cynthia. "It's going to be expensive, Cynthia. I don't work for peanuts."

Cynthia laughed. "You'll be well paid, Felix."

• • •

Julie's bedside phone rang at eight o'clock on Saturday morning. She pushed Heidi away and took the call. "Yes?" She knew her voice sounded weak and scared, echoing her fears and exhaustion. Even with Heidi beside her, she had slept little as she recalled last night's horror.

"This is Officer Kelley," a firm feminine voice said. "Can you come to the courthouse this morning? We'd like a statement." There was a long pause. "I hate to ask you, Mrs. Rogers. You've been through hell, but we need to have details."

"I understand. I'll be there." Julie replaced the phone and wanted to hear Russ's voice. Maybe he'd come. Oh, please, dear God, send him to me, she pleaded. Stroking Heidi, she called Russ's office, and when she heard his voice, sobs interrupted her words.

"I'm okay, but Jim Perruda came last night and tried to rape me."

She listened as Russ's voice exploded with astonishment and worry. Julie assured him he hadn't finished the job.

"Heidi, the Saint Bernard next door, saved me, and she slept with me last night." Julie patted the dog, and Heidi licked her ear.

"My God!" Russ said. "I can fly down today. I want to see you, to know you're all right."

"I want to see you too." She began to cry. "I have to go to the courthouse this morning. If you can come, call on my cell phone. I'll meet your plane."

Salt Marsh Sinners

Julie dressed and took Heidi next door. Lisette hugged both Julie and Heidi, offered coffee to Julie and a doggie treat to Heidi. "I'm sure you didn't sleep much," Lisette said, "but I'm glad Heidi stayed with you."

Julie's smile was rueful. "Heidi saved me last night." Julie accepted coffee and joined Henri at their breakfast table. "I'm going to the courthouse, and I hope to pick up Russ this afternoon."

"I'm glad you won't be alone now," Henri said. "We didn't sleep much either." He stirred his coffee. "That man is going to pay for his crime. Sitting will be painful. Heidi has sharp teeth."

Julie nodded. "I should feel sorry for him, but I don't." She shuddered. "If you hadn't come…" She looked down at her coffee. "I don't even want to think about it."

Julie finished her coffee and drove to the courthouse. She was relieved to find a woman at the desk. As soon as she identified herself, the woman introduced her to another officer.

"I'm Amanda Rieger. I'll help you through this meeting."

They walked together into an office, and Julie felt more at ease as she studied Amanda, thirty-something, with short blond hair, dimples, freckles, and an empathetic smile.

"I work with a lot of men," Amanda said. "Most of them are almost brotherly, answering my questions, encouraging my work, but last year I had an experience like yours." She sat, offered Julie a chair, and took her hand. "The attack happened right here as I was leaving. He pulled me into a room." Amanda stopped and looked through Julie into her memory. "No one could hear me, and he was strong, mean."

Julie gasped. "What happened? Did he…"

"No. Another officer opened the door, said he heard something and came to investigate. He saved me." She smiled. "We were both lucky." She turned on a tape recorder. "We need to have the full story. I know it's painful. It was for me, but it's important and necessary."

The woman at the desk entered with coffee, and Julie relaxed. Living through the horror wouldn't be easy, but perhaps it would be a catharsis, an opportunity to let it all out and move on with her life.

Amanda walked her through the ordeal. Julie cried often as she relived Friday night's experience. When she described Heidi's actions, Amanda turned off the tape recorder and laughed.

"Wow! Saved by a dog! Did she have a flask of whiskey around her neck? I've seen pictures of Alpine rescues."

Julie smiled. "The whiskey came later with Lisette and Henri."

Amanda reactivated the tape recorder. "My report states that you won't press charges."

Julie nodded. "Jim isn't a professional rapist. He was high on something, and he's going to suffer. I don't know his wife, but I'm sure this will be difficult for both of them." Julie stood and paced the floor. "I don't want to make it any worse." She looked at Amanda. "If Heidi hadn't interrupted, I'd have pressed charges."

Amanda nodded "I understand. James Perruda is in a cell right now. A doctor has treated him." She smiled. "Mr. Perruda is a weird sort of celebrity around here."

"What happens next?"

"His lawyer will probably post bail and get him out, but he's committed a crime. I know you don't want this to go any further, but James Perruda is a criminal."

When they reached the front desk, an officer took Julie's arm. "Mrs. Rogers, James Perruda's clothing was searched, and a controlled substance was found. Now it's more than attempted rape. We've talked to his wife and his lawyer. He'll stay here until he's formally charged."

Julie nodded. There was nothing more to say. She returned home and waited for Russ's call. As she straightened the living room after last night's chaos, she listened with one ear to the radio and the other to the telephone.

Russ's voice on the phone was a welcome respite from cleaning and worry, and the thirty-minute drive to the airport soothed her agitation. Welcoming embraces and another thirty minutes filled with Julie's report added to a release from past events.

"I don't know what will happen," Julie said as she opened her garage door.

"What was the controlled substance?"

"I don't know, but I knew he was high on something. Liquor, drugs, maybe both."

"You said his speech was slurred. What else?"

"He staggered."

Julie watched Russ as he processed her remarks. "It sounds like cocaine or heroin. I'll call Chief Turner at police headquarters and Sheriff Jack Ryder. Maybe there's a connection between Jim Perruda's drug possession and his father's murder."

"I haven't heard anything at the center, and there's nothing from the media. Maybe they'll never know who killed Frank Perruda."

"That's a possibility. The longer the time span, the harder it is to solve the case." Russ touched Julie's cheek. "Let's forget the case and enjoy a sunset at the pier."

CHAPTER THIRTEEN

Tony Perruda stood on the beach in front of his Vanderbilt Beach Drive condo and watched the sunset. The sky was a spectacular panorama of color. Brilliant orange faded slowly into a pale peach, and a faint lavender became deep purple. Tony kicked the sand and swore. To hell with sunsets in Naples!

His wife, Emma, had returned to their home in Minneapolis to care for their two daughters. No telling what two teenage girls might do without adult supervision. He envisioned wild parties with beer and high-school boys with high testosterone levels. Emma was needed at home, but Tony also needed her. The condo was empty and full of unpleasant memories. Because Phil had accused him of lying to the police, he was now a prime suspect in his father's murder, and long, ugly sessions with Officer Doyle and Detective O'Hara awaited him in a windowless, oppressive room at headquarters.

He sat on the beach and pulled out his cell phone. Maybe Jim would invite him for dinner at their condo. He'd appreciate a home-cooked meal. Laura answered, and Tony listened, shocked and sickened by her report.

"I can't believe Jim would try to rape the concierge or anybody, and drugs? I don't believe any of it."

"It's true, Tony. He's in jail and will appear in court on Monday."

"Where's the jail?"

"At the courthouse on Airport Road."

"Can I see him?"

"If you wish. He's not very presentable."

"He's my brother, Laura." Tony paused, horrified but hungry. "Would you like to have dinner with me tonight?"

He was disappointed when she said, "No, I have other plans."

He said good-bye and dressed for fast food and a trip to the jail. He dreaded to see Jim, but hell, he was his brother. Laura hadn't sounded like the grieving wife. He sensed bitterness, not compassion.

He drove to the jail, signed in, and gave proof of identification before he was admitted. An officer led him to his brother's cell, and Tony was shocked. Jim was curled up on a bunk, pale, rumpled, and desolate. He struggled to his feet as Tony entered the cell.

"I called you at home, and Laura told me what happened. I'm sorry."

"Everybody's sorry, especially me. I'll be in court on Monday with Mark Holtz, Dad's lawyer." Jim wiped tears. Tony gave him a tissue.

"Can I get you anything?"

"A new body complete with a full set of brains." He touched his back end. "The damned dog bit me."

Tony hid his laughter. "Maybe you were lucky. The gal too."

Jim sighed. "I guess it could have been worse." He lay down again, guarding his wounds. He stared up at his brother. "Laura may leave me, and if this hits the papers, my business won't survive."

Tony put his hand on Jim's shoulder. "People have short memories, Jim. Don't write off your business." He paused. "You and Laura will have to work this out together. Emma could have left me for good reasons but didn't. Don't give up."

"Thanks, Tony. Will you come to the courthouse on Monday?"

Tony was startled. He and Jim had never been close as children. Their father had driven a wedge between them with accusations and threats. Now they were adults, and Frank was gone. If the fires of sympathy and support had been extinguished years ago, was it still possible to kindle a brotherly relationship?

"I'll be there." Tony walked to the door. "Try to sleep." He studied Jim. "For God's sake, clean up and shave. Call Laura and ask for clean clothes. You look like hell!"

Jim laughed. "The same old Tony." He stood and put his arm around his brother. "We Perrudas got to stick together."

Tony smiled as he signed out. His brother Jim would survive. *Brother.* The word had a new meaning.

As he drove back to the condo, his cell phone vibrated. He pulled over and listened as an unfamiliar voice said, "Mr. Perruda, this is Dr. Chambers at Fairview Southdale Hospital in Minneapolis. I have bad news. Your wife, Emma, was involved in an automobile accident and is here in intensive care."

"Oh God!" Tony exclaimed. "Is she all right?"

"It's too early to tell. A car ran a red light and hit the right side of her car. She's unconscious, but so far her vital signs are good. We found your numbers. No one answered at your home, so we called your cell phone."

Tony, almost too stunned to speak, whispered, "I'm in Naples, Florida. I'll charter a plane and come as soon as I can. I'll try to contact our daughters."

Tony called a charter service at the Naples airport. "Yes, we can fly you to Minneapolis tonight."

"I'll come to the airport as soon as I can. My wife's critical. Auto accident."

He packed and boarded the jet at eight o'clock. The hours dragged as he envisioned the worst. He pleaded with God to heal and mend. He offered a bargain. "Let her live, and I'll be a better husband." He left messages on his daughters' cell phones and on his home phone.

It seemed an eternity before he was able to see Emma, who lay in a curtained area in the hospital's intensive care unit. Tubes were attached to her arms. Oxygen tubes were inserted in her nostrils. Medical people with clipboards and caring expressions entered, checked the patient, the IVs, and a heart monitoring machine, and left. One nurse remained. Tony sat by the side of the bed and held Emma's hand. Did she know him, hear his words? He scarcely remembered the forms he signed, the required information. It was a blur of worry and fear.

"Daddy, we're here. What happened?" His daughters rushed in and brought comfort by their presence but compounded his worry and fright.

Tony gave them a brief account. "I don't know much, but she's alive."

Two staff members entered. "We're taking her to X-ray. It won't be long. There's coffee in the waiting room." They rolled Emma's bed and the IV apparatus into the hall.

Tony took the girls' hands, and they walked to the waiting room. They found coffee, a soft drink machine, and plates of cookies. Other families, burdened with anxiety and fear, huddled in small groups, voices hushed. Tony led Kim and Stephanie to a corner table, three more worried people who blended into the waiting room's aura of grimness and anxiety.

"Where did it happen?" asked Kim, the eldest.

"On the corner of France Avenue and Sixty-Sixth Street. She was driving north. Maybe she had been shopping at the Mall of America. The other car was going west and was speeding. I read the report, but I don't remember much. I just thought about your mom."

They walked back to Emma's cubicle and watched her return from X-ray. An attendant said, "We'll have the results soon."

Emma was quickly attached to monitors. Her facial bruises had darkened and spread. "She looks like an opossum," Stephanie whispered, and Kim giggled. Tony threw them an icy stare, but a second look at Emma confirmed Kim's analysis.

"Mm, oh," Emma moaned, and three Perrudas rushed to her side.

"Emma, honey, I'm here," Tony whispered. "Can you hear me?"

"Mm." Emma nodded.

The nurse who had stayed with Emma during the X-ray trip checked her pulse and smiled. "You're all right, Emma, and your family is here." She spooned chipped ice into Emma's mouth.

Tony stroked Emma's left hand. "You had an accident. I flew from Naples."

"I'm glad," Emma whispered and closed her eyes.

Dr. Chambers entered and checked Emma's vital signs. He felt Emma's forehead and patted her arm. "You're going to be fine, Emma." He motioned to Tony, who followed him into the waiting room. They sat at a table, and Dr. Chambers studied the reports.

"Emma has serious fractures. Her pelvis, right shoulder, and right ankle. We'll operate as soon as she's stabilized."

"Oh God," Tony said. "Are there internal injuries?"

"We're monitoring her vital signs, and they look surprisingly healthy. She's breathing properly, her heart's okay. We won't know for several hours about other damage, but so far she's all right." He smiled. "She's lucky to be alive, Mr. Perruda."

Tony sighed. "I suppose I should ask about the guy who hit her, but I'm not sympathetic."

"That's natural." Dr. Chambers studied his notes. "The man was taken downtown to Metropolitan. We don't know his condition."

"I hope he's well enough to face charges."

They returned to Emma's bed, and the doctor checked her again. "We'll call you when we can operate," he said. "You and your daughters might want something to eat." He looked at his watch. "I don't know what's open at this hour, but you should find an all-night café. I'll order pain medication for your wife so she can sleep."

Dr. Chambers left, and Tony motioned to the girls. "Let's have dinner somewhere nearby. They may not operate until tomorrow."

They kissed Emma's forehead and stepped into the hall. "I have to make some calls, girls, so pick me up at the emergency entrance." He found a quiet corner in the waiting room and called Officer Doyle's extension at Naples police headquarters. Using Doyle's voice mail, he described his sudden departure.

"My wife's alive but needs extensive surgery and God knows what else. You have my cell phone number." He left messages for Carla and Jim's wife, Laura. His anger toward Carla's husband and his worry about Jim faded in the reality of Emma's condition. Nothing else mattered, not even his being charged in his father's death.

At the emergency entrance, the girls waited for their father in Kim's BMW. Kim drove slowly and carefully, and Tony knew she was deeply affected by her mother's accident. Dinner was bearable as Kim and Stephanie gave their reports of their trip to Martinique.

"We had our school assignments, and we practiced French," Kim said.

"The beach was super," Stephanie added. "Mom bought us bikinis."

"And Mom bought bedroom furniture," Kim said. She began to cry. "When it arrives, I hope she can enjoy it."

Tony took her hand. "She's going to be fine, and we'll take care of her when she comes home." Tony almost bit his tongue. How could he take care of her if he had to be with those damned cops in Naples? He shrugged off the "ifs." There were too many.

• • •

In Rosewood Center's garage, Felix Schmidt studied Diane Perruda's Bentley. Frank Perruda's young, sexy widow had wasted no time leaving the penthouse and returning with Saks and Nordstrom's boxes. This afternoon he noticed a dent in the Bentley's left front fender and considered a report, but he knew she'd accuse him of driving her car and causing the dent. Better to ignore the damage.

He sighed as he thought about Cynthia Frost's concern regarding Tomas, the boy who worked at Sharon's accessory shop. "The kid has to be silenced," she had said. "He knows too much." The boy, Tomas, did know too much, but he was just a boy, about the age of Felix's son, Tommy, who died too soon, too suddenly. He'd warned his only child, just a teenager, about drugs and hoped his message got through, but on Chicago's South Side, it wasn't possible for a son to follow a father's advice. Tommy was killed in a gang fight. No evidence, no charges. Just another crazy kid dead in a Chicago alley. Now Felix faced the killing of another boy.

He knew Tomas was a druggie and a loser with not much of a future, and his own allegiance to Cynthia Frost was cemented with mutual involvement in the drug trade. He provided transportation and detailed knowledge of the inner workings of Rosewood Center. He remembered an incident that could have triggered suspicions when she forgot her shopping date with Mrs. Johnson. The staff had even entered her apartment! He had preserved her identity with a quick report that her car was missing, and nobody asked questions. He remembered how she had avenged his son's murder in Chicago. They had worked together for five years. He'd do the job with strict attention to all details.

His desk phone rang, and he was quick to respond. "What are your plans regarding Tomas?" Cynthia's voice was commanding, terse.

Felix paused and said, "I want him desperate for a fix. I'll call tomorrow."

Because no one was in the garage, Felix checked his .38 and the silencer. Too bad the kid had to be eliminated, but he had no choice. Alive, he was a potential danger, a loaded gun.

When Frost arrived, Felix repeated his concerns. "I know he's a threat, but he's just a kid. I hate what has to be done, Cynthia.

Tomas reminds me of the hell we endured with Tommy, the pleading, the threats. Nothing worked."

"I know, but you tried." She put her hand on his shoulder. "At least we know there'll be no more killings by that gang."

"I don't know how you did it, Cynthia," Felix said. "One by one, each member of that gang either left town or was killed."

"I knew people in Chicago." Cynthia sat in front of Felix's desk. "I wonder why Russell Jones, the DEA agent, is back in Naples. I saw him in the lobby."

"I don't know. I'll ask around, casually, of course. Maybe his mother is sick."

Felix spent two sleepless nights at home as he planned his meeting with Tomas. Before leaving for work on Monday morning, he kissed Mary, his wife, and said, "Don't wait up for me tonight. Peter Watson's called a staff meeting concerning some resident problems."

"I hate those meetings, Felix," Mary said. She sat at the kitchen table and poured a second cup of coffee. "Don't be too late."

"I'll do my best." He left the house and called Tomas from his office. His invitation, with the promise of drugs, was easily accepted. "I'll pick you up at five thirty." He paused. "Better cancel your night work. We might want to visit the casino."

Felix's day at the garage dragged. He watched the clock too often, ate sparingly, and was relieved when five o'clock finally arrived. As he drove to the accessory shop, he planned conversations and actions, nothing to suggest impending death. It would be quick and painless.

He parked at the rear of the store, and waited for Tomas, who appeared five minutes later.

Felix rolled down his window, and Tomas asked, "Did you bring the stuff?"

"Yes. Do you have a car?" Tomas nodded. "Good," Felix said. "Follow me, and we'll go to my favorite sports bar. You can park in their lot, and I'll give you the coke."

Tomas stayed behind Felix and parked next to him. Felix motioned him inside his car and gave him a packet of cocaine. "Slow and easy," he said.

Tomas nodded but ignored the advice.

Giant TV screens lined the sports bar's walls, and crowds of fans cheered for their favorite teams. Felix ordered beer and watched Tomas, who placed his hand firmly on the waitress's round bottom and mouthed a kiss. She responded with a giggle and a wink as she delivered the beer.

When they finished, Felix said, "If you're free, leave your car here, and we'll take my car to the casino in Immokalee. I'll bring you back after a couple of hours."

"Great. My girl doesn't want to see me right now. I don't understand women."

"Who does?" Felix responded.

Felix staked Tomas at the blackjack table and watched as his money enriched the owners' bank accounts. After dinner Tomas's losing streak ended, and Felix almost forgot that soon Tomas's winnings would be safely hidden in the glove compartment, next to his gun with one bullet missing.

As they walked to Felix's car, Tomas said, "That was fun, Felix. How much do I owe you for the coke?"

"Nothing. Forget it."

"No. You bought beer and dinner."

Felix laughed. "You can pay me later."

Because he knew the area, Felix looked for a familiar road. He'd spotted it during one of his trips past Immokalee, an almost abandoned, one-lane road, thick on either side with brush, palmettos, and kudzu. Tonight it was an ideal setting for a killing. He drove onto the highway and turned right instead of left toward Naples.

"Where are you going?" Tomas asked.

"Just a little detour. Trust me." Felix drove slowly and saw the road, rutted and narrow, an abandoned and desolate road. As he drove farther into the woods, he reviewed his planned attack. He'd stop, open the glove compartment, and kill Tomas before the kid knew what happened. This was a perfect location. He could drag the body away from the road and, with the shovel stowed in his trunk, cover it with underbrush.

He stopped the car. It was time. As he opened the glove compartment, he glanced at Tomas, hoping the kid would suspect nothing unusual, nothing threatening. He stared at Tomas. Oh God! It wasn't Tomas. It was Tommy, his son, his only child, dead in a Chicago alley! Felix slammed shut the compartment door and covered his face with his hands. He leaned against the steering wheel and moaned softly in his native German. Beads of sweat dripped into his eyes.

"What's wrong?" Tomas asked. "Why are we here?"

Felix leaned back, his hands limp at his sides. He gasped, fighting for breath. "This isn't what was planned, Tomas. I can't tell you everything, but you're not safe here. You've got to get out of town."

Tomas turned to Felix and shook him. "Tell me what's going on."

Felix shook his head. "I can't answer."

"Crap!" Tomas yelled. "I saw you going for the glove compartment." He put out his hand and opened the compartment door. "Shit! You got a gun!" He pulled out the automatic and aimed it at Felix's head.

"Go ahead and shoot," Felix said. "I couldn't do it." In that instant he knew Tomas could pull the trigger, and his body, not Tomas's, would lie under the dead vines and brush. "Don't," he said as he slowly raised his hand and grabbed the gun.

Tomas made no effort to fight back. He lowered his head and shut his eyes. "I couldn't kill you either." He turned to Felix. "Why did you plan to kill me? What have I done?"

"I can't tell you." Felix sighed and gave him a wry smile. "Neither of us is dead, and my job is done. I can't protect you." He found gum in his jacket pocket and shared it with Tomas.

Salt Marsh Sinners

"You need to leave Naples. If you don't, someone else will kill you."

Tomas grabbed Felix's right arm. "No, I can't go away. What about Edilia, my jobs, my car?"

"Either you disappear, or you won't have your girl, your jobs, or your car. You'll be dead."

Tomas's body went limp. In the dim light, Felix saw tears. Between sobs Tomas asked, "What can I do?"

Felix thought of possible solutions. The kid had to leave, but where could he go? He brightened as he thought about his cousin, Henry.

"I have a cousin in St. Louis who owes me one. He manages a drug and alcohol rehab center." He paused and looked at Tomas. "I can't change your life, Tomas. I couldn't even help my own son, but I hate to see a wasted life, especially a young one."

"Yeah, my uncle wants me to quit." He chewed his gum and sighed. "Maybe I could do it. A different town, a new..." He stopped and looked at Felix. "But what about my girl, Edilia? She'll wonder where I am, maybe even call the cops. And what about my car?"

"Give me the keys, and I'll take your car to my house. It's safe there. You can't contact your girl now. It's too risky. I'll let you know when it's safe."

Tomas sat up and sighed. "Okay, I don't have a choice. How do I get to St. Louis?"

"We'll drive to the bus station in Fort Myers tonight. I'll buy your ticket, and you'll take the first bus out of town. I'll alert my cousin. He runs an excellent rehab, Tomas. This is an opportunity for you to put your life back together. It won't be easy, but you're young. Lots of years ahead, good years if you kick the habit and stay clean. He'll work with you and might even find you a job." Felix took out his wallet and gave Tomas some money.

"Thanks," Tomas said, turning the bills over in his hand. He pocketed the money. "I hope I can pay you back, and it's lucky I won at the casino. I'll be okay." He gave Felix his car keys. "When can I come back?"

"As soon as I call. Not until then." Felix wrote his cousin's name and address on a card. "I don't have his phone number with me. You'll have to look it up."

Felix turned the car around and drove to the main road. Neither spoke during the trip to Fort Myers. Felix shivered as he thought about averted murders. He could have killed Tomas, and Tomas could have killed him. It was a miracle that they were now en route to a bus depot, not to a morgue.

• • •

Tomas watched the highway as Felix drove to Fort Myers. He fingered an earring and worried about his future. Could he endure weeks of treatment at the rehab center? Would Edilia miss him, maybe find another guy, maybe get married? He shoved future thoughts away. Felix hadn't shot him, he hadn't shot Felix, and now he felt a mysterious bond with this man, old enough to be the father he couldn't remember. Crazy, crazy, he thought.

The bus deport was quiet at midnight. The man behind the ticket counter yawned as he handed Tomas a one-way ticket to St. Louis. "A bus leaves for Atlanta in ten minutes," he said. "You can transfer there."

Tomas walked with Felix to his car. "I'll call your cell phone when I'm in St. Louis," he said. He put out his hand and was surprised when Felix ignored the gesture and hugged him briefly.

"Don't forget what happened tonight, Tomas. I could have ended your life instead of giving you a new one."

Tomas nodded. "I didn't want to shoot you, Felix. I was too scared to think straight."

"I know." They watched a bus pull up to the curb in front of the depot. Its sign read "Atlanta."

Felix touched Tomas's shoulder. "Now get on that bus. I'll wait for your call."

Tomas climbed aboard and waved to Felix, who stood outside his window. He thought about jumping off the bus as soon as Felix left. He could get a refund on his ticket and hitch a ride back to Naples. He and Edilia could find jobs together in Orlando. They'd go to Disney World on their days off. Tomas smiled. Yeah, Felix would find him, maybe use the gun this time. The driver closed the bus door and started the engine. So much for idle dreams. Tomas leaned back, and thought about his future. For starters he'd need clothes and a toothbrush. Maybe he'd find them between buses in Atlanta. He fell asleep with thoughts of new jeans and a T-shirt reading "Get a Life" floating in his mind.

• • •

Julie and Russ went to sleep together in her bed Sunday night, cozy in a spoon position. Russ knew she wasn't ready for sex, not after Friday night's horror, so he kissed the back of her neck.

"I'm glad I'm here," he whispered.

"Me too," Julie murmured. He smiled as he heard deep breathing almost at once. His girl needed at least eight hours of uninterrupted slumber.

The next morning Russ heard the shower and knew Julie was preparing for work. He planned his day. He'd take a cab to Rosewood Center and visit his mother. With his own car, he'd drive to the courthouse and see Sheriff Jack Ryder. Lunch with Julie. He'd contact DEA headquarters in the afternoon. Dinner with Julie. In his mind the day improved as the hours passed.

Breakfast was easy, as Russ was now familiar with her coffee maker and refrigerator.

"Where's lunch?" he asked.

"There's a new place at the Pavilion. Pick me up at noon." She kissed him and drove to her garage.

Before calling for a taxi, Russ called DEA headquarters in Arlington, Virginia, and explained his absence. He hoped this would be an "up" day for his mother and was relieved to find her cheerful and alert.

"So nice to see you, Russell," Mrs. Jones said. "Marjory took me shopping yesterday." She shook her head. "Everything is so expensive now. I'm glad I don't need new clothes." She laughed. "When you move, your old St. John's knits look new to everyone."

They sat in her lanai, and Russ admired the view. "The mangroves look healthy, and the Gulf is filled with sailboats this morning."

Mrs. Jones nodded and sipped tea. "Yes. The estuary is beautiful. So many birds." She smiled. "One day I'd like to walk there."

Russ laughed. "But don't get too close. You'll get your feet wet."

"Don't worry, Russell. I know my limitations."

Russ kissed his mother, blew another to Julie at her desk, and found his car in the garage. He punched in the sheriff's number before leaving Rosewood Center.

"Glad you're in town," Ryder said. "We'll talk."

When Russ entered his office, the sheriff shook Russ's hand and ordered coffee. "I wish I had good news," he said, "but we've batted zero." He scratched the back of his head. "James Perruda has been arrested for attempted rape and possession of a controlled substance. He'll be arraigned today. The judge will probably set bail and release him temporarily."

"I know about the rape," Russ said. "Julie and I are…" He paused and added, "a couple."

Ryder smiled. "My informants tell me you have good taste." He picked up a paperweight and stared at it. "And we just received a voice mail from James's brother, Tony. He'd been told not to leave town, but he flew to Minneapolis because his wife had a serious accident. A speeding car drove through a stoplight and hit her broadside."

"I can't blame him for leaving," Russ said, "but what about his testimony?"

"Officer Doyle and Detective O'Hara have learned nothing in spite of threats. If he agrees to a lie detector test, we might solve the case."

An officer brought a welcome mug of coffee, and Russ sat back and sighed. He had no encouraging words or possible solutions. "My FBI friend and I went to an identification building and searched their criminal files."

"Did you find anyone with a possible connection to the Perruda case?"

"We spent the day there but didn't find anyone. I found one name, John Thurston, but it's too remote to consider. I'll just keep it in mind. Anything new on the Jeff Parker case?"

"No. The autopsy proved he'd been stabbed that night in the shipping bay at Perruda's Fine Furnishings. His wife didn't even know he'd gone to the store. We interviewed everyone who knew Parker. No suspects."

"And Sam Kolinsky was innocent." Russ smiled. "He saved my life, Jack. Somebody upstairs must have planted him and his need for bar stools in the furniture store that day."

Ryder grinned. "The SWAT team is still laughing about their raid in Everglades City."

Russ laughed. "Sam's business must have blossomed after all that commotion." He sipped coffee. "If we can't close the case soon, I'll remove the drugs from your safe and take them to headquarters in Arlington."

"I'll be happy to turn the stuff over to you." Ryder slouched in his chair. "Damn! I wish I'd never heard of Frank Perruda and his family."

Russ smiled. "Sometimes you win one, Jack. Don't give up." He checked his watch and stood. "I'm having lunch with Julie. Thanks for the coffee."

Russ and Julie sat at a beach-front table at the Turtle Club. "Sheriff Ryder is discouraged," Russ said. "No more leads, Jim's in jail, and his brother, Tony, is in Minneapolis with his wife, who is badly injured."

"What happened?"

"An automobile accident. A guy ran a red light and almost killed her. Tony sent a voice mail from Minneapolis. Ryder could have had him arrested and returned to Naples, but he understood the circumstances." Russ paused. "Nobody in law enforcement likes Tony very much. He's cocky, a smartass, and they know he's lying about his whereabouts the weekend his dad was killed."

"And they won't get much out of Jim." Julie shivered. "I hate what he did. Maybe I'll need counseling, Russ. I'm trying to do my job at the center, but I can't forget what happened. This morning one of our residents, a nice old man, tried to take my hand, and I froze."

Russ nodded. "Maybe counseling would help, honey." He almost reached for her hand but pulled back.

Julie reached for his and smiled. "The last two nights were comforting. I needed you. It felt good, and I slept." She looked at her watch. "I must get back. After work we'll stop at the grocery store. Cooking will be therapy."

Russ laughed. "I'm no doctor, but I can toss a salad."

• • •

Jim Perruda sat in his prison cell and thought about his chances in the arraignment. He'd asked an officer to call his wife and request a change of clothing and a razor. Headquarters gave him a toothbrush and a comb, and Laura brought his clothes. She didn't see him. The package was delivered by an officer.

Two officers escorted him next door to the courthouse. "We won't need handcuffs, Mr. Perruda," an officer said. "Your record is clean so far."

Jim winced. He heard "so far" and knew in law enforcement circles, he was recognized as a suspect in his father's murder.

Mark Holtz met him outside the courtroom and walked with him to a table in front of the judge's bench. They stood when the judge entered the courtroom.

"I'll ask for your release with bail, Jim," Holtz said. "If you're lucky, all you'll get is a slap on the wrist, but attempted rape and possession of a controlled substance are serious crimes."

Jim nodded. "I know, and I'll accept his decision."

The judge listened as Holtz introduced his client with a detailed account of his background, his occupation, and the events that led to his entering Julie Rogers's home.

After studying his notes, the judge spoke. "You're free to go, Mr. Perruda. I'm setting bail at fifteen hundred dollars, payable immediately."

Jim nodded, stood and shook hands with his lawyer. "Will there be a trial?"

"You'll be in court again, and the state's attorney will be present," Holtz said. "It won't be a trial unless Mrs. Rogers files a complaint, and I'm told she won't press charges."

"That's a relief."

"Yes, but possession of a controlled substance is a felony." He picked up his briefcase. "You're lucky, Jim." They walked out of the courtroom. "I'll help you get your things at the jail and sign out." He looked intently at his client. "I hope you've learned through this experience, and you and Laura can work it out together. It's difficult for both of you."

Jim nodded. "It won't be easy."

• • •

After Russ drove Julie back to Rosewood Center, he went to police headquarters and asked to see Chief Turner. Their meeting was cordial but fruitless. Turner had no more information regarding the murders of Frank Perruda and Jeff Parker.

"Tony Perruda's voice mail to Officer Doyle muddied the waters even deeper," Turner said. "We could throw the book at him for leaving town, but what good would that do?"

"Not much," Russ answered. "It's almost a dead end."

"And as time goes by, it gets deader." Turner shook his head. "I care more about finding Jeff Parker's killer. The guy was wrong to hunt for the drugs, but that's a horrible price to pay for an error in judgment."

"Yes, it's sad. He'd been married for just two months." Russ stood. "Thanks for your time, and good luck with the Perrudas."

Russ returned to his apartment and groaned as he listened to his messages. When Julie called him Saturday morning, he erased DEA on his mental blackboard and replaced it with her name. Now DEA reappeared in bold letters with details of emergencies that needed prompt attention. He spent the day connecting with DEA operations, and by five o'clock he had finished his assignments.

Dinner with Julie at an Italian restaurant was a welcome respite from his work, and Julie seemed more relaxed. He knew he had to get back to the agency, but was Julie ready to move ahead? She'd mentioned therapy. Perhaps he should encourage her.

"I hate to leave, honey, but it's time. Will you be all right?"

Julie nodded. "Yes. You being here saved me from a meltdown, but I know you have a busy schedule. When will you leave?"

"I'll take a late-afternoon plane tomorrow." He took her hand. "You might consider getting some help. You'll know if and when you need it."

"Yes, I'll know." She smiled. "Let's go home. I'll bring you back to the center in the morning."

Hurried kisses flavored with orange juice and bacon. Russ and Julie exchanged promises for "next time" without trauma and unsolved police work. Russ knew his efforts to solve two murders and break up a drug trafficking operation had failed. There was nothing more he could do, and Julie would survive her ordeal with the knowledge that help was available when needed.

Julie drove to Rosewood Center and made plans for lunch. Russ went to his apartment and opened his briefcase. Two hours later he was ready for a quick run to Starbucks. As he picked up his car keys, his cell phone vibrated and rang.

"This is Marjory, your mother's caregiver. Come quick. I've lost your mother!"

CHAPTER FOURTEEN

Russell Jones's mother had disappeared! As he stood in his apartment ready to enjoy a latte, Marjory's voice on his cell phone sent shivers through his spine. He lost breath for a moment.

"Oh God!" he exclaimed and took another breath. "When did she leave?"

He heard sobs. "I went downstairs to mail a letter. She'd been napping. Just now I returned, and she's gone! Oh, Russ, what have I done?"

"Don't blame yourself. We'll find her." Suddenly he remembered the center's protection system. "Was mother wearing her emergency response pendant?"

"No. I found it on her dresser. She must have removed it before her nap." Russ groaned. If she'd worn the pendant, she'd have been found immediately.

Suddenly he realized Marjorie didn't know he was next door in his apartment. He could have been anywhere answering his cell phone. He ran next door and rang the bell.

Marjory answered, a startled look on her face. "You're here?"

"Yes. I'll call Julie and the director. They know what to do." He called, gave the information, and ran to the elevator. In the lobby he was relieved to see staff members already outside searching under parked cars.

Julie ran to him. "Everyone's alerted." She took Russ's hand. "Our people know what to do. This isn't the first time a resident has disappeared, Russ. Folks with any kind of dementia are apt to wander, and the staff knows how to respond. There will be people searching on both sides of the building. I'll go with you." She took his hand and led him to the south door.

As they joined a group of staff people, Marjory ran up to him. "What can I do?"

Russ took the caregiver's cold, trembling hand. He knew Marjory was close to panic. "It looks as though the entire staff is looking for her. Stay cool."

As Russ tried to calm the caregiver, his own worries played giant leapfrog inside his brain. His mother had run to the highway, her body splattered across two lanes of traffic. She had drowned in the estuary. Fish gnawed at her lifeless body. Russ shook nightmares out of his head.

"What was she wearing, Marjory? Something bright, I hope."

She shook her head. "Just a brown dress and sweater. She might be hard to…" She stopped. "I mean, the clothes don't matter." She patted Russ's arm. "I feel terrible about this, Russ. It's my fault."

"Don't beat yourself up, Marjory. You said she was napping. You can't be a watchdog twenty-four-seven." With a wan smile, he gently pushed her toward the north group. "Go with them, and don't worry."

"Nice try, honey," Julie said. "I know you're bleeding inside." She looked out at the estuary. "I don't know how I missed seeing her leave the building." She paused. "A lecture was held in the theater next to the lobby, and when it ended, residents and guests walked out and went to the front door. She must have mingled with the crowd and left the building with them."

He and Julie walked to the south door and joined other searchers. As they approached a narrow stream in front of the salt march, Russ asked, "Should we call 911?"

"Not yet. Peter Watson, the executive director, usually waits for a few minutes."

Salt Marsh Sinners

As they hurried to the edge of the salt marsh, they heard a shout from the northbound team. He and Julie ran to the north side of the building.

Felix, who had left the garage called out, "I found a purse. It could be hers."

Russ gasped for breath, took the purse, and said, "This belongs to my mother. Where did you find it?"

"Right here."

Marjory, who had joined the north group, turned around when she heard Felix's call.

She ran to Russ and took his arm. "Your mother liked to talk about the marsh, wondering what was out there beyond the lawn."

Peter Watson checked his watch. "If she went into the estuary, we'll find her. It's low tide now. The water is only about a foot deep."

Jason, a staff member, appeared with three pairs of waders.

"These are hip-high." He sat and pulled on a pair. Russ and Felix joined him on the grass. They shoved their trouser legs into the waders as they pulled them on.

"There's a saw grass area south of the center," Jason said, "but the mangroves are more interesting. We'll walk forward together about twenty feet apart."

"I'm going back to my desk, Russ," Julie said. "If the executive director calls 911, I must be ready."

Russ nodded. "I have my cell phone. We'll keep in touch."

• • •

Julie ran back the concierge desk and was surprised to see Doris Johnson pushing her walker toward the south door. She was followed by six other walker-bound women.

"We'll take the pool area, Julie," she said. She turned to her followers. "Come on, girls. On the double."

Julie's thoughts brightened momentarily, knowing "on the double" meant walking faster than their usual pace. As she watched Doris Johnson's posse exit the lobby, her phones rang. Although her responses were meant to soothe anxious residents, she felt no inner calm. Fear mounted with each minute. Mrs. Jones could slip under a mangrove tree in the estuary, walk into a passing car on the main street in front of the center, or collapse on any stairway or hall within the center. Mrs. Jones was the proverbial needle in the center's haystack.

She answered a call from Diane Perruda. "Tell Felix I need the Bentley," Diane ordered. "I called the garage, and he didn't answer."

Julie fought anger. "Mrs. Jones is missing. Felix is helping the search teams."

"When they find her, call Felix."

The call ended as Julie stared at the ceiling. Her cell phone rang, interrupting her desire to strangle Diane Perruda.

"We're in the estuary," Russ said. "It's slow going. I can see Jason and Felix on either side of me. Any news from the lobby?"

"Mrs. Johnson organized a pool search. I haven't seen the parking lot people. I'll call when they return."

• • •

Russ walked carefully into the salt marsh, feeling his way around tree roots, and was reassured to see Jason and Felix twenty feet away on either side of him. The mangrove leaves were a cushion, but the water was murky, too dark to discern objects below. As he waded farther into the marsh, voices from the center faded. A blue heron, perched on a low tree branch, flapped its wings and soared into the sky, and two snowy-white egrets followed.

He walked slowly, bumping into tree limbs and roots below the surface of the brackish water.

He was only about thirty feet from shore when he saw an object wedged against a mangrove trunk. As he walked closer, he was surprised to see a weathered canoe braced against a mangrove and leaning precariously into the water. He waded quickly to the side of the canoe. He looked inside and saw his mother sprawled face up on the floor of the canoe. She leaned against the middle seat, arms at her side. Her eyes were closed, but he saw she was breathing heavily.

Relieved to know she was alive, he paused to notice her shoeless feet and her clothing—matted, torn, and wet.

"Mother!" he cried. "It's me, Russell. Can you hear me?" He reached for her hand, and she whimpered.

Felix and Jason, the staff member, had heard Russ's voice and joined him at the side of the canoe.

"Praise the Lord!" Jason shouted. "You found her!"

"And she's alive," Felix added. He studied the canoe, tilted against a mangrove trunk. "It's wedged in. We'll have to move it carefully."

The three men worked slowly as they moved the canoe away from the tree. Mrs. Jones whimpered as her body shifted to the craft's center. Russ reached into the canoe and adjusted his mother's body to a new position. Although he wanted to pick her up in his arms and carry her to the shore, he knew lifting her now could have serious aftereffects.

Jason must have read Russ's mind. "We'll push the canoe back to shore," he said. "She'll need medical attention before she's moved."

As they shoved the canoe ahead, Russ called to the executive director on the lawn. "We found her, Peter. She's alive." He looked down at his mother more closely and saw welts and bruises on her arms. "Mosquitoes?"

"Lucky it isn't snakebites," Jason said.

When they reached the shore, a man in a doctor's white coat met them. "I want to examine her," he said. "How did she get into the canoe?"

Russ smiled. "My parents spent years in canoes. They traveled the Everglades before anyone had powerboats. Both of them knew how to climb into a canoe without tipping it over." He looked down at his mother. "Some things you never forget."

The doctor leaned over the canoe and with his stethoscope, checked her heart. He gently moved her arms and legs.

"She's breathing well, but I don't like other symptoms. We need to get her to a hospital at once. She may have had a slight stroke." He pulled out his cell phone and punched in 911.

Smiling and panting staff members came to the edge of the marsh.

"So glad you found her."

"What a blessing!"

"We're so relieved she's okay."

Russ acknowledged their greetings as he sat on the grass and pulled off his waders. Felix brought towels from the garage, and as he studied his bruised legs, he remembered his struggle for survival at a roadside palmetto jungle in Everglades City. He had survived, and so would his mother.

As the search parties left with backward glances at the canoe, the doctor continued to check Mrs. Jones's heart.

Jason stayed with Russ. "The ambulance will be here in a minute. Can I get you anything?"

"No, I'm okay." He stood by the canoe, feeling helpless but relieved. They'd found her, and she was alive.

Russ heard sirens and watched as two EMTs ran to the edge of the marsh. With the doctor's help, they lifted Mrs. Jones onto a stretcher and carried her around the building to the front entrance. Russ and Jason followed and watched as Mrs. Jones was moved into the ambulance. Russ heard soft moans, each a welcome indication of life.

"I'll follow you to the hospital," he said to the driver. He ran back to the lobby and saw Julie surrounded by residents who had worried, expected the worst, and were anxious to share their concerns.

"I'm going to the hospital," Russ called over the residents' heads.

Salt Marsh Sinners

He ran to his car as the ambulance left the center. He followed closely and parked at the hospital's emergency entrance. As his mother's stretcher was lowered and moved inside, Russ stayed with the EMTs until they moved her into the intensive care unit. He watched the hospital staff as emergency procedures were carried out and at last was able to sit by his mother's side. Now he was no longer a key player, only a caring member of the audience.

• • •

Julie watched the ambulance pull away and heard its siren fading in the distance. The residents had left the lobby, and the phone was quiet. When her noon replacement arrived, she knew it was lunchtime. With a ham and cheese and a soda from the deli, she walked around the building toward a gazebo on the north side where she'd seen Russ and Jason with the canoe. She was surprised to see Jason and another staff member moving the canoe toward the garage. Another employee carried two oars.

"Where are you taking it?" she asked.

"To the dumpster," Jason said.

Julie paused and thought about Russ and his involvement in Frank Perruda's murder. "Wait," she said. "Russell Jones might want to examine it. Can you leave it in the garage until he returns from the hospital?"

"Sure," Jason replied. "We just need to remove it before someone trips or tries to take it back into the water."

She watched as the men carried the canoe to the garage, where Felix met them and gestured to a far corner. Satisfied, Julie found an empty table in the gazebo. She wanted to call Russ but good sense prevailed. He'd be busy at the hospital.

She finished her lunch and returned to the lobby. Mrs. Johnson sat with a young man who carried a notebook and iPhone. "This is my grandson, Trevor. He's a *Naples Daily News* reporter," she said with pride.

Trevor stood. "I covered Frank Perruda's murder here, so they sent me to do a story on Mrs. Jones. I've talked to the executive director, and I'd like to ask you some questions."

"Of course." Julie answered phone calls and gave directions to guests as she answered the reporter's questions. Did she know Mrs. Jones? Where was the caregiver when she disappeared? Did anyone suspect foul play? At the last question, Julie smiled. Mrs. Jones's disappearance would have been front-page news if she'd been attacked by a python or a drug-raged prison escapee. Given the facts, Mrs. Jones might possibly make page six in the second section.

"Sorry, Mr. Johnson," Julie said. "This isn't sensational."

Johnson laughed. "Better luck next time," he said as he pocketed his iPhone. He kissed his grandmother and whistled as he left the building.

"He's such a sweet boy," Mrs. Johnson said. "Just like his father."

"Your son?"

Mrs. Johnson nodded. "And he married a lovely girl." She sighed. "I wish they lived here. It's a long trip to their home in Honolulu." She laughed. "I can't swim that far."

"I'll bet you do laps in our pool."

Mrs. Johnson laughed. "When there's time. I like to go after dinner sometimes when there's no one around. I hate bumping into my friends. It's bad press." She paused. "Now I sound just like Trevor."

She pushed her walker to an elevator, and Julie studied her computer. Life at Rosewood center had returned to its normal routine.

•••

Russ Jones watched "normal routine" at the intensive care unit where his mother lay on a bed surrounded by machines and plastic bags suspended by tall, moveable poles. Hospital staff came, went, listened, probed, punctured, and manipulated monitors and machines. The patient mumbled a few garbled words, and when she smiled at Russ and squeezed his hand, tears of relief rolled down his cheeks.

An hour later a doctor appeared and motioned to Russ. They walked to a desk by the nurse's station, and as he motioned Russ to a seat, he put on his glasses and studied his chart.

"Your mother survived, Mr. Jones, but she has had a stroke. You may have noticed the right side of her mouth isn't working well."

Russ nodded. "I'm not surprised."

"Our people did everything possible and as soon as they could, so she's better than expected. Time will tell how much damage she's experienced. Medication will improve her condition, but we can't promise miracles."

"I understand. You know she has Alzheimer's on top of this." He shook his head. "I wonder what the future holds for her."

"God knows, and He won't tell." He smiled at Russ. "I wish I had better news or a magic wand." He stood. "We'll move her to a private room tonight and keep her here for two or three days. You can leave now and be assured she's comfortable and getting good care."

Russ thanked the doctor and returned to his mother's bed. To the nurse he said, "I'm leaving now, but I'll be back tonight. I'll find her if she's been moved."

He kissed his mother's forehead and drove back to Rosewood Center. As he opened the front door, he checked his watch and knew it was Julie's quitting time.

"We'll celebrate with dinner," he said. "Mom will be moved to a room tonight, and there's nothing more I can do."

Conversation was stilted as both Julie and Russ silently relived their agonies, she at her home with Jim Perruda and Heidi, he in the estuary with his mother in a beached canoe. As they finished a dessert coffee, Julie said, "I think I can stay alone tonight, honey. You can go back to your mother's apartment and get some sleep."

Russ nodded. "You're right. I'm beat, and I still have work to do. I'll be glad when my new furniture is delivered. It's hard to stay in Mom's apartment now."

"I understand. The place must feel so empty."

"Yes. I didn't make a plane reservation for this afternoon, and now I don't know when I can get back to work."

He drove to the garage at the center and left Julie at her car. "I'll see you tomorrow. I'll be at the hospital early in the morning. I hope we can have lunch."

"I'd like that. We could pick up sandwiches at the deli and eat at the gazebo." She paused. "The canoe is stored here. You may want to examine it before it's hauled to recycling."

Russ brightened. "I want to check it. The canoe looked like it had been there for weeks. Maybe it's involved in Frank Perruda's murder. That's a long shot, but right now the short ones are useless."

Sleep was welcome and dreamless. The next morning he found cereal and coffee and drove to the hospital before eight o'clock. At the desk he was given his mother's room number. He was relieved, knowing she was no longer in ICU.

"Come in," a nurse said as he opened her door. "She's having breakfast."

With effort Russ smiled and took his mother's hand. She wasn't the one he knew, this worn, wrinkled, bedridden person. Her hair was combed, but her face was almost disfigured. Her left lower lip sagged, and her cheeks looked as though they had sunk to the bone. Her eyes were red and unfocused.

The nurse must have recognized his disbelief. "She's endured real trauma, Mr. Jones. Shock is terrifying, and at her age, it shows."

Russ nodded. "I hope she knows me."

"She will. Give her time."

The nurse left with a breakfast tray, and Russ settled into a chair by the bed. As he stroked her hand and forehead, he talked quietly about music, Julie, shorebirds, whatever came to his mind. When she dozed, he read. Had she heard him, recognized his voice? At noon he was ready to meet Julie.

He stopped at the nurses' station. "I'll be back this afternoon," he said. "If there's a change, call me."

As planned, he and Julie ate sandwiches in the gazebo. "It's quiet here," Russ said.

"A nice change from yesterday," Julie added and paused. "The canoe is in the garage."

"Good. Let's see it."

With help from Felix, Russ moved the canoe to an open area. He studied the craft carefully and was surprised to find a damp, wadded-up scarf under the bow.

"Look at this." He exclaimed. "It's my mother's."

"She must have been wearing it yesterday," Julie said.

"I don't think so, but we can ask Marjory." He spread out the fabric with his hands. "This has been in the canoe for weeks. Look at it, Julie."

"You're right. It's an Armani, and it's faded. I know that pattern."

"Is this an exclusive design?"

"No. You can find them everywhere. I always wanted one, but they're too expensive."

Russ kissed her cheek. "There's always Christmas." He looked at the scarf. "If this isn't Mother's, it could belong to the canoe's owner."

He pulled out his iPhone. "Sheriff Ryder, please." He waited and spoke again. "Jack, Russ here. I'm at Rosewood Center with a canoe that might be tied to Frank Perruda's murder." He listened and added, "It's my gut feeling. No proof. Can you come to the garage?"

"Darn," Julie said as she looked at her watch. "I have to get back, honey. Fill me in later."

They kissed, and Russ returned to study the canoe. Felix offered coffee, and the two men sat in his office with steaming mugs.

"Were you here the night Frank Perruda was killed?" Russ asked.

Felix shook his head. "I heard about it the next morning. The center was alive with rumors, police, and media people."

"You knew the Perrudas, of course."

"Yeah. Frank was a decent sort, demanding but decent." Felix snorted. "Diane the trophy wife is something else." He stared at Russ. "Yesterday when everyone was busy trying to find your mother, she calls me and wants the Bentley."

Sheriff Jack Ryder arrived and shook Russ's hand. "Glad you're still here. Life is pretty dull when you're not around."

Russ grinned. "Just helping you earn your salary, Jack." As they walked to the canoe, Russ gave him a detailed report of his mother's disappearance, finding her in the canoe, and now, finding her scarf.

"Julie recognized the design and knew it had been in the canoe long before we found my mother."

Ryder examined every inch of the canoe, inside and out. "We'll dust it for fingerprints, but I'm afraid it's futile. I'll take the scarf also." He walked with Russ to the elevator. "I'm interested because the canoe may have been involved in the killer's escape. We know he couldn't use a window on the eighteenth floor with no lanai or outside ledges. He had to have left the building somehow, eluding the police and center staff. We don't know how he did it, but the canoe might be proof he's still at large somewhere."

Russ was surprised to hear Ryder's speculations. "I know you suspect Perruda's family, but if one of them had done it, there'd be no need for a canoe."

Ryder nodded. "One of the Perrudas would have escaped in his car, conveniently left in the guest parking lot. We've questioned many people, and no one saw or heard a vehicle leave at that hour." He sighed. "We're almost at a dead end, Russ. A lie detector test can pick up the lie, but what's the truth?"

As Ryder walked to his car with Russ, he asked, "How is your mother?"

"Not well. She has Alzheimer's, and yesterday's experience triggered a stroke."

"I'm sorry. If you have time tomorrow, come for coffee."

After Russ watched the sheriff drive out of the garage, he helped Felix move the canoe to its corner. "I'm going back to the hospital," he said. "Thanks for your help and the coffee."

Russ spent the rest of the afternoon sitting with his mother, who slept, tried to speak, and slept again. When he left to have dinner with Julie, his thoughts were in a jumble of unanswered questions. Would she know him and speak his name? Would she remember her adventure in the estuary? Would she be able to live in her apartment with Marjory's help? He needed to share his apprehensions with Julie.

• • •

Sally Torrino, Frank Perruda's lover and confidante, said goodbye to her last customer at the Shear Beauty Salon on Fifth Avenue. Her phone rang.

"It's me, Sharon," the voice said. "Do you have time to see my new lamps?"

"Of course. I need a lamp for my computer room. I'll come as soon as I close the shop."

Sally smiled. A lamp and possibly dinner with her next-door neighbor. She and Sharon were busy proprietors on Fifth Avenue, offering excellent quality at reasonable prices, and as they became friends, each recommended the other to their customers.

Sally: "You'll find lovely accessories for your condo at Chez Nous."

Sharon: "Shear Beauty does excellent perms and cuts."

Sally locked her doors, activated the alarm system, and opened Sharon's back door. "I like the scent," she said as she walked to the lamp section.

"The new ones are from Mexico," Sharon said. She locked the front door and hung a Closed sign. "I like the animals."

Sally laughed. "The iguana is priceless, and the color is perfect. Wrap it for me."

She followed Sharon to the back room and lit a cigarette. "I was in my back room when the truck arrived," Sally said. "I saw the lady with a cane."

"That was Cynthia Frost. She's one of my customers, lives at Rosewood Center, and spends money."

Sally stared at Sharon. "I knew someone at the center. Frank Perruda. He owned the furniture store." She leaned against the wrapping table. "He was my friend, and he was killed."

"I read about it in the paper. I wonder if Cynthia knew him." She finished wrapping the lamp. "I miss my helper, Tomas, and I'm upset because he never called to say he wouldn't be back."

Sally nodded. "It's hard to get reliable help." She snuffed out her cigarette and wrote a check. "I'll take the lamp to my car and meet you at our favorite restaurant."

As Sally drove to the wharf, she thought about her last night with Frank Perruda. He hadn't lost his ability to send her into orbit and, as they lay together, sweating and panting, he massaged her breasts and asked her to keep his secrets. They shared a bottle of merlot together before he left with promises to call the following week. Because Sally knew his information was important to him, she transcribed everything he'd said into a notebook. With the Mexican lamp stowed in her trunk, delivered by a woman who lived at Rosewood Center, she remembered Frank's secrets, and a heavy burden descended upon her shoulders. She could share her notebook with law enforcement, but they might discredit her report. She parked at a curb and lowered her rearvision mirror. The face that peered at her looked tired and too heavily made-up. Her hair, blond and curled, didn't complement a sagging chin line.

"Liar," the mirrored image shouted. "They'd never believe you. We know your type." She reentered the traffic and thought about the reactions of her family in a small town in Oklahoma. Again, disbelief and shock. Their sister, grandmother, aunt involved with a married man? Horrors!

By the time she found Sharon's wharf-side table, Sally knew her notebook and her memories must remain silent.

• • •

Jim Perruda was escorted from his prison cell at the county jail by a policewoman who carried his belongings in a plastic bag. She stayed with him as he signed out and walked with him to a waiting cab.

"Good luck, Mr. Perruda," she said and waved as the cab drove away.

Jim lay back on the seat and closed his eyes. Free at last, he thought. No more prison food, bars at the door and window, prison personnel on patrol duty. He especially hated the sounds that filled his nights with fear and torment, sounds of men fighting off hidden demons, cursing, pleading. He paid the cab driver and ran to Luna de Ciel's front entrance. It was good to be home.

Laura met him at the door with a cup of coffee and a newspaper. "Welcome home," she said. Flat tones, no smile.

"Thanks." Jim took his coffee and suitcase to the guest bedroom. This wasn't the home he remembered, but it wasn't prison either. He followed Laura to the kitchen, and as he accepted a coffee refill, he noticed her hand shook.

He sat down slowly, sipped his coffee, and chose his words with care. "I know I made a mess for both of us, and I'm sorry. What else can I say? That it won't happen again? That I wish I were dead? Tell me what you want to hear."

Laura stood and stared at the refrigerator. "I don't want to hear excuses, guilt trips, explanations. There are no excuses for what you did, Jim." She turned and faced him. "I've lived with your gambling addiction and Atlantic City, but I didn't expect drugs and rape."

Jim placed both hands over his ears and leaned on the table. His words came between sobs. "You're right. There are no excuses." He raised his head and looked at his wife as tears made wet paths down his cheeks. "What can I say?"

"Nothing now. You'll appear in court again and accept whatever the judge decides. I won't be with you." She left the kitchen and called from the doorway. "You can take your things and move to Tony's condo on the beach. I don't know how long he'll be in Minneapolis."

Jim ran to the doorway and took her arm. "Why is he in Minneapolis? I was really upset when he didn't come to my hearing. He said he'd be there."

"Emma was badly injured in an automobile accident. He flew there before your arraignment."

"Why didn't he call?"

"Maybe he didn't know how to reach you. He called Carla and me."

Jim shook his head. "I was furious when he didn't show. Now I understand. Is Emma all right?"

"We don't know. He hasn't called. His extra condo key is on my desk." Laura picked up her briefcase. "I have an appointment to show a house. Please leave before I get home." She closed the door behind her.

Jim walked back to the kitchen. As he poured another cup of coffee, his cell phone rang.

"Jim, this is Mark Holtz. The judge had a cancellation. Can you be in court at nine o'clock tomorrow morning?"

"I'll be there. Maybe they'll return my bail money."

Holtz laughed. "That's a minor detail, Jim. I'll discuss your case with the state's attorney this afternoon. We might arrange a plea bargain, but don't expect miracles. Possession of a controlled substance is a felony, and we haven't heard from Julie Rogers. If she's changed her mind and is pressing charges, you could be in serious trouble."

"I have enough trouble right now, Mark. I don't need any more. I'll be there at nine o'clock."

Jim went to the bedroom and threw clothes and toiletries into a suitcase. He locked the front door behind him and considered throwing his key into the garbage chute, but hope springs eternal, he thought. Maybe Laura would remember the good times and change her mind.

Tony's condo displayed signs of a quick exit—an unmade bed, dresser drawers and closet doors open. In the kitchen a coffeepot sputtered on its warming pad. Jim removed the pot and checked the refrigerator. He found lunch meat and milk, made a sandwich, went to the lanai, and stared out at the Gulf. Because sitting was still agony, he cursed the Saint Bernard and stretched out on a chaise.

He answered his cell phone and smiled when he heard Carla's voice. "How's my wounded brother?" she asked.

Jim heard a giggle and lost his smile. "It wasn't funny, my dear sister," he snapped. "I can't sit. I went to the hospital and to jail."

"I know," Carla said, "and I'm sorry. Laura told us what happened. She's angry, and I don't blame her. What are you going to do?"

"I don't know. I'm at Tony's condo." He paused. "Have you heard from him?"

"He called this morning. Emma is alive but has serious injuries. Tony informed police headquarters and told them he wasn't leaving Minneapolis. They'd have to drag him back to Naples."

"Doyle and O'Hara might hop on a plane and do it. They don't like us."

"Why should they, Jim? My husband has told me about your meetings at police headquarters. You've refused to answer their questions, and Tony and Phil haven't said exactly where they were the night my dad was killed."

"I know, and I have to be in court at nine o'clock tomorrow morning." He was silent and finally spoke. "Will you come to the courthouse, Carla? I need family support."

"If you need me, I'll be there."

• • •

Carla Perruda Stevens, Frank Perruda's youngest child, sat in front of the TV in the condo she and Phil had occupied ever since her husband and her brother had argued. She knew Phil would never accuse Tony of killing his father. Maybe the cops were desperate, hoping to find the killer with a false accusation. It made sense, but Phil didn't accept her explanation.

"You watch too many TV crime programs," he told her. "Your brother is a liar, and I hope I never have to see him again."

Carla bit her lower lip and frowned as she thought about the fears that disturbed her sleep at night and stirred up daytime suspicions. It started the day she received Mark Holtz's letter regarding her father's proposed will change. She'd discussed it with Phil and couldn't forget his words "*He'll have to be stopped.*" Tony's proposal after dinner at Jim's condo cemented those fears, drove them into her brain with fierceness. Did Phil draw the spade king, and did he follow through with its intended result?

Her father was dead, smothered in his own bed. Visions of his last terrifying struggle to breathe haunted her. Were her husband's hands on the pillow, that instrument of death? Phil had killed in a boxing match. Could he do it again? Although her love for Phil was tarnished, she maintained a cheerful façade. The children must never know of her tortured anxiety. Her trip to be with them in Boston had been a welcome relief. She missed them and considered another visit. How long Phil would be detained in Naples was anyone's guess.

There were plusses. Her speech impediment had miraculously disappeared, a joyous event even though it occurred at her father's interment, and her visit with Laura following the reading of the will had deepened her friendship with her sister-in-law. But the plusses didn't outweigh the worry and anguish.

Now she had added another jab with the knife of unspoken terror. Jim wanted family support at his hearing. She had seen signs of desperation in his eyes, and after hearing Laura's report, she knew he suffered, alone and powerless.

Although Jim hadn't given details regarding his appearance in court, Carla expected a trial of sorts, perhaps with a jury and press coverage. The next morning she was relieved to find Jim alone in the courtroom with Mark Holtz and another man. She sat behind Jim and smiled when he turned and took her hand.

"Who is he?" she whispered, nodding to the stranger.

"He's the state's attorney. He met with Mark yesterday."

The men stood when the judge entered, and Holtz approached the bench.

"Your client has posted bond," the judge said. "His cashier's check can be returned after this hearing." He looked at Jim. "I have reviewed your case, Mr. Perruda, and if the state's attorney agrees, I will not recommend a jury trial. You have a clean record, and the cocaine in your possession was for your own use." He turned to the state's attorney. "Is that agreeable?"

The state's attorney nodded. "I agree with your decision, Your Honor."

Before Jim was able to breathe normally, the judge added, "After a thorough review of your case, I'm ordering six weeks at a rehab center. Your presence will be monitored."

Jim stood, and the judge continued. "You are free to go, but I warn you to avoid any further trouble with the law."

Carla left her seat and noticed Jim shook his head when he spoke to his lawyer. "I understood his instructions," Jim said. "He must know about my pleading the Fifth at headquarters."

Carla put her hand on Jim's shoulder. "I hope the police have given up and there won't be any more interrogations. Phil and I want to go home."

Jim nodded. "Let's have coffee." He shook Holtz's hand. "Thanks, Mark. You saved me."

Holtz smiled. "Stay clean, Jim." He took his briefcase and left the courtroom.

Carla followed Jim's car to a bookstore and punched in Phil's phone number. After a brief report of the court proceedings, she said, "I want to go home, Phil. I can't help you, and the kids need me."

"I agree. I'll make travel arrangements."

Coffee with her brother reinforced Carla's decision. Jim's hand shook as he reached for his coffee, and he looked around the area as though he was being watched. She wasn't surprised when he told her about his move to Tony's condo.

"Go to rehab, Jim. Get your life back together." Silently she added, "And stay away from Rita." Damn, she thought, wishing Laura hadn't told her about Atlantic City. She had enough worries about Phil in Naples and the children in Boston. And what if the stuttering returned?

She finished her coffee. "I'm flying home, Jim. Please follow the judge's orders."

As they walked to their cars, Jim said, "I don't know what will happen to my marriage, the business, or me. Dad's death has changed my life." He studied his sister. "Yours too, Carla. You were always the quiet, meek one. You avoided Dad's beatings by hiding in the basement, and you never said much because of the stuttering." He hugged her, stepped back, and lifted her chin.

"You're a fine woman, Carla. You're strong. You know what has to be done, and you do it. I'm proud to be your brother."

Carla wiped her eyes with a tissue and looked up at her brother. "I think our family is being tested. Let's hope we all don't fail the exam."

She went to her car and sat in the driver's seat. She leaned back and closed her eyes. Jim had said she was strong, and the word tugged at her mind. Strong? She put her head on the wheel and moaned as a flood of memory washed over her. She was a child again, lying in her bed. Daddy would come again. She heard his voice whispering, "I want my baby tonight" as he moved closer. Carla shuddered and beads of sweat appeared on her forehead. Waves of guilt, fear and dread washed over her. "No!" she whispered. "No, please."

"Are you all right?" A woman rapped on her window. Carla sat up and returned to reality.

"Yes, I'm okay. I just met my brother."

The woman nodded and moved away. Carla breathed deeply. Her vision shocked and frightened her. She lay back against the seat and sobbed. A past horror had suddenly emerged. Denial ,confusion, agony, all there as she remembered being a child again, afraid and alone, a child who huddled in the basement with her dolls, crying silently, hoping no one would hear. A child again, fearing the night.

She sobbed again, her body shaking. She looked at her hands that trembled against the steering wheel. A memory had thrust itself into her entire being, a vision she had pushed away, too terrible to reappear. She sat up and steadied her hands. Why now, she wondered. As she recalled the events leading to her meeting with Jim, understanding and acceptance cleared her mind. The plan to murder her father, the interment storm, Jim's actions and her constant worry about Phil's innocence or guilt. Weeks of torment had led to another time of anguish.

She started the car and thought again about Jim's praise. "You're strong," he had said. She doubted at first but now realized that, yes, she was strong. She had survived.

She drove back to the condo and found a note from her husband. "I got flight reservations for you and am at the bowling alley." She packed and prepared some quick, easy meals for Phil. When he returned, he gave her the itinerary and boarding pass.

"This is a one-way ticket," he said. "I don't know how long I'll be here, but the kids need you." He paused. "How was the trial?"

"The judge released him and ordered six weeks of rehab. Jim's in bad shape and needs help."

"I can't help him, Carla. I can't help Tony, and nobody can help me. We're like three separate islands." He sat and stared at the ceiling. "Everything's changed since that dinner at Jim's condo." He looked at Carla. "Our relationship isn't the same either, is it?"

"How could it be? You agreed to kill my dad, Phil. I've tried, but I can't forget it."

Phil nodded. "I can't forget it either. I'm glad you'll be home with the kids. The truth will come out eventually, and it will be a relief for all of us."

Carla nodded and went to the bedroom. Phil was right. They were all islands, she thought, stranded with no means of communication. When would a ship come along and rescue them, and who would be on that ship? Three spouses? Law enforcement? Carla smiled. She knew the answer. The name of the ship, painted broadly on its side, would read *Truth*.

CHAPTER FIFTEEN

Cynthia Frost lounged on a chaise in her lanai and watched the sunset. She sipped a scotch and thought about her next operation. The lamp shipment from Mexico had crossed the border with no detection, but removing the drugs from the chandelier pendants had been a slow process, and retrieving the packets of cocaine sewn into the shades had been tedious and time-consuming. Luckily, she had talent with a needle. She had worked with Frank Perruda into the early-morning hours repairing the damage needed to uncover hidden caches of drugs inside upholstered furniture.

Damn Frank, she thought. Why did he get himself killed just when their operation was such a success? And who killed him? Probably his wife. Maybe his kids. She sat up and stared at the horizon. Yes! She remembered a conversation the week before he died, something like, "I'm going to build a university. The kids don't need the money." One of them had done him in before he could change his will. Of course she didn't know them, but the plot was obvious. She hoped the police were smart enough to find the killer. Cops! She snorted. A bunch of incompetents. They were the same all over.

She called catering service and ordered dinner. Eating with other women in the dining room was a total bore as they chatted about bridge and their grandchildren. She smiled as she considered a possible conversation.

"What do you do, Mrs. Frost?"

"I'm a drug dealer."

Chairs tip over, wineglasses smash, ladies faint.

She called Felix on his burn phone, knowing the phone and all conversations would be destroyed. "Did you take care of the kid?"

"He won't be a problem. I do my work carefully."

"I'll need a new driver. Who was Frank's driver? He wouldn't tell me."

"He didn't want me to know either. He said the less I knew, the better it would be for me."

"Okay, so now I have to find another. I don't want to use Edilia. She might get pregnant again." She paused. "I'm also considering a different transportation method. Maybe by air."

"Border patrols are getting wiser. It might be possible to fly a small seaplane into the Everglades. I've heard rumors."

"I'll talk to my buyers. They know people."

"Call if you need me," Felix said. "I was busy yesterday looking for an old lady with Alzheimer's who disappeared. We found her in the estuary."

"Was she alive?"

"Barely. We found her inside an old canoe. Don't know how long the canoe had been there."

"It probably belonged to a tourist from Omaha who didn't know how to paddle. He must have jumped out and waded back to shore."

Cynthia dismissed Felix's report, sat in her lanai, and considered delivery from Mexico by air. Possibilities multiplied as she watched the setting sun.

• • •

Dreams were nightmares for Tomas Fuentes as he dozed in the bus's rear seat. His trip from Fort Myers, Florida, to St. Louis, Missouri, was a death march through hell. He had rationed the contents of his packet of cocaine, hoping to ward off symptoms of total withdrawal, but the hours were filled with mental and physical anguish. He remembered every moment in Felix's car, the gun, the intent to kill as they confronted each other. Escape was impossible. Felix had given him a choice: stay in Naples and die, or go to St. Louis and live. Now he faced new surroundings with strangers who might or might not accept him.

He shivered in his T-shirt and shorts as he staggered out of the bus at his final destination. Clutching his meager Atlanta purchases, he walked two steps and bumped into someone. He looked up at a tall black man dressed casually but neatly in chinos and a heavy gray jacket.

"Are you Tomas Fuentes?"

Tomas nodded before he fell into the man's outstretched arms. He heard a soft chuckle. "We're glad you're here. I'm Leroy," the man said and led him to a minivan. Tomas fell asleep next to the driver and awakened when the van stopped in front of a two-story, white-shingled building. A sign on the front lawn read "Hope Springs Manor."

Tomas took his belongings and with chattering teeth, said, "I'm cold."

The man laughed. "It's not Florida. You'll need warm clothes."

"I fell asleep. It was a hell of a trip." He straightened up, brushed back his long black hair, and looked at the house. "Nice," he said. "I'm expected?"

"Felix Schmidt in Naples, Florida, called, said he was worried, thought you might not make it."

"No choice."

Leroy led him into a reception room, where a woman greeted him from her desk. "Welcome," she said and gave him a clipboard. "If you're not too tired, please fill these out. Henry Schmidt, the director, is waiting to see you."

His meeting with the director was brief but cordial as he listened to schedules and activities. "You're not ready for this yet, Tomas," Schmidt said. "When was your last fix?"

"Monday night, about ten o'clock."

Schmidt nodded. "You have to dry out if you want to stay here. We have a detox section in our small hospital with a staff trained for this duty." He studied Tomas. "Are you willing to go through the process? If not, you'd better leave now."

Tomas looked at his hands. Because they shook, he stuffed them in his pockets. He thought about the night with Felix, his nights with Edilia, his nights when he couldn't find cocaine, the torture of even a brief withdrawal. Did he want to endure programmed torture? Hell, he told himself, what else could he do? He remembered Uncle Jose's advice, "Get the monkey off your back." Maybe this was the time. He hadn't thought much about God. Now he wondered about divine intervention. The threat of death by a guy whose cousin ran a rehab center? It had to be more than coincidence.

Tears fell as Tomas nodded. "I can do it, Mr. Schmidt. I'm ready." He breathed a gut-busting sigh.

Schmidt stood and offered his hand. Tomas grasped the director's hand, a hand that might pull him up out of the quicksand of drug use.

"The worst is over because you've made a decision," Schmidt said, "You know it won't be easy, but once you're no longer under a doctor's care, you'll be back with us." He smiled wanly and shook his head. "The road ahead will be filled with bumps, ruts, and detours. You're the driver, Tomas. We can give you a road map, a good vehicle, and tools to keep it running, but the rest is up to you."

Tomas nodded and studied the carpet under his feet. "My uncle did it and says I can." He looked up at the director. "He and your cousin Felix sent me here. I'm ready."

"You'll have a nice room, and you can stay there tonight before you go to detox."

Tomas thanked the director and followed Leroy to the dormitory area. "You have a bedroom with a nice view," Leroy said. "The bathrooms are down the hall." He opened a door and gave Tomas a key.

Tomas sat on the bed and studied his living quarters. The room was clean and furnished with a dresser, nightstand, reading lamp, and a lounge chair. A chintz-curtained window offered a view of leafless trees and clumps of dead flowers drooping in front of a denuded cornfield. Winter drab, Tomas thought. No palm trees, green grass, and red bougainvillea. Flowers reminded him of Edilia, red lips, and a special scent. Would she wonder why he hadn't called? Would she miss him? He wanted to use his mobile, but the promise he'd made to Felix was stronger than a phone call. He scratched his head, wondering why Felix hadn't confiscated his mobile. Pointless, of course. Phones were available anywhere. He lay back on the bed and closed his eyes. A nap before dinner might calm his jitters. Seconds later he was asleep.

• • •

In Minneapolis, Tony Perruda sat beside Emma's bed at Fairview Southdale Hospital. Accompanied by IV bottles, a heart monitor, and two nurses, she had been moved out of ICU to a private room. He checked his watch. Ten hours had passed since Dr. Chambers replaced Tony's idle and boring interlude as a murder suspect in Naples, Florida, with hours of nail-biting anguish. An aide brought dinner on a tray, a waste of food and effort. Emma was semiconscious, and Tony's appetite had vanished in Naples.

Emma moaned, and Tony caressed her forehead between her bandaged hairline and her swollen eyes. "It's okay, honey. I'm here," he whispered.

She nodded and mumbled words he couldn't understand. Strange, he thought, how a slight nod and two or three garbled sounds could engender his high-octane delight and relief. An extra cause for rejoicing was her half smile, off to one side between swollen and battered cheekbones. A nurse brought chipped ice and spooned it into her mouth.

"Mm," Emma whispered.

Their two daughters rushed into the room and embraced their father. Tony smiled. "Your mom's better." Silently, he worried about internal bleeding, bones that might not heal.

As the girls hovered over their mother, Tony's cell phone rang. "Mr. Perruda, this is Sheriff Ryder. When are you returning to Naples?"

He paced the floor. "I don't know. My wife's critical. She may have a concussion and internal injuries. She has a broken pelvis, shoulder, and ankle." He glared at the phone, hoping Ryder understood his emotions. "I don't give a damn about my dad's murder right now. I didn't kill him, and I don't know who did. Can't you leave me alone?"

"We each have a job to do, and sometimes they conflict." The sheriff gave a massive sigh. "I could get extradition orders and bring you back, but your situation doesn't warrant legal action." Another sigh. "I hope your wife improves and you'll be back as soon as possible."

The call ended, and Tony's sighs echoed those of Sheriff Ryder. Emma's recovery was foremost on his mind. Nothing else mattered.

"Are you going back to Naples?" Stephanie asked.

"Not yet. I need to be here with your mom." As Tony walked to her bed, Dr. Chambers knocked and entered. "We have some test results, and they look good," he said. "She has a slight concussion, not severe enough to postpone surgery. I want to repair bone damage, and we have a surgical team ready to operate. We'll do her shoulder and ankle now." He gave Tony a clipboard. "Please fill out these forms."

Four hours later Emma was back in her room. Her right ankle was casted and elevated in a metal frame. A sling and cast protected her left shoulder. A nurse and an aide, dressed in operating room scrubs, smiled at Tony and moved Emma onto her bed.

"We'll do her pelvic area in the morning," Dr. Chambers said. "X-rays indicate clean breaks."

"More than one?" Tony asked.

"Yes, but operable. You might as well go home and sleep. Your wife is sedated and will be carefully monitored all night."

Tony nodded. "Thanks. It's been a tough day for us. You have my phone numbers."

He and the girls found a quiet restaurant and soft beds at home. Tony dismissed Ryder's call and, although his worries about Emma were intense, exhaustion induced peaceful sleep.

He awoke the next morning refreshed and ready to cope with anything, everything Emma needed in her recovery.

• • •

In Naples, Russ Jones awoke in his mother's guest room, looked at a bedside clock, and phoned Julie. "Hi, sweets. It's seven o'clock. Are you up?"

"I've already made coffee. I missed you, and…" She laughed. "I missed Heidi too, but I slept well. Lunch?"

"Of course. I'm going to work on agency business this morning. When I called to report my mother's disappearance, they sent casework and gave me time off. I'll see you at noon."

Russ was deep into a drug raid in Alaska when the doorbell rang. "I'm Edilia," the young Latino woman said as she pushed her cleaning cart into the apartment.

Russ laughed. "I don't have my mother's cleaning schedule, but come in. Coffee?"

"I haven't time. Our assignments are made out for us. I was gone for a few days, so I'm making up time."

"I hope you had a nice vacation."

Edilia shook her head. "It's a long story. I had to drive a truck to Texas, and I was sick." She went to the kitchen and began to wipe counter tops. "Anything special?" she asked.

"Just the usual. I'm not here often. You can see what needs to be done."

He returned to his laptop as Edilia did her work. Patiently he lifted his feet as she vacuumed the carpet and was startled when he saw her studying his laptop. He quickly covered his work.

Edilia smiled. "I didn't mean to snoop, Mr. Jones. You just looked so serious."

"I help people in my work, and it is serious."

Edilia turned off the vacuum. "I shouldn't bother you, but…" She began to cry.

Embarrassed by the girl's tears, Russ gave her a tissue. "Can I help?"

"Probably not." She sniffed. "It's personal. My boyfriend has disappeared."

Russ shook his head. "That's a shame. My mother disappeared too. We found her in the estuary."

"Is she all right?"

"I think so, but she's old and has Alzheimer's."

"My boyfriend, Tomas, is only eighteen, and he's gone."

Something inside, a gut feeling, nothing that made any sense, nudged him. "Sit down and tell me about it."

Edilia sat and wiped her eyes. "He's gone. I called his uncle, Jose Fuentes, and he didn't know either."

Russ stared at Edilia. "If your uncle lives in Golden Gate, I may know him."

Edilia nodded. "Jose told me he'd seen Tomas last week. I shouldn't tell you this, but Tomas takes drugs sometimes, and his uncle tries to help him."

Russ hid his expression that read "Eureka" in bold type. "I may be able to help you, but I need details. Can you come back after work?"

Edilia nodded. "I'll come." She rose and went to the guest room. Russ continued working his laptop, but his thoughts weren't focused on a drug raid in Alaska.

He met Julie at her desk as the clock's hands met at twelve. "I need a favor after lunch," he said in a hushed voice. She nodded and took her purse as Rosita, her replacement, arrived.

During lunch at the Trail Café, he told her about meeting Edilia. "She's worried because her boyfriend, Tomas Fuentes, is missing. I think I interviewed his uncle who did drugs."

"It's a small world," Julie said. "I've seen Edilia. What do you want to know about her?"

"Anything that might involve drugs. She said she took time off and drove to Texas. It might be a lead." He took Julie's hand. "Maybe you could talk to the woman who supervises the cleaning staff. I have to keep my identity as invisible as possible."

She stared at him. "You want me to involve Shirley Green in your case? I can't do that, Russ. Shirley runs a tight ship with those young women, and they know what they tell her goes in one ear and stays there."

Russ didn't respond. He paid the bill and stood. "Let's leave. We'll talk in the car."

He parked in the garage at Rosewood Center and turned to Julie. "I don't like my job sometimes, but if I can stop drug traffic even in a small way, it's worth every effort."

"Even if it means hurting people and ruining lives? If I ask Shirley to question any of her girls, she'd refuse and maybe wonder about the girl. I'd be opening a can of worms. Shirley suspects the girl, the girl's innocent, but loses her job because Shirley doesn't want problems." Julie stared at Russ. "You want to stop drug trafficking and solve Frank Perruda's murder, and you don't care who suffers. Frank Perruda was a dirty old man, and he deserved to die."

Tears came as she continued. "I never told you, but he came on to me just before he was killed. He called, asked me to come up to the penthouse, and when I walked in, he hit on me." She glared at Russ. "I'm an employee, and he's a resident. I can't report him. Penthouse residents get special treatment."

"I'm sorry, sweets. I didn't know. Did he…"

"I broke away. He sort of apologized, but he didn't mean it." She continued. "The whole family is rotten. When Frank's son, Tony, flew in from Minneapolis, he was rude, impatient, demanding."

"I remember. He almost knocked me down. He said something like, 'Get out of my way.'"

Julie was silent, then spoke slowly. "And his other son, Jim..." More tears fell. "I won't help you. I hope you never find Frank Perruda's killer. He did the world a favor."

"How can you say that, Julie? The victim's character or behavior is none of my business. Murder is a crime. I want to find the killer and, I hope, break up the drug ring. That's my job."

"You'll have to find the killer without my help." She sobbed as she removed Russ's sapphire ring from the third finger of her right hand. "It's over. You go your way, trampling over innocent people." She pointed her finger at him. "Don't forget what your SWAT team did to Sam Kolinsky's bar. All he did was buy six bar stools, and you treated him like a common criminal, tearing up his place."

"I know, but they cleaned up the bar, and Sam wasn't mad."

"That's because he's such a nice guy. Another person would have screamed and sued."

He slumped in his seat. "I don't want the ring. It's yours, even if you never wear it."

She dropped it into a cup holder. "Thanks, but I don't want it, ever." She opened the car door "You go and find your killer, Russ. Good luck." She slammed the door behind her and ran to the elevator.

Russ sat in his car, head down. Hell, he thought, what next? His mother maybe close to death in the hospital, and now Julie was turning on him, challenging his reasons for being who he was, and what he did with his life. She would never accept his beliefs, his core values. Yeah, what next?

He left the garage, drove to the hospital, and sat in his car reliving his conversation, his confrontation, with Julie. Selling drugs is a crime, but murder is also a crime. So a criminal act is performed on a criminal. Does one crime cancel the other? His mind did handsprings in a haze of bewilderment.

As he recalled their disagreement, he knew Julie still suffered pangs of anxiety. Attempted rape takes its toll, and the trauma doesn't end the next day. Patience, Russ, he told himself. Give her time and understanding.

He left his car and went to his mother's room. Maybe his mother would have had a miraculous recovery, no stroke symptoms and, please God, no Alzheimer's. She'd be whole again. They'd travel. He'd take her to England. Reality struck with one look at the struggling old woman in her bed. Right arm flailing, she cried and moaned.

Beside the bed a nurse spoke softly and placed a wet compress on her forehead. The nurse looked up at him. "I'm sorry, but your mother has had another stroke—not severe, but she's not coherent. Maybe you can bring her back."

"I'll try." He took his mother's arm and massaged it. "Mom, I'm here. Can you hear me?"

Mrs. Jones stared at her son. "Oh, Llewellyn," she mumbled. Her next words were a jumble of sounds.

Russ shook his head. "She doesn't know me. I'll stay here, and I'll call if I need you."

"Press this buzzer if you want anything," the nurse said and left.

Russ stayed with his mother until four o'clock. Hospital staff came, performed duties, and shook their heads. He stopped at the nurse's station and gave them his card. "Call me if there's a change," he said.

When he returned to his mother's apartment, he received a call from Perruda's Fine Furnishings. "We can deliver your furniture tomorrow morning at eight thirty. Will you be there?"

"Yes. Call me when you arrive."

"We're sorry for the delay, Mr. Jones. Two items had to be back ordered."

"No problem." He smiled. Now he'd have a home again. He opened his laptop and waited for Edilia. When she arrived, he offered a soda and led her to the lanai.

"Do you mind if I take notes?" he asked. "I need help."

Edilia sighed. "I'm not much help, because I don't know what happened."

"Okay, let's start at the beginning. How long have you known the guy, and what was your relationship?"

An hour passed, and Russ learned of Tomas's three jobs, his drug addiction, and their relationship that ended in a miscarriage. "Tell me about your trip to Texas," Russ said.

"Mrs. Frost hired me and said I wasn't to tell anyone, so I made excuses to my sister. I didn't tell Mrs. Frost I was pregnant."

"I saw her one day at lunch. Does she use a cane and walk with a limp?"

Edilia nodded. "She gave me travel money, and I drove a truck to Houston, where a guy from Mexico met me."

Russ sat up and spilled his can of soda. "From Mexico? What was in the truck?"

"I don't know. I helped him move the boxes into it." She giggled. "He was cute and wanted me to stay, but I didn't feel good, and I wanted to get home."

"And then?"

"I had to stop in Beaumont, where I had a miscarriage. Nice people at the convenience store took me to the hospital, and I was there overnight. Mrs. Frost was furious because I had to pay for hospital costs and was a day late."

"You poor kid! I'm glad I don't know her."

"She gave me some money and told me not to tell anyone about the trip. I really tried, Mr. Jones, but she wasn't concerned about my miscarriage, and I was miserable."

"Did you tell Tomas?"

Edilia nodded. "He treats me like dirt sometimes, but he was so sweet about the miscarriage."

Russ patted her hand. "So what happened to the boxes you delivered?"

"I don't know. I left the truck in the garage here, and I haven't seen her. I'm working on this floor now, and I don't want to clean for her again."

Russ stood and took her hand. "Edilia, I understand why you didn't keep your trip a secret, but now I must ask you never to repeat what you've told me. I can't tell you my role in this, but your worries about Tomas could stir up more trouble. Do you still love the guy?"

She blushed. "I think so. I was mad when he asked me to have an abortion, but he didn't gloat when I told him about my miscarriage. I want him to get off drugs and finish school."

Russ ushered her to the front door. "I'm sure he's okay. If he contacts you, please call me." He scribbled two numbers. "I may be at the hospital with my mother, so use my cell number."

"Thanks for the soda. I won't tell anyone, but I sure hope you can find him soon."

Russ watched her enter the elevator, and as he closed the apartment door, he shook his head. He wanted to find Tomas also, but for different reasons. He sat down and studied his notes. A shipment from Mexico. Drugs, of course. How could he get information without disclosing his identity? Julie could have solved his problem. Women! Even though he understood her anxiety after attempted rape, he still couldn't accept her reasoning. Two unsolved murders, and the drug trade still flourished with another shipment from Mexico.

He leaned back in his chair and thought about Jeff Parker, the second victim. Frank was guilty as sin, but Jeff's only vice was eavesdropping. As he stood and paced the floor, he remembered his own trashed apartment and his encounter with the Carlson brothers. Damn Julie, he thought. If the Carlsons had killed him, she probably would have found someone else. Russ worked himself into a self-righteous rage. He too was a victim, and nobody cared.

He slept fitfully and waited for the furniture truck. Julie called to report the truck's arrival with no sign of affection. He sighed as he went to his apartment and unlocked the front door. He remembered Julie's laughter when he had purchased the Venus clock. Would she ever see it on his coffee table? He welcomed the delivery crew, who made three service elevator trips. By nine o'clock his apartment was completely furnished. He confirmed the time on Venus's navel.

He made coffee and thought about the places where Tomas had been employed. He considered the chickee hut because of its location close to the beach, where he might have hitched a ride with a tourist en route to his northern home, possibly too drunk to question a young, tattooed Latino.

He found the chickee hut nestled between two beach-front, high-rise condominiums on Vanderbilt Drive. He knew he was conspicuous in a crowd of early beach walkers and swimmers as he approached the bar in his collared white shirt, chinos, and black oxfords.

"Bloody Mary?" the bartender asked.

Russ shook his head. "I'm looking for Tomas Fuentes, who works here."

"We're looking for him too," the man said. "He never showed up for work, never called. We don't know where he is, and we don't care. Guys like that aren't worth chasing down."

"Did he pick up his last paycheck?"

The bartender scratched his head. "That's strange. The boss still owes him for his work last week. I'll bet he'll be back to collect."

"I hope you're right. Did he have any special visitors, people who might have spent extra time with him?"

"I never saw anybody. He just did his work." He chuckled. "He had a nice smile, and the younger girls in their bikinis flirted with him. Tomas would grin and go to another table."

"Did he ever talk about his family or people he knew?"

"Never. He didn't talk about himself." The bartender leaned over and spoke quietly. "It's just my hunch, but I think Tomas used drugs. He'd leave for a few minutes during his shift and come back smiling. I'd never accuse him because he was a nice kid and a good worker."

"Thanks for your help. Please don't mention my coming here." He gave the man a sheet of notepaper. "Here's my phone number. If anyone else asks you about Tomas, please call."

He left the chickee hut and traveled south to Mel's Diner. When Russ inquired about Tomas, the waitress called the manager, who motioned him to a booth and asked the waitress for coffee.

"Tomas didn't show up for work this week," the manager said, "so I can't help you."

"Did he say he was leaving?"

"These kids come and go. I can't keep track of them. Tomas was a good worker, but I kept him in the kitchen and back rooms. His tattoos and long hair would have turned off our customers. We're a family restaurant. His image didn't fit."

Russ nodded. "Did he have visitors, people who asked for him?"

"I don't think so, but I'll ask." He left the booth as a waitress brought two coffee mugs. He returned five minutes later. "I asked the folks in the kitchen. No one had ever seen him with anyone."

Russ sipped his coffee and wrote his number on a note pad. "Here's my number. If anyone asks about him, please call."

The manager frowned. "Is he in trouble? Can we help?"

"We hope he's all right, and I'll call if I need you." He paused. "This is confidential. Please don't mention my visit to anyone. Thanks for the coffee. How much?"

"It's on the house. Come back for dinner."

As Russ drove to his last lead, Chez Nous on Fifth Avenue, he considered reasons for Tomas's disappearance, and none of the reasons was pleasant. The kid did drugs and knew about Edilia's trip to Houston. What else did he know?

He parked, and as he opened the boutique's front door, he admired the store's merchandise—lamps, glassware, china, silver, items to please a connoisseur's taste. He noticed a handsome, fifty-something woman at a desk at the rear of the store and introduced himself.

"I'm Russell Jones. Are you the manager?"

The woman smiled and held out her hand. "I'm Sharon Long, and I own the shop. How can I help you?"

"This is highly confidential, Miss Long. I'm looking for Tomas Fuentes."

"He's not here, and I don't know where he is."

"Can you tell me anything about his last working day with you? I've talked to his other employers, and no one knows anything."

Sharon ran fingers through her auburn hair. "I remember it clearly. A friend brought me some new merchandise, and Tomas helped unload the truck."

Russ pulled up a chair and sat. "This is the first lead I've had. Tell me more." He punched Sharon's information into his iPad as she described the lamp and chandelier shipment.

"I don't know Mrs. Frost well. We met at a reception I attended at Rosewood Center. She knew I owned a boutique and called to ask if I could use the imports. My customers admire quality pieces from Mexico, so she brought them here. We agreed on a price, and I gave her a check." She stood. "Would you like to see them? I still have two lamps and a chandelier."

He followed her to a table and admired the lamps. Each ceramic base was a brilliantly painted figure of an animal in attack mode. The shades were black silk, lined in a gold fabric.

Russ picked up a jaguar and studied it from all angles. Drugs could be hidden in the base, he thought. "I'll buy it," he said and reached for his wallet. As he removed a credit card, he asked. "May I see a chandelier?"

Sharon led him to the rear of the store, where several chandeliers hung from the ceiling. She brought one down, and he took it to a table. The wrought-iron arms were painted a dusty green, and dark green pendants hung from each of the five branches.

"I won't buy it, but I'd like to borrow a pendant."

Sharon's quizzical glance demanded an explanation. "Let's go back to your desk," Russ said. "This is important."

They sat and exchanged details and concerns. Russ identified himself, asked for complete secrecy, and told her about Edilia's Houston trip and her relationship with Tomas. Sharon described the truck's arrival and Tomas's listening to the conversation and studying the merchandise.

"I thought his interest was strange, but I dismissed it."

He rubbed his right ear. "Who drove the truck?"

"The man. His name was Felix."

He leaned back and sighed. He remembered Felix, who'd helped find his mother and offered to store the canoe. A man of many parts, he thought, and weren't we all?

"I believe this was a drug shipment, Miss Long. I don't know how the drugs were hidden, so I'll take the lamp apart and examine the pendant." He sat up. "Did you suspect Tomas might have done drugs?"

"I thought he did. He'd leave the store for a few minutes, not often, but enough for me to ask questions."

Russ stood and put out his hand. "You've helped more than you know, Miss Long. Please don't tell anyone about our visit. Tomas could be in trouble, and I want to help."

"Mr. Jones, you've told me you're with the DEA. Now it's important that you know something about me. Sit down."

He sat, glued to her confession. "I worked for the FBI before I bought Chez Nous. I was assigned to the Identification Division building in West Virginia. I learned to keep secrets."

"That's a surprise. I was just there." He grinned. "I was with a good FBI friend who arranged our trip."

"Then you know the dungeon." Sharon smiled. "It was fascinating work until my nerves reacted. Too much tension and frustration." She leaned back. "So I bought a business in Naples, Florida, and it's tension and frustration all over again."

"But you're not chasing criminals." He stopped. "Until today." He gave her his business card. "Please call if anyone asks about

Tomas or Mrs. Frost." He shook her hand. "Two people have been killed. We don't need any more victims."

"I understand, and I'll keep my eyes and ears open."

Russ left the store and found a Starbucks coffee shop. As he sat outside with a scone and a latte, he knew he'd reached a turning point in breaking up a major drug operation in southern Florida.

CHAPTER SIXTEEN

Russ left Starbucks, returned to his car, and studied his notes. Sharon Long's information had pushed aside heavy, dark draperies of the unknown and revealed a view of infinite possibilities. Because of the Mexican connection, it was obvious Cynthia Frost had worked closely with Frank Perruda before he was killed. He still had Frank's Mexican furniture invoices, and he'd study them again. His mind took a sudden detour off the main road. Did Cynthia kill Frank? Why? Because he didn't have enough information to answer those questions, the detour made no sense. He returned to his mental highway and called Sheriff Ryder.

"Jack, I think we're about to crack the Perruda murder case. You can forget about my suspect, John Thurston. It's a woman named Cynthia Frost. I'll be at the courthouse in fifteen minutes."

When Russ opened the sheriff's door, Ryder had two mugs of steaming coffee on his desk. Ryder gave him a mug and two files, one labeled "Perruda," the other, "Parker."

"I reviewed the cases after your call," the sheriff said, "and I'm relieved you have a lead. Tell me more."

Russ told him about Sharon Long's shop, her lamp purchases from Cynthia Frost, and Tomas Fuentes's role as employee. "Can you analyze the lamp and pendant? I'm sure there'll be traces of cocaine in them."

"You'll need to send them to your DEA lab, Russ. They'll know what to do."

"Right. I'll send them this afternoon." He sipped coffee. "Another problem. Tomas is missing. I talked to his girlfriend, Edilia, who works at the center and drove Frost's truck to Houston. Fuentes got her pregnant and wanted her to have an abortion. He was probably relieved when she had a miscarriage."

Ryder shook his head. "That's tough. When did that happen?"

"On her way back from Houston. She's all right but worried about Tomas."

"Would she testify?"

"Good question. She opened up to me, but it was confidential, and I must respect her privacy. We'll need proof, Jack. This is too big to allow for mistakes."

Ryder nodded. "You might have a class-act drug bust, but that doesn't necessarily solve two murders, and they're my main concern."

Russ considered Ryder's priorities as he finished his coffee. He looked at the files. "One murder inside city limits, and one outside. What's most important?"

"Frank Perruda's. As county sheriff, I have a large area of responsibility. Parker's death is more of a local concern, and we're working with Police Chief Turner. I hope he's found more evidence."

"But the murders must be connected to the drug operation, Jack. It's all tied together."

"Possibly. So far the evidence points in that direction. Assumptions aren't enough. We need proof." Ryder leaned back in his chair. "We've batted zero with our interrogations. While you were gone, we brought Diane Perruda in again, and it was the same routine. She flirted with the men, but if one of them even touched her, she'd scream rape.'" He paused. "Her testimony is full of holes. I'm considering a phone tap, but they're hard to get. We'd need a judge's okay, and the chances are slim."

"I could help. Drugs are involved. Maybe she's working with Frost or another person."

"With DEA support, a judge might okay the tap. I'll call and report back."

"What about Frank's kids? Any changes?"

Ryder frowned. "It's even worse than zero. James was arrested for possession and attempted rape."

Russ nodded. "I know. Julie's my girl." He stopped. "She was."

Ryder picked it up. "What happened?"

"She thinks I don't care about people, that I only want a verdict. Not true, but she's convinced." He sighed and changed the subject. "What about the others?"

"Frank's son, Tony, is in Minneapolis. When his wife almost died in an auto accident, he flew home. I could go after him, but he'd give the same old testimony, and I'm tired of repeats. It's the same with Phil, the son-in-law. When Tony returns, I have another plan. We have to get a confession."

"But what if none of them is guilty?"

"My plan will pry open the truth, no matter what it is."

Russ stood. "Thanks for the coffee. After I've sent the lamp and pendant to the lab, I'll go to the hospital. My mother wandered into the estuary, had a couple of strokes, and is critical."

"I'm sorry." Ryder stood and shook his hand. "It's hard to lose a mother. I lost mine last year, and there's a gap in my life, a hollow place that can't be filled."

Russ nodded. "We'll exchange information. I'll be here for a few days with my mother."

He left Ryder's office and arrived at his mother's hospital room as a nurse was changing her IV.

"She's resting with no pain, Mr. Jones, but the doctor asked if she has a living will."

Russ's heart skipped a beat, and he frowned. "It's that bad?"

"We can't predict, but she's had a serious insult to her body and at her age, recovery is difficult." She put her hand on Mrs. Jones's forehead. "I remember her work with abused women and latchkey kids. She helped so many people. I wish we could help her."

"You're helping the only way you can, and I thank you for your concern."

After the nurse left, Russ sat by his mother's bed. "There's so much I want to tell you, Mom," he said as he stroked her hand.

He was surprised when she raised her head. "Nice boy," she mumbled.

Russ smiled. She knew him.

• • •

As Cynthia Frost finished breakfast in her Rosewood Center apartment, she considered an alternative drug-importing method. Furniture had been a success when Frank Perruda was alive, and one shipment to Sharon Long's boutique had survived, but hiding cocaine in accessories was impossible. No hiding places in belts, scents, or scarves. Purses and candles were too obvious. She remembered considering air transport, and the Everglades offered wide expanses for seaplane landings. She had once visited with an Everglades City school board member who told her of kids who picked up drugs.

"How can you keep them in school when they can earn big money following a plane into the saw grass?" The board member shook her head. "We can't compete."

Cynthia picked up her cane, car keys, and purse. She'd have lunch in Everglades City. As she drove into town, she wanted to find a store or bar that catered to the locals. Tourists wouldn't have a clue. As she drove through the town, she noticed a building painted in bright orange. On the roof, a ten-foot sign, red with black letters, "Sam's Roarin' Twenties Bar and Grill." Cars and pickup trucks with Florida license plates were parked at the curb.

Cynthia parked behind a green Chevy pickup and limped into the bar. A short, stocky, bald-headed man wearing a soiled white apron leaned over the counter.

"Welcome," he said. "I'm Sam Kolinsky. What are you drinkin'?"

Salt Marsh Sinners

"Miller Lite, please." She stepped back and looked at six white, leather-upholstered bar stools with chrome legs. A coincidence?

"I like your stools," she said.

Sam laughed. "Me too. I bought them in Naples at a furniture store." He winked at her. "The cops thought I was smuggling drugs."

Cynthia smiled. "And you weren't?"

"Hell, no. I gave that up years ago."

Cynthia gave him a long look. "But you still might know about drugs around here. I know someone who's interested."

"I might locate a guy," he said. He left and wiped the far end of the bar before he returned. "If your friend wants more information, he can call me." He looked around the room. "The locals come here and know I keep my mouth shut."

Cynthia opened her purse and wrote her cell phone number. "You and my friend might do business. Here's the number."

She finished her drink, paid, and drove to the garage at Rosewood Center. When she noticed Felix at his desk, she stopped and told him about her trip to Everglades City.

"It has possibilities," Felix said. "Call Pedro in Vera Cruz. He may know someone who flies seaplanes."

"I'll call today." She smiled. "We're still in business."

• • •

Sam Kolinsky watched Cynthia Frost as she limped to the door and left the bar. A smart cookie, he thought. She had a friend who might be interested? Sam smiled. Of course, "friend" was Cynthia Frost. He knew that line. He also knew that DEA guy, Russ Jones, who should have this information. He pulled out his cell phone and punched in Russ's number.

"Russ, it's me, Sam Kolinsky. A dame named Cynthia Frost was here. My first clue was her noticing the bar stools, and when she asked about getting the stuff for a friend, I knew I had to call you."

Sam answered as Russ asked questions. "Yes, I have her car's license number." He waited as Russ copied the number. "A good-looking dame. She limped and used a cane. I'll wait for your call." Sam paused. "How's Julie?"

Sam listened to Russ's account of their argument. "Julie had a bad experience," Russ said, "and I was too wrapped up in my own frustrations."

"I'm sorry. I hope it's only temporary." Sam frowned. "You know I'm not upset about the SWAT raid, Russ. I want you to catch the bastards who peddle that stuff. I know what drugs do to people."

• • •

Diane Perruda stared at her Apple computer's twenty-one-inch screen and punched in a row of exclamation marks on the keyboard. She sat back and thought about the nights she'd spent in her bedroom alone at the computer. *"I'm going to watch TV, Frank. I don't care much for your sports programs."* Her husband, a half-crazed Boston Red Sox fan, always agreed with her decision.

Her written report of the last interrogation at police headquarters filled two pages of anger and frustration. Like all men, Doyle and O'Hara were stupid letches who hid their bestial desires under a blanket of innocence and law enforcement red tape. She printed her report and hit Save, where it would join her special file marked with only one word. *Men.*

She smiled as she printed her last experience with the male sex. Her career as a night nurse was a complete chapter filled with passion in a hospital bed and promises of undying love, followed by returns to former lives with wives, mothers, or children.

Her experiences began in middle school as a prepubescent blond child, eager to know what occurred in her parents' bedroom, with its paper-thin walls. She found answers from seniors on the high-school football team.

Diane practiced what she learned and added new positions, new movements, and new locations. She enjoyed sex but learned quickly promises made in bed were often postponed, forgotten, or intentionally broken. Although she flunked high-school English I and II, her creative instincts provided enough skill for a journal, and by the time she had nailed Frank Perruda, writing had become second nature.

As she glowered at the screen, she recalled a few of her former sex partners. Carlos, who preferred whipped cream, and Igor, twine and knots. Sadly, both Carlos and Igor returned to wives in their own countries. Wives! All of them misunderstood their husbands and were cold in bed. She thought about Larry and smiled. She'd found him on the Internet, young, unattached, with a career that matched her needs as the wife of an old, wealthy businessman. Meetings with an accountant were acceptable, and now that Frank was out of the way, she had no need for alibis.

She logged off and called his cell phone. "Are you free this afternoon?" She listened and frowned. "When?" The frown disappeared. "Tonight I'll wear something I bought just for you."

She went to her closet and chose a lilac-colored silk dress with a scalloped hem and spaghetti straps.

Bringing wine and flowers, he arrived at eight thirty. Diane brought chilled wineglasses and a bottle of Chardonnay to the lanai. The chaise accommodated two bodies, legs entwined. At nine thirty they went to her bedroom and moved together, accompanied by soft moans and wild laughter.

"Honey plum," Larry said as he stroked her breasts, "it's eleven o'clock. We need to talk business."

Diane bit his ear and laughed. "Now?"

"I have to leave soon, and this is important." He rose, pulled on his jockeys, and took papers from his briefcase. "Financially you're in such great shape that you have too much in your checking account."

"I could move it to savings."

"I have a better idea. How would you like to double that amount? You could buy a yacht, and we could sail around the world together."

Diane sat up and smiled. "How can I do that?"

Larry removed another file. "I know a company that invests in foreign operations. The president called me, said because I was such a good and trusted friend, he'd let me in on a new venture in Africa. He said it's legal and can't fail." Larry stroked her upper thigh. "What do you think?"

"I'd like a yacht. Do you have a prospectus?"

"Not yet. My friend said he'd fax one to me, but didn't have time. His company has to move fast before others learn about it. He says it's a once-in-a-lifetime opportunity."

Diane moved her hands closer and felt his erection. "Let's talk about it later."

Later was midnight. Larry dressed, and Diane found a robe. He stuffed files into his briefcase, and she followed him to her front door. "This is a great chance for us, honey plum," Larry said. "Think it over, but not too long."

Diane stroked his cheek. "How much would it cost me?"

Larry put down his briefcase and embraced her. He put his mouth to her ear and whispered, "Only fifty grand. It's a steal at that price."

"How much are you investing?"

"Seventy-five grand. We'll be in this together."

Diane smiled. "I'll call you tomorrow." She kissed him deeply. "Early tomorrow."

Larry left, and Diane went to her computer. The next morning she made some calls before phoning Larry on his cell phone. He'd asked her to use his cell, not his landline. He lived with his sister, who was too ill with diabetes to answer the phone.

"You'll meet her one day," he said.

"Good morning, sugar honey," Diane said, her raspy voice couched in a southern drawl. "I thought about your offer all night, and I've decided to take the plunge. What's money but to spend?"

"Not spend, honey plum. This is investing, and you won't be sorry."

Diane laughed. "I'll have no regrets as we sail to Rio on our yacht." She sipped coffee before she continued. "I'll have to go to the bank this morning. Will a cashier's check be all right?"

"Of course. When can I get it?"

"Come here about eleven this morning. I can't wait to see you again. Last night was magic." She giggled. "So hurry on back for a repeat."

Diane dressed in bright yellow shorts and a see-through tank top that revealed a yellow bra. She tied a yellow scarf around her blonde chignon and admired her image in the full-length bathroom mirror.

At nine o'clock she drove to her bank and obtained a cashier's check for fifty thousand dollars. No eyebrows were raised. Mrs. Perruda's deposits and withdrawals were well-known. She left the Bentley at Rosewood Center's front door, leaving instructions with the concierge.

"Tell Felix to drive it to the garage," she said and half smiled at Julie. "Parking is such a bore."

As planned Larry knocked at eleven o'clock. Diane opened the door and embraced him, her right leg positioned tightly in his crotch.

"Mm," he whispered. "You're the best." He untangled himself, sat, and opened his briefcase. "I have the papers here. Sign them, and soon you'll be cruisin' Naples Bay."

Diane detoured around the coffee table and sat next to Larry on the davenport. "Here's my check." As Larry took it, Diane stood and yelled, "Okay, guys, he's all yours!" She watched Larry's face as a happy grin became raised-eyebrow surprise and morphed into monstrous terror.

"What the hell?" he shouted as three men rushed from the den into the living room.

Before Larry could stand, escape, or strike a blow, he was handcuffed by a uniformed officer.

"Thanks, Lieutenant Callahan," Diane said. "I hadn't seen you since Frank was killed. I'm glad it's not another death, although—" She glared at Larry. "Shooting's too good for him."

The second man in civilian clothes, with Collier County Sheriff's Office badges on his sleeves, picked up a tape recorder that had been hidden behind a pile of books on the coffee table.

"Glad you turned it on, Mrs. Perruda," he said.

Diane smirked. "Detective O'Hara, that's your first decent remark after two sessions at police headquarters. I didn't know you were human."

O'Hara laughed. "You're still a suspect in your husband's murder, but this is a different scenario. You're the victim this time."

Diane smiled at the third man. "I'm glad you came, Mr. Holtz. As Frank's attorney, you'd need to know how I'm spending his money." She turned to Larry, who stood, head down, hands cuffed behind him. "You worm!" She sneered and shook her head. "You stupid worm! Did you really think I'd fall for a scam that's as old as the hills? I'm blonde, but I ain't dumb."

Callahan laughed. "Your information last night was all we needed to learn that Larry Kellogg, alias Laurence Durant, served ten years in Leavenworth for embezzlement, and now he's wanted in New Jersey with the same charge. He'll be extradited tomorrow." He paused and glared at Kellogg. "His wife, Glenda, has three children by a previous marriage. They live in Estero."

"No sister with diabetes, Larry?" Diane asked. "What other lies have you thrown at me?" Before Larry could answer, Diane continued. "Don't tell me, sugar honey. I don't need any more." She turned to O'Hara. "Will I have to testify? I'm sick of police business."

"I understand," Callahan said. "A written statement may be enough. We'll call if we need you."

Callahan and O'Hara put Larry between them and walked to the door.

Larry looked back at Diane and sneered. "Maybe you'll find somebody else to buy the yacht."

Diane watched the men as they went to the elevator. Words and sentences formed in her mind and remained unspoken. She found leftover pizza in the refrigerator, nuked it, and sat in the lanai. She sighed between bites. Another chapter formed in her brain. There was no joyous, smug "gotcha." This morning's revelations, coupled with nights of passionate hours together, produced a melancholy jumble of emotions. She looked out at the Gulf and envisioned herself aboard the yacht Larry had promised. Maybe someday she'd find someone who owned a yacht.

• • •

Two sisters-in-law in different cities and in different kinds of beds shared the same fear. "Did my husband commit murder?" Emma Perruda's hospital bed in Minneapolis was surrounded by IV poles, and Carla Stevens's bed was in Boston, surrounded by her son and daughter and four classmates.

Emma moaned as hospital staff adjusted her right shoulder splint. Tony sat by her bed and stroked her left hand. "It's okay, Emma. Your CAT scans and MRIs look good. Maybe only one more surgery."

Emma nodded and looked up as her parents entered the room.

Tony stood and shook hands. "Emma's doing well. I'll leave you with her and get coffee." Emma didn't see Tony shake his head as he left the room, and painkillers had dimmed her recollections of his lack of understanding that had plagued his relationship with Emma's parents. As a city-bred boy, he had no interest in farming. Milk came from cartons, not cows. Rain meant a canceled golf game, not much-needed crop income. Emma's parents had grudgingly accepted him, but his South Dakota visits were infrequent and awkward.

Emma acknowledged her parents' visit with a weak smile and a slow extension of her left hand. She listened and sobbed briefly as they spoke words of love and concern. Emma squeezed her mother's hand and whispered, "I'll be okay. Don't worry."

As Mr. and Mrs. Olsen stood to leave, Tony returned. Emma watched as her husband shook hands with his father-in-law and kissed Mrs. Olsen's cheek. Although Emma's time in Naples had been a nightmare of death and accusations, sleepless nights and tortuous days, she had seen a hopeful change in Tony's character. He'd been fantastic in bed and genial at breakfast. She stared at her right leg, suspended above the bed.

"Mend," she ordered. "I want to walk the beach with Tony."

• • •

Carla, at home in Boston, got up from her afternoon nap and asked her children to escort their friends to the front door. She was still tired after her Naples flight and tormented with images of a murdered father and her husband, the suspected killer.

As Carla prepared dinner, she thought about her sister-in-law, Emma, who shared her worries and now fought for her life. Life for Carla in Boston was far easier than Emma's. A smile formed. Life could be worse. She called Phil, and when she heard his voice, she pushed tortured fears aside.

"I wish I could come home," Phil said. "I asked the sheriff and was told to stay here and wait for Tony's return. He wants to meet with us again."

"Again? I'll come back if you need me. The kids are fine, and I miss you. I'm working a few hours this week at the crisis center. They help abused women and need someone to answer the phone."

The conversation ended, and as Carla filled her children's plates, she remembered her last meeting with Jim. He'd praised her, said she was strong. She wondered what strength would be needed if Phil had drawn the spade king.

• • •

"Rosewood Center. May I help you?" Julie's telephone voice hid her misery. She had returned Russ's ring because she couldn't agree with his methods. People were expendable in his fight to stop the drug trade. Spy on Edilia? Never!

As though summoned by her thoughts, a young woman approached her desk. "Mrs. Rogers, I need to see you. Are you leaving now?"

"It's five o'clock. I'm just checking out." She recognized Edilia and motioned to a quiet corner in the lobby. "Let's sit there." She noticed trepidation and fear as Edilia sat close to her.

"I talked to your friend, Mr. Jones," Edilia said.

"There are no secrets in Rosewood Center." Julie laughed. "This place is a sieve."

"I could lose my job, and I need people who will support me."

"I know you're a good worker." Julie stroked Edilia's hand. "I'll help if you need me."

"Mr. Jones is a nice man," Edilia said. "He asked me questions, and I knew he cared about what happened to me."

Julie stared at her. "He cared?"

"He wants to break up a drug ring, and I hope he can. My friend Tomas got hooked, and I hate what it's doing to him. Tomas has disappeared, and Mr. Jones wants to find him. I want to help Mr. Jones, but I need this job."

Julie took Edilia's hand. "Don't worry. I'll help you." She pulled Edilia up and hugged her. "You'll be fine. Now I have to make a call. We'll talk tomorrow." She ran to her desk and pulled out her cell phone.

• • •

Russ Jones sat by his mother's hospital bed and patted her hand. He sighed as he watched for recognition and found none. He was almost relieved to answer his cell phone. A break in his lonely vigil.

"Julie?" As he listened, his body relaxed, and a broad grin appeared. "I want to see you too. Can you come to the hospital?"

Time dragged before Julie entered the room. A welcoming embrace, a chair beside his, a threesome now. He watched as Julie stroked his mother's forehead, tears falling.

"I'm so sorry, Russ. I hoped she'd recover from her ordeal in the marsh."

Russ shook his head. "She's had another stroke. She's lost out there somewhere, really lost this time." He stood. "I can't reach her. Let's have dinner." He took Julie's hand. "I want to share good news."

Dinner at the pier was a clash of tourists' greetings and farewells, a clatter of plates and glasses, and a crush of diners as they were led to bayside tables. During after-dinner coffee Russ leaned toward Julie and told her about Edilia's visit.

"She's scared and worried, sweets. Tomas worked at the accessory shop and must have realized Edilia had transported a drug shipment from Mexico. He's disappeared."

"And Tomas knew too much? No wonder she's worried."

Russ nodded. "I sent a chandelier pendant to the lab for drug verification, and I'm sure the results will be positive." He laughed. "I also bought a table lamp. It's crazy." He sipped coffee. "There's more." He stroked Julie's hand and told her of Sam Kolinsky's call. "Everything points to Cynthia Frost. I think she worked with Frank Perruda and maybe killed him. She may have murdered Jeff Parker also. Maybe both she and Parker were looking for drugs in the bar stools. It's falling into place."

"What are you going to do?"

"Move carefully. I want Cynthia Frost arrested and alive." Russ sat back and watched pelicans as they dived into the water, plopping down, wings outspread. "We don't know the scope of her operation, Julie, but it could involve many dealers in this area. We need Frost alive."

"Will she talk?"

"Let's just say she can be persuaded."

Julie nodded. "Do you remember seeing her at the Turtle Club?"

"Vaguely. I was more interested in you."

Julie squeezed his hand. "What are you going to do?"

"Set a trap, of course. We'll need Sam. He hates the drug trade. I hate what drugs do to people, sweets. Jim Perruda was high on drugs and booze when he attacked you."

"I know, and I'm still a victim." She paused. "I'm sorry about what I said in the garage, honey. I overreacted."

"So did I, sweets. We were both too intense and not thinking clearly. I was worried about my mom and you—"

Julie finished his words. "Were still suffering from Jim's visit." She smiled. "I want my ring back, honey, and I'll never take it off again."

Russ took it out of his wallet and put it on her finger. "Thank God," he said. "I might have given it to someone else."

"Give me her name, and I'll kill her."

They laughed as they went to Russ's car. "My place or yours tonight?" Russ asked.

"Mine. We don't want to run into Cynthia Frost at Rosewood Center."

• • •

Jim Perruda sat at his desk and studied invoices and work orders. He had unlocked the back door at Perruda's Fine Furnishings at seven, knowing his last day at the store would be filled with a staff meeting and personnel changes. He turned his chair and stared at his safe that once held packets of cocaine. Those packets had started him on a downward path from a mountain built by hard work with dedicated employees. He'd reached the bottom that night at Julie's home. Could he ever climb back up?

The court had ordered six weeks of rehabilitation, and a local center had accepted his application. He looked up at the calendar. Summer would end before his release, and then? Because Laura had told him to pack up and get out, he'd obeyed and moved to Tony's condo. Following his staff meeting today, his assistant would assume Jim's duties. How much influence would a rehab patient have in the store's daily life? His life's a mess, he thought, and only he could change it. He sighed as he sorted, tossed, and filed.

When his assistant arrived, Jim, sparing details, gave him his new assignment. "I'll be back in six weeks, and you can always call me at the rehab center."

The assistant nodded. "We'll do our best. The season's winding down, and summer's not as busy."

At five thirty, Jim had completed his work. He handed a set of keys to his assistant and drove to the rehab center.

"Mr. Perruda?" The receptionist, a smiling young woman, stood and shook his hand. "We're glad you're here. That's the first step."

Jim laughed. "The court-ordered step."

The receptionist grinned. "You're not the first. The 'why' isn't important. You're here. That's what's important." She gave him an admittance form. "You can fill this out later. Dinner is being served. Will you join us?"

Suddenly Jim remembered he hadn't eaten since breakfast. "I'd like that."

As she led him to the dining room, the tension and fear eased, as though he'd dropped them off in the hall. He almost turned to see if they had materialized into sinister forms that slithered away into remote doorways far behind him.

CHAPTER SEVENTEEN

Sheriff Jack Ryder sat at his desk and stared at his calendar. More than three weeks had passed since the body of Frank Perruda had been discovered in his bed at Rosewood Center, and with each passing day, the trail grew colder. Because Perruda had planned to disinherit his three children, they were prime suspects. Ryder learned about the violence and abuse that could lead to a second generation of more violence. James and Tony Perruda could kill. Their sister, Carla, however, seemed too fragile to commit murder, but what about her husband? He'd been a boxer. Yes, he too could kill.

His last visit with Russ Jones was encouraging. Because Russ was convinced Cynthia Frost was in the drug business big-time, she could have killed both Perruda and Parker, but they had no proof. They would move carefully. He hoped Russ would learn more from Edilia.

Ryder buzzed his assistant, Arturo Lopez. "I want to review the Perruda case, Art. Please come to my office."

As Lopez entered, Ryder scratched the back of his head. "James and Tony Perruda and their brother-in-law, Phil Stevens, have been interrogated separately, and we've learned nothing. It's time to change our procedure."

"You're right, Jack. What's the plan?"

"I'm going to bring them all in together. Maybe they'll change their testimonies. It's a crap shoot, but worth a try." He looked at his calendar. "Art, contact James Perruda at the Robert Ackerman Center, Tony Perruda in Minneapolis, and Phil Stevens here in

Naples. Tell them to be at police headquarters at one o'clock Friday afternoon."

"That gives them four days. Will Tony be able to leave his wife in the hospital?"

"Ask him when you call. Let's hope she's recovering. I want all three of them here together."

• • •

Jim Perruda sat in his room at the Robert Ackerman Center and listened to Arturo Lopez's call on his cell phone. He shook his head. "They won't let me leave here. I'm stuck for another five weeks." Damn! He didn't want another session at police headquarters, but Lopez was firm, demanding, and if Tony could leave his wife in Minneapolis, Jim had no choice but to agree. He sighed.

"Okay, Lopez, I'll check with the office. I guess I can be there."

He stared out of his window and relived his nightmare that began on Tuesday, March 8, when his brother Tony had suggested the unthinkable. Why had they all agreed? He made circles on his forehead. Almost a month of worry had passed, complicated by his own stupidity that night at Julie Rogers's home. He groaned. Maybe it was time to spit it all out, tell the police about his trip to Atlantic City with Rita. He hadn't drawn the spade king, and he could prove his innocence. He paced the floor. He hated to divulge his affair with Rita, but after almost a month of lying, he was ready to let it all hang out, dirty linen, all of it.

• • •

"Next Friday?" Tony asked. "Mr. Lopez, my wife isn't critical now, but she needs me." He held his cell phone with one hand and stroked Emma's forehead with the other. He had brought flowers to her hospital room and was relieved to see a sparkle in her eyes, and her smile told him that casts, splints, and bandages were mere trifles.

Emma looked up at her husband. "You must go, Tony. I'm healing, and the girls are here."

Tony nodded, mouthed a kiss, and answered Lopez. "Okay, I'll be there." He replaced his phone and stroked Emma's left hand. "I hate to leave you, but maybe the police have found Dad's killer." He sighed. "I'll be glad when it's over."

"Yes, but you know who started it, Tony."

"My dad was a demon. He hated us. I can't forgive him even now. We deserved his inheritance, Emma. We earned it with bleeding sores. You can't imagine how we suffered."

"No, I can't. My parents loved us and taught us respect and honesty." She laughed. "They also taught us how to milk cows and harvest corn."

"I envy your happy home, but not milking or harvesting." Tony stood. "I need to reserve a flight and then pack a bag, baby. I'll see you this evening." He blew Emma a kiss at the door and ran to the elevator.

• • •

Phil Stevens held a bowling ball in his right hand and with his left hand, held his cell phone, listening to Arturo Lopez. He studied the remaining tenpin and considered his best position as he heard orders from the sheriff's department.

"Okay. If my team loses, I'll be there." He heard loud, unfamiliar Spanish words. "All right. I'll be there."

Phil pocketed his phone and stared at the tenpin. "Fall, dammit," he whispered and missed the spare. Shrugging his shoulders, he returned to his seat and glowered at his right hand. "Sorry I missed," he mumbled. It had been a bad day ever since seven thirty, when his cell phone rang. He pulled it from his pocket and answered.

Carla's voice betrayed worry and fear. "The kids just left on the bus. It's been three days since your last call. Are you all right?"

"I'm fine but lonesome. I wish you could come back soon, but the kids need you."

"I know, but our sitter's sister is in the hospital. Back surgery."

"I'm sorry about her sister, but I wish you were here."

And now he faced another trip to police headquarters. He stared at ten newly placed pins at the end of his alley and hoped he could knock all of them down with his first ball.

• • •

At two o'clock on Friday, April 8, Jim, Tony, and Phil arrived at police headquarters, each in his own car. They walked apart and followed a police officer into a larger version of the room they had all inhabited twice. Jim studied the floor. Tony turned and eyed the camera above the door. Phil looked at a microphone on the table.

The officer who admitted them left as Officer Doyle and Detective O'Hara entered. They were followed by a tall man with wavy brown hair flecked with gray. He wore a blue sport coat, chinos, white shirt, and a navy-blue tie. The man nodded to the three suspects and motioned them to chairs.

"I'm Sheriff Jack Ryder," the tall man said. "I've set up this meeting, but I'm not staying. Officer Doyle and Detective O'Hara are in charge." He stood at the door. "It's been almost a month since Frank Perruda was killed. You've been interviewed, and all of you say you're innocent. Personally, I don't believe any of your stories. Today we're going to get the truth, and I don't care how long it takes." He left, shutting the door behind him.

Jim sat and glared at the two officers. He didn't look at Tony or Phil. They were on their own, and he couldn't help them, even if he wanted to. "All right, Officer Doyle," he said, a sneer accenting each word. "What do you want?"

"Just the truth," Doyle said. He turned on the tape recorder.

Salt Marsh Sinners

Half an hour later, Jim had listened to the tapes of his interviews and read his testimonies.

"Well?" Doyle asked. "How long do you want to stay here?"

Jim looked at Tony and Phil. Four eyes were glued to the ceiling. He was angry and frustrated. He knew he hadn't killed his father, and he was tired of protecting his family. Tony had never been a real brother, never stood by him when accusations spewed out of his father's mouth. Tony was a sneaky little kid whose innocent black eyes pleaded with his father.

"Jim did it. I didn't," he'd say, and Jim would be punished. His father liked to pull the boys' pants down and hit their bare buttocks. Jim could almost feel the blows now as he sat across from his brother.

Jim also remembered Sheriff Ryder's sudden departure. He turned and looked at a large window behind him. The pane was blank, but Jim had seen enough police programs on TV to recognize a one-way window. Ryder surely was behind that window, watching and listening. Sweat poured out under his arms. He felt his face and knew that fear shone like an ominous red beacon. He couldn't remain silent any longer. It was time.

He stood and glared at Tony.

"Okay. I've had it. I didn't kill my father, and I can prove it. I lied to protect you, Tony." Jim looked at his brother-in-law. "You too, Phil, because of Carla."

Tony looked up at Jim. "So big brother is going to jump ship." He glared and beat his fist on the table. "Go ahead. Make an ass of yourself. You always were so damned self-righteous."

"I also lied, Tony, because I did make an ass of myself."

The room was silent as four men looked at Jim.

Jim sat, his elbows on the table, his head between his hands. "I didn't go to Las Vegas. I flew to Atlantic City with another woman."

Tony broke the silence with a loud guffaw. "So big, honest, clean-living brother two-timed his wife. That's a laugh, Jim. Was she a real dish?"

Jim walked around the table, shook Tony's shoulders, and shoved him to the floor. He stood over him. "Don't ever laugh at me again, Tony." He walked back to his chair. "Laura knows, and the party's over. No more lies." He looked at Officer Doyle. "You can check with the flight service here and the hotel in Atlantic City. I can even give you our fake names."

Tony got up from the floor and brushed off his pants. He walked around the table and looked down at his brother. "I won't laugh at you, Jim, but don't push me around ever again. When we were kids, you were bigger and stronger. I took a lot of abuse from you then, and I don't want any more." Tony paused and breathed deeply. "You told us where you were Friday night, so you didn't kill our dad, but you didn't talk about the cards."

Jim stared at Tony. "I thought that was our secret. Are you going to admit what you cooked up? I don't want to fight, but, damn it, Tony, this was a private family matter,"

O'Hara looked at Tony. "What about the cards?" He nodded to Doyle. "We'd like to hear it."

Jim glared at Tony. "Go ahead. I'm sure these two gentlemen will be interested in your little scheme to kill our father."

Tony went back to his chair, frowned at Jim, and looked at Doyle. "They all agreed," he said. "We all received letters from his lawyer telling us our father intended to change his will. We knew we had to do something."

Doyle studied his notes. "Diane Perruda told us her husband intended to disinherit his family and build a university. Is that correct?"

Jim nodded. "I tried to reason with my dad, but he wouldn't listen. He said we weren't entitled to anything, he'd done it all himself, and we had enough without an inheritance."

"Yes," Tony added. "I talked to him, and he didn't care. He had a penthouse and a trophy wife."

"We've questioned Mrs. Perruda and haven't ruled her out as a suspect," O'Hara said. "Now we want to hear more about your plan, Tony."

Amazed, Jim looked at his brother. Gone was Tony's bluster and pompous gestures. Jim remembered Tony as the little boy he once was, cowed by an abusive father and a big brother who had no time for him.

Tony leaned back in his chair and blew his nose. "I didn't want to do it. Nobody did, but we couldn't think of an alternative. We knew we were entitled to his money. Hell, we'd earned it, but he just got mad and wouldn't listen to us."

"So what was your plan?" Doyle asked.

"I had cards. Three kings. The one who drew the spade king would do the job. Nobody saw another's card, and I tore them up." He looked at Jim. "You said you didn't draw the spade. Is this another lie?"

"God, no," Jim said. "I'm sorry." Jim was sorry. As the older brother, he was sorry about the decision they'd made together, sorry about his anger as he left his father's penthouse for the last time, and sorry about his childhood that could never be reversed. "I didn't draw the spade, thank God. None of us wanted it."

"I know it was my idea," Tony said. "I probably should have drawn the spade." He looked at Phil. "But I didn't. I drew a heart."

"So you went to Key West," Doyle said. "We have your statements twice, and you refused to give details."

Tony sighed. "I had to lie to protect Jim and Phil. If I could prove my presence in Key West, that would leave Jim and Phil as prime suspects. I did go to Key West, and I stayed at the Bottle Inn. I have the receipts to prove it." He stood and walked around the table to Jim's chair. "I won't ever laugh at you again, big brother, and at least I didn't incriminate you."

Jim stood and put his hands on Tony's shoulders. "We've been through hell for too many years. It's time to climb out together."

Doyle stood. "I'm glad there's no more violence, but let's get on with your revelations. It's getting late, and we're nowhere. I'm still convinced one of you killed Frank Perruda." He stared at Phil. "All right, Phil. Let's hear from you."

Phil had sat in the interrogation room with his two brothers-in-law and listened to Jim's admission of adultery and Tony's pathetic response. He knew the brothers had a history of accusations, blame-shifting, and abuse. Carla had told him about the threats and beatings, and he worried about his wife. She had told him about hiding in the basement, how she tried to talk, but the words weren't there. Carla was vague about the abuse she and her brothers had endured and didn't want to talk about it. Now these two men faced each other in a dreadful, frightening situation. Yes, it was Tony's idea, but the entire family had agreed. As the lone brother-in-law, he now faced the same predicament.

Doyle's "Let's hear from you," jarred Phil back into reality.

"Oh, I, well, if Tony and Jim didn't draw the spade, I guess I did."

There! The truth was out, the moment he had dreaded. Waves of anguish and torment flooded his mind. He covered his face with his hands and sobbed.

Four men stared at him. Jim was the first to speak. "You killed my dad?"

Tony exploded. "Fuck you!" he yelled as he ran around the table. He grabbed the back of Phil's shirt collar and tried to pull him up. The shirt collar ripped, but Phil didn't move.

Seconds later Phil stood and looked at Tony, who was three inches shorter, maybe ten pounds lighter. Phil wiped his eyes. "Yeah, I got the spade king, but I didn't kill your father."

"You're a fucking liar!" Tony yelled. "You killed Dad and told the cops that I did it. You're a murderer, Phil." He stood and drew back his fist, ready to strike.

"Wait a minute," Doyle said. "Sit down, all of you." He glared at Tony. "It was your idea to kill your father, and now you're accusing Phil of doing just what he was supposed to do. He was following your plan, Tony."

Salt Marsh Sinners

Tony shrugged. "I guess you're right." He glared and kept his eyes on Phil as he shuffled back to his seat.

"Take it easy, Tony," Jim said. "One of us was to kill my dad, and poor old Phil got stuck." He looked at Phil. "Sorry, Phil. We're all pretty messed up."

Phil sat again and looked at the officers. He didn't want to look at Jim and Tony. He didn't want to be a part of their craziness. Jim, a gambler and an adulterer. Tony, a braggart and maybe a wife-beater. His wife had taken their daughters on a trip without telling Tony. Maybe she wanted to escape.

"Yeah, I drew the spade king, and I knew what it meant. I didn't want to kill Frank, but I'd agreed to Tony's plan. I couldn't talk to anyone, not even Carla, so I didn't sleep much all that week."

"You said you went to Orlando," O'Hara said. "Is that true?"

Phil nodded. "I knew I should carry out the plan, but I couldn't do it. I never could have done it." He looked at O'Hara. His hands shook, and his voice cracked. "I killed a friend when I was in high school. It was a fair fight. My friend and I were in the ring together, and something snapped in my head."

Phil stared at the ceiling. He remembered each blow he'd struck and the horror that built inside his head as he watched his friend fall and hit a pail beside his corner of the ring. He shuddered as he saw again the blood and his friend's lifeless body.

"My friend severed his jugular vein when he fell. I've lived with that horrible scene all my life, and I still can't forgive myself. Yeah, I killed, and nobody, no authority, no plot of any kind, could make me kill again. I didn't care if Frank Perruda lived to change his will. Carla hated Tony's plan and tried to find an alternative to murder. She finally agreed, knowing there was no other choice. She didn't want her dad's money. I didn't want it either. I don't understand why I agreed. I must have been as crazy as the rest of the family."

He put his head on the table and covered his ears. He had admitted his own crime. He was no better than Tony or Jim.

"So you didn't have the guts to carry out the plan, and you accused me of killing my dad," Tony said. He stood, walked around the table again, and lifted Phil's head. "Look at me, damn you!" Tony shouted. "You knew I didn't draw the spade, but you accused me."

"Shut up, Mr. Perruda," Doyle said. "The accusation was wrong. Phil Stevens didn't accuse you. There was an error in the transcript."

Tony left Phil's chair and faced Doyle. "An error in the transcript? What are you saying?"

O'Hara put his hand on Tony's shoulder. "We work that way sometimes when all else fails." He glared at all three men. "You people have made a mockery of our interrogations, with your lying and accusations. Frank Perruda was killed weeks ago, and we've wasted valuable time trying to get the truth out of you."

Doyle nodded. "After a murder the trail gets colder with each hour, each day. We've spent almost a month with you because you are prime suspects. We even hoped you'd hang yourselves with phony accusations, and we'd finally know which one of you killed Frank Perruda. Now we're back to square one, and with luck the Collier County Sheriff's Office will never have to see any of you again."

Leaving the door open, Doyle and O'Hara left the room while three men slumped in their chairs, facing one another, speechless.

• • •

Officer Doyle and Detective O'Hara joined Sheriff Ryder in the room next door and watched the three men, who still sat motionless.

"I wonder what they'll do when they leave here," Ryder said. "They've accused and attacked one another. Their emotions are down to the bare bones with nothing left to hide."

Doyle wiped his forehead. "We've been through a lot of interrogations, but this was the most intense. Three men together who hated one another's guts."

"And a background of resentments and abuse," O'Hara added. "Frank Perruda's death brought out the worst in the two sons, and Phil, the brother-in-law, has his own issues." He took a bottled water from the cooler and swallowed half of it.

"Write up your reports," Ryder said. "We have the tapes, but I want your own impressions. Now I want to review every ounce of data we have about the murders of Frank Perruda and Jeff Parker. We know they're connected, but we don't know why. I'm calling Russell Jones, the DEA agent. He needs to work with us."

He picked up his jacket and files. "I need your reports tomorrow." He returned to the courthouse carrying a load of unfinished casework, two unsolved murders, and a massive headache.

• • •

Russ Jones sat in his car in the courthouse parking lot and relived his morning at Julie's home. When Julie's alarm clock rang at seven, both she and Russ jumped out of her bed, followed by a quick kiss and a hurried breakfast as they discussed their day's activities. Julie faced her usual routine, answering the residents' requests and assisting visitors, caregivers, and maintenance staff. Her phone and intercom rang frequently. "Rosewood Center, may I help you?" was a phrase repeated between requests at her counter.

Russ knew his day would not be routine as he made notes on his iPad. Call Sam Kolinsky, Sheriff Ryder, and the lab in Miami. He buttered toast and between bites, mouthed kisses to Julie.

"I want you with me when we set our trap for Cynthia Frost, sweets. You know her. Maybe we can strike a bargain. Of course she'll be searched. No chance for a hidden automatic, and a lady's purse isn't large enough for an assault weapon."

She laughed. "You've lived through these experiences. You know how to handle them. I'm not worried. Where will you meet her?"

Russ sat back. "When I talk to Sam, we'll agree on a place that's safe, well-guarded. I'd like to meet at Sam's bar. We know the area, and Ryder's people can hide in the storage room."

As they cleared the table, Julie hugged him. "Be safe, my love. I almost lost you once."

"Don't worry. Sam saved me last time. Maybe he'll do it again."

They drove away in separate cars. Russ put his driving on automatic as he considered his options. With an opportunity to break up massive drug traffic in southwest Florida, the stakes were high. His plan had to succeed.

In his car he brought today's schedule into focus. Cynthia Frost was a drug dealer and possibly Frank Perruda's and Jeff Parker's killer. Now it was time for action. He called Sam Kolinsky in Everglades City on his mobile.

"I'll be in Sheriff Ryder's office. Can you call Frost and convince her you've found guys to pick up the shipment in the Everglades?"

"No problem. Honesty will drip into the phone." Sam laughed. "This time I'll call the shots, and Russ, tell that cute officer Rieger I'll buy her a beer after we nail our drug dealer."

Russ found the sheriff at the reception desk and followed him to his office. "Sam's setting up a visit with Frost," Russ said.

"Where?"

"He didn't say. Have you any suggestions?"

Ryder nodded. "His bar in Everglades City is out. Too many customers. A hotel conference room in Naples would be perfect. We can alert the manager and station our officers in a room next to the meeting. Many hotels have sliding walls between large areas. It would be easy to open a wall quickly and arrest her."

Russ nodded. "I'll call Sam as soon as you've selected the hotel. I'll get coffee while you make the arrangements."

Ten minutes later Russ's iPhone buzzed, and Sheriff Ryder spoke. "The Edgewater has agreed to our plan. Call Sam."

Russ followed Ryder's request. "Sam, the sheriff has located a hotel here. Call Frost. I'll wait for her response."

Russ read a newspaper and sipped coffee until his iPhone buzzed again. "She said no, Sam? What do you mean?" Russ listened and made notes on a scratch pad. "I'll tell the sheriff. Hold on." He lowered the phone. "Jack, your plan won't work. Frost's car is at a repair shop. She wants Sam to come to Rosewood Center at six thirty tonight. He'd arouse suspicion entering the lobby, so she wants to meet him poolside. She said everyone would be in the dining room, and no one goes to the pool at that time. What do you think?"

He held his phone and waited, knowing Ryder's thinking process meant scratching the back of his head. "Okay," Ryder said. "Our people can be in the shower room or behind the shrubbery. I'll send someone out this morning to check the area and take photographs."

Russ nodded. "Okay, Sam," he said. "Be ready to give her names, addresses, and times for a drop. Answer her questions, even if you have to fake them." He paused. "After you've given her that information, ask questions as if you're ready to buy into her operation. We think she killed Perruda and Parker. Tell her about the SWAT raid. Curse the police who tore up your bar."

"I can do that," Sam said. "I might even tell her I bought the stools expecting to find cocaine. I was in a high-school play once and thought about a career in Hollywood." He laughed. "I expect to win an Oscar for my performance."

Ryder interrupted. "Ask Sam to come to my office at four o'clock. We'll have photographs of the pool area."

Russ relayed the information and Sam agreed.

When Sam left the line, Russ said, "Sam will do okay. Let's hope his act will work, and if it doesn't, your people must protect him."

"Of course. We owe him one."

"I'm going to call the lab and see my mother this morning. I'll be back at four o'clock."

"Use my phone. I want to hear the test results on the pendant you borrowed from the boutique."

Russ called and nodded as he listened. He replaced the phone and smiled. "The pendant showed traces of cocaine, Jack. Cynthia's our man." He laughed. "I mean, our woman."

His visit at the hospital was discouraging. Mrs. Jones showed no signs of recovery and didn't acknowledge Russ's presence until he was ready to leave. "Nice boy," she mumbled and returned to her own world.

He and Julie bought sandwiches from the snack bar and ate lunch in the gazebo. The warm rays of a March sun danced on the Gulf's surface, and palm tree fronds swayed in a gentle breeze. It was a quiet afternoon outside the gazebo. Inside, Julie and Russ excitedly made plans for Sam's meeting with Cynthia Frost.

"She'll probably meet him at the south end of the pool by the bar," Julie said. "There are tables and chairs, and it's close to heavy foliage and a maintenance building."

"I hope she chooses that area. We'll make that suggestion when we meet with Sam this afternoon." He took her hand. "I'm glad but almost sorry this job's about finished, sweets. Being with you has changed my life. I thought I'd be alone forever, and now I can't wait to spend my life with you. My life is crazy sometimes. I take orders from the DEA. That's my job."

He stood and knelt in front of her chair. "Will you share this crazy life with me, Julie Rogers? Will you marry me?"

"I thought you'd never ask." She put her arms around his shoulders and knelt in front of him. "I'll marry you, Russell Jones. I want to share your crazy life."

Russ fumbled in his pocket, brought out a diamond ring and placed it on Julie's fourth finger of her left hand. "It's my mother's. She'd want you to have it."

"Oh, Russ, it's just like my grandmother's ring, the one I lost." Tears fell as she stroked Russ's cheek.

They stood and embraced. "We'll make wedding plans as soon as this case is over," he said. "Will you miss Rosewood Center?"

Julie pushed away and stared at Russ. "I thought we might live here. I love my job, and your agency has an office in Miami. Can't we live in my house?"

Russ's thoughts were a jumble. He needed her, but his office was in Alexandria, Virginia. "We'll work it out, sweets. What's important is I love you." He kissed her and caressed her breasts. "We'll find our home together. I promise."

"I love you too, honey." She checked her watch. "I have to get back. Call me when you're ready. Maybe I can help."

Russ returned to his apartment and worked his laptop. Correspondence had piled up, along with directives and information from the main office. At three thirty, he drove to Ryder's office.

"Sam's here," the sheriff said, "and we're studying the photographs of the area."

"Frost wants to meet me on the south side of the pool," Sam said.

"It's a good spot. There are tables and chairs in front of a bar. Our men can stay behind the bar and listen."

"I've rehearsed my lines, and I feel like I'm on stage."

Russ laughed. "But we don't have a prompter. You'll have to wing it." He studied the photographs again. "Julie wants to be there because she knows Frost and hopes to convince her to reveal her contacts. It's a crapshoot, but she's hopeful. We'll station ourselves behind that maintenance shed. It's close to the pool, and if there's trouble, my gun will be off safety."

• • •

At six o'clock Ryder and his two officers, Julie, and Russ were securely positioned. Sam sat at a table and clipped his fingernails. At six thirty Cynthia Frost appeared. With her cane she limped toward Sam.

Sam stood as Cynthia came to his table. When he put out his hand, Cynthia ignored the gesture, leaned her cane against the table, and sat.

"You have the information?" she asked.

"I asked around. Everglades City is a small town. Everybody knows everybody. No secrets." He gave her a sheet of paper. "Here's four names for you. They're high-school kids who want to earn extra money. They know the area."

Behind the shed Russ held Julie's hand and smiled. Sam had memorized his lines.

As she put the list in her purse, Sam looked around and spoke softly as though someone might hear. "I know your friend has a big business here, Mrs. Frost. I knew the system in California, worked with a guy who had connections in Tijuana. Maybe your friend and I could work together."

Cynthia laughed. "Let's skip the 'friend' stuff, Sam. You know I'm the one who needs this information." She took his hand. "We might work together. You told me you were raided."

Sam picked it up quickly. "Yeah. Those bums came to my bar even before we opened and tore the place apart. They said they were looking for coke."

"Why?"

"It was the stools. I bought them at Perruda's for the bar." He snorted. "God, if I'd known they were shipped here full of snow, I'd have paid double."

Cynthia stared at him. "You didn't know?"

"Hell, no. Did you?"

"Of course. Frank Perruda and I worked together for about five years. He told me about the shipment, but when I arrived at the receiving dock, someone was there already."

"Who was the someone?"

Salt Marsh Sinners

"I wish I knew. I thought I did, but I was too late." She looked up at the sun that moved slowly to the west, its fading rays reflecting in the pool.

"What happened?"

Cynthia laughed. "You ask too many questions. Why do you want to know?"

Sam paused. Cool it, he told himself. You're on her side, remember? He leaned back and smiled. "Hell, I've been through too much in California, I guess. Life's cheap if the stuff's available, and sometimes you had to eliminate a life. We had it pretty good, being close to the border, but you had to know how to handle problems. You have a bigger transportation problem, but some things don't change. You still have to be in control if you want a successful operation." As Sam watched Cynthia's facial expressions, he knew she believed him.

"I guess I can trust you." She sat back and smiled. "If I can't, you're in this as deep as I am. We'll swing together." She smiled. "I knew where the drugs were hidden, and I had to get there before someone else got them. I went to the store's loading dock about midnight. I coordinated my visit with the cop's surveillance schedule."

"Wow! Where were the stools?"

"They were on a top shelf. I was mad when I saw someone on a ladder trying to remove a stool, a guy who maybe worked there and knew about the drugs. I went to the shelves, pulled the ladder with the guy on it away from the shelves. He screamed when he hit the floor."

"Was he hurt?"

Cynthia sighed. "He was banged up when he hit the floor, and the ladder fell on top of him. He wasn't dead, and he could have identified me." She sighed again. "I had to kill him. I had no choice."

Sam had no time to respond as Sheriff Ryder, Russ, Julie, and two police officers rushed to the table. Cynthia jumped up. An officer tried to grab her wrists, but she was too quick. She grabbed her cane with her right hand and Julie with her left, holding both of Julie's arms tightly against her left side and gradually moved a squirming and screaming Julie in front of her.

She pointed her cane at Russ. "Don't come any closer." She tightened her grip on Julie and moved back, and with a sudden hand movement, the cane became a lethal weapon. An eight-inch knife protruded from its base.

Sam, too startled to remember his lines, watched in horror as Julie, with arms held at her side, became a human shield. He looked toward the opposite side of the pool and saw a woman get up from a chair and use her walker to move to the edge of the pool. He wondered if Russ and the officers had seen her but knew he had to concentrate on Julie and Cynthia. Any distraction could result in Julie's death.

Russ, who must have seen the action across the pool, said, "Don't do this, Cynthia. You're outnumbered. You can only kill one of us."

Cynthia laughed. "I planned to give your idiot friend, Sam, a fake list, Mr. Jones. If you want real names, you'll have to let me go. I don't mind killing again. I've already admitted I killed the guy at the receiving dock." She sneered and moved her cane from side to side. "My cane is useful at times like these."

Sam watched Russ, the sheriff, and the two officers as they stood facing Cynthia. No one moved. Julie's life became more precarious as Cynthia gradually moved her right hand closer to the end of the cane.

"I might kill Julie first. You'd like to watch, wouldn't you, Mr. Jones?"

Because the event was life-threatening, Sam didn't notice Julie's movements as she slowly edged Cynthia backward toward the pool. Suddenly everyone heard a splash. Someone or something had hit the water behind Cynthia and Julie. Cynthia, startled by the sound, turned her head toward the pool and lowered her cane. Her action was brief, but Julie found the chance to push Cynthia backward . Again, she pushed up against her and shoved with such force that both of them fell backward into the water. Cynthia screamed and released both Julie and her cane. Julie swam away, and Cynthia's cane sank to the bottom of the pool.

• • •

At five thirty that evening, an hour before Cynthia's rendezvous with Sam, Doris Johnson, Rosewood Center resident, forgotten friend of Cynthia Frost and grandmother of *Naples Daily News* reporter Trevor Johnson, pushed her walker to the pool. She treasured her solitary swim at five thirty without residents and their grandchildren who bumped into her during daytime hours. At six o'clock, she pulled herself out of the pool, took her walker and a towel, and sat in the shadows of an overhang.

Because most of the residents were in the dining room or out for dinner, she was startled to see activity across the deep end of the pool. She recognized Cynthia, who wore a pink sweater and matching slacks. She and a stocky gentleman sat at a table and seemed to be involved in a serious conversation.

Suddenly Julie and Russ Jones appeared, followed by two police officers and another man. How exciting, she thought as she punched in Trevor's number on her cell phone.

"Come to the pool," she whispered. "It looks like trouble."

She replaced her cell and stood in the shadows. "Oh dear God!" she whispered as she watched Cynthia grab Julie, pointing her cane at Russ. What was happening? Because she wanted a closer look, she pushed her walker to the edge of the pool and dived. When she came up to the surface, another surprise occurred. Julie had swum to the edge of the pool, and Cynthia, still in the deep end, screamed and swore, her arms flailing wildly. Mrs. Johnson remembered her lifesaving course and swam behind Cynthia. She grabbed her hair, hoping to pull her to the pool's edge. She pulled, but Cynthia remained in deep water. Mrs. Johnson held only a mass of gray hair!

More splashes sounded as Russ and an officer dived in and grabbed Cynthia. Each took an arm as their victim screamed and swore in a voice that lowered with each outburst. The men pulled Cynthia to the shallow end as a reporter's video camera recorded the activity. Mrs. Johnson was startled and embarrassed as she watched Russ begin to undress Cynthia. He tore off her sweater and jerked a padded bra from a hairy chest. Embarrassment became horror. Cynthia was a man!

She heard Russ call to the other men, "Here's your killer, Sheriff. John Thurston."

CHAPTER EIGHTEEN

At eight o'clock, two hours after Sam's appointment at the pool, Julie and Russ, still wet from their unscheduled swim, sat alone in Sheriff Jack Ryder's office. They sipped coffee and shivered.

Julie snuggled close to Russ. "I still can't believe what happened. How did you know Cynthia's real identity?"

"I didn't know until I saw him in the pool. Remember I found John Thurston's name in the FBI files? He was always in the back of my mind because his body had never been recovered. When he fell into the pool and panicked, I suspected it was Thurston, a guy who nearly drowned in a lake between Mexico and Texas."

"Most of our residents use the pool or go to the beach." Julie smiled. "And our pool isn't large. Cynthia over-reacted."

"Yes, and Mrs. Johnson proved I was right when she pulled off his wig."

"She, I mean he, had everyone fooled. What an act."

Russ laughed. "I've seen two movie actors pull it off. Eventually the act becomes easy and natural."

"Will Thurston give you the names of his buyers?"

"He can be persuaded. He has bargaining chips, and he knows we want to crack the whole operation."

Sheriff Ryder opened the door and smiled. "I needed to brief Arturo Lopez," he said. "I've ordered more coffee and dry blankets. "Don't go away."

Russ laughed. "We're too wet to go anywhere. More dry blankets will help."

"I'm cold too," Julie said, "and I lost my new pair of sandals."

A policeman brought more coffee and blankets, a welcome gift.

"Lopez gave me more information," Ryder said. "Thurston's in a cell at the county jail next door. He was read his Miranda rights, and he's calling a lawyer. He's been given a shower and a prison uniform."

"Julie and I need to get into dry clothes," Russ said. "Sam furnished you with a complete report before he went home, and we gave our versions of what happened. We can come back either later tonight or in the morning."

Ryder agreed. "It's late. We'll take you home now, and Russ, I'll see you in the morning." He stood and shook Russ's hand. "You never gave up. I'm proud to know you."

A sheriff's car delivered them to Julie's home. "I hope the neighbors don't see us dressed in blankets," she said.

Russ laughed. "They'll just think we went to a pool party."

• • •

At eight thirty the next morning, Russ and the sheriff reviewed the case.

"You identified Thurston as soon as Mrs. Johnson pulled off his wig. How did you know his name?"

"Remember when I went to West Virginia with my FBI friend, Dwight Holbrook? We studied criminal files all afternoon, and I copied Thurston's dossier. It was only a gut feeling, but he had a Mexican connection." He opened his briefcase and gave Ryder the report.

Ryder read the report aloud as he scratched the back of his head. "John Thurston. Born in Phoenix, Arizona, on May 10, 1948. Married to Frieda Hunt, June 21, 1969. Divorced January 3, 1975. No children. Arrested in Tampico, Mexico, suspected in a drug-related murder case but never convicted. Prison record: one conviction. Sentenced to three years in Omaha, Nebraska."

"Fingerprints and other identification were listed, but I didn't copy any of it. Read on, Jack. That's what interested me."

"He's listed as a missing person. His fishing boat, an Argos, was found upside down on Lake Falcon in Zapata, Texas, in June 2003, and his body was never found."

"A severe thunderstorm was reported at the time Thurston's boat overturned." Russ looked at Jack. "Storms can come up quickly. No wonder his boat capsized."

"I remember that lake," Ryder said. "Half of Lake Falcon is in Mexico, and the other half in the United States. A water skier was shot a few years ago."

Russ nodded. "I kept the information but disregarded it as being too remote, no tie-in with a drug operation in Naples, Florida."

"Until Mrs. Johnson hit the water." Ryder laughed.

They heard a knock on the door, and Trevor Johnson entered. "Have you seen the paper? I got my first byline, and I'm a hero."

Ryder laughed. "Your grandmother didn't waste time when she called you."

"I was in the area, so I got good coverage. I'd like to interview both of you."

"It will be brief," Ryder said. "Our first job is to break up the drug ring, so we need to interrogate Thurston. We can't give you much information."

"I understand." Johnson smiled. "The editor liked my work and said I could have exclusive rights to the story. That's what every reporter dreams about, and I got my dream, thanks to Grandma."

Russ laughed. "You're lucky, Trevor. Most grandmothers don't swim after hours."

"I'll bet you didn't know she was on the Olympic swim team in 1944, but she never had a chance for a gold medal. The event was canceled because of World War Two."

The sheriff and Russ answered some of Johnson's questions and sent him back to the paper's main office.

Together, they worked on Thurston's interrogation format. The killer might reveal the scope of his operation and provide the names of his buyers in exchange for what? The question weighed heavily. The man was guilty of murder, but a drug ring could be uncovered and destroyed.

"We still don't know what happened to Tomas Fuentes," Russ said. "He's the guy who worked at Sharon Long's boutique and probably knew too much. Maybe another dead body."

Ryder nodded and made notes. "We also need to find Thurston's accomplices. We know he worked with Frank Perruda." Ryder scratched the back of his head. "Maybe he murdered Frank too."

"Yeah, we know he's a killer."

They mapped out their agenda. Ryder called the jail, and fifteen minutes later, he and Russ sat facing Thurston in an interrogation room. Thurston lounged in his chair and stared at the ceiling. Although he was handcuffed, with legs tethered in chains, the man displayed an air of total relaxation.

"I haven't called a lawyer yet," Thurston said. "I'm in the driver's seat. You guys want information, so here goes. I was born in…"

"Cut the details, Thurston," Ryder said. "We have your record. We need to know about your Naples operation."

"In exchange for what, Sheriff?"

"Do you want the chair or life?"

"It doesn't matter. One's as bad as the other." He stared at Ryder. "You have my confession of Jeff Parker's murder, but you don't know much else." He turned to Russ. "You're a narc. You want to bust up my drug business." He snorted. "If I sing, you'll be heroes, and I'll be in the can." He raised his cuffed hands above his head. "For how long? That's the real question."

"We can't promise anything. That's up to the courts."

"Yeah, but you can testify on my behalf and ask for leniency." He looked at Ryder. "A plea bargain maybe?"

Ryder nodded. "It's possible. Are you willing to take that chance?"

Thurston shrugged. "What have I got to lose?" He lowered his hands to his lap and spoke quietly. "I had help. If I give you the name of a killer, my sentence ought to be cut by at least twenty years." He laughed. "Yeah, good old Felix needs to join me in prison."

Russ stood and stared at Thurston. "Felix who works at the garage at Rosewood Center?"

"Yeah. He carries out my orders."

"There are no surprises in this business," Ryder said. "I'll go back to my office and contact the man."

After Ryder left the room, Russ questioned Thurston. He needed names, but Thurston refused to talk. They sat in silence, waiting for the sheriff's return.

"We're bringing Felix Schmidt in for questioning," Ryder said as he entered. "Let's talk, Thurston."

• • •

At nine thirty, as Sheriff Ryder and Russ began to question Thurston, Felix Schmidt sat at his desk in the garage. He read and reread the *Naples Daily News* front-page story, and sweat dripped from his nose and under his arms. Cynthia Frost was John Thurston, a murderer? He, Felix, his trusted helper, should have known, at least suspected the disguise.

Now his former boss was in jail. Had he revealed their relationship? As reported in the news release, Julie had played a major role in Thurston's arrest. Perhaps she had the information he needed. He called the concierge desk.

"I'm sorry, Felix," Rosita said. "Julie is helping one of our residents." She cut the connection.

As furrows deepened on his forehead, his phone rang.

"Yes?" Felix's hand shook as he held the phone. A summons to the county jail meant trouble. "When?" He checked his schedule. "I can come to the courthouse in an hour."

Oh Lord! Cynthia must have implicated him. A mountain of fear rose up into his mind, a mountain he couldn't climb.

Maybe he could go around it with a diversion, a different path. He leaned back and thought about Tomas Fuentes at his cousin's rehab in St. Louis, and the thought became the path around the mountain.

When Henry Schmidt answered his call, Felix asked, "How is Tomas?"

"Doing well. I'm glad he's here. The worst is over. He's dried out and attending group meetings." Henry sighed. "He's worried about his girlfriend, Edilia. How long before he can call her?"

"I don't know. Stall him. I'll call again as soon as I have more information." Felix bit his upper lip. What information would be available now that Cynthia was John behind bars? He struggled through an hour in the garage and then drove cautiously to the courthouse. A speeding ticket would only add to his worries.

His knees shook as he followed an officer to the jail. He signed the register and was led to a room that held two chairs separated by a glass panel, each at a phone-connected desk.

"Am I the prisoner, or am I going to meet one?" Felix asked.

The officer shook his head and left the room. Felix fell into the chair and wiped his forehead. Minutes later he watched, puzzled and frightened as a handcuffed and foot-chained prisoner was led to a chair on the other side of the glass.

Felix stood and stared at the man. "I don't believe it," he exclaimed as he recognized a masculine Cynthia Frost.

"It's over, Felix," the prisoner said. The voice was deep, a man's voice now.

Felix fell back into his chair, speechless.

The officer looked at Felix. "John Thurston has admitted killing Jeff Parker and selling drugs. You have ten minutes."

The officer left, and Thurston sneered. "You're in this deeper than I am, Felix. I have bargaining chips and one murder. You have nothing, and you've killed two people, the hit-and-run gal in Chicago and now Tomas. I'll be free, and you'll get life or the chair."

Felix leaned back and bit his upper lip. "We worked together for five years. I followed orders because you knew about what happened in Chicago." He stared at Thurston. "You lied to me, pretending to be a woman. I wonder what other lies you told."

Thurston laughed. "You'll never know, Felix. You're too stupid." He stood, ankle chains rattling as he moved to the door. "Guard," he yelled. "Get me out of here. I can't stand this piece of shit."

After Thurston was led away, Felix sat and thought about his five years at Rosewood Center. He and Mary had fled Chicago, glad to get away from past memories of their son Tommy, killed in a South Side gang fight. The hit-and-run accident cemented their decision to escape. Because he'd had a few beers, he knew he'd be slapped with a DUI citation plus a murder charge. They left town and found a new life in Naples, Florida. Mary cooked at a fast-food restaurant, and Felix, who filed an application omitting his accident, found work at Rosewood Center. Worries that he'd be hunted down by Chicago authorities diminished as time passed, and when he met Cynthia, he found a person who sympathized and appreciated his work in the garage and his knowledge of drug sales. He didn't remember why he had told her about his accident.

An officer interrupted his memories. "Detective O'Hara wants to see you."

Felix followed the officer to the sheriff's department in the courthouse next door and slumped into a chair by O'Hara's desk.

"Thurston says you killed two people," O'Hara said. "Considering the source, we're not ready to book you, but we need an explanation."

"Only one murder, sir," Felix replied. "Thurston ordered me to kill Tomas Fuentes because he knew too much. I didn't kill him. He's at my cousin's rehab center in St. Louis."

O'Hara made notes. "Give me the rehab number." He picked up a phone. A receptionist answered and paged Henry Schmidt.

After O'Hara explained the reason for his call, he listened and smiled. "You can tell Tomas he's free to return." He replaced the phone and sat back. "Now tell me about the other murder."

"It was a hit-and-run in Chicago six years ago. I'd been drinking, and a gal walked right in front of my car. I panicked and drove home. I knew my alcohol level would convict me, and I was scared. We left town."

"How do you know she died?"

"I just knew, that's all."

"And you told Thurston?"

"Yes. He knew I'd faked my application, and he never let me forget it. 'Follow orders or lose your job,' he'd say."

O'Hara nodded. "Thurston lived a lie too. A big one." He paused. "Give me the accident victim's name. We need to verify the death."

"Louise Cartwright. I'll never forget it. Here's the address." Felix printed the information, and O'Hara picked up the phone.

• • •

Tomas Fuentes sat in the director's office and listened as Henry Schmidt spoke the words he'd dreamed of and hoped for. "You're free to go home, Tomas."

"Wow! I can leave now?" He smiled. "You saved my life, Mr. Schmidt. I can't thank you enough."

"Thank Felix for sending you here. He paid for your treatment. You owe him, not me."

Tomas nodded. "I'll pay him for everything."

"Your best payment is to stay clean. Too many folks relapse."

"I won't. I can't." He stood and shook the director's hand. "When can I leave?"

"Pack and be ready for the next bus. Leroy will take you to the station."

Tears fell as Tomas thought about Edilia. "Can I call my girl?" he asked.

Salt Marsh Sinners

"Of course." Schmidt smiled as he reached for the phone.

• • •

At seven o'clock that morning, Julie and Russ had finished breakfast and relaxed with coffee and the newspaper. Russ smiled as he read a front-page report of the arrest of John Thurston, aka Cynthia Frost.

"Only one typo," Russ said, "and Trevor's report is accurate."

"I'm glad it's over, honey. No more murders, and when Thurston realizes the odds are against him, he'll provide the names of his buyers."

"It will be a huge roundup, so my work here is done." He sighed. "This means I have to return to headquarters. Can you come with me?"

"There isn't time to find a replacement. I'll speak to the director, Peter Watson. Maybe I can leave in a week or two."

The doorbell rang as she stood, coffee cup in her hand. Julie opened the door, and Russ heard barks and laughter. Julie introduced her next-door neighbor, Lisette, and Heidi, who bared her teeth and lunged at Russ.

"Nice doggy," Russ said as he picked himself up from the floor, straightened his chair, and with his napkin, wiped spilled coffee.

Julie and Lisette laughed. "*Mechent chien,*" Lisette said and laughed again.

Julie said, "Heidi thought you were another attacker, honey. She protects me." She took Russ's hand and pulled it onto Heidi's neck. "Don't move, and be gentle. She's smart and won't bite."

Heidi turned and licked Russ's hand. "I guess she likes me," Russ said. He checked his watch. "I have to leave you girls and meet the sheriff." To Julie he said, "I'll pick you up for lunch." He was eager to see Ryder again, probably for the last time. He liked the man, his concerns and his honesty.

When Russ entered the sheriff's office, Ryder stood and shook his hand. Russ smiled. "I'm going home, Jack. My work here is finished."

"You did a great job, and you have the scars to prove it. A broken arm is nothing compared to almost being killed by the Carlson brothers."

Russ nodded. "And my apartment was trashed, but hey, I found Julie and met some fabulous people." He sat facing Ryder. "Working with you has been a real pleasure. I'll miss you."

"Come back anytime. Your mother's here, and I'm always looking for a partner in crime."

"You'll be busy rounding up the pushers. Call my people in Miami if you need more help."

"Will do. Thurston has thrown in the towel. Maybe years of hiding have been a struggle." Ryder scratched the back of his head. "Thurston admitted he killed Jeff Parker in the store's loading dock, but we're still looking for Frank Perruda's killer. His three kids are innocent. We checked motel receipts and Jim's plane trip to Atlantic City."

"What about the wife?"

"We'll bring her in again." He paused. "I have good news about Felix Schmidt. Detective O'Hara traced the name of the person Felix thought he'd killed in Chicago. The woman is alive and well and won't press charges against Felix. She told O'Hara she'd had too many martinis and just walked into the traffic. O'Hara called Schmidt and said Felix cried."

Russ smiled. "I'm glad for Felix. He deserves some good news after being Thurston's gofer." He stood, moved to the door, and looked back at the sheriff. "But you still have an unsolved murder on your hands."

"Yes. I wonder about the person who drove the trucks from Mexico. I've studied the invoices. No name is listed. Thurston was questioned, and I believe his testimony. He says Frank refused to give the driver's name because he wanted to keep that part of his operation separate from local drug sales."

Salt Marsh Sinners

"I wonder what Perruda did with all his money. His lawyer, Mark Holtz, has no record of large deposits."

"Lots of unanswered questions. We'll keep digging." He stood and shook Russ's hand. "Come back soon, Russ. Maybe I'll have some answers for you next time."

• • •

Three months after Frank Perruda's murder, Frank's driver, Patrick Davis—now Andrew Stahl—lounged on a beach chair in front of the Turtle Bay Hotel on Barbuda, a small Caribbean island near Antigua. The man whose last job was transporting six bar stools from Texas to Naples sipped a gin and tonic and watched a flock of pelicans as one by one, they swooped down into the ocean searching for a quick meal. A tour boat driver, he'd finished his last trip to the frigate bird sanctuary near the island, and at five o'clock he was ready to relax. He looked back at the hotel and hoped the manager wouldn't see him in the tourist area. Patrick smiled. The tourist season ended in May and now, on June 15, only a few rooms were occupied.

Patrick looked up at the pelicans and waved. Maybe they were the same birds that had hovered over his escape route in Naples, Florida, three months ago. He drained his glass, looked up at the birds, and laughed.

"Hi, guys, remember me? You watched while I ran through the estuary to my canoe and paddled out to Chuck's boat."

His mind, soothed by the drink, sent him back to the month of March, to his last days in Florida. They had begun in Tampa after a night with friends. Because his truck broke down in Panama City, he wanted a respite before facing Frank Perruda at the furniture store. Frank was mad about the delay with the shipment of bar stools, but what the hell. Frank was mad most of the time. Mad at delays in McAllen, Texas, while the border patrol searched the van from Vera Cruz. Patrick was mad also, mad at his Mexican counterparts who wanted American cigarettes and complained about the long drive home.

This would be his last trip. Good-bye to Naples and Frank Perruda. Patrick's bank account was healthy, and now he'd ask for an increase in his wages. "Consider the risk, Frank," he'd say, and Frank would accept his request.

Last month, in February, he met his friend, Chuck, at a chickee hut near the Naples pier. "I need a new life. I'm sick of my boss and the trips to the border. I'm scared, Chuck. My luck's bound to run out."

"What do you want to do?"

"I want to be somebody else in a new location, maybe in the Caribbean. I can drive trucks, and you could teach me to drive a boat."

Chuck squeezed half of a lime into his beer and drank. "That's a challenge, Pat, but I think I can help you. I know people in Tampa. There's a funeral home that sometimes takes care of bodies with no families. I could talk to the funeral director. He has contacts who can work miracles, sometimes just this side of the law, and sometimes…but we don't inquire."

Two weeks later Chuck called. "The funeral director says it's possible. He can fake a death certificate. You'll need a new passport, so send me a photo. The funeral home collects all sorts of unclaimed stuff."

"How much?"

"Don't even ask, and don't ask for details either. The guy wants to stay in business, and the less you know, the better it is for him."

Patrick nodded and reviewed his bank account. "I'll send a photo, and I can get the money." He pulled his left ear. "I want this bad, Chuck. Can you take me to Antigua? I've checked the area. Boats take tourists to a frigate bird sanctuary in Barbuda, a little island near Antigua."

"My boat isn't big enough, but my buddy, Jake, takes people to Antigua. He has a thirty-eight-foot sailboat, a Catalina, and you could sign on as a deckhand."

Salt Marsh Sinners

Patrick's last two weeks in February were a mad jumble of conspiracy, and when Frank called ordering him to pick up a shipment in McAllen, he smiled.

"What's the cargo?" he asked.

"Six bar stools. The legs will carry the drugs."

"Okay, Frank. I'll deliver them to the store."

Now, with a definite schedule, Patrick called Chuck and made his final escape plans. "I'll hide my backpack in a canoe in the estuary behind Rosewood Center and meet Frank at his apartment. Stay close because I won't know the exact time."

"Everything's set," Chuck said. "You're going to be Andrew Stahl because your photo almost matched his."

"Andy!" The hotel manager's voice interrupted Patrick's memory. "Take some towels to room six. The maid's gone for the day."

"Sure, boss. Right away." Patrick drained his glass and ran to the laundry building. He delivered the towels and returned to his room. He lay on his bed and stared at the ceiling. Life was good here. The hotel staff was friendly but not curious, and when the manager learned of his experience on the sailboat and his driving ability, he was asked to pilot a tourist boat to the sanctuary. Naples and Frank Perruda were history.

His mind went back to the events that changed his life. He'd made the trip to McAllen, met his Mexican counterpart, and exchanged the cargo with ease. Border guards checked the stools and waved him ahead, no questions asked. Relieved, he relaxed until the truck broke down. Cursing, he stopped in Panama City. As soon as the truck was ready to travel, Patrick drove to Tampa, met Chuck, and reviewed his escape plan.

"I'm ready," Patrick said. "I hope there'll be no problems with Frank."

"Keep me informed. I'll be waiting for you."

Patrick's mind swirled as he drove to Naples. New name, new world. He remembered his mother's last words, *"I want my boy to be happy."* He's happy now, Patrick thought.

When he drove to Perruda's Fine Furnishings and parked at the loading dock, Frank met him and watched as Pat unloaded the bar stools.

"I'll pay you tonight at my condo," Frank said. "Come about nine o'clock. Don't come through the lobby. Leave the truck in the garage, and use my private elevator." He chuckled. "When you leave, you'll have enough cash for a taxi."

With visions of a four-figure payment, Patrick drove to a local bar and called Chuck. "I'll meet Frank at Rosewood Center tonight. I'll have the money, I'll find the canoe, and I'll be at your boat about ten. I'll call if there's a delay."

At nine o'clock Patrick drove the truck to Rosewood Center's garage and took Perruda's private elevator to the penthouse. Frank opened the door, finger to his lips.

"Diane's in her bedroom with the TV. Be quiet." He led Patrick to his bedroom on the other side of the spacious penthouse and closed the door behind them. "This is just between us," Frank said. "I'll give you cash. Checks can be traced."

He opened his closet door, and Patrick heard a drawer open and shut. Frank emerged with three $100 bills.

Patrick stared at the money. "Is that all? I risked being caught at the border, Frank. I could have spent the rest of my life in prison."

"That's the risk you took when you accepted this job. I've paid, haven't I?"

Patrick sat on the bed. "That's not enough."

"I got big expenses. Diane spends money like water."

"That's your problem. You married her." Patrick's temper rose. "Dammit, Frank, I gotta have more. I earned it."

"You sound just like my kids. More, that's all you ever want. More, more."

Patrick grew angrier with each *more*. As he stood, his heart pounded against his chest, and perspiration dripped from his forehead.

"I need the money, Frank." He paused and sat again.

Frank stood over him and sneered. "You little pipsqueak! I can get a hundred just like you to drive for me." He pulled Patrick up by his shirt collar. "Now get out." He glared at Patrick.

"You're through as my driver. I never want to see you again." He pushed Patrick to his bedroom door, opened it, and shoved him. "You know your way out." He shut the door behind Patrick.

As Patrick walked through the living room to the front door, he thought about the money he deserved, money that would take him to Antigua. He remembered the long drives to the border and back, the risks he'd taken. He needed more, and the money was in Frank's closet.

If he could hide in the penthouse until Frank was asleep, he could sneak back into the closet, find Frank's money, and leave before the old man awoke. He walked toward the kitchen and found a laundry room. He checked his watch. Nine thirty. He'd wait there until ten.

Time seemed to stand still. At last it was ten o'clock. He got up from the floor and rubbed his aching knees. In his jeans pockets, he carried a pair of gloves he'd used to move heavy furniture. Might come in handy, he thought, as he put them on and crept toward Frank's bedroom.

He heard snoring as he slowly opened the door and crept toward the closet. He was only inches from the closet door when he heard a loud snort, followed by "Stop!"

Patrick didn't move as more light flooded the room. "What the hell?" Frank roared. "I thought you left." He got up and faced Patrick. "You little pipsqueak! I'll kill you!"

Patrick's mind closed down in the next seconds, and his actions were automatic. He shoved the old man onto his bed, and as he forced him down, he grabbed a pillow and covered Frank's mouth and nose. He spread his legs, jumped on Frank's body, and pushed, pushed hard until there was no more movement.

Minutes later Patrick stood beside Frank's bed and removed the pillow. Frank lay on his back, eyes glaring, mouth open. His lips were spotted with drops of blood. Patrick bent over and listened for breathing. There was none. Frank was dead.

Swallowing panic, he rushed to the closet and pulled open a drawer. He pushed aside jockey shorts and found a pile of bills. He shoved them into his pocket, straightened the shorts, and shut the drawer. He looked down at Frank's body and shivered. Frank's death was not in his escape plan. He turned off the light and crept quietly to the front door. He was out of the penthouse, ready to shut the door behind him, when he heard a voice.

"This is Diane Perruda at Rosewood Center. Someone's here. I heard voices. A fight, I think. Hurry!"

Patrick didn't linger to hear the rest of Diane's call. He had to get away, find the canoe, and get the hell out of Naples!

He considered the elevator but knew its opening in the garage might find him face-to-face with the cops. His only escape was the stairway. As he ran down one flight, he heard sirens. He ran down another flight and heard voices. He knew the police would climb the stairs.

He needed a place to hide in the building until the search ended. Quickly he left the stairs and tried to open apartment doors. At last, the door of apartment 1613 was unlocked, and Patrick stepped inside.

"Hello. You must be my new caregiver."

Patrick gasped for breath as he saw an old woman seated in a chair across the room. He stood at the door and considered his options. Escape meant possible capture. Being a caregiver was a better choice.

"Yes. The agency sent me." He checked his watch. "It's late, but I wanted to meet you tonight."

"That's nice. I'm Carolyn Jones."

"I'm Bill." Patrick sat and smiled.

"My son, Russell, worries about me and hired a caregiver. You don't need to stay all night. The mice are here."

Patrick stared at her. "You have mice?"

"Oh yes. I feed them sometimes." She struggled to stand and reached for a cane. "I want to go to bed now. Will you help me?"

"Of course. I always helped my mother."

"Nice boy. Come with me."

As Patrick walked to her chair, the doorbell rang. Oh God, Patrick thought. It was the cops.

"You should answer it, Mrs. Jones. I'll wait for you in the bedroom."

"Yes, and don't step on the mice."

Patrick shut the bedroom door behind him and heard men's voices. Helpless, he ran to a closet and hid behind a row of clothing. Minutes passed, and the bedroom door opened. He moved farther into the closet, terror clutching every bone in his body.

"Bob, those nice policemen have left. Where are you?"

Patrick relaxed, pushed aside the clothes, and came out of the closet. "I'll help you, and I'll come back when you need me."

"You're a nice boy." She took a scarf from the dresser. "You'll be cold when you leave. Wear this."

"Thanks," he said and helped her into bed. He sat in the living room and waited until he heard cars leaving the area. At last the building and the parking area were quiet. Still wearing his gloves, he closed Mrs. Jones's apartment door behind him and slowly inched his way down the stairs to the garage. He saw no one but heard a car approaching the double entrance doors. He hid behind two large crates next to the doors and waited as the car passed through. Quickly he ran out behind the car as the doors began to shut and ran to the estuary.

He pulled out his cell phone. "Chuck, sorry to be late, but I'm on my way as planned. I'll find the canoe and meet you at your boat."

Because it was low tide, he waded into the estuary. With a flashlight he followed the route he and Chuck had planned. The canoe, hidden under a mangrove, was ten feet from shore. He climbed in, tossed Mrs. Jones's scarf under a seat, and thought about the old lady. She'd said, "Nice boy" as he left her bedroom.

Now in the canoe, he paddled toward the Gulf where Chuck's boat waited.

"I thought you'd never come," Chuck said as Patrick pushed the canoe back toward the estuary and climbed aboard.

"Our plan didn't work too well. I had to wait, but I have the money. Let's get out of here."

• • •

Patrick left his room, returned to the beach chair, and watched the sun as it slowly settled into the blue waters of the Caribbean. Life was good. Here on Barbuda he'd found a home and another vehicle that needed a driver. He sighed. Driving trucks had been his life, his passion. There was no trucking business on this small Caribbean island, but there were boats that needed drivers, boats that took tourists to the frigate bird sanctuary. When the hotel manager learned of Patrick's driving skills, a new career opened.

"Andy, come here." His boss's voice interrupted his reverie, and Patrick trotted to the manager's office.

"Is it a sunset cruise?" he asked.

The manager laughed. "No, it's June, and that means weddings. We'll have honeymooners here for the entire month." He studied his schedule. "Your first passengers will arrive tomorrow."

"Who are they?"

"It's a couple from Naples, Florida. Julie Rogers and Russell Jones.

EPILOGUE

Five years have passed since Julie Rogers and Russell Jones were married and spent their honeymoon on the island of Barbuda in the Caribbean. They had enjoyed their week on the island and admired the frigate birds. Their boat captain said little during their trip to the sanctuary, but they admired his skill at the helm.

Sadly, Russ's mother died in May, a month before their wedding. They divide their time between Russ's apartment at Rosewood Center in Naples, Florida, and his condo at the Rotonda at Tyson's Corner in McLean, Virginia. When Rotonda management learned of Julie's concierge experience, she was hired as the director. Russ is also a director; his new appointment with the DEA in Arlington, Virginia.

The Perrudas are busy. After Jim, now single, completed his six weeks of rehab at the Robert Ackerman Center in Naples, he stayed on assisting new patients and is now a high-ranking administrator. His ex-wife, Laura, and her partner Janet, own an art gallery in San Miguel de Allende, Mexico. Janet paints and Laura sells.

When Emma's parents retired, they gave their South Dakota farm to their daughter. Emma whose bedroom furniture from Martinique has a rural home. Reluctantly, Tony agreed to abandon his position at the brokerage in Minneapolis and is now the president of the Kingsbury County Farmers' Union. Because his knowledge of the stock market has enriched the organization's treasury, he may, with Union endorsement, become a candidate for the US Senate.

Carla's work with abused women has been recognized in Boston, and she is now a featured speaker and advocate for centers throughout the state. Her husband's position with Waverly Dechtonics is assured as he moves up the corporate ladder.

Perruda's Fine Furnishings continues as an upscale furniture store offering exquisite items for all generations. It's new owners, Kimberly and Stephanie Perruda, Tony's daughters, travel the world in search of the exotic yet practical, youthful but classic. Sales have doubled.

Diane Perruda is a featured guest on TV talk shows. Her first book, *Men I Love to Hate,* was an instant success. Gone is her raspy voice with its pseudo-southern accent. Thanks to expensive elocution lessons, her well-modulated voice is perfect for TV, and her wardrobe choices delight her male audience.

Sheriff Jack Ryder considers retirement and has been honored by the chamber of commerce for his work in law enforcement.

Tomas and Edilia Fuentes own a modest home and have two children. She continues her work at Rosewood Center. Tomas works two jobs and studies for a degree that will qualify him for work with the DEA. He is a frequent speaker at Alcoholics Anonymous meetings.

Sally Torrino sails the seven seas in her yacht appropriately named *Bella Fortuna.* Her friend Sharon Long often accompanies her in search of unique items for her shop in Naples. Sally kept Frank's secrets and his envelope for six months, and when she followed his instructions and identified herself with Frank's Swiss bank officials, she received Frank's entire fortune. She endowed a special chair at Boston College in Frank's name and continues to establish scholarships and endowments in higher education. Although Frank's dream of Perruda University in North Dakota never materialized, Sally has established the Frank Perruda scholarship in the University of North Dakota's Masters in Business Administration program. When chosen to receive an honorary PhD at Columbia University, she accepted the honor in Frank's memory.

John Thurston, aka Cynthia Frost, was sentenced to twenty years in a plea bargain. He had given the sheriff the names of drug dealers, pushers, and users, a treasury of drug trafficking. Although he was moved often and given a new identity, he was unable to avoid detection from dealers who also languished in prison cells. His body was discovered in a locked vat filled with hot water in the prison's kitchen. The perpetrators were never discovered.

Patrick Davis, now Andrew Stahl, has moved from Barbuda and was last seen in Cusco, Peru. He and his Barbuda-born wife, Della, operate a tour bus to Machu Picchu. Patrick continues to suffer from nightmares. When Della wakens him and says, "Nice boy," Patrick falls back to sleep, a cherubic smile on his face.